Chris Ryan Extreme: Most Wanted

Chris Ryan

CORONET

First published in Great Britain in 2013 by Coronet
An imprint of Hodder & Stoughton
An Hachette UK company

1

Copyright © Chris Ryan 2013

The right of Chris Ryan to be identified as the Author of the Work has been
asserted by him in accordance with the Copyright, Designs and Patents Act 1988.

A CIP catalogue record for this title is available from the British Library

HB ISBN 9781444756647
TPB ISBN 9781444756722

Typeset in Plantin Light by Hewer Text UK Ltd, Edinburgh
Printed and bound by Clays Ltd, St Ives plc

Hodder & Stoughton policy is to use papers that are natural, renewable
and recyclable products and made from wood grown in sustainable
forests. The logging and manufacturing processes are expected to
conform to the environmental regulations of the country of origin.

Hodder & Stoughton Ltd
338 Euston Road
London NW1 3BH

www.hodder.co.uk

acknowledgements

To my agent Barbara Levy, publisher Mark Booth, Charlotte Hardman, Eleni Lawrence and the rest of the team at Coronet.

one

John Bald observed Memphis Hay from behind the wheel of a VW camper van. Headlights set to full dark, engine still tap-tapping out its death song. The van was parked amid the yard clutter of a scrap-metal dealership forty metres due south of Hay and his Lada Niva 4x4, in the shadowy underside of a concrete overpass on the outskirts of Almaty.

Bald looked on as Hay popped the boot on the Niva and a goon from the local Tengir drug gang elbowed him aside, ran his bare-knuckled hands over the contents. The Tengir goon wore a pair of ball-hugging jeans and a white V-neck T-shirt, and he looked like a swollen testicle. He had rocked up to the drug meet a minute ago in a battered Mazda 6, parked eight metres further down the road from the Niva. Testicle's buddy was propped against the Mazda's hood. Guy was decked out in a Brazil national football team tracksuit. Six foot two of bright yellow and green douche bag.

Bald watched Hay lug a brown suitcase out of the Niva's boot, dump it on the ground in front of Testicle. The guy nodded, waved to Brazil, who retrieved a black gym bag from the back seat of the Mazda. Bald knew two very important facts about the meet. The brown suitcase belonging to Hay contained thirty keys of opium base, the shit that got processed into heroin for the street crackheads. He also knew the black gym bag contained the money: 120 grand in clean US bills. And in roughly thirty seconds the money and the opium would change hands, and then Bald would strike.

Brazil carried the gym bag over to the Niva. Posters were lathered onto the walls of a derelict warehouse between the two vehicles, about the only strokes of colour in an otherwise monochrome landscape. Posters of the Kazakh and Russian presidents pressing the flesh, the Kazakh flashing a chummy smile at the camera, dumb-looking borik fur squatting on top of his head.

Brazil chucked the gym bag to Hay. The hippie caught it like he was catching a baby. He weighed it up for a moment. Then he stuffed the bag into the front passenger seat, and Bald sat up in his seat. He was inching closer to a big fuck-ing payday. Now all he had to do was wait for Testicle and his mate to piss off. Then Bald would ambush Hay and make him an offer he couldn't refuse. The kind of offer best made with the business end of a semi-automatic handgun.

'Baby, do you think they have animal sanctuaries in Panama?'

The voice belonged to a Dutch blonde hippie Bald had been plugging called Saakje Wolfswinkel. Saakje was a tight package of slappable arse and punchbag tits, good enough to make Bald forgive her Marxist bullshit and dreadlocks. She was seated at a laminated folding table set way back in the camper van's living area, and she was sparking up a joint. Bald smelt the sweet fumes filling the cab.

'Yeah. No. Fuck should I know?' he said.

'I was thinking about it, and I'd like to run a sanctuary. Help the animals, you know.' Saakje paused and sucked hard on the joint. 'Baby? We're gonna live down on the beach, right? In a hut, just like you promised?'

'Just like I promised,' said Bald.

'And we'll grow old together? Like, for ever?'

'Nothing lasts for ever,' he said distractedly. 'But yeah, whatever lasts less than that.'

Bald tried to phase out the sound of her voice. He phased out, too, the constant drone of traffic roaring along the overpass. All his energy and senses were focused on the drug deal going down beneath it. Now Hay was parading around to the driver's door of the Niva while Testicle was lugging the suitcase back to the Mazda. Brazil had a hand wrapped around a shotgun shaped kind of like a clunky AK-47, a weapon Bald immediately ID'd as a Saiga twelve-gauge.

Almost time, Bald told himself. He tightened his grip around the TT semi-automatic pistol on his lap. The TT was a weapon way past its sell-by date, but he liked the heft of the grip. Could feel the eighty years of killing engrained in its moving parts.

'Tell me the plan again,' he said, keeping his eyes on the Mazda.

'But we've been through this, like, already,' Saakje replied, saying the last word like a child.

'Yeah. And now we fucking go through it one last time. So we get it right.'

Saakje shrugged and said, 'You're gonna block the road so Hay can't escape from the overpass. Then you're gonna get out and do things to him I don't want to know about. Then you're gonna get our holiday money, and I'm gonna take the wheel and put my foot to the floor.'

She was stroking Bald's arm the way other people stroked cats.

Bald hated it when she did that.

Up ahead Hay was flipping open the driver's door of the Niva. Was about to climb inside when he stopped short. For a cold second Bald wondered what the fuck was going on. Then he heard a noise, like ice being stabbed with a pick. Footsteps treading on broken glass. Bald couldn't see where the footsteps were coming from. Not to begin with. Then Hay spun around and looked beyond the Niva, and Bald chased his eyes and saw it too. Movement in the gloom. Twenty metres south of the Niva. And in the same moment Bald realized his plan was fucking sideways.

two

Bald counted two of them.

They came into view at Hay's six o'clock. Emerged from the warehouse and gunned towards the Niva. They were both wearing football tracksuits too. Guy on the left wore Turkey's national team's colours: red and white with an Islamic crescent on the back. He had a shaven head that revealed a bumpy scalp, and the kind of squat frame that indicated serious steroid abuse. Guy on the right wore Germany's, and had a face like a sack of gravel. The pair of them were kitted out with PP-2000 submachine guns. Both fitted with laser optics and tactical light attachments on their Picatinny rail systems. They looked like a couple of ex-squaddies who'd robbed a discount clothing store.

'Who are they?' Saakje asked. She had propped herself between the two front seats.

'Fuck knows,' said Bald. 'But I do know that Hay just walked into a trap.'

Saakje frowned. Somewhere behind that curtain of marijuana haze, she dimly understood that this was bad news.

Now Hay was turning to face the muscle charging at his six. He glanced back at Testicle. The Kazakh shrugged and smiled apologetically, but Hay just stood rooted to the spot, his hippie brain desperately trying to process the scene playing out in front of him.

He was still trying to figure it out as Turkey raised his PP-2000 level with his torso.

Then he figured it out.

He tried to run.

He'd made it about a metre and a half when a tongue of flame lashed violently out of the PP-2000, three hot slashes of 9x18mm Parabellum zipping out of the barrel and shattering his ankle. He dropped to the ground, clutching his ankle, the joint jutting out like a strip of splintered wood. His body was shaking. Bald heard Saakje whimpering behind him. Brazil swaggered over to Hay. Stopped at the foot of the hippie prick and cocked his head at him curiously. Hay's face was stretched with pain. Brazil booted Hay onto his front and traced the Saiga twelve-gauge up from his shattered ankle to a spot between his eyes. Then he traced the Saiga back down to his bollocks.

Squeezed the trigger.

The shotgun barked. Hay jolted. A large dark-red stain splattered his jeans. There was a hole where his manhood used to be, wretched and flabby. A brown pool quickly formed under him. Brazil laughed as Hay voided his bowels. He patted Hay on the head and ruffled his hair. Bald watched Germany approach Hay and lower the PP-2000. Aimed the muzzle at his skull.

But Germany didn't shoot.

Instead he raised his weapon at a spot due south of the Niva. Turkey did the same.

Their PP-2000s pointed directly at the camper van.

'Baby, what—?'

Bald frantically shoved Saakje's head between her legs, ducked down behind the dash alongside her. Two rounds cracked through the air and pounded on the side of the van. The shriek of metal shredding metal was ringing inside Bald's ears. The rounds ricocheted off the plywood in the back of the van, where Saakje had been sat thirty seconds ago.

Bald heard two more bursts discharge from the PP-2000s. The rounds spattering against the windscreen, the van shuddering. Then he heard the windscreen glass shatter and cascade over the cab, shards of it raining down on the back of his head.

And then, just like that, the shooting stopped. Bald glanced over the dash. He spotted Germany and Turkey beyond the shattered windscreen. They were shouting at Testicle and Brazil. Testicle was ten metres to their right. He was hurrying into the driver's side of the Mazda and frantically gesturing for his mates to follow. Bald realizing, way too late, that the Tengir were making a grab for the cash and the opium. They'd seen Hay show up to the meet all by himself, done the math, and naturally concluded that they could work both angles. In their shoes, Bald would've done the same.

He pulled back the slider on the TT and looked for the reassuring gold nugget of a 7.62mmx25mm Tokarev bottleneck round snug in the chamber. Found it. Smiled and snapped the slider back into position. Grabbed the spare eight-round clip from the key tray behind the gear shift.

Said to Saakje, 'Soon as I'm putting rounds down on these fuckers, fire up the engine.'

Saakje was trying to hawk up words from deep in her throat. 'Hay, he—'

Bald blanked her. He had no time for this shit. He prised open his door, slid out of the van and slammed the door on Saakje, dropping to a kneeling firing position behind the right front wheel. His training had taught him that the wheelbase offered the best protection against incoming rounds. He shuffled a step to his left, holding the TT in a two-handed grip for stability, his eyes keeping the rear notch in focus and the front blade sight slightly out of focus, index finger applying a little pressure to the trigger. Ready to give the Tengir the good news.

Then a siren sounded, and Bald froze.

The wailing was distant but crisp. Bald scoped the underpass. He couldn't see the crack and pop of police lights anywhere up ahead. They had to be coming from somewhere deep within the bowels of the underpass, he figured. But the sirens were enough to put the frighteners on the Tengir. Germany and Turkey were spinning away from Bald and tearing towards Testicle in the Mazda. They dived into the rear seats, the engine thundering already as the car K-turned in the middle of the road and raced north, heading in the opposite direction from Bald and Saakje in the camper van. Away from the sirens wailing in the Kazakh night.

Leaving the gym bag behind.

Bald told himself he had one chance to act before the coppers arrived. He pulled out from behind the camper van and shuttled down the road. Made it to Hay in eight powerful strides. Saakje shouting at his six o'clock, 'Help him, baby! Help Hay!' Bald gritting his teeth and wishing she would shut the fuck up.

Hay was in rag order. He was lying on his back. His chest was limply inflating and deflating. A soft, flopping sound coming from his lungs. His groin was a gout of red. He was slipping in and out of consciousness. Hay rolled his eyes skyward and looked at Bald. They were bloodshot and he was almost fucking gone. Then he did a funny thing. He grinned at Bald. A big, goofy, red-toothed grin.

Cunt.

Bald sidestepped Hay. Beat a path to the Niva. Then he reached into the front passenger seat. He snatched the bag. It was surprisingly light. But then money didn't weigh all that much. Even a million dollars felt pretty light. Bald knew such things, because he thought about money a lot. By the time he was hurrying past Hay on the return trip, the hippie fuck had almost slipped over to the dark side. He was taking his time about it, and Bald was just fine with that. He sprinted back to the camper van. Jumped behind the wheel. Dumped the bag on Saakje's lap. Twisted the keys in the ignition. The engine cleared its throat.

'What about Hay?' Saakje said. 'We can't leave him behind.'

Bald said nothing. He just trod down. The sirens were urgent now. They had to put some distance between themselves and the carnage before the cops joined the party.

'We have to do something.' Saakje's eyes were glued to Hay.

Fuck it, thought Bald. I'm not wasting my time listening to her crap. In his mind Hay had got exactly what he deserved. He wanted to play with the big boys, that was his choice. But if you rocked up to a drug deal on your own, unarmed, to meet a bunch of guys who extracted people's teeth for shits and giggles, you were fucking asking for it.

They sped away from the road, Bald pushing the VW as hard as its engine and age allowed. By the time they had steered onto the artery of main roads that snaked around Almaty, clusters of police lights were blinking at the underpass. Bald drove in silence. Saakje retreated into the bullet-riddled darkness of the living area, hollow-eyed with shock. In the rear-view mirror Bald watched her rolling another joint. She layered the giggle weed on big time, sprinkled a few token tobacco leaves on top and rolled up the joint, lit it and took a long drag. A sign at the side of the road told Bald he was three kilometres from the overpass. Hay and the Tengir were already ancient fucking history.

'What happened?' Saakje was smoking the joint hard and fast. 'Baby, talk to me.'

Bald gritted his teeth.

'They were lying in wait to ambush Hay. They must've taken up positions before we arrived. Planned to drop the cunt and keep the drugs and the cash for themselves. They were probably waiting there hours ago and saw us arrive.'

Another road sign announced they were ten kilometres north of the overpass. The road became a rough, desolate track. No streetlamps out here. Nothing but vermin for company. They were heading east towards the Charyn River Canyon. Their view consisted of stark desert and a whole lot of sky. Once he was sure no one had tailed them, Bald pulled over to the side of the road. Killed the engine, climbed into the living area and lifted the gym bag. Big smile stickered to his face.

A hundred and twenty large. This was more fucking like it.

Bald unzipped the bag. Several wads of fifty-dollar bills were nestling inside. He snatched one of the wads. Counted eighty notes in the bundle, which came to four thousand bucks. But then he dug a little deeper into the bag. Something was wrong. Bald frantically rummaged through the bag, paper spilling out onto his lap.

He had twenty grand in his hand.

The rest of the money was missing.

three

Bald checked it again, just to make sure his eyes weren't going all David Blaine on him. They weren't. Five measly wads of fifty-dollar bills stared out at him from the bag. Twenty thousand pissy dollars. Screwed-up balls of newspaper filled out the bag. Balls and balls of it eyefucking him.

'What's wrong, baby?'

Bald looked across at Saakje. She was sitting in the front of the cab and looking dazed.

'You told me Hay had thirty keys of morphine base in the suitcase. That shit has a wholesale value of four grand a key. There's supposed to be 120 fucking grand in here.'

Saakje bit her lower lip. Bald sensed she was holding something back. 'What is it?'

'Nothing, baby.'

'Tell me, or you and me are history.'

Saakje was silent for a beat. Weighing things up inside her head. Then she said, 'The first time Memphis dealt with the Tengir, the cops stopped him on his way back to the Farm. They searched the car and found the money. They took it. All of it. Ever since, Memphis only picks up a little money from the Tengir. In case the cops are watching him.'

'What about the rest?'

'He picks it up from someplace else.'

'Where?'

'The location changes every time. Way it works is, the Tengir tell him where to pick it up and he goes there the same evening. Sometimes it's a bin, sometimes it's another car parked across town.'

'And where is it this time?'

Saakje glanced uneasily at Bald.

'I don't know, baby, I swear.'

Bald thought back to Hay. Thought about him lying on the slick tarmac. Blood fountaining out of his shotgunned groin, flashing that strange smile at Bald. He'd wondered about that smile. Now he knew what had made Hay so fucking merry. He knew where the 100 grand was, but Bald didn't. And now all he had was a bounty that hardly stretched to buying a decent set of wheels, and a headache brewing in the back of his skull.

Bald had been recuperating at the Farm ever since Joe Gardner left him for dead in the Kazakh desert. Saakje had been the one who'd found him. She'd taken him to the commune. Nursed him on the long road back to health. There had been no booze there – and no bad memories either. Bald had lost weight, and the sex with Saakje had been legendary. Enough to keep him entertained for a few months.

Bald had discovered something else on the Farm too. The home-grown waccy baccy had put the brakes on his migraines. Six months and he hadn't suffered a single attack. But the constant diet of tofu and pacifist bullshit had him aching for a change of scene. Bald was on top of the Firm's shit list and keeping his head low had been his number-one priority. But then he had found himself sharing a bed and a spliff with Saakje and listened to her venting steam about her ex, Memphis Hay, and how he was two-faced because he preached peace and love but dealt heroin on the sly, and the acorn of a plan had formed in Bald's head.

His only problem had been where to go with the cash and the bird. Britain was out of the fucking question. He couldn't go anywhere the Firm had a presence, and the Firm had a notoriously long arm. The list of countries he could live in had been narrowed down to about a dozen. He settled on Panama, a state as corrupt as his own soul. He planned to use the opium loot to muscle in on the local cocaine business. Work his way up. His plan also involved ditching Saakje as soon as they touched down in Panama City.

Bald wiped down the TT's grip on his shirt, emptied the clip and the chamber, and tossed the pistol out of the window. A kilometre on, he ditched the clip and the chambered round, surrendered them to the stark desert. They continued with their original plan, heading for Almaty International Airport. Even with a lot less money, Bald had no time to cook up a new plan. And they couldn't very well go back to the Farm. Not without Hay. Too many questions. News of his death would reach the other hippies soon enough, and though high on weed, it wouldn't take them long to figure out that something was wrong.

Eighteen kilometres and twenty-eight minutes later Bald arrowed the camper van into the short-stay car park at Almaty International. He parked as far away from the terminal as possible. Then he joined Saakje in the living area. She was seated at the table with her legs pulled tight to her chest and her chin resting glumly on her knees. The birch plywood panelling above her head was pockmarked with bullet holes.

'I've never seen someone die before,' she said to the wall.

'Welcome to my world,' was all Bald said.

He tipped the five bundles of cash out of the bag onto the floor. Grabbed a roll of silver duct tape and said, 'Take off your clothes.' He watched Saakje undress. Got a semi from seeing her naked body. It took him a couple of minutes to fix the cash to her arms and around her slim waistline. He strapped eighteen thousand to Saakje and stuffed the other two grand in his pocket. Then he locked up the camper van and they hit the tarmac.

'Baby,' Saakje said, 'you're sure no one's going to search me?'

'You'll be fine.'

'But what if they do stop me?'

'You're a good girl. Nothing's going to happen.' Bald smiled. 'Trust me.'

'I don't know, Maybe this is a bad idea.'

Bald stopped her. Looked deep into her eyes.

'I told you already,' he said, keeping his voice low. 'The staff here are all blokes. If they try and frisk you, you just say you want a woman to do it. End of problem.'

Saakje nodded, not yet convinced, but not yet ready to back out of the plan. The maximum amount of cash a person could take through customs undeclared was $9999. So Bald was happy for Saakje to take all the risk. And if the agents did pull her aside, he'd simply put on his best innocent mask and say he didn't know the girl.

They reached the terminal. There was only one at Almaty International. It was white-tiled and glass-fronted with a curved ceramic roof shaped like a handlebar moustache. Bald took a final look back at the VW and checked his Aquaracer. Nineteen forty-four. In ninety sweet minutes he'd be boarding an outbound Lufthansa flight to Astana. Then onward to Frankfurt on a connecting Lufthansa flight. Then a KLM flight to Amsterdam and a three-hour layover before catching another KLM to their final destination, Tocumen International in Panama City. Total flight time thirty hours and five minutes.

In a little over a day Bald would be starting with a clean slate. Twenty grand was a hell of a lot less than he'd anticipated. But still it would be enough to get him started in the coke trade. He had the contacts. He could cash in a favour or two. Establish a foothold and work his way up.

They made their way through the river of car rental and bureau de change outlets. At the Lufthansa check-in desk Bald flashed his brand-new passport at the middle-aged trollop behind the desk. He'd obtained it two weeks ago on a visit to the British Consulate in Almaty. Showing his mug there had been a risk, but a necessary one, since he had no other way of getting his hands on a passport that looked legit.

The Lufthansa trollop scanned his passport indifferently and handed it back to him. Wished him a safe trip, but sounded like she meant the opposite. Now Bald and Saakje hot-footed it to the security zone. He motioned for Saakje to go first. They were almost home and dry. Saakje had calmed down. The dope was working its magic. She took a deep breath, flushed all that tension out of her neck and shoulders, and joined the queue. Bald looked on as she breezed cheerily through the scanner, no fucking questions asked.

Bald was up next. He tossed his keys and loose change into the plastic tray. Unlaced his Corcoran leather jump boots and placed them on the rollers. Whipped off his leather Belstaff jacket and bunched it next to the boots. Passed through the scanner. No fuss, no bullshit. Collected his possessions from the tray. Laced up his boots, slipped on his jacket. Clocked Saakje ahead of him, sauntering towards the duty-free shops.

He shaped to catch up with her.

Then he spied them. Two guys. Grey suits the colour of cigarette ash. Faces like jugs of milk, eyes like drill-holes. Heavies loitering five metres ahead of Bald. He spun around. A third heavy was already at his back and seizing his hands. Now the two heavies in front were steaming into him, grabbing his arms and dragging him away. Bald quickly gave up the fight. Three on one in a busy airport terminal, he had no fucking chance. The second heavy gave him the silver-bracelet treatment. Bald saw Saakje wander into a duty-free shop, unaware of what was happening to him.

The three wise men manhandled Bald down an artery of poorly lit corridors that reeked of antiseptic. They came to an industrial-grade fire door with a small wire-reinforced glass window. One of the wise men yanked the handle, bundled Bald into a small room. The heavy slammed the door and blocked it. Bald looked at his new home. Cream walls, lino floor warped like an old shammy leather. A small wooden table in the middle. A quilt of fluorescent panel lights spitting light onto a chair behind the table. Onto a man sitting cross-legged on the chair.

Leo Land smiled at Bald and said, 'You've been a very naughty boy, John.'

four

Two thoughts struck Bald as he stood there staring at the man who'd screwed him over. Thought number one wasn't really a thought, more an instinct that rushed up from the lizard part of his brain and urged him to punch Land's lights out.

But then thought number two told him Land looked bad. Life had beaten Bald to the punch, and left the MI6 agent looking like a bag of shit tied up in the middle. His hair was greasy. He had bags under his eyes like iron burns. The Savile Row suit had gone, replaced by a cheap black nylon number overlong in the sleeves and frayed at the lapels. He looked like he hadn't washed in a week.

'You really didn't make that very hard for me, John,' said Land.

Bald said nothing. He stood there and felt like a cunt.

'Presumably I don't need to tell you how I found you? Even you're not that dim-witted.'

'The passport,' said Bald.

Land clapped his hands.

'Spot on, John. You really ought to have kept your head down, old boy. Tell me, what have you been up to all this time?'

'Trying to avoid posh wank buckets like you.'

Land grinned at Bald. Gestured to the empty chair opposite.

'Do take a seat,' he said. 'We've got a lot of catching up to do.'

Bald didn't move. He looked at the chair like it had AIDS. Land nodded to the heavy at the door. The guy strolled over to Bald. Stopped in front of him. Grinned. Then he dropped his shoulder and jabbed a balled fist into Bald's guts. Bald didn't see the punch coming. It had zero backlift. The blow pushed his guts up against his abdominal muscles and sucked the life out of him. He collapsed into the chair.

Land was smiling at Bald, but only with his lips. Hate was brewing in his eyes. It was a look of such intensity that it seemed unnatural somehow, like it did not belong on that reserved face.

'In case that didn't give me your full and undivided attention, I'd like you to consider something,' he said.

'Let me guess,' said Bald. 'You're finally coming out of the closet. I'm cool with that.'

'Very droll, John. But no. The Kazakhs, as I'm sure you know, have a rather large problem with drug smuggling. There's a sergeant by the name of Sukharov waiting outside and he's just itching to arrest you. I hear Kazakh jails aren't the most pleasant of places. Matter of fact, the boys back at Vauxhall are already having bets on what kills you first. The daily rape or the TB.'

Land made a gesture as if weighing the odds. 'Luckily for you, there is an alternative.'

'Not interested,' Bald said.

'I'm glad you asked. I have a job that requires your particular skills.'

'Don't you have some other sucker on speed dial?'

Land drummed his fingers on the table and glanced at Bald.

'Let me be blunt. I need you as an asset for Six.'

Bald belted out a laugh, involuntary and strained, like a spasm. 'I'm not in that game any more. That's not my rag.'

Land steepled his fingers on the table.

'And what is your rag, John? Smoking dope? Robbing Kazakh drug dealers?' He was staring lethally at Bald. 'You're not grasping your predicament. Unless you help me fix my problem, I can't save you from prison.'

'I'll take my chances.'

'But you don't even know what the job is yet.'

'It's working for you. That's all I need to know.'

'Do this one job for me and the slate is wiped clean.'

Bald said nothing. Just warily eyed Land and felt a pressure building inside.

'I'm serious. No more running away from your past.'

Bald still said nothing.

Land leaned across the table. 'I'm offering you a once-in-a-lifetime opportunity, old chap. One last mission, for a new life. New name, new country. You'll be a new man. Christ, John, we'll even throw in a nice house. Can't say fairer than that.'

Bald thought of the streak of pink, plasticky flesh on his left temple. The scar of a bullet that had penetrated his skull and damn near killed him in the wilds of Serbia two years back. The scar reminded Bald that Land couldn't be trusted. That he should tell Land to go fuck himself. But the logical part of his brain saw things differently. He was backed into a corner. Leo Land had a vice grip on him, and he fucking knew it.

'Madeira,' said Bald.

Land whistled.

'A bit exotic for your tastes, don't you think?'

'Somewhere on the beach.'

Land made a face.

'And a kitty to get me started.'

Land frowned. 'How much are we talking about?'

'Two hundred and fifty large. Something to get me started.'

'That's a big ask, what with all the cuts and—'

'Sterling,' said Bald. 'None of that euro shite.'

'Two hundred? That's all I'm authorized to sign off on.'

'Two hundred and fifty or I'm out of here.'

Land sighed, then looked at the heavy and jerked his head at the door. The heavy moved around behind Bald, fiddled with a set of keys and uncuffed him. He turned like an oil tanker and left the room. They were alone now, just the two of them.

Bald soothed his swollen wrists and said, 'What's the job?'

Land tapped the desk and drew Bald's attention to an A5 manila envelope. Bald hadn't noticed it before. The words 'DO NOT BEND' were stamped on it in a faded red ink that reminded Bald of cheap lipstick. Land opened the envelope and tipped out a photograph. He placed this flat on the table and rotated it so Bald could get a proper look.

It was a portrait of a guy. Late forties, maybe early fifties. Roughly the same age as Land. First impression, Bald thought the guy looked like a bum. But his eyes were strange. Spectral and grey. Dull at first glance. But a closer look revealed an intensity shimmering beneath the surface. Like misted diamonds. They spoke of a man who had a lot of money but was constantly worried about losing it.

'His name is Viktor Klich,' said Land. 'He's a Russian oligarch.'

Bald studied the photograph again. It had been taken in a rush, Klich marching purposefully at the head of an entourage of corporate-looking men in dark suits.

'This was taken three weeks ago, outside the Royal Courts of Justice. Yesterday Viktor Klich fled London on a plane to Venezuela. I need you to track him down and bring him in. And I need him alive.'

Bald said, 'What he'd do?'

Land looked at him. 'Klich killed a parliamentary aide.'

five

'They call him the "Invisible Billionaire",' said Land. 'Viktor Klich is the oligarch you've never heard of or read about. There was a time, not so long ago, when he was one of the richest men in the world. Now he's not even one of the richest in Russia. The chap is practically down to his last hundred million.'

'My heart fucking bleeds,' said Bald.

Land made a snorting sound with his nose. '"Rich" is a relative term. If you used to be worth billions, and now you're worth mere tens of millions, are you still rich?'

There was the scrape of wood on metal as Land slid out of his chair. He was full of nervous energy, unable to sit still for a second. Bald was surprised to see him acting out of character. The guy was normally so smooth you could spread him on toast. Something was putting him on edge.

'Klich made his fortune in the aluminium wars. Do tell me if you've not heard of them, there's a good chap. I'm assuming that the geopolitics of Russia isn't exactly your forte.'

Bald shot Land a look.

'You mean the bad shit that went down between the oligarchs.'

Land looked amused. Bald felt a distant, hollow scratching at the base of his skull. He closed his eyes. He could hear Land doing circuits of the room, his steps eliciting a solemn echo, like a detective retracing the steps of a killer at a murder scene.

'When the Soviet system collapsed, Klich was thirty and worth a couple of hundred million. He was the right man in the right place at the right time. He turned 200 million into a billion practically overnight.'

'He should go on fucking *Dragons' Den*,' Bald said.

Land gave a polite laugh.

'During the aluminium wars murders happened on a daily basis. Smelting plant managers were decapitated. Metal traders buried alive. Journalists car-bombed. Klich hired ex-Spetsnaz operators to protect his interests. He quickly established his dominance. Then the murders stopped. They used to say the safest place to sleep in Russia if you were rich and powerful was beside one of the smelting machines at Klich's factories. He was suddenly the most powerful man in Russia. He bullied other oligarchs into paying him protection money. Klich collected his payment mostly in the form of shares. He turned one billion into ten. Are you keeping up?'

'Just crack on with it,' said Bald.

'Klich had a disagreement with an old friend. Chap by the name of Valery Favorsky. I presume even you have heard of Favorsky?'

Bald nodded. 'He's the guy who owns the football club.'

Land nodded back.

'Favorsky also owns a submarine, the world's largest private yacht, an island in the Maldives and a mansion in an exclusive gated community in Moscow designed to look like Kensington Palace Gardens. He got all this through acquiring ownership of a very small gas company in eastern Russia. Then he bought other, much bigger gas companies.'

'I'm guessing for that kind of action, he didn't go to his bank manager and ask for a loan.'

Land shook his head. 'The money was gifted to him by the Kremlin. By the President himself. As a way of undermining Klich. You see, Klich had incurred the President's wrath.

He was pumping millions into the Communist Party and the Russian Christian movement. He'd accused the government of bribery and cronyism. He exposed corruption inside the Kremlin, leading all the way up to the President. So the President needed to silence Klich. He used Favorsky to achieve that goal.'

The MI6 man loosened his collar. Like he couldn't breathe.

'The President provided the funds for Favorsky to launch a hostile takeover of Klich's aluminium giant. Klich protested. The Russian judiciary upheld the sale at a knockdown price. In one blow Favorsky had become the richest man on the planet and Klich was buggered.'

Land tapped a finger on the photograph. 'That's why Klich was going to the High Court. Which is where all the oligarchs take their cases, even though they have nothing to do with British law. They don't trust the justice system in their own country, you see. And they love all things British. So this was Klich's last throw of the dice. His last chance to claim back the billions he'd lost to Favorsky in the takeover.'

'What happened?'

'He lost the case.'

Bald shrugged, like he gave a solid crap.

'The same day Klich left court, his financial adviser called him from Moscow. We picked up the chatter at GCHQ. Seems there were three men spying on him outside his house. Next day police found his body in a grave in Ramenskoye, forty kilometres outside Moscow. Klich never took that flight back to Russia.'

Bald scratched his elbow. 'Why even bother going to court? If he knew the President and his mates would come after him, he'd have to go into hiding even if he won the case.'

Land squirmed, all the soft lines on his face cracking up. He looked at Bald the way ruperts had looked at him in the Regiment, contempt and curiosity etched into his features.

'Not necessarily, old fruit. If Klich had won, he would have been able to pay a small army to protect him. Buy a football club, too, make himself a public figure. That way the Russians would never be able to touch him. But when he lost, the gloves were off. He knew that. We did too. And that's why we decided to make him an offer.'

'What kind of offer?'

'Protection, John. In exchange for intelligence. The inside track on the Kremlin.'

Land had now completed his ninth circuit of the room. He stopped behind his chair and propped his manicured hands on the back rest, then stared at Bald long and hard. He was trying to look his usual smarmy self. But the corners of his mouth were twitching, his eyelids too. Land was a bundle of nerves, and he was having trouble hiding it.

Bald said, 'So Klich was good mates with Putin and he got fucking rich, and now he's only got the odd million, you try and work the old charm. What the fuck's this got to do with killing some aide?'

Land harrumphed, gave his back to Bald. He paced to the door and gazed out through the wire-mesh window, humming a thought. 'Zara Axline, the aide, was working for a Lib Dem MP by the name of William White.' He waited for the name to mean something to Bald. It didn't. Bald didn't do politics. The MI6 man frowned at the floor and said, 'William White sits on the Parliamentary Defence Committee.'

Bald blinked at him.

'Axline was sleeping with William White. At the same time Axline was also sleeping with Viktor Klich.'

Bald said nothing. Land fidgeted and made a pained face, like he was trying to cram a cricket bat up his arsehole.

'We found her body yesterday in the master bedroom of Klich's pad in Mayfair. She'd been there for a few days. Advanced state of decomposition, face unrecognisable.' Land was back at the table now, reading from a report he had taken out of the envelope. 'She had, quote, "severe bruising to her breasts and marks consistent with cigarette burns on her face and neck. The victim's hair had been torn from her scalp. There was also tearing of the victim's anal passage. Post-mortem suggests she would have been conscious for the majority of her ordeal", unquote.'

Land pushed away the report, like it was dirty. He inspected his fingernails, frowned at his index finger. Picked away at a crumb of dirt trapped under the cuticle.

'Anyway, here's the gist of it,' he said. 'Prior to Axline's unfortunate passing, White confided to her about various state secrets.'

'What kind of secrets?'

'The kind you don't need to know about,' Land snapped. 'God knows what White was thinking. A desperate attempt to impress her, perhaps. The fool told her everything. Apparently he knew things that even I am not privy to.' Land's voice was haughty, his eyebrows arched.

'Since this Axline slag was nobbing Klich on the sly, you reckon she spilled her guts to the Russian?'

Land shifted uneasily. Trying to accommodate the rest of that cricket bat. 'The truth is, Axline is nothing to me,' he said. 'Just a name. But a Russian oligarch hopping around the globe, knowing every dark secret there is to know about our intelligence services, that's potentially the biggest security breach we have ever suffered.'

Silence. Land let it settle, like dust. Bald grinned back at him. 'I see what's going on here,' he said. 'You've been caught with your fucking pants down. And now you want me to come in and clear up the mess.'

'A clean slate, John. Come on. It's a good deal. You know it.'

'Where's Klich now?'

'He boarded an Iberia flight headed to Madrid from Heathrow late yesterday morning. From Madrid he took a connecting flight to Venezuela. To Caracas. He's cashing in a cheque down there.'

'What kind of cheque?'

'A favour, John. Klich is a personal friend of President Chávez. Some kind of dodgy arms deal that he helped smooth over with the Iranians. Chávez owes him. Big time. He'll never grant extradition and Klich damn well knows it.'

Bald said, 'So you want me to go and snatch this prick?'

Land nodded. 'Before he disappears off the radar.'

'What about Interpol?'

Land looked at Bald like he had just suggested a threesome. 'Klich is still of great use to us. But if Interpol get their hands on him it'll go public. They'll be judge and jury and the rest of it. And our chance of squeezing intelligence out of him will be gone.'

Jolting out of his chair, he said, 'Come on, your plane is waiting.'

They bugged out of the room and threaded their way through a maze of utilitarian corridors. Land led from the front, Bald sandwiched between heavies one and two.

'There is a complication,' Land said to the space in front of him, not even looking at Bald. 'GCHQ picked up traffic in Moscow. We know that the Russian security services have been alerted to Klich going on the lam.'

'FSB?'

Land nodded. 'They think they can extract intel from Klich and use it against us. It's imperative that you reach Klich before the Russians do.' Land had stopped walking. They were standing beneath a light panel flickering on and off and emitting a factory hum. 'Klich is staying at a villa in the Country Club suburb in the north of the city.'

'Does he have a BG team?'

'Three men. Or women, I should say. Klich has a particular taste for black women. They're all highly trained. Jujitsu,

Krav Maga, kick-boxing, firearms.' A smile crawled from one corner of Land's mouth to the other. 'You don't have a problem with hitting women, do you, John?'

Bald looked at him. 'I don't think so.'

'Good.'

Land walked on quickly. Bald followed. After seven turns they came to an emergency exit. Land pushed down the crash bar and light splintered through the crack. A smell of jet fuel and burned rubber greeted Bald. They emerged onto a small runway adjacent to the main air park where the commercial liners were taxiing and roaring. Closer to Bald sat a mid-size business jet he recognized as a Falcon 50. French-manufactured. Land was marching ahead powerfully, a vigour and a spring in his step now.

As Bald thought some more about the set-up, gears clicked inside his head. Catching up with Land, he said, 'So what's the plan? I just turn up at the villa, pull a gun on the cunt and leg it?'

Land stopped. 'I appreciate it sounds a little, ah, thin.'

'It's a size fucking zero.'

'We don't have the luxury of time on this one, John.'

'And what about the BG team? That's four on one.'

Land grinned.

'More like four on two, actually.'

Bald felt his guts tighten like taut rope.

'What the fuck are you talking about?'

Land held his hair down against the wind. Pulled his jacket tight across his chest.

'Look, I can't trust you do this mission alone. Not after what happened in Florida. Klich is of strategic importance to the UK. So you'll have a partner.'

Bald felt the veins in his head pull tight.

'Who is it?' he said.

Land hesitated before saying, 'It's your old chum, Joe Gardner.'

Land cocked his head at Bald and gave a nervy smile.

'Something the matter?'

'No,' said Bald. 'It's all fucking gravy.'

'Good. I know you and Joe have a chequered past. But bringing Klich back to London is vital to the national interest. It's not a job for one man. So I need to know there won't be any bad blood between the two of you.'

Bald shrugged.

'I feel worse about the yoghurt I left in my fridge.'

Land studied Bald for a long time. Then he nodded.

'Your flight will get you in for just after 1500 hours local time. There are two of my best men are waiting for you on the plane. They will accompany you to Caracas, sort you out with papers and a phone. Rendezvous with your man Gardner. Once you detain Klich, you are to contact a local snatch team and rendezvous with them. They'll escort Klich to a secure airfield for immediate exfiltration.'

Bald said, 'What about the Russians?'

'Our best estimate is that they will be three hours behind you. They're planning to corner Klich and cut a deal with him. His life in exchange for everything he knows.'

Now Land raised his eyes at Bald. They were pearly white and wide. And Bald saw in them something he had never seen in the man before. He saw fear in its purest form. Land looked like he was about to puke. Bald just peered back at him and felt kind of queasy himself.

Then Land briefly regained his composure and said, 'If we fail to bring Viktor Klich home, I'm done for. The knives are out for me. But know this: if I go down, you're going down with me.'

six

The passenger door sucked open, and as Bald sat up he got a ruthless blast of air con in his face. He'd been lying in the back seat of a Ford Explorer SUV for the ride from Maiquieta Airport to Caracas, thirty klicks due south. A bunch of pains had been shockwaving his jaws all through the ride. Now they were working their way up his face and smashing coloured spots across his vision like a pool break. He glanced out of the passenger door. Saw hundreds of clay-brick shanty huts stacked on a hill. He heard the catcalls of kids playing and mopeds buzzing like flies and Latino rap thudding out of big fucking sound systems. Then Wellfoot stepped into view, thrusting a skinny arm across the passenger exit.

'Rise and shine. We've arrived.'

Bald shuffled out, Wellfoot dropping his hand and standing to one side of the door to make way. A smell of fried maize and spiced meat hit Bald. He was suddenly very hungry. He stretched in the road, working the jetlag out of his muscles, and blinked at the sun. It was the first time he'd seen the sun since boarding the Falcon at Almaty sixteen long hours ago. It was a blazing, blinding gash.

'I thought Joe was supposed to be RV'ing with me?' he said.

'He'll be along any minute,' Wellfoot said as he consulted his Citizen Eco-Drive. He wore beige trousers, pointed brown leather shoes and a crinkled white shirt. Looked like he was headlining the Colombian version of *The Apprentice*. Curious faces were popping out of the shadows. A couple of kids in shorts and baggy T-shirts had stopped up the street, sitting on their bicycles, sizing up the two men. They pedalled back into the maze of huts, calling out to unseen friends. Wellfoot seemed unaware of the fact that he was in a poverty-stricken neighbourhood and looked about as conspicuous as you could get. A white guy with a nice watch and an iPhone, he was a magnet for muggers.

Bald watched the kids disappear, then asked, 'Where the fuck are we?'

'Blasted GPS isn't working properly,' Wellfoot said, frowning in deep concentration at his iPhone. 'What did you say there?'

Bald was about to repeat the question, but the iPhone stole Wellfoot's attention again. Wade, the second agent, was still sitting behind the wheel of the Explorer, arm hanging out of the window, Marlboro Light dangling from a bony thumb and forefinger.

'We're supposed to be on Avenida Cinque de Mayo. But I'm not sure this is the right place. Looks a bit rustic, don't you think?' Wellfoot squinted at the sea of huts, like he had never seen poor people before. 'Quite a view from up here, though,' he said, swivelling his eyes down the hillside.

Bald looked that way too. Found himself staring down into a valley basin, maybe fifteen kilometres wide and the same deep. It was situated about three hundred metres down and a kilometre along from the spot Bald and Wellfoot occupied. The basin was a brown and grey diagram of skyscrapers and tower blocks and decaying concrete edifices. The city was covered by a thin veil of smog. Looking at it was like viewing a city through seventies newsreel. The Avila mountain imposed itself at Bald's three o'clock. In the map in his head the mountain stood north of the city, which meant he was currently somewhere east of downtown Caracas.

'Oh, and before I forget. Happy birthday.'

Wellfoot chucked an envelope at Bald. It was brown and thinly padded. Didn't weigh much. A couple of hundred grams. Bald fumbled inside the envelope. A Blackberry slipped out. A prehistoric model, the kind of thing that a property tycoon would have been tapping away on five years ago. Kind of thing a teen in a hoodie would have been organizing riots on a year ago. The screen was scratched. The casing came loose in his hands.

'Sometimes the signal goes a bit haywire,' Wellfoot said. 'But it should do the job.'

Bald clumsily reset the casing on the BlackBerry. 'Fucker sends us halfway round the world on a private jet, but he won't give us a decent phone.'

'The BlackBerry is on an encrypted frequency,' Wellfoot said. 'Now, soon as you get to our Russian friend, call the number stored on the SD card. We'll come and find you using the BB's internal GPS. Any questions? No? Good.'

Wellfoot paced over to the Explorer, stopped, and inspected the caps of his shoes. 'Oh, and one more thing. The chief says, if you make a hash of this mission, you can forget about setting foot in England ever again. Just so we're clear. Best of luck.'

Then he climbed into the Explorer and slammed the door, and the engine was growling into angry life, bringing curious faces out from the shadows. They watched the Explorer pick up speed and hurtle down towards the city in the basin, spewing grit and dust over the dirt road.

Then they stepped out of the shadows.

There were nine of them. Angry young men. They looked like a gang. Eight of them had the padded physiques of guys who hung out all day at the gym. Giant pecs and beer guts, arms that were overloaded on the biceps but slender at the triceps. Frames skewered by too much power-lifting and not enough cardio. One kid was younger than the rest. Mid-teens, skinny as fuck, a human Twiglet with bad teeth. They were all giving Bald the cold stare. They were decked out in basketball tops and tattered jeans, scuffed white sneakers.

Bald instinctively tensed up. He'd heard all about the shanty towns in Caracas from a mate who worked kidnap-and-ransom cases in Latin America. The people who lived here had no jobs. No money. No way out. Primary-school kids got shot for looking the wrong way at somebody in the street. Cops took backhanders from gang leaders and ran assassination squads, doing the drug dealers' dirty work.

The nine guys formed a loose circle around Bald. Three metres and closing. Four were armed. Two were packing switchblades. A younger kid, maybe twelve, had a pair of knuckledusters. The fourth guy had a baseball bat. Blood smeared on the sweet spot. This guy was older than his mates. Maybe late twenties. A little taller than Bald, he was twice as wide. His skull was covered in tats and his skin was the colour of roasted peanuts. The guy tapped the sweet spot against the palm of his fat hand. Then he took a step closer to Bald.

'You got any friends round here?' Peanut said. His accent made every word sound like he was squeezing out a shit a mile long.

'No,' said Bald.

'Well, you got some now.'

Bald said nothing. He thought about Gardner. Wished he would hurry the fuck up.

'Where you from?' said Peanut.

'Scotland,' said Bald.

Peanut made a face.

'Where the fuck is that?'

'A long way from here.'

'Why you come to my back yard, brother? This ain't no Hilton Hotel. This is rancho territory.'

'Believe my fucking luck,' said Bald. 'Travel halfway round the world and I'm still bumping into cunts like you.'

In the next instant Peanut surged at Bald, lifting the bat high and back across his right shoulder, like a crazed lumberjack.

Bald saw it coming. A blind guy standing the other side of the city could have seen it. Peanut was loaded down with about 250 pounds of muscle, and muscle weighed more than fat. He moved in a graceless, exaggerated way. Bald weighed 100 pounds lighter thanks to his months of clean living on the Farm. He gave away three inches in height and five inches on the arms. But he was agile, and he knew how to throw a punch. So when the bat rushed on a downward arc at him he simply sidestepped it in a fast, smooth motion, though it was close enough for him to feel the air rush over his skin.

Peanut followed through with the swing. Now he was exposed. Bald was a step to the guy's right, his upper torso leaning a little further to the right than his legs, like a man leaning out a window to look at something on the roof. He had a good angle, facing the left side of Peanut's head. He bunched his right hand into a fist. Not a loose arrangement of knuckles, but the real deal. His fist was solid as Aberdeen granite. He dropped his left shoulder and pushed forward on the balls of his right foot. He didn't swing with his arm. Only amateurs did that, and Bald had been punching people for longer than he could remember. He concentrated all the power in his right shoulder and the glutes and quads of his right leg. The move began as a split-second blur of energy, and ended with his knuckles smashing into Peanut's lower mandible.

It was a good hit: right on the point where all the major nerve endings are concentrated. Peanut's head jerked back and he gave out a yelp as the nerve endings ignited and the blood in his brain instantly compressed. Then his head flopped forward. His arms and legs gave out, invisible hands unplugging him from the mains. He hit the ground with a violent shudder. Bald took a step back. Stood there and admired his handiwork.

Then, all around him, the other eight guys charged.

They came at him from all angles and all at once. Bald was ready to pounce on the first fucker who came within striking distance, but then a pang of pain shot up his right calf and his leg buckled involuntarily. Someone kicked him in the back. Then his left leg gave way too, and Bald dropped to his knees, then fell flat on his face. He moved his hands to shield his head. Multiple fists pounded away at him. It was like every punch reset his brain to zero. He felt a pair of hands grab him by the head and put him in a headlock. Bald tried rocking his head from side to side. Then he looked forward and saw the kid with the knuckledusters saddling up. Big fucking smile breaking out from ear to ear. Like he'd been waiting for this day his whole life. The kid just walked right up to him, wound up his puny arm and socked Bald in the face. For a kid with no muscle, he got a lot of power behind it. Curved metal slamming into his right temple.

Leo Land's voice in his head, saying, 'Crap way to die, old fruit. Beaten to death by a bunch of low-lifes.'

Then Bald heard something else. Not a voice. Not coming from inside his head, but coming from his six o'clock. Gears grinding. Gravel churning. Stones cracking. Engine droning. Then he felt the arm around his neck slink free and he lifted his head up from the ground and spat dirt out of his mouth. He rolled over onto his back and looked down the road at his six. A vehicle had stopped four metres away. MPV the size of a tank, timberwolf grey, Chevrolet badge tacked to the grille. Guy standing by the side of the Chevrolet, gripping a Glock 17 semi-automatic in his right hand. Glock aimed at the gang. Shouting to Bald, 'Get in, mate!'

Joe fucking Gardner.

The kid with the dusters legged it. His mates too. Disappearing back into the cracks. Bald laughed. His ribcage exploded. He scraped himself off the road. His body ached in about a hundred different places. Muscles were swollen and twisted. Bones were flashing up warnings in his brain. He felt like he'd been run over by an Eddie Stobart truck. He hobbled over to the Chevrolet and dived inside, and in the same moment Gardner was gunning the engine. He U-turned in the dirt road. Hit the accelerator. They hurtled forward. Bald glanced at the clock. Gardner was doing the kind of speed that could break a swan's neck. The slum shrank in the rear-view mirror. Soon it was nothing but a bad memory. Bald slumped his head against the headrest and closed his eyes and listened to the rhythmic throb of his muscles.

'Thought I'd lost you there, mate,' said Gardner.

Bald kept his eyes and his gob shut.

Gardner glanced across at him. Bald was sweating like a gypsy in a room full of spoons. He snapped his eyes back to the road.

'Land told you, right?'

Bald opened his eyes.

'Told me what?'

'It's a clusterfuck, mate. The Russians are already here.'

seven

Gardner was pushing the Chevrolet hard. Bald watched the needle pass 110 kilometres per hour. Half a klick on, the dirt road smoothed out and curled steeply down into the valley basin, where Caracas exploded into dirty life. The sun was hooked high above the city and throwing harsh shafts of light through the windscreen. Inside his head, Bald felt a bag of spanners split open and rattle.

'Land said we had time,' he said. 'He told me the Russians were three hours behind.'

Gardner shook his head. 'That int was wide of the mark, mate. They ambushed the villa thirty minutes ago. Guess our Russian mates had the same plan as us. Rock up, nab Klich and bug out. Piece of piss. But they walked into a trap. Turns out Klich wasn't alone at the villa. He had company.'

'You're talking about his BG team, right?'

'Not just the BGs.'

'Then who?'

Gardner sly-grinned, and Bald hated him even more.

'The President sent twelve of his top-level advisers to the villa. Like a welcome party. They had a government security detail with them, see? Six BGs. Plus Klich and his BGs, twenty-two people were at the villa when the Russians came knocking. They weren't expecting a bunch of hard-as-fuck BGs. The Russians couldn't take instant control of the villa then. They got pinned down by the choppers. We're on our way to RV with the Venezuelan SF team planning the assault. That's all I know.'

Bald studied Gardner out of the corner of his eye. Gardner never really changed. He was a little older in the eyes. A little more frayed at the edges. His hair was buzzcut to hide his receding hairline. The beard had been shaved down to a belt of salt-and-pepper stubble. His skin was still hard as clay. Three leather bands were strapped around his right wrist. Kind of things surfers wear. Gardner trying to look young and cool. But to Bald he was still the same old prick, with an artificial piece of crap for a left hand.

They pelted onto a three-lane highway that drifted west into the heart of the city, ripping past apartment blocks with rooftop billboards displaying images of Chávez looking real presidential. After a kilometre Gardner slid into the right-hand lane and took the next turn-off, nosing onto a two-lane stretch of gleaming new tarmac. Avila swelled in the distance. Bald could see the Humboldt hotel perched like an antennae on top of the mountain. Could see, too, the sagging lines of the cable car slinging down from the old hotel all the way to the valley floor.

'What about Klich? Any word on where he is?'

Gardner shrugged. 'My best guess is he's still at the villa.'

'If the place is under attack, then how the fuck are we supposed to get to him?'

Gardner popped a strip of gum into his mouth and pointed with his eyeballs to the glove compartment.

'Have a peek in there,' he said.

Bald sprang the latch. The mouth of the glove box sagged like someone had told it bad news. Bald expected to see a stack of maps and manuals inside. Instead he found a manila folder. He flipped it open and several photographs gushed out onto his lap. He skimmed through them. They were surveillance snaps of a black woman in her mid to late twenties. She had hair that flowed down her shoulders like poured coffee and eyes that could suck the light out of a black hole. She had attitude. Bald could see it in the aggressive line of her jaw and the defiant pout of her lips.

'Odessa Stone,' Gardner said. 'She's one of Klich's bodyguards. The other two women are Yanks. But Stone's a UK national.'

Bald nodded approvingly. 'So the Venezuelans have to cooperate with us.'

'Land got on the phone to the Justice Department chief. Laid his cards on the table. Says he has a couple of guys who want in on the assault, and if we were denied, they'd expel the diplomats from the Venezuelan Embassy in London. They didn't like it, but fuck 'em. We're here now. Orders are to hook up with a guy called Ray Monzant. Captain of the Special Ops Brigade.'

The road plunged into a tunnel whose roof was a lattice of wooden beams and slats. The walls were decorated with brightly coloured tiles, each one slanted, so that the overall effect was like an infinite line of collapsing dominoes. Wooden beams and support slats criss-crossed the tunnel roof.

'There's another thing,' said Gardner. 'Land reckons Stone might know something about the Axline murder. Says she's our secondary objective. If we can snatch her as well as her boss, then we're in line for a bonus.'

'What sort of bonus?'

'A hundred large each.' Gardner was grinning again.

'And if we can't get her?'

'Land says Klich is the top priority. If the bird gets slotted, that's too bad, but the Firm won't lose any sleep.'

'Do they ever?'

Gardner fell silent. Bald likewise. After half a klick they bombed out of the tunnel and Gardner hooked the first right.

The traffic hushed. The streets were lined with Art Deco buildings and bronze statues. Gardner arrowed the Chevrolet a hundred metres up the street and as he took the first right he said, 'Thought I'd never see you again.'

'You don't always get what you wish for.'

They fell silent again. The neighbourhood went from pleasant to minted. They passed whitewashed villas built like compounds, brooding behind two-metre-high concrete walls and gates with mounted cameras. National flags draped from flagpoles outside a few of the residences.

Gardner straightened in his seat. 'Fuck it. I'm sorry about what happened in Kazakhstan. I was wrong to leave you there like that. I was bang out of order. There. I did it. I said sorry.'

'Give yourself a medal.'

'You got a short memory. You forget that you had a gun pointed at me. Or does that bullet in your brain give you amnesia as well?'

Bald didn't rise to the bait. He rubbed his temples and dreamed about a cold pint of lager. Christ, it had been a long time since he'd touched a drop of the stuff. Coping without it had been all right on the Farm, with the shagging and the weed. But now he was back in the shit, with a face he'd never wanted to see again, alcohol was his bestest best friend.

'Got any booze in here?' he said.

'Sorry. Land made me promise.' Gardner rustled up a semi-smile, weak and flimsy. Like the man himself, thought Bald. 'But hey. When this is over, first round in Hereford is on me. What do you say?'

Nothing, was what Bald said.

Gardner slowed the Chevrolet down to a fast walk. He took the next left, easing off the gas at the turn and waited forever for a crowd of locals to waddle across the street. South America, thought Bald. The continent that turned laziness into a fucking art form. The road cleared about ten years later and then Gardner put his foot to the floor, but after a hundred metres he slowed again. A static train of cars and crowded buses stretched into the horizon. They weren't moving.

'Shit,' he said, slapping his palms against the wheel.

The street was heaving with a large crowd. Bald checked the time: 1649 hours. Gardner had said the Russians had attacked the villa at around 1550. That made it nearly sixty minutes since the first shot had been discharged. Sixty minutes was a fuck of a long time for a bunch of bodyguards and cops to be holding out against highly trained Russian gunmen. They would be closing in on Klich now. If they hadn't got to him already. Gardner honked his horn, Bald banged a fist on the dash. The two ex-Blades angrily gesturing at the crowds to move out of the fucking way. Their protests went unnoticed. Everyone was too busy craning their necks at a police roadblock a hundred metres ahead.

Most of the locals were seven shades lighter than the gang guys Bald had seen in the slums. The men were dressed in loud shirts and light chinos and had too much facial hair. The women were all hotter than the hottest girl in Europe. They had skin the colour of Fort Knox gold, hair black as midnight. Bodies with curves in places Western women didn't even have places. Bald allowed himself to forget about the migraines and Klich and the Russians for a few precious seconds. In the travel brochure of his mind, he reckoned the closer you ventured to the equator, the better the talent. And Caracas backed up his theory in a big way. He could see himself maybe sticking around the place for a while once the mission was over. Have himself some fun.

'That roadblock up ahead?' Gardner said, snapping Bald out of his daydream. 'That's where Land said we'd find Monzant.'

'Yeah, and these arseholes aren't moving.'

'Fuck it.'

Gardner gave up trying to steer through the crowd. He just yanked the handbrake, killed the engine and jumped out into the middle of the road. Bald flung open his door and hit the ground running. Followed Gardner as he threaded his way through the street. Elbowing fucking people out of the way. Sunlight was thudding against car roofs. A Hawker Beechcraft helicopter circled overhead, decked out in the livery of the National Air Force. Bald pushed on, keeping Gardner in his sights. It was hard going. The heat was close and thick, like a physical thing.

Forty metres from the roadblock Bald spotted a clutch of red and blue lights, throbbing in the heat. He counted four cop cars. Twenty cops. They were separated from the crowd by a ribbon of bright yellow police tape. The cops eyed Bald and Gardner suspiciously. One of them approached Bald. Guy had a look on his face like he was chewing tar but couldn't spit it out. He was bony and dark-skinned like a burned matchstick. He had a nose that probably showed up on Google Earth.

'Stay back in line, gringo,' said the guy.

'We're here to see Captain Monzant,' Gardner told him, offering up the fake passports given them by the Firm.

The guy studied each passport for what felt like a very long time. Flicked his eyes at Gardner, then Bald. A glimmer of recognition flashed across his ugly mug. 'Yeah. OK. I was told to look out for you guys.'

'You're Captain Monzant?' Gardner asked.

The man shook his head.

'Sergeant Elvis Rodríguez. Second in command, Special Operations Brigade, Caracas Division.' He didn't offer a hand. He kept both passports. 'I'll take you to the captain. We gotta hurry.'

Rodríguez turned and took off down the street, away from the crowd. Bald and Gardner ducked under the police tape and followed. Way back on the horizon the sun was setting.

The sky was blue in the west and purple in the east. To their right a line of palm trees ran parallel to the street. Bald peered through a gap between them and glimpsed a golf course. He imagined Land playing eighteen rounds there with some crooked Asian diplomat.

'What's the spread?' Bald asked Rodríguez.

'Captain Monzant will fill you in,' the cop replied, acting superior, like Bald was something he was trying to scrape off the bottom of his shoe. Bald had seen a hundred guys like Rodríguez during his time. Mini-ruperts, he called them. In some ways they were worse than the real thing. Ruperts were just cunts. Mini-ruperts were cunts with a grudge, boiling up with bitterness at having to do all a rupert's dirty work and taking it out on the squaddies.

'How do you like my country?' Rodríguez said.

'Great,' said Bald. 'I can finally cross it off my bucket list.'

'You have a bucket list, amigo?'

'Yeah. All the shit places I want to laugh at.'

Rodríguez didn't seem to have heard. They had stopped outside what appeared to be an old church fallen into disrepair. The façade was mottled, degraded to the colour of stained teeth. The miniature statues of martyrs and saints looked more like gargoyles. The Venezuelan flag draped from a pole above the main entrance.

'This is the big plan?' Bald joked. 'Ask Jesus for forgiveness?'

Rodríguez shook his head sombrely. 'This place used to be the Church of Our Lady of Coromoto. She is our patroness. Now it is our headquarters.'

They raced through the double doors and found themselves in a gloomy nave. The pews had been removed. Decorations had been ripped off the walls. There was a smell of damp and sweat festering in the air. Water dripped from the ceiling and had formed a big puddle on the floor, inches from a band of power cables. The cables snaked down the chancel and into a generator stationed at the base of the pulpit. From the wall behind the pulpit a crucifix was still hanging.

Bald let his eyes slowly adjust to the darkness. A dozen men were loitering in the aisles. Their clobber marked them out as specialist operators. Ticked all the SF boxes. Fire-retardant assault suits, ballistic vests, elbow and knee pads and utility belts. Each man was equipped with an FNC assault rifle primary weapon and a Glock secondary. They all wore bright-orange armbands with the word 'POLICIA' printed in black on them. Some of the guys were chugging cans of Red Bull. Others were chain-smoking their way through packets of Marlboros. There was a nervous buzz about them. Bald could see it in their eyes, white studs in the gloom. The men were getting ready to go head first into the shit. Bald suddenly realized how much he missed the adrenalin of being on a mission. There was nothing else fucking like it.

Then Bald heard gunshots thunderclapping across the sky, clear and lethal. Like a hundred carburettors backfiring. He spun round, looked out through the doors, at the street. The gunfire was coming from the east, from the direction of the villa.

Then Bald saw something else outside the church. A figure skulking between the palm trees, looking right back at him. It was a face Bald had seen before.

The kid with the knuckledusters.

eight

Rodríguez muscled his way through the throng of operators, Bald and Gardner chasing his shadow. Then the cop
took a right and swept into the transept, where big slabs of
rose light from the stained-glass windows were cast onto the
stone floor. At the far wall there was a shrine to the Virgin
Mary, who wore a halo of fake gold. A guy stood there,
beneath a window, dust motes swirling around him, his face
tense. He was busily thumbing rounds into an ammo clip.
Each round made a heavy clack as it locked into place. A
Glock 19 semi-automatic pistol was lying on a table next
to the shrine. Two clips laid out on the table, and a box
of ammo. The God of Hair had looked kindly on this guy,
as He did to all Latinos. The guy was five-six and about
the same wide. His sleeves were rolled purposefully up to
his elbows. His skin was darker than a Madeleine McCann
joke. A pair of colourful insignia sewn onto the epaulettes
of his assault suit marked him out as a captain. Monzant,
Bald decided.

The captain stopped thumbing in rounds. Snapped his
eyes to Bald.

'Who the fuck are you?'

He had a voice like water being poured over hot coals.

Rodríguez said something to the captain in Spanish.
Flashed the two passports at him. Monzant grunted. Jerked

his head at Bald and said, 'My sergeant tell me you wise guys are the British soldiers?'

'That's right,' said Gardner.

Monzant harrumphed and turned his attention back to the table. Cunt, Bald thought. Monzant plucked a round from the box of ammo. The front of the box was red with a white bar running down the side. White text on the red stripe read, '9mm LUGER. 9mm PARA. 9x19.' There was a logo in the bottom-right corner, a diagonal 'B' with an 'S' on top. Bald recognized the logo. Sellier & Bellot. Czech company, French owner. Bald had used their .38 Special in a full-metal jacket, and it had been a sturdy round. He figured the niner would be just as dependable.

'You look too old to be soldiers.'

'What we've got, you never fucking lose,' said Bald.

Monzant shot Bald a look straight out of the *Eyefuck Manual*. Grunted again.

'Way I see it, the only reason you're here is because some fuckhole in a suit signed a piece of paper. But on this operation the fuckholes can go fuck their own bitch mothers. I'm calling the shots on this one. You do as I say, and you do it when I tell you to do it. I don't care if you're fucking SAS.'

'Sure, mate,' Gardner said, holding up his hands in mock surrender. 'Whatever you say.'

Bald gritted his teeth. Sweet Jesus, he hated working with this appeasing prick.

Monzant thumbed in another round.

'How much do you know?'

'About as much as I know about your love life,' Bald said.

Monzant laughed.

'I got no time to tell you every fucking detail. These gunmen, they attacked the villa about an hour ago. The security guards at the villa, they stopped the guys in their tracks, but some of the gunmen made it through the back door. Got the drop on our guys. We lost couple of good men. Those gunshots you heard? That's the gunmen shooting at the cops from the first-floor windows. Pushing us back. But see, now we gonna strike from the south. Hit 'em with everything we got.' Monzant punched his right fist into the palm of his left. 'In eight minutes these bitches gonna regret the day they popped out their mammas' chochos.'

Bald thought about the set-up. The Russians were holed up inside. But there was no way they would ever be able to slip away with Klich now. Not with half the fucking army on their case. He thought about this while Monzant pressed the final round into the clip. The captain gently slid the clip into the underside of the Glock 19 pistol grip and it clicked decisively into place.

'How many gunmen are we talking about?' Bald asked.

'Six. They came dressed as golfers.'

Monzant saw the look of confusion scrawled over Bald's face and laughed.

'The villa backs onto the golf course,' he said. 'The gunmen dressed so they wouldn't attract attention. They just looked like six guys going for some rounds, shooting the shit. Fucking assault rifles in their golf bags, believe that?'

Bald believed. He knew exactly what the Russians were capable of. They were sneaky and fearless. If he was up against some local toughs, he wouldn't be worried. But Land had said these guys were ex-Spetsnaz. They had SF training. They would be heavily armed and hard as fuck to dislodge.

'What about the hostages?'

Monzant shook his head, like a guy who had bet on black and wished he'd bet on red.

'We just got reports they killed a diplomat.'

Gardner and Bald swapped worried looks.

'Any idea who?'

'Yeah. Some fucking adviser to Chávez. Name of Rincón.' Monzant looking puzzled at the relief playing out on the two

Brits' faces. Forgot about it, and went on, 'They dragged his ass into the toilet and blew his fucking brains out. That's why we're moving in now. Orders of El Presidente. We got to stop the gunmen before they kill anyone else.'

So Klich is still alive, Bald thought. But what the Russians were planning to do with Klich troubled him. He pressed a hand to his left temple and could feel his veins thumping away beneath the skin.

'You're worried about your citizen? The black bitch? Don't be,' said Monzant, a crafty smile tickling at the corners of his lips. 'We'll do everything we can to bring her back safely to you. You have my word.'

'I'm not worried about that,' said Bald.

Monzant tugged back the slider. Released it. The slider snapped forward, half a dozen parts clicking and clanging as the first round boosted out of the clip and crashed into the chamber. Then he stashed the Glock in his hip holster, before looking at Bald.

'So tell me what's beefing you, gringo. Because that look on your face – I seen guys on death row look less stressed than you.'

Bald stiffened his gaze at Monzant. 'You're planning on crashing through the front door.'

'Give them a friendly Venezuelan welcome.' There was a glint in the captain's eyes. 'Got a problem with that, gringo?'

Bald boiled up inside, rising to the bait. 'Yeah, I do. You're gonna turn the villa into a fucking bloodbath.'

Monzant shot around, snorting through his nostrils, neck muscles pulled tight like cables. 'You need a reality check,' he said. 'This ain't no polite European siege. The first thing happens in a siege, you get the gunmen calling with a list of demands a mile long. They want a hundred million dollars, they want their bros released from jail, they want Scarlett Johansson sucking their dicks night and day,' Monzant making a blowjob gesture with his hand. 'They only kill people later. When they realize they ain't getting shit. These guys, they started killing people *first*.'

'Any demands?' This from Gardner.

Monzant nodded. 'They want a helicopter, take them all the way up to Havana. It was me in that villa, I'd ask for Scarlett Johansson. They got more chance of getting pussy than a free passage to Cuba.'

Bald now understood how the Russians planned to bug out of the shit. Cuba still enjoyed a cosy relationship with their old Soviet pals in Moscow. Strings would be pulled. False identities arranged, they'd be smuggled back east with Klich. The plan had balls, and in any other country it might just work. But with Monzant calling the shots, it was going to end up as a killing spree. And Klich would be caught in the crossfire.

Bald said, 'You need to change your plan. These guys you're dealing with? They're not your average local toughs. They're serious players.'

Monzant stuffed the two spare clips into a pouch on his utility belt. 'Tell you what,' he said. 'How about I don't change the plan, and you go fuck yourself.'

'People will die,' said Bald.

'People are already dying. Rincón was the first. Pretty soon they'll start shooting up the rest. Maybe they already are. The sooner we go in, the quicker those assholes are fucking history.' He suddenly stopped and eyed Bald suspiciously. 'Unless there's something you know that we don't?'

'No,' Bald said with a straight face. 'We're in the dark about these guys, same as you.'

'Good. Then shut the fuck up and get ready to move out.'

'But—'

'No more talking. Now we act.'

Gardner made a face at Bald. The face told him not to protest, that Monzant had made his mind up. Monzant had already tuned out. He was hurrying past Bald and steering out of the transept. Rodríguez and Gardner filed out after him.

Bald felt his BlackBerry spark up. He fished it out of his hip pocket. The display beamed a number at him. Bald recognized the first five digits: +44208 – 44 for the UK, 208 for London. He knew who the caller was before he'd even tapped the answer key.

'Can you talk?'

Land's voice crackled down the line. There was background noise, sounded like radio interference. Bald held the BlackBerry close to his right ear and plugged a finger into his left. He said in a low voice, 'Your toughs dropped me in the shit. Almost got me slotted in some fucking slum.'

'Yeeeees,' Land said. 'Terribly sorry about that.' He cleared his throat. 'How's Joe, by the way? I hope you two are getting on OK, mmm?'

'Like a paedo in a prison shower.'

'Once the mission is complete,' Land went on, 'I need you to tie up a loose end.'

'You didn't mention anything about a loose end before.'

'You should have read the small print, old bean. You signed up for the job. No ifs or buts. And you'll damn well do what I say, or I call off our little arrangement and pass your file to Interpol.'

'I'm getting bored of your threats,' said Bald.

'No joke, John. One click of my fingers and you'll be bumped right to the top of their wanted list. And believe me, that is not a very comfortable place to be.'

Bald dug his fingers into the palm of his hand, like he was digging them into Leo Land's throat.

'What kind of loose end?' he said.

There was a long pause.

Then Land said, 'I need you to kill Joe.'

nine

Land said something else, but the signal weakened and his public-school voice disintegrated. Then the line cut out. Bald tried pointing the BB around the room like a guy angling an antenna. He still got nothing. Monzant was calling out after him now. Bald heard the stamping of boots on concrete, and the clattering of weapons, and realized he was flat out of time. The operators were moving out.

The assault was beginning.

Bald rushed down the nave. Watched the operators filing out into the street in a flurry of motion and racing across the street towards a waiting pair of Pinzgauer high-mobility all-terrain vehicles with the symbol of the National Armed Forces of Bolivarian Republic of Venezuela stamped on the side of the cabs. The Pinzgauers were the six-wheel-drive variants. One look at them and Bald had a little less faith in the mission. The Pinzgauer had been used by the Brits in Iraq and Afghanistan, but became renowned as a death-trap if you happened to ride over an IED. Monzant watched the last of the operators pile into the back of the lead Pinzgauer. Medical staff and a couple of logistics guys clambered into the second. Then Monzant ditched Bald and trooped across the street towards the third vehicle in the train, a Jeep Wrangler SUV. Monzant was deceptively quick on his feet. The way his fat little legs scuttled along made Bald picture a pig on a treadmill.

Monzant shouting back at Bald and Gardner, 'You and your friend will stick by me and Sergeant Rodríguez. The guys ahead of us, they're gonna crash through the front door. We'll wait out front. Once our guys have swept the building, we'll secure the hostages. Prep 'em for interrogation.'

'What about guns?' Bald said.

'You guys don't get none.'

'The fuck we don't. We're going into an armed siege. There'll be rounds flying all over the fucking place.'

Monzant chuckled, his shoulders dry-humping his neck.

'This is my operation. My unit. I call the shots. You and your friend? You're here as a fucking courtesy from my country to yours. Officially you're advisers. And guess what? Advisers don't get to carry guns.'

Monzant climbed into the front of the Jeep, wedged himself behind the wheel. Rodríguez shuffling after him like an obedient dog. The two Pinzgauers roared down the street. Bald held back for a brief moment, then pulled Gardner aside.

'The plan's fucked, Joe.'

'What are you talking about?'

'We're on the clear-up crew,' said Bald. 'Monzant is sidelining us. We'll be standing outside like a couple of spare dicks at a gangbang, and meanwhile the Venezuelans will be busy turning the villa into Bullet City.'

'Explains why he's being such a cunt to us. But what's he getting out of it?'

'He doesn't need a reason. He's a Latino,' said Bald. 'He has to show us how big his balls are. It's in his fucking blood.'

Gardner squinted at the sun. 'What are we going to do, mate?'

Bald bristled at the way Gardner threw 'mate' in there. Like things were kosher between them. Like Bald could just flick a switch inside his head and forget everything. He hoisted himself into the back of the Jeep. Gardner did the same.

Then Monzant fired up the engine and they took off after the Pinzgauers. The road swiped north, handrailing the golf course. Bald looked out of the window at its contoured green carpet bevelling like a bent horseshoe, sloped with deep pockets of sand. Palm-tree shadows creeping like smudged fingers across the fairway.

'What do you say, John?' Gardner said. 'Let's forget about the past. Mates again?'

'Sure,' Bald answered, putting the lid on his rage. 'Why the fuck not? Mates again.'

Gardner smiled, not fully convinced.

'I know people think you're a wanker and a crook,' he said. 'But I know the real John Bald. And he's a good mate. Always will be.'

Bald thought back to Land. He didn't know why Land wanted Gardner out of the picture. He really didn't care. His mind was already racing with possibilities about how he'd do the prick. Put one in the back of his head. Make it look like he got slotted in the crossfire. *Then* we can call it even. Bald smiled inside as he pictured the business end of a gun sparking up and a shard of hot brass pencilling through Joe Gardner's brain.

The road snaked east at the northern end of the golf course. The Beechcraft circled overhead. Now Bald spied the villa, fifty metres away, across the road at his twelve o'clock. To his eye the villa looked more like a fucking palace. Wrought-iron gates out front. Exterior the colour of wedding cake, front lined with stone pillars, eight of them. At the front a south-facing balcony extended from the first floor. The rooftop doubled as a terrace, edged with a stone balustrade. A huge porch decorated with exotic plants contained a set of marble steps that led up to the main doors.

Monzant slowed the Jeep to fifty. The Pinzgauers were twenty metres ahead and slowing down too. Gunfire whipped and cracked from the villa. Bald couldn't see where the shots were coming from, but he figured that rounds were being put down somewhere deep inside. He worried that the Russians were executing more hostages. He willed the vehicles to get a fucking move on. They were now forty metres from the villa, at a point where the road divided. The left fork led away from the villa, the road running like a gravel tongue up the side of the mountain, where a few token shanty huts somehow clung on for dear life. The other fork went past the front of the villa, the road cutting a line between the villa and the golf course.

Bald watched the two Pinzgauers halt fifteen metres from the gates. Twelve operators debussed from the lead vehicle and pounded across the road, its surface gleaming in the last light. They manoeuvred towards the wrought-iron gates, moving as a single unit. In Bald's view the whole plan was half-baked. Any immediate action, first thing you did was to attack from multiple angles. You used speed and their own confusion to overwhelm the enemy. You went in under cover of darkness and you didn't advertise your approach with loud trucks and choppers thumping away overhead. But Bald wasn't in charge. Monzant was calling the shots. And calling them badly.

The operators reached the gates. Bald counted three bodies sprawled at the gates: casualties from the earlier gun battle. The bodies were black bundles sprawled on the lawn. Impossible to tell if they were gunmen or operators from this distance. Half a dozen operators huddled at the walls either side of the gates.

Bald saw a glint coming from one of the first-floor windows of the villa. A gunman popped his head out and started putting rounds down on the operators. Down below four of the guys returned fire, providing cover while one of the operators stooped down by a metal panel screwed to the wall beside the right-hand gate and set about short-circuiting the locking system, his hands working overtime. He unscrewed the box panel and separated a bunch of wires inside. Rifle jolting in the hands of the guy beside him, the round striking the gunman on the first floor, the other guys whooping and hollering as the gunmen fell from view. The guy at the gates cut one of the wires and a shrill alarm sounded. He pushed the gates open and all twelve operators poured through into the porch.

Monzant pulled the Jeep over to the side of the road, twenty metres short of the gates. Bald flew out and beat a quick path towards the villa. He felt frustration gnawing at his bones. Eating him up. He was so close to Klich he could almost smell the guy. And yet he was stuck on fucking guard duty with Monzant and Rodríguez.

Bald was fifteen metres from the villa. His blood was up. He could smell Klich. He could taste the air on Madeira, and the wine and the women too.

'You look sad,' Monzant said to him. 'Why? It's almost over. Be happy. Like Marley.' He brought up and spat a bucketload of phlegm. 'I fucking love Bob Marley. No woman, no cry, eh?'

The twelve operators had broken into two groups of six. The first group was six metres ahead of the rest and charging up the steps. The six guys at the rear moved slowly, assault rifles trained on the first-floor windows, putting down indiscriminate three-round bursts to keep the other gunmen pinned down. Shattered glass and fists of dust rained down over the porch. Five of the operators each unloaded a clip at the windows. The sixth man, Bald saw, was wielding an AK-94 assault rifle equipped with a GP-30 Obuvka underslung grenade launcher. Bald knew the type because he had studied Russian armaments in the Regiment. The GP-30 UGL fitted under the barrel of the AK-94, took a 40mm caseless grenade, and was good for up to four hundred metres. The guy had tilted the weapon up at the first-floor windows, his finger on the trigger mechanism. There was a distinct pop as he depressed it and a grenade pumped out, flew through the shattered window and detonated inside the villa. But, instead of a devastating explosion, Bald heard a long hiss. Then he saw tongues of feathery smoke filling the first floor and flooding the balcony.

'CS gas,' said Monzant, beaming with pride. 'Bet you gringos didn't think of that, eh?'

The gunfire from the first floor ceased. Now the rear group upped the pace and joined their six mates at the entrance. Two of them took up position either side of the doors, backs against the wall. The one on the left thrust his hand across and banged the doors open and the operator on the right pulled the ring on a flashbang and tossed it into the entrance hall. There was a blinding gush of light. Smoke billowed up inside. Bald looked on enviously. It's all kicking off, he thought.

Monzant stopped eight metres shy of the gates. Just stood there, rigid and hesitant. Like he didn't want to get any closer to the action. Bald had wondered why the captain hadn't put himself on the main assault team. Now he could see why. Cut through the macho bullshit and deep down the guy was a pussy. While his men were crashing through the doors and launching themselves into a desperate firefight, Monzant would be parked out front, away from the bullets and the screams, grooming himself in preparation for when the TV cameras rolled in. Like all ruperts, Monzant wanted the glory without getting his hands dirty.

'We should be in there,' Bald told him. 'Me and Joe, we've done hundreds of house clearances. We can do the fuckers in our sleep. We're wasted out here. Let us push through with your lads.'

'I don't think so.'

Bald scowled at him, but Monzant seemed not to notice. He was busy taking a pack of Dutch Masters cigars from his pocket. He plucked one out, wedged the uncut end between his teeth and bit off the cap. Bald watched as the captain blanked him, and felt his anger straining at the leash. 'Your men are going to get whacked,' he said. 'If the gunmen are holed up inside, they'll be training their weapons on the front doors. The lads are passing through a fatal funnel of fire. You know what the fuck that means?'

Monzant spat out the cap and struck a match. He cupped the flame to the open end of the cigar and sucked smoothly on it.

'Sure I do,' he said. 'It means I get to have some Anglo pussy screaming in my ear.'

Monzant twirled the cigar between his thumb and forefinger, puffing away. 'You say you're both soldiers. Brother, that cracks me up. I mean, you ask me, you and your friend look like wash-up. Shit, I seen guys in the slums in better shape than you. So why don't you do yourselves a favour: go find a bar and sit this one out. Or you can stay and watch how real men take care of business.'

Mild-mannered smoke wafted over Bald. 'Fuck this,' he growled.

Then he was barging past Monzant and knocking the Dutchy out of the guy's hands and bombing towards the gates. Monzant shouted after him. Gardner did too. Bald made it in a couple of strides and next thing he knew Rodríguez was seizing him by the shoulder and tugging him back, screaming, 'Get back, I said. Get the fuck back!'

Bald spun around and in one quick move he pushed forward on his right foot and followed through with a punch. Lamped Rodríguez square in the face. *Bang!* Rodríguez stumbled backwards, cupping his busted nose. Then Bald turned back to the villa, marching towards the gates. The punch was justified, he told himself. He had one chance to get to Viktor Klich. One chance to finish the mission and start afresh in life. No fucker was going to stop him completing the mission. Not Joe Gardner, not some piss-taking gang. And not some jumped-up mini-rupert like Rodríguez. Bald had let too many chances slip by him in the past. This time, he promised himself, things would be different.

Then he heard a metallic click at his back.

Monzant said, 'Turn the fuck around.'

Bald turned the fuck around.

Monzant had drawn his Glock 19 semi-automatic. He was pointing it at Bald.

'Hands in the air,' he said.

Bald heard a hiss at his back. The ground shuddered, and a wind whipped past behind him, a sudden, torrential blast, blazing and violent, scorching his neck. Next thing he knew, smoke was frothing out of the gates and swarming over him.

And then his world went black.

ten

The smoke suffocated Bald. Hot clumps of debris rained down on him. A million grains of sand and mortar sprayed his face. Glass scalped his cheeks, scraped the flesh from his knuckles. He forced his eyes tight shut. The smoke was like a tunnel. Felt a mile long. Felt ten miles long. His eyes were streaming. Smoke flooded his nostrils and lungs. Bitter and scorching, like someone was shovelling hot gravel down his throat. He couldn't see a fucking thing.

The smoke cleared a little. Bald saw shapes playing in front of him, like shadows projected onto a screen. The smoke cleared a bit more. He spotted the wrought-iron gates eight metres away from his position. Busted off their hinges, twisted out of shape.

Bodies were sprawled across the porch. New bodies. Not ones from the earlier firefight. They were dead operators. They looked somehow unreal, their arms and legs contorted into weird arrangements, as if they were trying to spell out letters that would be visible from the sky.

Bald looked to his six. Monzant was stunned. Four metres further back Rodríguez was on the deck, face down on the ground, his hands locked in a jittery brace over the crown of his head. Gardner stood beside Rodríguez. Looking past Bald's shoulder. Looking west, towards the road that led away from the villa. Bald spun around, traced his line of sight. Then he saw them, too.

Two men. They looked like insects from a distance. They were roughly two hundred metres away, on the fork of the road that corkscrewed up into the slums perched on the mountainside. The gradient was steep and gave the men an ideal line of sight overlooking the porch. One of them had adopted a kneeling firing position, a long brown tube resting on his shoulder. Exhaust fumes sneezed out of the back of the tube.

From this distance Bald couldn't distinguish faces. But he could see outlines and skin colour and clothes. The two men wore basketball shirts and cheap white trainers. They had overblown muscles. He recognized them from the gang that had jumped him in the slums. The long tube the guy was supporting was an RPG launcher. The grenade had smashed like a fist into the operators, who'd been bunched up close. The explosion had simply chewed them up and spat them out. They didn't stand a fucking chance.

Now the other guy was reaching into a rucksack and retrieving another RPG round. Preparing to reload the unit his mate was holding. At the same moment Monzant had returned to the land of the living and was shouting frantically at Rodríguez in Spanish, and Rodríguez turned to Bald and Gardner, yelling, 'We have to get out of the line of fire. Inside the villa – now!'

More members of the gang were joining their two muckers on the road. Ten of them. Bald broke into a sprint. Felt his tired muscles working overtime. His heart going at a hundred per. His mind was totally focused on getting out of the line of fire of the RPG. He was going to get Viktor Klich, kill Joe Gardner, line his pockets, then tell Leo Land to go fuck himself.

But he needed a gun.

Picking his way past the gates, Bald darted into the porch. Twelve metres from the gates to the porch steps. Inside it was carnage. The kind of damage the RPG had done, Bald figured the gang guys had to have fired a thermobaric round. Regular warheads didn't cause this kind of damage. But a thermobaric round relied on oxygen in the surrounding atmosphere to create a crushing overpressure rising to temperatures of 3000 degrees in the centre. Which made him wonder. Where the fuck did a slum gang get hold of a thermobaric round? It wasn't exactly the kind of thing you could pick up in your local mini-mart. That question led to another. What did the fucking gang want in the villa? He snapped his head left, to his ten o'clock. Saw the guy re-arming the RPG. Saw his gang buddies streaming down the road back towards the villa. They were all brandishing assault rifles.

Bald pushed on towards the entrance. An operator lay spread-eagled on the ground, pawing at his face with one hand, his lower jaw nestling in his lap. Screams gurgled deep in his throat. He had his FNC assault rifle by his side. Bald stooped down beside him and yanked the weapon free from the guy's other hand. He had to move quickly before the gang took another pop at the villa. Thermobaric rounds had a kill zone of five metres and impact zone four times as big. If the round impacted anywhere close to the porch, Bald was fucked. The overpressure would crumple him up like a paper bag. He grabbed the two spare clips of 5.56x45mm NATO ammo in a rush. Thirty rounds per clip plus the full clip in the mag gave him ninety rounds to play with. Then he stashed the two clips in his hip pockets and legged it to the entrance. Left the guy with no jaw to die.

As he hurried up the marble steps there was blood and spent brass everywhere. Bullet holes riddled the walls. Monzant hadn't been bullshitting him. The earlier fighting around the villa had been intense.

Heavy breathing at Bald's back. He turned to see Gardner racing through the gates. Monzant, five metres further back, was putting down rounds at the RPG guy. He fucking missed, but it did the job of forcing the guy to displace to get out of the line of fire, while his mate returned fire at Monzant with his assault rifle. Bullets whizzed through the porch, kicking up furious clouds of dust. Monzant broke into a run, weaving a zigzag pattern towards the steps.

Now Bald pulled back the FNC's cocking lever and checked a round was engaged in the chamber. The weapon had a weight to it that told him it was fully loaded. He checked anyway, hitting the release catch on the side and catching the mag in his left hand. He glimpsed inside the clip. Saw the rounds sitting side by side. Full clip. Best news he'd had all day. He pushed the clip gently back into the feed. Whole thing took a couple of seconds. With the fire selector notch switched from 'S', safety, to '1', single fire mode, he adopted a standing firing stance and lined up the gang shooters in the sights of his new toy. He would rather see Gardner riddled with hot lead, but the logical part of his mind said he needed to keep him alive. Until the mission was complete. Then the gloves would come off.

Bald aimed at the nearest gang guy. His mind went through the calculations in a millisecond. He started zeroing the FNC on the shooter. All he needed to do was get a general mark on the guy. Make him realize he was in the killing zone, and force him to shift to cover, buying Gardner and Monzant valuable seconds to get their shit together and reach the villa. He pulled the trigger. Let off three single rounds. They missed the shooter by a good ten metres. But the guy was spooked. He dropped into a low run and started running towards a clump of trees, getting out of the line of fire. Bald checked on Gardner. He was crouched beside the guy with no jaw, flipping open his pistol holster and seizing his Glock 19 semi-automatic. Satisfied that the coast was clear, Bald turned back to the villa.

There was a crater where the doors had once stood. Splinters of wood scattered across the steps. Wounded operators were screaming in the entrance hall. Small fires were breaking out and squirting toxic fumes down the steps. Bald saw silhouettes shuttling across the hall, veiled by the smoke and fumes. They were shouting. Sounded Russian. Bald glanced back at the gang. The guy he'd been shooting was coming back at them now. He was ninety metres from the villa, veering off-road and moving down the green slope. The guy was peering down the sights. A split second later the AK-47 kicked up in his grip, a flame licked out of the snout, there was a sequence of violent cracks, like someone chopping through a stack of wood, and three rounds spattered the ground four inches from Bald. He thundered up the last steps and hurdled over body parts, shutting out the fear. Didn't give it airtime inside his head. Same as any guy who had done time in the Regiment and been in the shit, Bald looked at the world differently to everyone else. He stared at the villa and the gang outside creating confusion, and the Russians stuck inside, and he saw a once-in-a-lifetime opportunity to get to Klich.

He ducked through the crater. Crashed into the hall. It was vast and garish, like something from a drug baron's wet dream. The floor was marble inlaid with gilt patterns. The walls were lined with gold-framed mirrors and paintings. A chandelier dangled five metres above Bald's head. The twenty-four-carat gold lights had been blown out, scattering glass across the floor like big pieces of ice. Bald saw an arched doorway on either side of the entrance hall.

The smoke cleared, and the silhouettes resolved themselves into the shapes of two men. They were ten metres from Bald. Guy on the right was facing away from him, distracted by something. He couldn't see what. Guy on the left had spun around to face him. He was wearing a look of surprise on his face, like a slap. Both of them toted AK-47 assault rifles. For a second Bald wondered whether they were blue or red. Russian or Venezuelan. Then he clocked their clothes. Bright polo shirts, cream trousers. Golfing clobber. Russians. The one on the left had the world's most popular killing instrument raised to shoulder height, finger on the trigger. His mate sensed trouble and began spinning around, bringing his rifle to bear on Bald.

With less than a second to get his shit together, Bald's muscle memory kicked in. He executed a move he had done maybe ten thousand times before. He trained his eye on the first guy's neck. The Russian was wearing a gold crucifix outside his polo shirt. Bald targeted it. Worked on the principle that if he concentrated on hitting that small target, he had a better chance of hitting the big one.

He exhaled, then depressed the trigger.

The FNC barked and jumped and threatened to angle off target. But Bald kept his posture firm, and the weapon stayed true. Gases squirted from the chamber. A round zipped through the air and perforated the Russian's neck. Smacked into his Adam's apple. He fell back, blood pumping out of his neck, like a burst pipe. Bald swung the rifle in a smooth, quick arc over to the guy on the right. He'd drawn the AK level with Bald, but he was slow and ungainly, and he was flat out of time. Bald gave the trigger a squeeze. Put three rounds in the Russian in quick succession, the hot lead perforating his torso, rounds pinballing through his body, smashing up bone and carving through his soft tissue. The guy did a little pirouette, blood jetting out of his exit wounds, and then he collapsed on top of his mucker, Bald building his own little stack of dead Russians, like a gambler piling up poker chips.

Now Gardner was at his shoulder. Bald could hear his nose doing all the breathing for him. Gunshots rattled outside.

The gang putting ferocious rounds down on Monzant. The captain now ran up the steps in a deranged gallop and dived into the entrance hall. Rounds grazing the marble steps where he had been a split second before. Bald couldn't see Rodríguez anywhere.

Monzant wheezed and snatched at the incinerated air. 'We can't stay here,' he said.

'What's going on?' Gardner asked.

Radio chatter squawked Monzant's walkie-talkie. The voice sounded like Rodríguez. Monzant said something in reply. Rodríguez repeated it. Then Monzant gave Bald a wide-eyed look. Gave the same to Gardner.

'Word got out to the gangs there's a billionaire holed up in here,' he said. 'Some Russian oligarch. The gangs hear some rich foreign fuck is in town, they figure on kidnapping his ass. Shake him down for a fat ransom and go retire to Beverly Hills.'

Monzant shot Bald the screw-face from hell.

'Someone leaked the word to the gangs. I trust my boys. That leaves you two fucks. You just caused the murder of Special Forces operators. You're both going to spend the rest of your days getting ass-fucked.'

Bald exploded.

'You idiot,' he said. 'Those gang fucks were shooting at us too. We've been in your shit country for five minutes. Got nothing to do with any gangs.'

But Monzant kept wearing the screw-face. 'Only reason I'm not arresting you both now is we got a bunch of crazy gang cholos on our fucking tails. But soon as this is over, you're both going down. I'll see to that.'

Bald just shook his head at this sad prick and said, 'What's the deal with backup?'

'On their way.'

'ETA?'

'Four minutes, maybe five.'

'That's too long for us to wait. They'll overrun us before then.' Bald nodded at Monzant. 'Stay here, put rounds down on the gang. Stop them from getting inside the villa.'

Monzant frowned. 'How do I know you won't shoot me in the back?'

'Same way I know you won't do a number on me. Because we're in the shit, and we need all the fucking firepower we can get.'

Monzant nodded warily, then reached into a pouch on his utility belt and pulled out a couple of orange armbands. 'Wear these,' he said. 'For when the backup arrives. Don't want them mistaking you for bad guys, eh?'

They slipped on the armbands, Bald doing a body count in his head. One sniper taken down on the first-floor. Plus the two guys he had just dropped. Three dead Russians. Monzant had said there were six gunmen in total at the villa. That left three more gunmen somewhere inside. But the ground floor looked deserted. Which meant the Russians had to be upstairs. The ground floor had been cleared in the search for Klich, and if they had gone upstairs, the odds were on him hiding out somewhere on the first floor. And if they were up there, that was where Bald would go too.

Monzant manoeuvred into a prone firing position facing out across the porch. Stacked his clips next to him, within easy reach. Bald and Gardner moved down the hall towards a spiral staircase set six metres back from the entrance. Beads of sweat were tracing down Bald's back. His migraine was muffled by the adrenalin pumping through his veins. The staircase, with frosted-glass treads, wound upwards like a snake being charmed out of a basket. Up on the wide, curved landing Bald could see three doors. He led the way up the stairs. Calves pumping, glutes burning up, heart pounding against his breastbone. His footsteps were heavy and sounded loud inside his head. Blood rushed in his ears, waves of it crashing through the sides of his skull. Like a fucking tsunami going on in there.

Bald flashed a look over his shoulder. Gardner was struggling up the stairs at his six o'clock, lack of fitness telling on him. Bald smiled to himself. In a few minutes' time he'd be putting the prick out of his misery.

'We'll clear the rooms one by one.'

'Just like old times, eh, John?'

'Yeah. Like old times.'

Bald snapped his focus back to his twelve. Hit the landing in four big strides. His eyes were fixed down the barrel of the FNC. Of the three doors, one was at his twelve o'clock, the others at his three and nine. Like marks on a clock face.

Bald followed the landing clockwise, heading for the door at the six o'clock mark.

Then the wall to his right exploded.

Plaster and wood hailstoned Bald. Lashed at him. His ears were assaulted by the whip and crack of bullets whizzing past his head. Instinctively he hit the deck. Rolled over onto his back with his head propped up against the wall. He got a clear view of the shooter: the guy was at the door at the twelve o'clock mark. The door was already back on its hinges. A cape of blackness flowed behind the shooter.

Bald had time. Not time to act, but time to grasp. Time for impulses from his retinas to travel through the optic nerves to his thalamus and relay the image in front of him to the visual cortex in his brain. Time for the signal to ripple out to that part of his brain which would process the information. He had time to grasp the basic facts of the matter. The basic fact was that he was fucked. The gunman had his AK-47 zeroed on him. Bald had the FNC by his side. It would take him a second and a half to hoist it and zero in on the guy.

Then Gardner burst into his peripheral vision, surging onto the landing. He angled his torso at the gunman. The Glock 19 was drawn and trained and his finger was on the trigger. He fired before the Russian could adjust his aim. The sound of the Glock was deafening. Four rounds thumped into the gunman. He jerked wildly. Like somebody was striking him repeatedly on the back with a hammer. Fragments of hot lead yawed and cleaved through his body, doing all kinds of sickening and irreparable damage to his organs. He grunted.

Four down, two to go.

Bald tasted metal on his tongue. His face was glazed with sweat and lead particles. He looked at Gardner, who was looking back at him, waiting for the thanks to come his way. But Bald wasn't in a thanking mood. He said nothing. Picking himself up, he had his eyes on the AK-47 in the dead man's grip. Thoughts were brewing inside his head.

Gardner was racing towards the open door at the twelve o'clock mark. Bald gave chase, sidestepping the dead Russian. His heart was pounding, telling him he was pissing distance from the big prize.

They funnelled into a room the size of a tennis court. Now Bald pushed deeper inside, clearing the right side of the room, while Gardner cleared the left. He kept the front aperture in focus and the rear notch out of focus. His index finger was applying a precise pressure to the trigger. Ready to give any fucker in sight a happy ending.

The room was gloomy and it had taken several seconds for Bald's eyes to adjust. It looked like the bailiffs had recently arrived and cleaned the place out. The walls were plasterboard, the floor bare boards. No shooters. Gardner was at his nine o'clock, relaxing his aim.

'Jesus,' he said. 'John, come and take a look at this.'

Bald faced him. Gardner was scratching his head. A large wardrobe, the sole piece of furniture in the room, had been pushed against the left-hand wall. Gardner was looking at it, puzzled, like a guy trying to decipher hieroglyphics. Then Bald looked again, and he realized in the half-light that the wardrobe wasn't a wardrobe at all, but towering stacks of what looked like bank notes.

eleven

The stacks were three metres tall. They touched the damn ceiling. Bald counted at least fifty stacks stretching in a neat row. It was long and tall and seven stacks deep. Bald took a couple of steps closer to the wall of money. Ran his hand over the edges. The stacks were arranged in bundles, each bundle the thickness of a brick.

'Fuck me,' he said. 'There's got to be tens of millions here.'

Bald eased out a bundle and flicked through it. Benjamin Franklin stared sternly out at him from the face of each bank note. The bills were crisp and clean. The smell of freshly printed money filled his nostrils, made him feel warm and fuzzy inside, made him feel good about himself and life.

'Let's get a move on,' said Gardner. 'Klich is still out there. And the gunmen.'

Bald stayed silent. He stared at the money, thinking about all the things he could do with it.

'Mate,' Gardner said, his voice rising. 'We're running out of time.'

Bald made a promise to himself, to come back here once he had Klich. Line his pockets. He bid his goodbyes to Mr Franklin and strode back out to the landing, the smell of greenbacks on his fingers, quietly congratulating himself on his discovery.

Moving anti-clockwise, the two ex-Blades manoeuvred their way to the door at the nine o'clock mark. Gardner was a couple of metres behind Bald. Gunfire sparked up on the ground floor. Crackled like loud radio static. Monzant putting down suppressive fire on the gang, shouting hoarsely above the *ca-racks*. His FNC was the only weapon Bald could hear being discharged. At least the guy's keeping his end of the bargain, he thought. Pinning the gang down. But he also knew there were twelve of them and only one of Monzant. The battle-hardened part of his brain knew that Monzant couldn't hold them off for ever.

They cleared the room. There was less money in this room. A couple of knee-high stacks of greenbacks piled against the far wall, a cavity at head height in that wall. The floor was littered with chunks of plaster and wallpaper. Someone had gone at the wall with a mallet. Several bundles of cash had been removed from the stacks. Each bundle was thick as a brick and sealed with elastic bands and shoved inside a clear plastic bag. Bald spied a few bundles crammed into the wall cavity in a desperate attempt to hide money from somebody. The stacks called out to him, sang him the sweet tune of money.

Gardner said, 'Two rooms down. One to go.'

Bald said, 'Our man's in that room.'

'And the Russians too. The hostages are there, we're still missing two gunmen—'

'They're guarding the hostages.'

Gardner nodded, then frowned. 'Unless the CS gas knocked them out.'

'Only one way to find out. I'm right behind you, mate.'

Bald waited a couple of seconds for the sound of Gardner's heavy footsteps on the landing. Then he liberated a couple of tightly wrapped bundles from the pile beside the wall. Each bundle was surprisingly light, thought Bald. Yet there had to be a couple of hundred bucks in each. He had a four hundred large in his fucking hand. More than Leo Land's pension fund. And nobody would notice it had gone missing. He stuffed the cash into the pockets of his Belstaff and exited the room.

Four rapid bursts of gunfire echoed up from the entrance hall.

'Guys, a little help down here!' Monzant shouted up the stairs, his tone rabid. 'The fuckers are getting close!'

Just another minute, Bald thought, that's all I need. He let Gardner lead the way to the door at the three o'clock point. Gardner arrived there two seconds ahead of him, turned and made a shush gesture, then pressed his ear to the door. He motioned for Bald to do the same.

Bald killed his breath in his throat. Put his ear to the wood and listened. The door was hollow and muffled voices carried through from the other side. Wailing, moaning and coughing. Among them was a woman's voice, throaty and hysterical. She was bawling something over and over again in Spanish, like an incessant fucking chant. Bald looked at Gardner. Gardner looked right back at Bald. Their minds clicked through the same combinations, their eyes glowing as they registered the same thought at the same time.

The hostages.

This is it, thought Bald.

He got down on his knees and bent down to peer under the door, at the half-inch crack of light between it and the floor. He could make out a pair of combat boots, black and weathered. Left foot tapping out a beat. The feet weren't pacing up and down. A gunman, Bald figured. Guarding the hostages. Lack of movement suggested the guy was sitting on a chair. Bald looked up at Gardner and signed to him to train his Glock on the door handle. Now Bald sat up and trained his FNC on an imaginary spot at waist height, where he figured the gunman's head would be. He gave Gardner a slight nod.

Now!

Gardner unloaded three rounds at the handle. The noise was thunderous. The force of the shots trashed the lock. Bald heard a wet thump coming from the other side of the door. A body dropping. Then Gardner booted the heavy door at waist height. It swung back on its hinges before it knocked against something and jolted, refusing to swing open beyond a forty-five-degree angle. Bald looked through the apertures at the imaginary head he was aiming at. The door swung open a few inches more, and the head became real. Bald had the gunman dead in his sights. He was rising from his chair, AK-47 in his hands. Looking up just in time to acknowledge Bald and the rifle barrel, and the world of pain coming his way.

Bald squeezed the trigger. Dropped the guy.

He spotted the second corpse immediately behind the door. The last gunman. Bullets stitching the guy's throat. There had been two gunmen behind the door, not one. They had unwittingly slotted the sixth and final fucker as he had been creeping up to the door. That's it, thought Bald with a deep sigh of relief. All the gunmen are down.

Gardner tried pushing the door fully open, but it wouldn't budge. He frowned. The cries from inside the room cranked up a few decibels. Sounded like a hundred people wailing away in there. Gardner tried to push the door all the way back. But it resisted. The fifth gunman, lying behind the door, was wedging it.

Bald watched Gardner wrestle with the door. Then he quietly backtracked and paced over to the gunman Gardner had dropped a few minutes earlier, when Bald had first reached the landing. The gunman who had come close to cutting his life short. He was still sprawled by the door at the twelve o'clock mark. The pool of blood under him was coagulating and was now thick and brown and gooey like molasses. Bald quietly laid down his FNC and relieved the dead guy of his AK-47. The clip was engaged with the recess in the mag feed and properly snapped into place, and the charging handle was in the release position. This indicated that a round was chambered and ready to discharge. The rifle selector on the right-hand side of the trigger guard was set to the middle position: full automatic. Then Bald stood up, holding the weapon in a two-handed grip, and fixed his gaze on Gardner.

Just in time to see Gardner pointing the Glock at him.

Bald froze. Gardner had a look in his eyes he had never seen before. His eyes were black and dead, like a spotlight with the bulb blown. Clay skin drained of colour. His face a blank.

Bald said, 'The fuck you think you're doing?'

Gardner said, 'Land told me to kill you.'

twelve

Bald slowly lowered his left hand from the AK's barrel, let it fall by his side. He kept his right hand wrapped around the trigger guard. Wanting to defuse the situation, but not willing to drop his guard. Gardner kept the Glock trained on Bald. Shifted on the balls of his feet.

'Easy, Joe,' said Bald. 'Don't do anything fucking stupid.'

The blank look on Gardner's face melted away. His eyes took on a new sheen. Glowed intense white, like bleached sand, and shrank his irises to pinpricks. 'Talk to me about stupid,' he said. 'You were about to put a bullet in my back.'

Bald inched closer to Gardner. 'Land told me the same thing as you. Said I had to kill you before the mission was over.' He smiled a chummy smile. 'But I was never going to go through with it. Never even crossed my mind.'

'Then what the fuck are you doing, grabbing that guy's weapon?'

'We're mates,' Bald said, ignoring the question. 'Remember, Joe? All the shit we've been through, you think I'd cap you? If I was going to kill you, like Land said, I could've done it outside, when the gang had us in range. I could've left you to die.'

Gardner frowned for a beat. Unsure. Then he shook his face. Shaking off the frown.

'Bullshit,' he said. 'You're lying. You're just saying that to fuck with me.'

'It's the truth. Swear on it,' said Bald. 'Land is the real enemy here, mate. Not me.'

Gardner all quiet and shit, his eyes darting left and right at empty spaces, like here was Bald telling him one thing and there was Land telling him something else, and which one to believe?

'Did Land say why he wanted you to kill me?'

Bald shook his head. 'Posh wanker just said you were a problem that needed taking care of. Why, what did he tell you?'

'Same.' Gardner shrugged.

The cries coming from the room were getting louder. Downstairs Monzant was screaming for help. The gang was closing in. They were almost out of time. They seized Klich now, or they didn't seize him at all.

'Looks like we're in a Mexican stand-off,' said Bald. 'Put the gun down, Joe.'

'Drop yours first.'

Gardner's neck muscles tensing like rope.

'You're gonna believe that twat Land over me?'

'Give me one good reason why I shouldn't.' Gardner smiled painfully and shook his head.

'You stupid cunt,' said Bald, taking a couple of steps closer to Gardner. 'We're on the same side. Think about it. Land doesn't give a shit about you or me. The only way we're going to get through this is working together.'

'One more step and I'll drop you, John. I mean it.'

Bald stopped. Raised his left hand. 'OK. Look. Shit. Let's call a truce. We need each other to get Klich out of here in one piece. We get him to safety. Mission over. Then we fucking sort out Land ourselves. How about it, Joe?'

Bald watched Gardner chewing his lower lip as he grappled with the problem of whether to trust a man he'd left for dead in the desert. The hostages were shouting at full volume now. Wild hollers were coming up from below too. Gardner gave a slight nod of his head. Deal. Bald breathed a sigh of relief. 'Go help Monzant pin down the gang,' he said. 'I'll grab our Russian mate.'

Gardner swung away and charged down the stairs. Bald turned to the door. Dropped the FNC by his side, lowered his shoulder, took a run-up to the door and shoulder-barged it. The door put up some resistance. The body of the gunman was blocking the other side. Bald slung the rifle over his shoulder by the strap, planted both his palms on the door and pushed. Felt the body begin to dislodge. The guy was over-heavy, like he was made of anti-matter. And then suddenly the body moved and the door was flying open and Bald was stumbling inside, his momentum carrying him a few steps into the room. He tripped over the fifth gunman, only regaining his balance at the last moment. Unslinging the FNC again, he cleared the corners.

Then Bald looked down. The gunman had a trauma wound to the neck. There was a collar of abrasion around the entry wound and a greasy rim of torched skin. Powder tattoos stippled the skin around the neck. The impact of the shot had created a star-shaped cavity, the surrounding skin over-stretched and torn by the tension of the bullet. The skin on his hands and face was reddened and the eyes were puffy. Effects of the CS gas, Bald realized. Entrails of CS smoke were rising to the ceiling, where they dispersed.

Bald stepped over the body and directed his gaze ahead. His buddy was two metres further back. Still seated on a chair. His head drooping forward, like he'd dozed off. Blood oozing out of his upper chest. Ten metres behind him, at the far end of room, ceiling-high windows provided a view overlooking the front of the villa. The windows were punched out. The sun was a purplish-red cuticle raging on the horizon, and there was a dead gunman covered in shards of glass by the window. The sniper that the operators had slotted during the approach to the villa. His skull had been split open.

The hostages were in a loose circle in the middle of the room. They were blindfolded and their hands were plasti-cuffed behind their backs. Half the hostages were prostrate, hacking up their guts or lying next to pools of vomit. They all had mucus streaming out of their noses and down their chins, crying between bouts of profuse coughing. The gas had rendered a couple of them unconscious. About a dozen of the hostages had the soft complexions and the prim clothes of people who had lived their whole lives on civvie street. Half a dozen guys were the size of tanks, dumb muscle shrink-wrapped in black suits. The security detail. There was a priest and a nun, neither blindfolded, but both with their eyes clamped shut, tears streaming down their cheeks, grimacing from the burning sensations of the gas. Bald couldn't smell the CS as it was odourless, but he could feel it. Particles of it itching his skin, making his eyes water and suddenly restrict-ing his breathing. Like walking into a room that had just been bug-bombed. Bald wiped away tears and did a quick head-count. Twenty people.

None of the men matched the profile of Viktor Klich.

Four gunshots boomed out from downstairs. Gardner and Monzant putting the drop on the gang. Gardner shouted up to Bald, 'Hurry the fuck up, mate! We're can't hold them off for much longer.'

Bald hurried to the door. He stopped by the dead gunman on the floor, struck by something odd. A hand was sticking out from beneath him. A delicate, feminine hand. Ebony. Bald rolled the guy over. A woman was pinned underneath. She was dressed in the same black suit as the security detail but had the slender, curved shape of a woman. Face down with her arms pulled tight across her chest. Bald turned her over. Recognized the face from the picture Gardner had showed him a couple of hours ago in the Chevrolet.

He was looking at Odessa Stone.

She stirred and with a light, weary moan wriggled free. Then she looked up at Bald and her eyes went wide as Coke bottle caps. She shook her head and glanced around, disorientated.

'Where is he?' said Bald.

Odessa didn't answer. She looked at the civilians. Then at the dead guy. She swung her eyes back to the gnarled ex-Blade six inches from her face.

'Where's Klich?' Bald said again.

Odessa raised a hand to her temple and ran her fingers along a large gash.

'He's in big fucking trouble,' said Bald. 'Where is Klich?'

Odessa looked away from Bald. Not looking at anyone or anything. Just staring at nothing, her face twisted, like she was having a bad trip. 'You're too late,' she said.

Bald gripped her shoulders. Three more shots echoing along the landing, like a hundred hammers smashing down on a lead pipe at the same time. Bald kept flicking his eyes back to the door. The battle was raging downstairs. The rate of fire increasing with each burst, the *ca-racks* followed by the clinking of spent brass on marble floor. That told him the gang was closing in. He shook Odessa.

'Where the fuck is he?'

Odessa wasn't tuned in. She ran her soft fingers down to her lips. They were purpled and cut and her jaw was swollen. Looked like she had a mouthful of ice. She was about to say something when sirens wailed in the distance. Bald sprinted the length of the room, looked out of the window. He spotted seven police cars screaming down the road and screeching to a halt at the gates. A double-dozen cops launching out of the cars and gunning for the gang. FNCs in their hands and menace in their eyes. The tide was about to turn. Across the road the guy with the RPG launcher was turning to the cops and bricking it. He took five rounds to his torso and dropped. His mate picked up the warhead and took a stream of bullets as well. His mates legged it up the road leading back to the slums. The cops began pouring into the porch.

Bald beat a path back to Odessa. He had already put behind him his disappointment about Klich. In the Regiment you were taught to think with clarity of purpose at all times. Emotions like regret or remorse were wasteful. You lived simply, in the moment, and you kept one eye on your next move. Bald didn't dwell on the disappointment at not finding the Russian. He knew Odessa was the only one who would know what had happened to him, so he made it his priority to keep her by his side at all times. He seized her hand and escorted from the room. Gardner was already on the landing, his face and body oozing sweat, like he'd just stepped out of the shower. He looked at Odessa and blinked his confusion.

'Klich isn't here,' Bald said before Gardner could pop-quiz him.

'Then where?'

'Fuck knows. I'm going to check on Monzant. You check out the other hostages.'

Then Bald was brushing past Gardner and bounding down the stairs, Odessa in tow. She was still groggy, but her five-six frame was supple and her muscles finely tuned, and she managed to descend without too much support from Bald. They cleared the treads two at a time. Bald ushered Odessa through the entrance hall.

Monzant was lying by the double doors. His head was slumped against the wall, his neck lacquered in fresh blood. His belly was stitched with bullets and his torso was springing a bunch of leaks. The civvies were hurrying out through the doors, towards the cops flooding the porch. The priest stopped to kneel beside Monzant and began reading from a dog-eared Bible. He was wearing an ankle-length black cassock with a collarino dress shirt and a white cloth insert at the throat. His plain black shoes were scuffed with blood and dust. He had a scraggly beard and thick-rimmed black glasses, and he kept glancing across at the entrance. Bald watched the cops storming up the steps. He gently set Odessa down by the stairs and approached the priest. Guy was reading the last rites. Bald kicked the Bible out of his hands. Sent it flying across the bullet-streaked marble.

'Move it, kiddie fiddler.'

The priest said nothing. Looked at the floor and pretended Bald wasn't there.

'You heard me, old man,' Bald said. 'Take your Bible and fuck off.'

The priest studied the floor very hard. Then he scurried off just as the first wave of cops poured into the villa. He scooped up his Bible and ducked out of their way as they swept into the entrance hall. Bald pointed to the stairs.

'*Agua,*' Monzant throated. '*Agua, amigo.*'

Monzant tried to explain himself with his right hand, trying to unscrew the cap on the water canteen latched to his utility belt. Trying and failing. Bald reached across to the canteen and unscrewed the cap. Monzant's eyes brightened. Bald started tipping water into his eager mouth. He watched the cops piling up the stairs. Leaned in close to Monzant. The guy greedily glugging away and coming back to life. Then Bald took the index finger and thumb of his free hand and, shielding himself from view of the last cops, clamped them over Monzant's nostrils. He kept on pouring the water, forcing it down his gullet. Monzant started to feebly kick and jerk his head away. But Bald held the canteen in place and went on clamping the guy's nostrils. His face turned blue, then purple. His eyes bulged in their sockets. He swiped a limp hand at Bald, like a puppet trying to swat a fly. Then the colour drained from his face, and he stopped kicking. Bald stood up and coolly watched the life seeping out of Monzant.

'Fucking cross me, you cunt, that's what you get,' he said.

Bald beat a path back to Odessa. He found himself attracted to her. Despite the bruises and cuts she still looked great. Scratch that. She looked better than great. She made great look like a fat bitch with a face like a bucket of smashed crabs. He slung an arm around her shoulder and lifted her to her feet. His leg muscles throbbed. His shoulder muscles ached. Every part of his body was off the pain scale. He told himself he needed to get clear of the villa. Hide up somewhere, wait for Odessa to get her shit in order. She had to have some idea of where her boss was. He started for the porch. Odessa was still totally out of it, her feet dragging a step or two behind the rest of her. She rested her head on Bald's shoulder. He liked the feel of her skin against his. He liked the warmth of her breath and the cinnamon smell of her hair.

He paused at the doors. More cops were gathering out front. Bald clocked Rodríguez. The sergeant was alive. A medic was tending to his broken nose. Then Rodríguez clocked Bald. Shot him an evil look. Bald remembered what Monzant had said. The Venezuelans were blaming Bald and Gardner for the leak to the gang. If he didn't want to reacquaint himself with a pair of silver bracelets, he needed to get as far away from the Venezuelans as possible. Rodríguez pointed furiously at Bald, barked orders at the cops. Bald reversed down the hall. Odessa whimpered, then said, 'I know another way out of here.'

'Where?'

'Middle door, past the staircase.'

'Give me one fucking reason why I should trust you.'

Odessa smiled faintly.

'Same reason I'm trusting you right now,' she said. 'Because I don't have any other choice.'

Bald was thinking, if Odessa knew another way out of here, the odds were good that Klich would have bugged out using the same route. So the trail wasn't cold. Not yet. A second wave of energy juiced his bloodstream. He barged open the middle door and crashed into a billiards room. Saw a body in an expensive flannel suit and an Omega 5 watch lying on the floor. The diplomat the Russians had executed, Bald realized. Rincón. Bald bypassed the poor cunt and gritted his teeth at the millions of dollars he was leaving behind. He had kissed a hundred grand goodbye in Almaty. Kissed a million more goodbye in Caracas. And he didn't have Klich. But he did have Odessa. He was still in the fucking game.

There was another door at the far end of the billiards room.

'Through here,' Odessa croaked.

'What happened to the other bodyguards?' Bald said.

Odessa said nothing.

Bald yanked open the door. A set of wooden steps descended into a cave-like cellar. Bald supported Odessa's weight as he carted down the steps. He was leaving Gardner behind, but he didn't feel bad about that, not at all. The cellar was muggy and the air was thick with dust. Naked bulbs illuminated rows of vintage wines. Bottle necks caked in generations of dust. Bald could hear his breathing echoing off the stone walls. Odessa directed Bald through the cellar. There was a space between two racks of vintage Bordeaux. The space widened into a low, cramped corridor, more like a tunnel.

'Down here,' Odessa said. 'We follow it all the way.'

'How long is this fucking thing?'

'You'll see.'

Bald shuttled into the tunnel. The going was slow. Odessa hobbled alongside him. Every step triggered a hundred pains.

His body was stiffening, his muscles hardening, like cement drying. There was no light: he was heading into a blackness that was flat and dense yet also endlessly deep. The air was Siberian. Water dripped through unseen leaks in the roof. Stones crunched under his boots. He had to bend and keep his head low and tuck his chin tight to his neck, and that slowed his pace even more. There was nothing but the blackness for the longest while. Bald had no up or down, no left or right. It was like he was submerged in a tar pit.

He felt Odessa stirring by his side. Leaning into him less, putting more weight on her feet. Another four or five steps and she was walking without his aid. He heard her footsteps stop for a moment. She was coughing her guts up. Then she spat something out, groaned, and started moving again.

'How did you know this thing existed?' Bald asked.

'Wherever my boss goes, he likes to be someplace he can leave in a hurry.'

Bald said nothing.

'Did you see the money?' Odessa asked.

Bald nodded, then realized she couldn't see him. 'There's millions in there,' he answered.

'Fifteen million dollars. That was my boss's payment to the Venezuelans. To guarantee his safe keeping. But they set him up.'

'Who? His mate the President?'

'The cops. They were gonna collude with the gangs. Split the takings between them.'

Rodríguez, thought Bald. Made all kinds of sense to him that the mini-rupert might spill his guts to the gang. He spotted a beautiful chord of light in the distance, the size of an aspirin pill. Willed his body on. A naked bulb flickered like a distant star, marking the end of the tunnel. There was a metal door beyond the bulb. Rusted lock. Odessa shoved a key into the lock and gave it a clockwise twist. Levers cranked. Then the door swung back and sunlight gushed through the opening, fierce and pristine, stinging Bald's eyes.

They emerged into an alley. Bald smelled the place before he could see it. It was not a good smell. Like rotten meat smeared with dog shit. There were more smells in a square metre of Caracas than in the whole of London or New York. He helped Odessa out of the tunnel. She locked the door behind her. It was an old metal thing disguised as a power station outlet, stickered with warning signs in Spanish, and graphic illustrations of a man getting electrocuted. Bald did a one-eighty and scoped out the alley. It was ten metres long and fanned out into a pleasant plaza buzzing with tourists and restaurants and sweet aromas. But the alleyway itself was a slum. Families were laying out flattened cardboard boxes and using soiled blankets as pillows. Getting ready to bed in for the night. Bald saw a police car flash past the plaza.

He hauled Odessa over to an unclaimed spot and lay her down next to a family of seven or eight. An old man with a face like a sucked orange gave Bald the evil eye. It was the only eye he had. There was a viscous, oozing welt where his right eye should have been. He barked something at Bald and pointed at Odessa. She was already crashing out. Bald got the message. Even in cardboard city, you had to pay rent. He reluctantly fished a Franklin from the bundle and handed it to the old man. The old man studied it suspiciously with his one eye. Like a jeweller trying to determine the value of a diamond. He'd probably never seen a hundred-dollar bill before. He slipped it into his shirt pocket and went back to his family. Bald making poverty history.

Then his BlackBerry vibrated. He dug it out. Land's number was flashing up on the display. Bald peeled away from Odessa and the bums and took the call. The signal was scratchy and kept cutting out. Land's voice came down the line like a badly tuned radio.

'Where the bloody hell are you?' he said.

'Cardboard city,' said Bald. 'The siege went tits up.'

'Jesus. What happened?'

'You lied to me. You set us up.'

'What the devil are you talking about?'

'Joe Gardner, that's fucking what. You told him to kill me.'

'John,' Land said, 'you're a fucking idiot. Do you really think I'd put the entire mission in jeopardy? If I got you both killed, no one would be around to escort Klich to safety. Let me speak to Joe.'

Bald clenched his jaws so hard he thought they might never loosen.

'He's not here,' he said.

Land paused a beat.

'Where is he then?'

'Joe got lost in the battle. Fuck knows where he is now. And Klich was gone, by the time we rocked up,' said Bald. 'If the captain hadn't been trying to audition for Rambo, we might have got him. But I do have Odessa Stone. The bodyguard. She's gotta know where we can find Klich.'

Land made a strange noise, like he was laughing through his nose.

'You bloody fool. You let Klich slip through your fingers. That's why I kept trying to call you. Couldn't get through. One of the diplomats tipped us off. It turns out that Klich was in disguise.'

Bald looked up at the sky. He had the funny feeling it was about to cave in.

'He was dressed as a priest, John.'

The sky didn't cave in. Bald felt like he was sinking into the ground. The words slugged him in the guts, left him reeling and unsteady. He spun on his feet and sprinted back down the alley. Odessa had pulled the wool over his eyes. He passed the family, the kids now extending their palms and begging for money. He reached Odessa and whipped off the filthy blanket she was sleeping under.

Then Bald did a double-take. Land's voice fizzling out of the BlackBerry limp by his side, faintly reaching his ears. 'John? Are you there? Chrissake, answer me.'

Odessa had disappeared.

thirteen

Caracas, Venezuela. 2003 hours.

The sign announced the bar as the Galway Hooker. Made it sound like a brothel with a sea view. John Bald sized up the joint from the street corner. The place was a pure Irish scumhole set a couple of winding streets back from Avenida Casanova, way the fuck down in the middle of Bello Monte district, a steep kilometre west of the villa in the Country Club suburb. From here Bald had a panoramic view of the city at dusk.

But he couldn't see much: night was settling like slow black snow across the city. At the front gates of the villa, he could make out ambulances racked up, medics ferrying slotted SF operators across the porch. Bald was lucky to have escaped the clusterfuck, especially since his mucker Joe Gardner had ended up in a pair of silver bracelets on a murder charge. But that was about all that Bald had to be thankful for. He looked again at the knackered old BlackBerry in his hand. The display was still black and dead. He had no way of reaching his contact at the Firm. Maybe that wasn't such a bad thing: all he'd get from Leo Land would be an earful of shit.

Sweet Jesus, he needed a fucking beer.

Bald sized up the other half-dozen bars lining the street. They were all cosmopolitan places with yuppie crowds and minimalist interiors and DJs beating out too-cool-for-school tunes. Bald felt like a plate of shit reheated for breakfast and if he tried frequenting any of those swank joints he'd stick out like a straight guy at a Glee party. So he headed for the Galway Hooker. The black paintwork was chipped and blistered like a picked scab. The windows were smeared with dirt so thick that from a distance you might easily have mistaken them for brown curtains. Bottle glass was sprinkled about the entrance. Bald broke out into a little cheer inside. He'd never been so happy to see a bar.

Bald stepped through the door. Nu Metal was playing, all death growls and aggressive riffs. The bar had its own microclimate. It was like shoving your face into a fat guy's armpit. A couple of old-timers were seated at a booth and masked behind a veil of fag smoke. Irish old-timers, thought Bald. Guys with mean fucking eyes and skin like petrified wood, looked like they had been sitting there longer than Google had been a word. Probably part of the wave of IRA pricks who'd fucked off to Latin America after the Good Friday Agreement, swapped the Emerald Isle for emerald-eyed birds. Bald ignored them and strode to the bar. He pulled up a stool, gestured to the barman. Short, skinny guy with just-got-out-of-bed hair and an XXL Celtic FC replica shirt hanging from him like a fucking tent. He had the words 'IRISH' and 'PRIDE' scrawled on his knuckles.

'What have you got?' Bald said, surprising himself with how thirsty his voice sounded.

The man narrowed his eyes at a stack of refrigerated lager. Like he had only just started working there and he wasn't exactly sure what beers they stocked. 'I got ten types of Polar.' The accent was Dublin via Croydon.

'Anything British?'

The plastic paddy fuck shook his head in disgust.

'A Polar then.'

The barman slid Bald a bottle of liquid gold with a cartoon sketch of a polar bear on the label. Droplets of ice-cold lager traced veins down the neck. Bald raised the bottle to his mouth. The cold glass rim kissed his lips. He took his first swig. Christ, but that felt good. He gulped down half the bottle in one go. Ahhhh!

He quickly drained the rest of his Polar. Waved to the barman for another.

After three beers, he felt relaxed. After six, he felt chilled. After ten beers and three double Jameson's he felt arctic. At 2200 hours a young couple, backpackers, Israelis, looked inside the bar. Quickly left. About an hour later the two old-timers unglued themselves from their seats and shuffled out onto the street, and Bald was left alone with the barman and the Polar for company. Around midnight the barman slapped a bill in front of him. Bald's eyes focused on the ton of zeroes at the bottom, and he sobered up a little. He dipped a hand into the pocket of his Belstaff leather jacket and sobered up a little more. Padded down his other pockets. Frowned.

'There a problem, pal?' The paddy was screwing his eyes at Bald and making a face like an airbag being crammed back into the wheel.

Bald rooted through his pockets. He pulled out a few balled-up receipts and a couple of coins. But that was it. A thought slapped him in the face. The hundred and sixty large he'd looted from the villa was missing. His mind scuttled back to cardboard city, on the other side of Caracas. To the alley he'd bugged out to after escaping from the villa. He thought about the homeless family and the old bastard with the sucked-in cheeks. He felt lead weights tugging at his guts, the thought growing legs and arms and telling him that he must have been pickpocketed while he had been distracted.

Fucking bums.

Then Bald looked up and found himself eyeball to eyeball with a shotgun.

fourteen

The weapon looked ridiculous in the paddy's grip, like he was trying to wrestle a crocodile. His left hand rested on the choke and his right hand was wrapped around the trigger. Bald tried not to think about the fact that the muzzle was eight inches from his chest, and weighed up the situation.

A Heckler & Koch FP6. Twelve-gauge pump-action with the barrel sawn down to fourteen inches from the regulation twenty. Sawn-offs were good for two things. One was concealment. The other was power. What the shorter barrel lost in range and accuracy, it made up for in the damage it did. The cone of fire was twice as wide, carrying enough destructive power to sever a guy at the torso. One squeeze of the trigger and a twelve-gauge slug would rip a hole in Bald that would make him look like he'd swallowed a hand grenade. The big mirror behind the bar gave him a view of the room behind him. Fucking empty. He was the only punter desperate enough to spend his evening in the Galway Hooker. He flicked his eyes from the shotgun to the barman and thought he saw a flicker of doubt in the black pinpricks that passed for his eyes.

'Pull that fucking thing on me you'd better use it,' said Bald.

'I don't want any trouble,' said the barman. 'Just pay up and leave.'

'I got robbed.'

'I hear that a lot.'

'I'll come back tomorrow. Settle up then.'

'Hear that a lot too.' The paddy fuck pointed with his eyeballs to the Tag Heuer Aquaracer on Bald's left wrist. 'That's a nice fucking watch.'

'What are you, my style guru?' said Bald.

'No, I'm your fucking mother. Now take off the piece.'

But Bald kept his hands where they were. He could put up with a lot of shit, but he drew the line at some two-bit Irish cunt stealing his watch. The Aquaracer had been a gift to himself, on his thirtieth birthday. No way was he giving it away to this guy.

'I asked nicely,' the paddy said. 'Don't make me ask un-nicely.'

Bald started sliding off his stool.

'Where you think you're going?'

'I'm leaving,' said Bald. 'The service in this place is shit.'

The barman tightened his finger on the trigger.

'Another step and you'll regret it.'

Then the door creaked open, the barman directed his gaze past Bald and in the same instant smoothly withdrew the sawn-off below the counter. Bald glanced over his shoulder. A woman had slipped through the door. At first he couldn't see much of her in the soupy gloom, but the closer she came the more he liked what he saw. She had the kind of body to make a guy eat his own face. Button eyes, slimline lips the colour of strawberries, long legs gift-wrapped inside a pair of denim knicker shorts. Tits bulging from a strapless bandeau crop-top. Her hair was brunette and shoulder-length and flowed like a gown. She looked Venezuelan. She looked like she had just stepped out of one of Bald's wildest fantasies. He'd once banged a Colombian beauty. Looks like a model and screwed like a high-class hooker. Venezuelan women were cut from the same cloth. But hotter. Bald watched the woman saunter up to the bar in the highest pair of platform shoes he'd ever seen, and prop herself on the stool next to him. 'You going to stare at me like a pervert, or get me a beer?' she said to the barman.

Obediently he fetched a Polar and popped the cap for her, all the time glaring at Bald. The woman removed a pack of Lucky Strikes from her purse and sparked up. Bald didn't know if there was a smoking ban in Venezuela or not. Maybe there was and the woman just didn't care. She looked like the kind who went around flouting the rules just for shits and giggles.

'I can tell you're not from around here,' she said to Bald. She had a smooth accent but a little husky around the edges. Like a bar of chocolate melting in a pan. She went on, 'Now let me guess. You're very white. You have big muscles.'

She nodded at the ten empty soldiers clustered in front of Bald.

'But you can handle your beer,' she said. 'So you're not American or Canadian.'

'What are you, a detective?'

'And you have a funny accent.' She toyed with a curl of her hair. 'You must be Australian.'

Bald grinned.

'Am I close?'

'I'm from Scotland.'

The woman pulled a face. 'What is that, a city?'

'It's a place where all the men are rock hard,' said Bald.

The woman shrugged and reached across Bald to pick up a glass ashtray, giving him a sneak preview of her rack. Her hair smelled of suntan lotion and sex.

'I love your accent,' she said.

Bald grinned again.

'Know what else I love?' she said.

The barman retreated.

'Fucking,' she said. She coolly tapped ash into the tray.

Bald's grin stretched out like a piece of elastic. 'Funny,' he said. 'We've only just met but we already have so much in common.'

She leaned into Bald again. Winked at him and offered her hand.

'Carmen.'

'Joe Gardner,' said Bald, using the first name that popped into his head.

'What brings you to Caracas, Joe? Business or pleasure?'

'Was the first.'

'And now?'

'Thinking maybe it's the other,' Bald slurred. He was feeling pretty tanked and doing his best not to show it. Which basically involved sitting upright and ignoring the fact that the world was spinning around him.

'I like the way you think,' Carmen nodded at him approvingly. She didn't seem to notice that he was pissed. Or maybe she didn't care. She drained the rest of her beer and stubbed out her cigarette. Fingers of smoke stroked the ceiling. She looked at Bald for a little while and toyed with her hair. Her eyes stared deeply at Bald, fucking the shit out of him.

Finally she leant closer and whispered, 'Want to know a secret?'

Bald nodded.

'My pussy's lonely,' she pouted. 'Want to give it some company?'

Bald drained his whisky in a hurry. Carmen left three crisp hundred-bolivar notes on the bar: enough to cover both their tabs. Then Bald hopped off his stool. He let Carmen walk a couple of steps in front, so he could admire her arse. It was curved and pert and it swayed like a pendant from hip to hip. He was fucking hypnotized by it. Bald rubbed his hands, pleased with himself. He had gone from having a shotgun drawn point-blank on him to having a crack at the arse of the century. He turned to the bar. Smiled a big old 'fuck you' at the plastic paddy.

'The fuck's so funny?' the guy said.

'You,' said Bald. 'And the fact that I'll be getting a ride on that later, and you'll be spending the rest of your life in this dump. That's not funny. It's fucking hilarious.'

The paddy made a smile like a slit throat.

What's he got to be pleased about? thought Bald.

It turned out that Carmen lived a couple of blocks up from Avenida Casanova, on a street populated by knackered old VW Beetles, potholes and wild dogs. She led Bald through an archway into a courtyard surrounded by a block of modest-looking apartments painted nail-salon shades of yellow and pink. Bald followed her butt up a wrought-iron stairwell, their footsteps backdropped by the chirps of crickets. Carmen ushered him into the apartment furthest from the stairwell, overlooking the courtyard.

The decor reminded him of a budget motel. There was hardly any furniture. What little she owned was cheap and tawdry. Carmen led Bald through the reception room and down a sparse hallway. The apartment smelled like bubble gum. Four short paces and he found himself in the bedroom. The bed had no duvet or sheets on it and the mattress was still wrapped in the original warehouse packaging. A rickety little table stood beside it and overhead there was a wooden fan. Dead moths had gathered like dried leaves in the wall lights.

Carmen pushed herself against Bald. She started rubbing his crotch and eyefucking him. Bald was taken aback by her direct manner. But then again he figured this was the way Latino women did their thing. He preferred it to the timid approach of English women. He ran his hands over Carmen's shoulders and down her back and clamped them over her arse and squeezed. She made a faint sigh. Then she traced her lips down his neck. He could feel her breath on him, fast and loose and heavy with the promise of sex. Bald went to kiss her, but she pushed him away and smiled playfully at him. Set him down on the edge of the bed, putting his eyes level with her chest. He had a raging hard-on in his pants as Carmen pulled her strapless crop-top up over her neck and tossed it at Bald. Underneath she was wearing a strapless black lace bra that barely suspended her tits.

She drew close to Bald and buried his face into the clammy crevice between her breasts. Bald went wild. He licked at her flesh and groped her arse while she ran a long-nailed hand through his hair and moaned dreamily.

'Kiss me,' Carmen said between gasps. 'Kiss me and don't stop.'

Bald wrapped his arms around her waist and pulled her towards him as he fell back onto the bed. She landed on top of him and started grinding up and down on his crotch. She tasted good. She tasted of cherry and rose wine and Marlboro Lights. Twirls of her hair stroked his face. Bald fiddled with the strap on her bra and was about to rip it off when he heard something, and froze.

A car pulling up. A mechanical growl followed by a squeal as it screeched to a halt. Sounded like it was in the court-yard down below. His eyes wandered from the flesh in front of him and focused on the front door. He heard the urgent thump-thump of car doors being slammed. Bald didn't like the sound of this. He tried pushing Carmen off but she kept him pinned down. Smothering him with kisses and her rack. Finally he rolled her to one side and leapt off the bed. Footsteps were clanking up the stairwell. Bald raced to the front door. Glanced out of the window. Did a double-take as he saw a lime-green BMW 3 Series rumbling down in the courtyard. Long experience had taught Bald that only one type of guy would dare drive a brightly coloured Beemer. He looked back at Carmen. She was standing sheepishly in the bedroom doorway, covering her tits with an arm and cocking her head curiously at Bald. The footsteps were getting closer. Now the footsteps paused on the other side of the door. A lone thought cut through the booze haze and struck Bald like a blade.

Carmen's a fucking hooker, he thought as a hand rattled the door knob.

And her pimp's just rolled up.

fifteen

The door cracked open and Bald knew he was in the shit. The pimp's after his cash, he figured. I'll have to fucking slog my way out. Knock him down with a punch to the face and fucking leg it. Bald clenched his fist. Then the door widened a little more, and the gap was filled by a face, swathed in shadows and with a fedora on top. A figure stepped through the door. Swaggered into the apartment like he fucking owned the whole block. Bald dumbly watched a slender hand lift the hat as the man entered the room. The spotlights blasted away the shadows and revealed a face with a stern jawline and precisely combed hair, and a pair of eyes like weathered marbles.

Leo Land.

Bald felt his fist loosen. Felt the tension draining from his head and neck. It was replaced with a boozy numbness. Land seemed not to notice Bald at first. He nodded at the bedroom door. At Carmen. She had finished putting the strapless top back on and was chewing gum loudly. Land plucked an envelope from inside his jacket and tossed it to her.

'There's two thousand in there,' he said. 'One thousand to cover your expenses and another thousand to keep your mouth buttoned shut.'

Carmen slyly peeked inside the envelope.

'Where's Manny?' she said.

Land blinked. 'Who?'

'My pimp.'

'He's busy.'

Carmen shrugged, then stuffed the envelope into a bright-red shoulder bag and blew a kiss at Bald. 'Adiós, honey.' She did a little pirouette on her platform heels as she sashayed towards the front door. A swing of her hips this way and that and she was breezing out of his life and into the dark of the night. As she left Bald glimpsed the silhouette of another agent standing guard at the front door of the apartment. He turned back to Land.

'What the fuck are you doing here?'

'Nice to see you too, old boy,' said Land. He pulled up a chair at a glass dining table next to the small kitchen area, gently placed the fedora on the table and ran a hand through his thinning hair. 'You should be thanking me. Manny was on his way to collect his fee.'

'I can take care of myself.'

Land said nothing. The spotlights were blinding Bald. Ice-picks of light rebounded off the walls and screamed inside his head. Bald closed his eyes, tried to shut out the pain.

'You set me up,' he said.

Land chuckled. 'If I hadn't got here in time, then just about now Manny and his thugs would have been nailing your hands and feet to the floor.'

Bald grimaced. The fog was beginning to lift from behind his eyes.

'What do you want?'

'What I want, John, is for you to explain why you went AWOL after the gunfight at the villa. A gunfight in which you singularly failed to apprehend our Russian target.' The MI6 man narrowed his eyes at Bald. 'You know what that means, don't you?'

'You finally realized you're a prize cunt.'

'It means you and I have unfinished business. You ought to know better than to think you can simply walk away from a botched job.'

Bald finally sat up. Slowly. His body ached in a thousand places. Land looked worse than the last time he'd laid eyes on him. His dandy leather brogues were in need of a good polish. His features were creased like an old suit. His suit was creased like an old face.

'You lied to me,' said Bald.

Land pulled a face. 'What are you talking about?'

'Joe gave me the spread. He had the same orders you gave me. First chance he got, he was supposed to put a bullet in the back of my fucking head.'

'And you actually believe him?'

'Joe's a spineless cunt, but he's not a liar.'

Land said nothing. Bald looked into his eyes. They were the colour of faint smoke. It was impossible to tell what he was thinking. Land summed up everything Bald detested about civvie street. No one ever sold it to you straight. In the Regiment, if something was shit, they'd tell you to your face.

'Give me one reason I should believe you,' said Bald.

'Christ, why would I ask Gardner to kill you? Who would be left to escort Viktor Klich to safety?' Land rustled up a cruel smile. 'Gardner played you like a drum set, old boy.'

Bald closed his eyes. His neck muscles were tugging on his veins, pulling them tight across his skull.

'So where is he?'

'Joe? En route to the worst jail in Venezuela. The authorities are pinning the murder of Captain Monzant on him. But what concerns me most is that Klich is still out there.'

A long moment of silence played out between the two men, Bald living in the blackness behind his eyelids. Then the moment passed and Land's clipped voice was breaching the emptiness.

'We know where he is,' said Land.

Bald opened his eyes.

'Klich?'

Land nodded.

'Where?'

'Dubai.'

'I hear the hookers out there rock your world,' said Bald. He headed for the front door of the apartment. But Land took a few steps and imposed his spindly frame between the Scot and the door.

'You're not quite getting it, are you? You're going to go to Dubai, John. And you're going to bring me Viktor Klich.'

Bald laughed.

'I'm done playing your fucking games.'

'In that case our deal is off. No clean slate. No villa on Madeira. And certainly no two hundred and fifty thousand pound payday.'

'Suck a bag of dicks,' Bald growled. 'We had a deal.'

'Conditional on your bringing Klich back to me. But you let him slip through your fingers.'

Bald balled his hand into a fist. Could he kill Land and get away with it? In a place like Caracas homicides went unsolved every day. Land would be just another body in a city teeming with corpses.

'I'm going to give you a simple choice,' Land went on. 'Retrieve Klich and get that one-way ticket to your new life on Madeira. Or you can walk away and take your chances flying solo. But a word of warning: the feeling at Vauxhall is that we're better off quietly rubbing you out. Quite frankly, you'd be lucky to make it to the end of the week.'

He patted Bald softly on the back. 'Choose wisely, old boy,' he said.

Bald felt a pain like a knife twisting through his guts. A couple of dead-cert thoughts hit home. Thought one was that

Land wasn't bluffing. The Firm had long arms, and sooner or later they'd catch up with him. The second thought was that they wouldn't go easy on him.

'What's the deal?' he said.

'Klich has a contact in Dubai. An Iranian he worked with. You recall the Bushehr deal?'

'The nuclear power plant the Iranians built?'

Land nodded. 'Bushehr was left unfinished for years. Klich supplied Russian engineers and parts to his Iranian contact. Chap by the name of Nima Hemdani. He wants Hemdani to help him disappear.'

Land smoothed his lapels, then continued, 'The attack at the villa clearly spooked Klich. He's looking to go deep underground, to a place where no one can find him.' Land paused, grinding his jaw. 'Hemdani undoubtedly intends to smuggle Klich into Iran. If that happens we've lost him for good. Iran is an intelligence black hole. Once there Klich will be out of everyone's reach. Even the bloody Russians.'

'What's the ETA for the meet?' Bald asked.

'As soon as Hemdani arrives in Dubai,' replied Land flatly. 'He's been red-flagged by the Firm for some time. We know his every move. He's currently tied up in China on business and he won't get into Dubai until the day after tomorrow.' Land narrowed his eyes at Bald. 'You need to stop Klich before he RVs with Hemdani. Forty-eight hours, John. Plenty of time.'

'I'll want a gun. And a mark-one eyeball.'

'Your local handler will supply both. Chap by the name of Skinner. He'll source weapons for you and show you the lie of the land.'

The guy who'd been standing at the front door entered the room. Bald now recognized him as one of the two agents who'd dumped him in the slums in Caracas the previous day. He remembered the name. Wellfoot.

'Fuck it,' Bald said. 'Let's do this.'

'Good boy.'

Then Land hurried out of the apartment and paced purposefully ahead. Bald lagged behind, his legs stiff and his brain jarring inside his skull with every movement. Land glided down the steps, bounce in his fucking posh step. Bald could see a dark-skinned Latino guy with a ridiculous haircut and a goatee slumped in the front passenger seat of the Beemer. Guy was wearing a pink jacket, a pair of silver bracelets and a pissed-off look on his face.

'Ah, the pimp,' said Land, waving at Manny. 'He kindly let us borrow his car.' Then he hardened his gaze at Bald. 'Skinner will be waiting for you at the Scorpion Bar in the Malibu Hotel. Your cover story is that you're a security expert in kidnap and ransom and Skinner is your business partner. You're looking to set up a new office. We'll set up a line here for the company front. If anyone gets suspicious, you tell them to ring the number on the BlackBerry. They'll be patched through to an actress working a desk at Vauxhall and pretending to be your PA. The name of the company is Argonaut Risk Management. Don't forget it.'

Land manoeuvred around to the rear passenger door on the Beemer. Hooked it open and gestured for Bald to clamber inside.

'No more excuses, John. It is absolutely imperative that you complete this mission. Fail and I'll haul you onto the first flight back to Caracas. And you can take Joe Gardner's place in prison.'

sixteen

Bald unfolded himself from the back of the Toyota Camry taxi and stepped out into the night. It was like stepping into a steam bath. On the Persian Gulf the temperature was more tropical than desert. Bald slipped the Indian taxi driver fifty dirhams for the fare. In the distance he could make out the hazy outline of the Emirates Towers, the two buildings shaped like the jaws of a monkey wrench. If he squinted real hard, he could just about see the spire of the Burj Khalifa tower, the tallest building in the world.

Bald gave his back to the skyline and walked the short distance to the lobby at the Malibu Hotel. It looked like a fucking dump. Twelve storeys of concrete with a tacky sign out front. Even the palm trees and hanging fruit were fake. But Bald didn't care about any of that. After eighteen hours in the air, six more kicking his heels at various terminals, he was jet-lagged and hungry. He was also looking forward to a shit and a shower and a shave.

A bellhop begrudgingly opened the door. He was an Indian guy with nearly black skin and grey streaks in his hair. Bald brushed past him and entered the lobby. The hotel lived up to the crap promise of the exterior. A maid and a waiter were racing across the lobby to place buckets below a number of leaks in the ceiling. So far everyone Bald had seen in Dubai had looked Indian, or maybe other Asian. Then he told himself that this was the Arab world and that, in his experience, the average raghead was too fucking rich and lazy to work. Far easier to import others to work for them.

Bald threaded his way across the lobby and rode to the eighth floor in a cramped lift with an overhead air-con unit blowing stale air over his face. Twenty shuddering seconds later the doors slithered open to reveal a glass door blocked by a couple of heavies. Arab guys with glassy eyes and trimmed beards covering granite jaws. The one on the right signalled to Bald to stop.

'Members only,' he said.

'I'm meeting a friend,' said Bald.

'That's too bad.'

Bald paused for a beat.

'How much is membership?' he said.

The heavy sized Bald up. He was amused by what he saw. 'For you my friend, two hundred dirham.'

Bald thought about it. Then he shrugged and dug out the clip of cash, greased both their palms with a hundred dirhams. Guy on the right padded him down, stamped some kind of a logo on his wrist and waved him through. Bald found himself inside a low-ceilinged room washed in pink and blue neon lighting. There was a roundhouse bar in the middle and a row of booths to the left and right, with a curtained area at the back and a sign above the curtain that said 'VIP LOUNGE'. A bunch of guys sat at the bar. Westerners in suits guzzling down flutes of champagne and checking out the action. Not an Arab in sight.

Hookers were working the room. There seemed to be an invisible line between the hookers to the left and those to the right. Left was home to Eastern Europeans, all high cheek-bones and narrow eyes that Bald knew would widen at the sight of a black AmEx. Right was a double dozen of the hottest Asian women outside of American porn, all fake tits and unbe-lievably slender curves. A five-foot-nothing Oriental from this group approached him and smiled with her lip-glossed mouth and said, 'Fuck and suck, mister. Four hundred dirham.'

She had those big, alluring Thai eyes like something out of an anime cartoon. She was wearing a ruched bra-top dress that curved in all the right places and a pair of angel wings on the back. She tapped Bald on the nose with her magic wand.

'Only four hundred,' she said. 'Fuck and suck.'

'Not tonight, love,' said Bald, gritting his teeth in regret.

The hooker made a cute face at him and did the whole batting eyelids thing. Stroking his crotch like she was rubbing a genie lamp. 'You drive hard bargain. Two hundred and fuck, then. But no sucky.'

'Maybe another time.'

'I find you later. We have good time. I give you best fucky-fuck in Dubai.'

'I bet you do,' said Bald.

Then the hooker spun away from Bald and wandered off in search of the next mug. Bald paced over to the bar, took a stool and ordered a double Ballantine's thirty-year-old whisky on the rocks. That set him back a cool two hundred dirhams, but fuck it, the Firm was paying, and he was determined to fleece them for all they were worth.

'You dodged a bullet there, fella.'

Bald swung around to his left. The voice belonged to a guy sat next to him at the bar. He was dressed in a short-sleeve shirt once blue but now the colour of detergent, khaki shorts, white socks and trainers. His hair was crewcut and his skin was lobster. He looked like a fat Yank on safari. He was so big he took up two stools and he had a layer of sweat on him like he'd just stepped in from a monsoon. The Essex accent told Bald that this might be Skinner, his handler, but he had to make sure. He started the pre-planned exchange that Land had explained to him during the ride to the airport.

'Know where I can find an internet café nearby?'

The man swigged his drink. The sharp smell of gin hit Bald from three feet away. Could probably smell the gin from the other side of Dubai. 'Sorry, mate,' the man said. 'I'm not from round here. Try one of the locals.'

'You sound familiar,' said Bald. 'Where'd you say you're from again?'

'I didn't. But just so you know, I'm from Chingford.'

That was the answer Bald was looking for. He relaxed a little. The guy tipped his empty glass in the direction of the Thai woman and said, 'You know what they say about hookers? You don't pay them for the sex. You pay them to fucking leave.'

Bald was puzzled by Skinner. For one thing, the guy didn't exactly look like a handler for the Firm: he was dangerously fat and stood out like a real tit at a beauty parade. Their handlers were generally smartly dressed and anonymous-looking. They were the grey men and women. And two, Skinner wasn't posh.

'Terry Skinner.' The guy offered his hand to Bald. 'You must be John. Drink?'

'Evan Williams, double. Thanks'

Bald shook the guy's hand; it was warm and sweaty and gross.

Skinner turned back to the bar and caught the eye of the bored-looking barmaid. 'They all drive a hard bargain in here,' he said, gesturing to the hookers. 'Especially the Chinkies. Before, it was just your Russians and Swedes. The odd black. Now you get half of Beijing in here on a Friday night, and the sweethearts from the old Soviet bloc get angry because the Chinkies undercut them. Cheap labour, and all that.'

Their drinks arrived. Skinner offered an ironic toast to the hookers and glugged down his gin-and-not-so-much-tonic. Bald sipped his bourbon. It tasted good.

Skinner said, 'Now that you're mellowed out, I've got some bad news and some worse news. What do you want to know first?'

Bald thought about it for a second. Then he downed half his drink and said, 'Give me the bad.'

Skinner eyed a matchstick Asian whore stroll past. 'We've lost track of Hemdani.'

'Land said he was held up in China.'

'But we now know he left China yesterday.'

'So Hemdani might already be here? He might be meeting Klich right this fucking minute?'

Skinner raised a hand. 'Easy, fella. He ain't hooked up with Klich yet. I know this because Klich is staying at the Seven Wonders Hotel, and right now he's in his penthouse suite.'

'Then what are we waiting for? I'll go and grab the cunt now.'

Skinner sucked his teeth. 'Not that simple,' he said. 'He ain't sitting up there on his lonesome. He's got his full coterie of bodyguards keeping watch on him twenty-four seven.'

'How many?'

'Three. Two women and a guy. Armed to the teeth. Even a tough nut like you doesn't stand a chance against those kind of odds.'

'So how the fuck am I supposed to get to him?'

'This is where Lady Luck parts her fanny flaps and lets you dip your fingers in her pudding, if you get my drift. Last night, Klich rocks up in town. Guess what's the first thing he does?'

Bald shrugged. 'Check in at the hotel?'

A crafty smile curled the corners of Skinner's lips. 'Wrong, sunshine. He goes to a labour camp south of the airport.' He let the int sink in, then drained his glass.

'What the fuck for?' said Bald.

'Boys,' Skinner said. 'Look around. You can get all the fanny you want in a club, but if meat and two veg is your thing, you have to cast your net a little wider. Know what I mean?'

Bald recalled his briefing with Land. 'What about the affair Klich had with that parliamentary aide?'

'So he bats for both sides,' Skinner said, dismissing Bald's comment with a wave. 'All the ragheads are the same. Four wives and a bunch of boys on the sly. Anyway, I went down to the labour camp early. Fucking rank place. Got talking to the local batty boys. Turns out Klich has booked another session.'

'When for?'

Skinner tapped his watch and grinned. 'Forty minutes from now.'

Bald nodded.

'I've been saving you the best bit for last,' said Skinner. 'Klich only goes to the camp with one BG. Obviously, he doesn't want the whole fucking world knowing about his dirty little secret.'

'Even better,' Bald grinned. 'What are we waiting for?'

Skinner toed a Nike gym bag lying at his feet. 'Your gun. As requested. Just call me fucking UPS.'

'Let's get this wanker,' said Bald.

He slid off the stool, scooped up the bag and slung it over his shoulder. The Thai hooker with the angel wings looked at him sadly, and Bald made a promise to himself to come back here once the job was done, and have his wicked way with her. Then he paused as he remembered something.

'And the worse news?' he said.

'Shit, I almost forgot.' Skinner slowly counted out a wad of dirhams onto a silver tray. He left a generous tip and pocketed the receipt. Then he turned to Bald. 'The Iranians know you're in town.'

Skinner was slurring now, his eyes glazed. 'They haven't forgotten about how you fucked them over with the nuke deal.'

'What the fuck are you talking about?'

'Fella, they've put out a contract on you.'

seventeen

They hurtled along the Jumeirah Beach Road towards downtown Dubai. Skyscrapers rose out of the desert floor and
gazed out triumphantly across the Gulf. Banks of sea mist
were rolling in from the coast. Skinner was wedged behind
the wheel of the Porsche Panamera. He had a tracking device
tacked to the dash with a pair of window suckers. It showed
the streets a few blocks ahead of their current location, a red
dot flashing as they headed south.

Skinner said, 'GPS satellite tracker. Klich left his car in the
underground car park, I slipped the valet a few shekels and
Bob's your uncle.'

'He's being careless for someone so paranoid.'

'Do us a favour, mate,' Skinner replied. 'There's some Bell's
in here somewhere. I'm gasping for a drop.'

Bald rummaged around on the back seat and found the bottle
buried under a muddle of sweaters and paperbacks about the
Third Reich. The bottle was half full. Bald took a hefty swig.
Warm, cheap whisky juicing his bloodstream. Then he passed
the bottle to Skinner. The guy had a thirsty look in his eyes that
suggested his body ran on alcohol, and large quantities of it.

Skinner gunned the Panamera up to 140 k per. The Burj
al-Arab Hotel, with its giant metallic sail, loomed into view at
their nine o'clock. Three or four kilometres farther along the
coast Bald spotted two large dark blobs.

'Left you've got the Palm Islands,' said Skinner, pointing to what Bald was looking at. 'World Islands on your right. Reclaimed land. Prime fucking real estate. You buy a pad out there, you know you've made it.'

At the public beach Skinner hooked a right onto Al-Athar Street. He put his foot to the floor. The speedometer eased past the 160 mark. Now they were looping their way south past Safa Park, fluorescent lights illuminating its postcard lawns and palms and waterfalls.

'So what's the rub with this Klich bloke?' Skinner asked. 'You gotta kill him?'

Bald shook his head.

'Land wants him alive. Makes no fucking difference to me. Let's tail him to the camp. I'll grab him before he gets a chance to get his end away.'

Skinner raised an eyebrow at Bald. 'What about the BG?'

'If there's only one with him like you say, I'll take the cunt down.'

As they ramped onto Sheikh Zayed Road and swept past Business Bay, Skinner was quiet for a while. Then he said, 'Three fucking years those arseholes in Whitehall have kept me posted here. In this sodding heat. I mean, it can't be good for my ticker. I should fucking sue.'

Bald laughed. 'The only person you should be suing is Ronald McDonald, you fat cunt.'

They drove on for another kilometre and merged onto Sheikh Rashid Road. Every driver was doing at least 150, Bald figured. In Dubai they didn't seem familiar with the concept of brakes. Skinner pointed wide at the thin line of traffic thirty metres ahead.

'There he is,' he said. 'The Lincoln. Second car along.'

Bald leaned forward. Craned his neck to see beyond the Cayenne in front of them. The next motor along was a Lincoln Town Car. Black, gleaming, tinted, and racing towards Dubai

Creek. Bald unzipped the bag on his lap and pulled out the gun.

It took him a couple of seconds to identify the weapon. Bald picked up the big old revolver. Fucking huge, it weighed almost two kilos. The barrel was eight inches of highly polished stainless steel and the grip was finger-grooved and moulded from rubber. Bald flicked open the cylinder. It was chambered for the .44-Magnum large-bore cartridge. Had 'COLT ANACONDA' stamped on the barrel. A hunting gun, thought Bald. Perfect for killing bears. But useless for keeping a low profile in Dubai.

'Well,' Skinner said. 'What do you think?'

'I need to capture a man, not kill a fucking whale,' said Bald. 'But it'll do.'

Skinner looked disappointed. Bald ignored him. There was also a box of Fiocchi .44-Mag 200-grain semi-jacketed hollow-point in the bag. Bald popped open the box. Fifty rounds: enough to kill a small army. He looked up at the rear-view mirror. The melange of beaches and skyscrapers were sliding towards the horizon. Paradise trundling along a conveyer belt. The Anaconda held six rounds in total. Bald began thumbing .44-Mag rounds into the cylinder.

'I hear you're ex-Regiment,' said Skinner.

'A long time ago.'

'I also heard you did some pretty crazy shit?'

Bald slotted in the last round, snapped the cylinder back into place in the barrel. 'That contract on my head,' he said. 'How much?'

Skinner hesitated. Like he was trying to work out how to answer without offending Bald.

'Fifty grand.' Then he added quickly, 'Could have been more . . . I'm not sure.'

Neither man said anything for a while. But Skinner wasn't the type of guy who could sit in silence. He said, 'I was in SIS. The Met's Special Intelligence Service.'

'Never heard of it,' said Bald.

'We didn't blow our own trumpets, mate. We worked under-cover. Infiltrated smuggling rings, the mafia, you name it. We saw some pretty bad stuff. I suppose you know all about that, being in the SAS.'

'How many times were you shot at?' asked Bald.

Skinner thought for a moment and said, 'Once. But it turned out it was an air rifle.'

'Ever kill anyone?'

'Never had the chance, mate.'

'Then you know fuck-all about my world,' said Bald. 'So stop pretending you do.'

They bombed over the Al Garhoud Bridge. Down below in the creek the Gulf mists were burning themselves up over hundreds of moored dhows. Bald was familiar with the route from his earlier cab ride and he knew the airport was two kilometres east of the creek. Now he could see its assortment of red and yellow lights suspended just above the desert floor. Planes were coming and going, lights blinking and zipping across the sky like tracer. The Lincoln turned south.

Another kilometre and it slinked onto Emirates Road 311. The lights faded. The traffic on E311 thinned out to just the Panamera and the Lincoln and a few fuel trucks. Felt like they were a long way from Dubai. Like they were on the dark side of the moon. Skinner eased on the accelerator and kept a solid forty metres between the two cars. Then, two kilometres east of the airport, the Lincoln's brake lights flared and it shed its speed, causing Skinner to ease off the pedal. A row of low buildings sifted out of the horizon, some four hundred metres ahead.

'Kill the lights,' said Bald.

Skinner switched off the headlights. The sun had fucked off. The downtown city lights were bleeding across the sky and spraying their garish blues and neon purples over the desert. At a hundred metres the buildings broke free of the murky darkness. They stood in uniform rows: drab breeze-block dormitory buildings three storeys high and each twenty metres long. They were shoddily thrown up, with a lop-sided roof, cracks running down the walls and plastic bags crudely taped across many windows. On one side the buildings were hemmed in by a mountain range of garbage.

'This is where all the poor cunts who work in the city live.' Skinner shook his head. 'Builders, cooks, cleaners, taxi drivers. I see them getting buses out of there every night.'

'Looks more like a housing estate than a camp,' said Bald.

'Fuckers used to sleep in tents. Now at least they get a roof over their heads.' Skinner grinned at Bald. 'Still no air con or Starbucks for these poor bastards, though.'

They trailed the Lincoln deeper into the camp. Linking the buildings was a network of walkways shaded by date palms and dimly lit by sparse streetlamps. The streets were rutted and unpaved, and without names. At one place along the roadside lay paving slabs, upended like gravestones. They passed a market stall with a battered Coca-Cola sign out front and a few scrawny chickens pecking at the ground. The occasional worker in uniform shuffling along the side of the road. Bald made out Indian faces, Chinese, and a few African ones. Everything was caked in dust: buildings, courtyards, trees, people. Beside the road, Bald saw a field carpeted with it.

Twenty metres ahead, the Lincoln stopped. Skinner came to a halt too. The building on the opposite side of the road to the Panamera had a brightly lit sign: 'LIANG CORPORATION LABOUR HOSTEL.' Four doors faced the street. Three were painted red, the fourth white.

'That's the place,' said Skinner, pointing. 'The white door.'

'Telling me there's a brothel in there?'

'It's a dorm. But there's a communal toilet area. That's where they do the dirty.' He shrugged. 'If you're looking for arse around Dubai, you can't be too picky.'

Bald didn't reply. He was too busy working out his attack in his head. He thumbed back the hammer on the Anaconda. It clicked as it locked into the cocked position. Ready to snap forward at the slightest pressure on the trigger mechanism. Now Bald spied movement at the Lincoln. A figure was stepping out of the rear passenger door. Walked a few paces from the vehicle. Stopped and scratched his elbow, and looked pensively over his shoulder.

'That's our man,' said Skinner. 'Klich.'

'You're sure?'

'Two thousand fucking per cent, mate.'

Klich was bigger than he'd looked in his photographs, and he seemed to have put on weight. Bald guessed being on the run probably wasn't good for your figure. He had a mullet haircut and wore a black cotton collarless shirt with gold embroidery around the neck. The shirt reached down to the mid-thigh of his stonewashed jeans. He had on a pair of red and yellow striped boots. He didn't look like a billionaire, more like a tosser in a glam-rock tribute band.

'Some traditional dress the Russians wear,' Skinner explained. 'Seen them all decked out in similar clobber around town. Some of them even wear it down to the fucking beach.'

'And there was me thinking he just wanted to dress like a cunt.'

Bald watched the Russian fiddle with his mobile phone and pop a cigarette into his mouth at the same time. The street was empty and the only sound was the distant hum of a generator. But something troubled Bald.

'Where's the BG?' he said.

Skinner scratched his head. 'Maybe already here? Waiting for him?'

Bald rolled his tongue over his teeth. If he'd been a regular squaddie he'd have sat this one out. Wait until he had all the int about the whereabouts of the bodyguard and had the whole plan mapped out in his head. But he had lived the life of a Blade for longer than he could remember, and he seized opportunities while other people shit themselves.

He told Skinner, 'Wait here, and don't do anything stupid.'

'Screw that. I'll come with you.'

'Like fuck you will. You'll die of a heart attack before you cross the fucking road. Besides, I need you here keeping your eyes peeled. You see anyone coming, you warn me.'

'How?'

'Sound your horn.'

Bald checked his Aquaracer: 2015 hours. Twenty-four hours since he'd bugged out of Caracas. That meant he had twenty-four left on the clock to complete the mission.

Then Klich began to cross the road. The Russian was twenty metres from Bald in the Panamera and twelve metres from the Liang Corp hostel. Bald tightened his hand around the Anaconda and quickly sprang open his door. He swung towards the same building but stuck to the side of the road, clinging to the shadows to make himself less visible to the driver in the Lincoln. Flies buzzed and zipped in front of his face. Hundreds of the fuckers. A vicious waft of curry and sewage hit Bald. He was fifteen metres from the hostel now. Klich was making a beeline for the white door. Bald quickened his stride. Ten metres between him and the Russian, and closing.

But now Bald spotted a sliver of movement in the corner of his eye. It came from across the street. Voices booming. He swung his head to his three o'clock. Two men were emerging from an alleyway between two dormitory buildings. They didn't look like workers. They were dressed in a drab olive uniform and wore steel-toecapped boots and both carried some kind of pistol and a torch. Security guards. Bald quickly backtracked around the corner of the Liang building, to where they couldn't spot him. He watched them head to their right and continue their patrol further down the street, in the opposite direction from the Lincoln and the Panamera and the two dormitory blocks. Bald waited until they had patrolled ten metres further from his position before he risked emerging out of the shadows. Then he froze.

Klich had disappeared.

He saw movement at the white door. The door was gently swinging back and forth. Klich must have slipped inside, thought Bald. He edged forward, keeping a watchful eye on the two guards as they continued their patrol away from his position, then he made for the door. The Anaconda felt heavy in his right hand. It dragged on his shoulder and the tendons in his wrist. Ten metres to the white door and the guards were melting into the shadows. Now Bald reached the white door and stopped. He gripped the Anaconda at chest height, his arm drawn close to his chest and his elbow tucked at his side. Finger applying a precise degree of pressure to the trigger. He paused for a moment. Listened. But he heard nothing except the patter of his heartbeat reverberating in his ears.

Bald counted to three.

Then he charged inside.

eighteen

2019 hours.

Bald's eyes swivelled from left to right across the dorm. It was a single large, rectangular room with four bunk beds crammed into the near-left corner and a clutter of cooking pots and pans and a forty-pound sack of rice to the right. The floor was warped lino and the walls were bare concrete decorated with old family snaps. The room was small. Bald had seen bigger parking spaces. Three men were curled up in the bottom bunks. Coffee-bean faces snoring loudly. Bald switched his focus to the far end of the room. Four metres away a frayed curtain divided the sleeping area from the shitter. A light source was glowing on the other side of the curtain, and Bald could see the silhouette of a man. Klich. Getting his fucking end away with some Indian kid. Bald powered across the sleeping area, his feet brushing aside pots and cutlery. He grabbed the curtain and yanked it back along the rail, preparing to pound Klich into submission.

The figure behind the curtain shot his hands in the air. He was alone, his face lit up by a naked light bulb. Bald lowered the revolver. The guy wasn't Klich. He was just some Indian kid, nineteen or twenty. Pants round his ankles. There was a hole in the ground beside him and next to it a coiled hose-pipe and a wooden bucket. The stench of steaming shit hung thick in the air. The kid's eyes were wide open and fixed on the Anaconda. He had a look of silent shock on his face. For a moment they just stared at each other. Then a drum beat of footsteps sounded from Bald's six. He spun around. Spotted a man storming through the open doorway of the room.

The guy was dressed like a bum. He wore a pair of olive-green camo trousers and a plain black T-shirt and a wood-camo army jacket. He held a stubby gun in a two-handed grip. The barrel caught the gleam from the light bulb and winked wickedly at Bald. Two bullets shot out of the snout in rapid succession. But they missed. Bald felt the heat of the rounds rip through his hair. The clatter roused two of the Indians from their beauty sleep. There was a slow second between that and the bum readjusting his aim. Less than a second for Bald to get a fucking shot in. He drew the Anaconda level with the mass of badly dressed target four metres away and depressed the trigger.

The weapon jolted in his hand. A flame licked out of the barrel and briefly lit up the room in a wash of acidic white. There was an overloud roar like a thunderbolt crashing through the roof. The round thumped into the shooter. He grunted and tumbled backwards, landing on the pots and pans, and the two Indians bolted out of the door, wailing and flapping their arms. A third guy, an old man with no teeth or hair, sat rigid in his bed. His lips and eyes trembling at something behind Bald.

Now Bald charged over to the bum. The guy was lying at the foot of the doorway. Still alive and pawing at his dick. There was a gout of brown-red across his groin where a .44-Mag round had made its mark. He was writhing around in agony, his head rocking back and forth against the sack of rice. Bald glanced back at the shitter and suddenly understood why the old geezer had been wailing. The skinny Indian kid was slumped against the wall. Trauma wound on his Adam's apple the size of a ten-pence piece. The bum had missed Bald but slotted the kid.

He looked back at the bum. His face was pale and he had an unkempt beard and he stank of piss and spent brass. But mostly piss. He tried to say something to Bald. But Bald didn't have time to quiz the guy. He pointed the tip of the Anaconda at his temple and fired. The revolver kicked up half an inch in his grip, the bum flinched and the round veered narrowly off target and took off a chunk of his forehead. Brain spattered the lino floor.

Then Bald looked up at the shitter and he noticed something else. As well as the Indian kid with the hole in his neck, there was a door to the right of the shitter. The door was open.

That's where Klich must have got to, Bald thought. He knew that the sounds of the firefight would have made Klich scarper. The Russian would likely be retreating to the Lincoln to make his getaway. Bald could feel the slim window of opportunity slamming in his face. He turned to resume the hunt for Klich. But then three rounds lit up at the main door of the room. Two metres from his position. The rounds bounced off the lino and slapped into the wall above the bunk beds. Bald spun around and looked to the doorway. Caught sight of a figure outside. Across the road, twenty metres away.

Racing towards him.

The guy looked like the long-lost twin of the dead bum on the floor. The old Indian guy leapt out of his bed and raced past Bald, out into the street. Bad timing. Two bullets punched holes in his upper torso. One of the rounds bored its way through his chest and a fractured second later it was exiting through his right eye socket.

Bald scooped up the gun lying by the bum. He was now the proud owner of a Heckler & Koch UMP submachine gun. Bald judged its weight to see if it was loaded. He didn't have time to fuck about with the clip. The UMP felt heavy with 9x19mm Parabellum. The fire selector was already switched to two-round burst. Bald looked through the doorway. The second bum was drawing near to him. Nine metres from the door now. Close enough for Bald to see him tensing his finger on the trigger. Ready to give Bald the good news.

Bald took aim at the shooter and fired.

Two rounds spat out of the UMP. Fucking missed. But the bum was unsettled by the fire coming his way. He steered away from the building. Away from the fatal funnel of fire. Bald calmly adjusted his aim. Relaxed his shoulder muscles. Eased the tension out of his guts. He lined up the shooter between the rear aperture and the front sight. Kept the rear aperture in focus and the body marginally out of focus. He aimed at the torso, not the head. With a moving target in poor visibility, your best bet was to go for the high-percentage shot.

He unloaded two more rounds at the guy. This time they felt surgical. They felt good. Bald got that same feeling a golfer gets when he hits a ball and knows he's chalked up a hole-in-one even before the ball has fallen from the sky. Seeing blood puffing out of the target's guts, and the guy crumple in a heap, he congratulated himself on a good kill.

Lights were flicking on in the dormitories on the other side of the street. Workers were rushing to the old Indian guy and the dead bum in the street. At first Bald thought they were being good citizens. Then he saw them squabbling over the dead men's coins and notes and phones. Somewhere in the distance a car horn blared. Skinner sounding the warning. Bald was running out of time. He wheeled away from the door and made a snap decision to ditch the Anaconda. The revolver was big and clumsy, and having it stuffed it into the waistband of his jeans would slow him down. He hurried back into the room and through the door near the shitter.

The door led into a courtyard hemmed in on all sides by other dormitories. The courtyard was twelve metres long and eight wide, with a shade tree in the middle. Washing lines sagged across the width of the yard, forming a soggy curtain that obscured his line of vision. Bald spotted a pool of raw sewage beside the tree. The smell was a hundred times more potent than in the shitter. Swiping aside the clothes hanging on the lines, Bald made for the far end of the courtyard. When he could see the end, he stopped dead in his tracks.

Six metres away from Bald a narrow alleyway tunnelled between two identical-looking three-storey buildings. The alley was six metres long and gave onto a rutted road. The Lincoln was resting at the alley's mouth and a grainy figure with a mullet and a black shirt was flinging open the rear passenger door.

Bald snapped the UMP level with his shoulder and lined up the sights with the Lincoln's wheelbase. He'd target the vehicle first. Immobilize it and stop Klich from making his getaway. Once the Lincoln and whoever else was inside were chop suey, he'd nab the Russian on foot and escort him back to the Panamera.

Then Bald felt something hard and bony collide with the back of his skull. The blow was devastating. It was like someone had wired up his jaw to a defibrillator. Next thing he knew his legs were buckling and his face was hitting dirt. A boot swung at him and struck him on the right side of his ribcage. Steel toecap slamming into bone. The blow winded Bald. He breathed in and needles of pain flared up along the length of his chest. Another boot connected and Bald heard something snap inside. He clenched his jaw. Get up, you cunt, a voice roared at him from his guts. Get up or fucking die. A third kick jabbed at his upper chest. Bald battened down the nausea. Spat out dust and mucus. Up ahead he saw Klich climbing into the Lincoln.

Then Bald reached for the UMP. The grip was three tantalizing inches from his fingertips. The figure standing over Bald side-footed the weapon. Then he rolled onto his front and caught a boot square in the guts. A massive wave of nausea exploded in his chest. Fuck the pain! he told himself repeatedly. Fuck it with bells on. Another kick fired down at him but this time he was ready and he thrust out his right hand and grabbed the guy's foot by the ankle. There was nothing martial-arts about his strategy. Lying on the ground and stricken by your opponent, you left all the fancy stuff at the door. You had to drag your enemy down into the trenches. To a dark and savage place. He leaned forward and bit deep into the ankle. Blood oozed out of the joint and the guy howled.

Now Bald wrapped both his arms around the leg at knee height and wrenched the leg to his left. Threw the guy off balance and sent him crashing to the ground. He landed a half-metre to Bald's three o'clock. Now Bald sprang to his feet and launched himself at the guy as he lay on his back. He was about to fucking get it, big time. Bald kicked him in the guts. Then lowered a boot into his balls and sent him into squeals of agony. The guy curled up in the foetal position, trying to shield himself from the blows. But Bald wasn't done. He kicked his back, blow after savage blow.

He shaped to boot him again.

'John!' the guy said. 'Don't fucking do it, mate.'

Bald froze. The voice was pure East End. Sounded familiar somehow. For the first time, Bald looked down at the face of his enemy. It was half hidden beneath a thick beard, but he recognized that face all the same.

'It's me,' the guy was saying. 'Your old mucker, innit? Dave Hands.'

nineteen

Bald took a step back from Dave Hands the way a guy steps back from a ticking bomb. He couldn't believe what he was seeing. Hands looked terrible. His skin was pale and stretched like a lampshade cover and his nose was shaped like a knuckle at the bridge, which told Bald it had recently been broken and then reset by a surgeon with paddles for fucking hands. He was dressed in a cheap black suit and white shirt polkadotted with blood. Bald manoeuvred quickly around him and scooped the UMP off the ground. Hands was in too much pain to make a play for it. Clutching his guts and groaning. Bald trained the UMP on him.

'The fuck are you doing here?' he said.

Hands said nothing. He scraped himself off the ground and coughed up a Hoover bag of dust. He stood in a kind of hunchbacked stoop, his hands splayed on his knees, blood drooling out of his nostrils and pooling onto a spot between his shoes. In the distance Skinner frantically sounded the horn. Three long blasts. Dogs barked.

'You've got three seconds to start talking,' said Bald. 'Otherwise I'm going to get Guantánamo on you.'

Hands laughed nervously. Eyes darting left and right, like he was looking for a magic escape route that only he knew about, except now it wasn't there. 'Come on now, mate.'

'Why the fuck did you try to kill me?'

'Security guards are on their way. Hired by the building firms to keep the peace. Mob fucking justice round these parts. They will have heard the gunshots, mate. They'll be here soon. Know what they do to people like you? They fucking necklace you.'

'Then you'd better start talking,' said Bald.

'You don't need to point that fucking thing at me, John. We're mates, right?'

'Wrong. We were never mates. You were always just a cunt.'

Hands screwed his face up at Bald.

'Then that makes us practically brothers,' he said.

Something snapped inside Bald, the only thing that had been tying down the tension rippling under his muscles. Now he whipped the UMP at Hands, smashing the bridge of his nose. Stainless steel on bone. Hands screamed and reeled backwards. Bald sprang forward. The regular John Bald was just a passenger along for the fucking ride. The inner savage had taken the wheel. He grabbed Hands by the neck and dragged his stunned body over to the sewage pond.

The smell was vicious. Like someone smearing shit across his face. Hands tried to claw himself away from the pond. His fingernails were digging into the loose soil. Bald booted him in the guts. Winded the prick. Then he manoeuvred his way around Hands until he was towering over him with his legs planted either side of his torso, and knelt on him, using his knees to pin down the guy's upper arms. Bald clamped his hands around Hands's head and positioned himself so that he was ready to plunge him head first into the sewage. Hands instinctively tensed up. He jerked his shoulders in a desperate attempt to throw Bald off his back. His legs were flailing and kicking like a wild animal. But Bald had a rock-hard grip on Hands and the irresistible downward pressure began to take its toll. Bald adjusted his stance and concentrated all his force on the dome of his head. He pushed down hard. Like he was plugging a leak in a water pipe. Hands kept kicking and twisting.

'Jesus, John,' he said. 'Think about what you're doing.'

'Talk to me,' said Bald.

'I don't know fuck-all, I swear.'

'Bullshit! Why did you hit me?'

Bald felt the resistance slowly drain out of Hands. His head dropped a precious inch as Hands wrenched his body from side to side. Another inch. Then another. Then the fight flushed out of him. Hands clamped his lips shut and trapped his breath in his throat.

That was when Bald plunged his head into the sewage.

The pond opened like a mouth. Bald submerged Hands until the warm, lumpy brown sewage was licking at the nape of his neck. Hands made a bunch of gargling noises in the back of his throat. After fifteen seconds the gargle became a retch. He yanked his body left and right in a desperate struggle to lift his head above the surface. Bald held firm. After twenty seconds Hands puked his guts up. Yellowish chunks bubbled to the surface. Then Hands groaned and went limp and Bald hauled his sorry arse out of the sewage. His face was caked in shit. Dollops of puke dripping from his eyebrows and the tip of his nose.

Hands took a deep breath. 'What do you want to know?'

'Why are you here?'

'To ambush you.'

'For who?'

'Justin Timberlake. Who the fuck do you think?' Hands spat out a mouthful of excrement and dry-heaved. 'The Russian.'

'Viktor Klich?'

Hands saw the look of confusion playing out on Bald's face. 'You didn't know about me working for Klich? Fuck me, John, you're well behind the game. I couldn't get a fucking job after Rio. Then the Russian made me an offer. An overseas BG gig.

Best decision I ever made. I'm fucking rolling in it. Telling you. Cushy hours, good coin. Ten grand a month in cash. No fucking thanks to you. For years I couldn't get a job on the circuit. Had to doss with my mum in her one-bed on the old estate down in Crystal Palace.'

Angry voices rang out above the rooftops, distant but clear across the velvet night sky. The security guards. Bald judged them to be a few streets away. Hands raised his eyes to Bald. They were blazing with hate.

'You blackballed me,' he said. 'Shut me out of the Regiment old boys' network. Every job I went for, same old fucking tune. "Sorry, sunshine, a mate in the know told me that you ain't reliable, you got a drug problem." That was your fucking handiwork.'

'Spare me the sob story,' said Bald. 'Keep talking.'

'Klich knew someone was on his tail. We hatched a plan. Lure the tail out here, then spring a trap and nail the fuckers.'

'He's not a paedo, then?'

'What, Klich? Do me favour. That man likes his pussy. Nah, it was all a trick, mate. And it worked.' Then Hands changed his tune. 'You have to believe me, John. If I'd known you were the one tailing Klich, I would never have gone along with the plan.'

'And your two mates back there?' Bald jerked his head at the dormitory.

'Couple of ex-Paras,' said Hands. 'Sleeping rough. Fuckers fell on hard times. Paid them next to nothing to lend me a hand.'

'Where is he now?' said Bald.

'Where's who?'

'Don't play games with me, Davey boy. You know who. Viktor fucking Klich.'

'Back at the Seven Wonders Hotel. He won't be popping his head above the parapet again until the RV with Hemdani.'

'Tonight was a decoy?' said Bald.

Hands nodded.

'The RV with Hemdani,' said Bald. 'When is it?'

Hands was silent for a moment. Pursing his lips and cocking his head, like he was trying to solve a maths problem. 'Let me see now. What's that int worth to you? We talking ten grand? Twenty? Fifty?'

'We're talking nothing. You tell me, or you can take another dip.'

Hands eyed the sewage.

'How do I know you won't kill me, after I fess up?' he said.

'That's a chance you'll just have to take.'

His mouth tight, Hands said, 'Eighteen hundred hours tomorrow.'

'Where?'

'I don't know. No one does except the man himself.'

'Don't fuck me about.'

'I swear on my fucking grave, John.'

Boots were trampling nearby. The guards were close. Bald levelled the UMP at Hands. All set to waste this cunt and bug out. Hands was pissing himself. His eyes looked like a couple of white snooker balls suspended over the rim of the pocket. The slightest nudge and they'd sink.

'You can't kill me,' Hands said.

'I know where Klich is and the time of the RV,' Bald said quietly. 'That's all I need. You're expendable.'

'And what's your big plan? Take down his whole BG team, plus the ragheads?'

Bald said nothing.

'You'll never get close enough to him, mate. The other BGs are shit-hot. You'll be dropped before you get within ten metres of Klich.' Hands paused. 'But there is another way.'

twenty

2217 hours.

The guards were almost at the courtyard. The Panamera's horn blared again. Bald felt the urgency of his situation in his veins. Hands grinned at him and said, 'I can get you on the BG team, John. Get you next to Klich.'

No time left, thought Bald.

'What about the guards?'

'I know a way out of here,' said Hands, scraping to his feet. 'Deal?'

Bald glanced over his shoulder. The door was swinging back on its hinges.

'Deal,' said Bald. Then, pushing Hands ahead of him, he hurried down the alley just as three guards raced into the courtyard. Wearing the same uniform as the two guards Bald had seen patrolling the main street. They were twelve metres behind him. Too close for comfort. Bald urged Hands to run faster. Hands almost tripped up and Bald had to reach out and grab him before he stacked it and fatally slowed them down. Now they broke onto the rutted road and Bald glanced back at his six and saw that the guards were halfway across the courtyard, eight metres back. They were swatting aside the washing lines.

As he scoped out the road, Bald had déjà vu. It looked identical to the road where Skinner had parked the Panamera. There was a grocery store and a row of date palms lining the walkways. But there was no sign of the Panamera. Then he spotted the company logo outside the dormitory to their right. 'BAXTER CONSTRUCTION,' it read. They were on a different street. He would have to be guided entirely by Hands, and that didn't sit right with Bald. Trusting the guy was a bad idea, in his experience. But right now he had no choice. So when Hands said, 'This way,' Bald followed.

The guards were now racing down the alley, shouting at them. Bald stopped, did a one-eighty and unleashed a two-round burst in their direction. The bullets thwacked into the wall and spat fistfuls of hot mortar into their faces. Then Bald rushed after Hands, who had darted to the other side of the road. His hobble was ancient history. He was flying and now Bald was struggling to keep up the pace. He willed his body on and joined Hands at the Baxter Construction building. The accommodation looked a little more classy than the hovel Bald had just fought his way out of.

'We need to get back to the main road,' he said.

Hands nodded. 'The Porsche? I saw you arrive, mate. That's our getaway?'

'Unless you've got a better idea.'

'We'll swing around through the alleys. Throw these pricks off our scent.'

'The shit coming off you, that won't be easy.'

Hands hooked a right at the 'BAXTER CONSTRUCTION' sign and bounded down a walkway that ran between the first and second buildings north of the sign. Bald throwing looks over his shoulder every three or four paces. The first two guards were hurtling out of the alley. Bald put them at fifteen metres away. His two-round burst had slowed their advance. But not by much. Bald chased Hands's shadow down the walkway, which led away from the main road. They powered past one dormitory after another, branded with company logos. The deeper they went into the camp the more Bald feared they'd never find their way out of this fucking labyrinth.

Then Hands veered left and the walkway disintegrated into a loose gravel path. There were no streetlamps here and the darkness was thicker than the fucking heat. Bald could make out almost nothing ahead of him. He was guided purely by Hands, by the suck and hiss of his breathing and the scuffing of his feet on the dusty ground.

'How do I know that Klich will put me on the team?' said Bald.

'My word is golden,' Hands replied. 'Saying you don't trust me?'

'Fuck off.'

Hands went quiet. 'Klich needs manpower,' he said at last. 'I was trying to get the ex-Para lads onto the security team. But you know what the Russians are like. They've got a taste for the finer things in life. That goes for personal security as well as their dinner. He wouldn't put no fucking tramp on the team. But if I tell Klich that you used to be a Blade, he'll be sold.'

Bald was struggling to keep up the pace. His calves were shot to pieces. His hamstrings felt like old rope. He gritted his teeth and pushed on. Twenty metres further along the walkway they emerged onto the main road and the darkness dissolved. The Liang Corp logo, scattering its gaudy glow across the street, lit their way. They were back where he'd debussed from the Panamera. Except the Panamera was nowhere to be seen.

'Where's that fat cunt?' Bald asked himself aloud.

He looked around. The road was lifeless and dull as a pair of dead eyes. The footsteps off to their six were still closing in. In moments the security guards would be on top of them. Bald dropped to a kneeling firing stance. Every second counted, and the kneeling position gave better accuracy than a standing stance. The nearest guard emerged from the shadows twenty metres back, his silhouette a faint cape of grey flapping in a sea of grainy black. Keeping his buttocks clear of the ground, Bald rested his left elbow on his knee to distribute his weight and maintain his balance. Then he pulled the trigger. The walkway lit up like a paparazzi shoot. The guard gave a throaty grunt. He stopped in his tracks like he'd just run head first into a wall of glass. He was clutching his guts. He fell against the wall and slumped to the ground. One less guard to worry about.

Bald did a quick calculation. Thirty rounds to a clip on the UMP. He'd spent four rounds in the dorm. Two in the alley. Another two rounds just now. That made eight rounds spent. Twenty-two left in the clip. At least two more guards on their case. Maybe more would be on their way. He spotted the wounded guard crawling back down the alley. Bald put another two rounds in his back. The guy stopped crawling. No sign of any more guards, and Bald wondered, have they dived into an adjacent alley? Trying to flank us? He hoped they had just bricked it and backed off, even though he knew deep down that was unlikely. But he couldn't keep them at bay for much longer.

Then a sound made Bald prick his ears. A bass note buzzing further down the road. He looked away from the guards and scanned the darkness. Saw a pair of headlights to the south. He watched the lights resolve themselves into the outline of the Porsche Panamera as it accelerated towards them, bouncing over a dozen potholes before it shuddered to a halt a couple of metres short of his position. Then Bald directed Hands into the back seat. He climbed in after him and shouted to Skinner, '*Go, go! Fucking go!*' Skinner was already putting his foot to the floor before Bald had even shut his door. His guts lurched as the Panamera shunted from zero to just under a ton in four shaved seconds, rear tyres spewing out swirls of dust that blanketed the walkway.

Skinner arrowed it north of the labour camp. They pelted along the highway at 140 per. The dormitories and the mountain of garbage sliding into the horizon. Ahead the road was empty. The sky was gleaming and black like a tar pit. The Panamera's air con was working overtime, but it made no difference. The heat coming off all three of them, they were sweating like gerbils at a gay bar. The sweat mixed with the smell of raw sewage and the brand-new leather of the seats to form a putrid cocktail. Skinner wrinkled his nose.

'Fuck me,' he said, rolling down his window. 'You two smell like shit.'

Bald eyefucked Skinner in the rear-view mirror. 'What happened to you?'

'Camp guards. Came out of nowhere. Four of them. I had to put the afterburners on. I did a circuit of the camp and spotted you two arse bandits legging it.' Skinner cocked his head at Hands. 'Who's your friend?'

'This cunt?' said Bald, pulling a face at Hands. 'Dave Hands is no friend of mine. But he's gonna help us get to Klich.'

Hands snarled back, 'If I'm going to help you out, I want something in return.'

Bald laughed. 'I already spared your miserable fucking life. That's the only thing you're getting, Davey boy. Put your Christmas list away, because it ain't happening.'

Hands poked a finger at Bald. 'Nah, mate. It don't work that way. You want the Russian, you give me my old life back. The one you fucking took away from me.' He paused. 'I want back in with the Firm.'

Bald was silent. They rushed past skeletal apartment blocks and vacant shopping malls. It was like someone had pressed the pause button on Dubai's relentless expansion and nobody had been able to find the remote. Bald felt his BlackBerry trilling in the front pocket of his jeans. He dug it out and saw the name lit up on the display and his day got a little bit worse.

'John?' There was a squawk of radio interference, and then a voice shot down the line. Schoolmasterish. 'Are you there? I've been trying to get you for the last hour. Do you have Klich?'

'It was a trap,' Bald replied. 'We were ambushed.'

Before Leo Land could speak Bald piped up. 'Klich knew he was being tailed. He led us into a trap. One of the welcome party was a familiar face.'

'Oh?' Land said airily.

'Dave Hands.'

Land made a pained sound like someone was pulling a splinter out of his dick. 'I knew it!'

Bald gripped the BB hard. 'What the fuck are you talking about?'

'His name was flagged up on our system a few hours ago.'

'You fucking lied to me.'

Land chuckled. 'No, dear boy. I've only just come across this intelligence myself. That's why I've been trying to call you.'

Silence filled the car. Out of the corner of his eye, Bald could see Hands kicking back and resting his hands behind his head, looking fucking pleased with himself.

'Hands says he can get me on the BG team,' said Bald. 'Means I can get close to Klich. Nab the guy in his own penthouse suite.'

Land hmmmed a moment, then said, 'I have a better idea.'

twenty-one

Bald caught a glimpse of himself in the rear-view mirror. He literally looked like shit. The struggle with Hands had flecked his own mug with sewage, and his hair was glued into dirty clumps. His eyes were bloodshot and puffy. He looked ten years older than he was, and he felt a hundred older than that.

Land said, 'Let me tell you my plan.'

What's wrong with mine?' Bald asked.

Land sighed. 'Where to begin? Let me see now. You believe you are going to waltz into the world's premier hotel, press the flesh with a heavily guarded and no doubt paranoid Russian oligarch, and spirit him away?'

'Something like that,' Bald grumbled.

'I see. And you're expecting his security detail to simply lay down their arms and hand him over to you? Or are you intending to use the power of persuasion?'

'I have a gun,' said Bald. 'I can persuade anyone I want.'

That enticed a tasteless guffaw out of Land, kind of how Bald imagined upper-class twats laughed at comedy. 'This is why wars are fought by grunts and won by generals,' said Land. 'You're good with your fists. And me? I'm well paid for a reason, John. I provide the brains to an operation like this.'

Bald squirmed, like he had maggots in his guts. He said, 'Just shut up and tell me your fucking idea.'

'It will involve a small risk on your part.' There was a pause, and what sounded to Bald like Land suppressing a snigger. 'But then, that's what you're paid for, isn't it?'

Silence. Bald let it play out like the fag end of a tune. The Gulf loomed on the horizon, a bar of shiny blackness beneath a dark-blue sky. He sat back in his seat, the closest he'd ever come to owning a Porsche, trying not to look at his shit-stained reflection in the rear-view and wondering why he was the one who always ended up getting his hands dirty. All the while, Land glided through life. Not so much as a speck stuck to Land. The man was Teflon.

'This is my plan,' Land said. 'Hands will secure your place on the security team as you suggest. But we have less than twenty-four hours until the meeting with Hemdani. What if there isn't a chance to spirit Klich away before then? That's a risk we can't afford to take.'

Bald frowned.

The line crackled as Land went on, 'Our best chance of securing Klich is to lure him away. No need for fisticuffs in a heavily guarded five-star hotel when a little ingenuity will do the trick.'

'But I'll only just have met the cunt,' said Bald, still frowning. 'How can I lure him anywhere?'

'You will need to prove yourself.'

Bald felt something like dread tying itself in knots around his bowels. 'How?'

'By taking a bullet for Klich.'

The knot tightened. Bald looked across at Hands wiping down his shitty face and hair with his sleeve.

'You need to act fast. As soon as Klich and his team exit the hotel,' said Land.

'You're going to fucking shoot me?' said Bald in disbelief. He clocked Hands at his side, shooting forward in his seat, a look of surprise on his mug.

'With a blank, man.' Land cleared his throat. 'You will dive in front of Klich to protect your quarry. Since the round will be a blank, you won't be wounded. But Klich will simply believe it missed. The mere fact that you were prepared to lay down your life will be ample demonstration of your loyalty.'

'OK,' said Bald. 'But if we do this, we do it right.'

'That goes without saying.'

'Skinner will need a rifle. And a box of blanks.'

'Of course.'

'Something that makes a lot of noise. A Ruger 10/22 will get the job done.'

'I'll arrange a weapons cache. Anything else?'

'Just one. When I give you Klich, I never want to see or hear from you again.'

'The pleasure will be all mine,' said Land.

Bald tightened his grip on the BlackBerry and imagined it was Leo Land's windpipe, but he had to listen to the posh old cunt as he went on, 'Once your bond of trust is established, you will take Klich aside and tell him that the situation is unstable. You will then say that you know a safe passage across to Iran – via Port Rashid. When you arrive, a snatch team will be lying in wait to apprehend Klich and lift him out of Dubai.'

Land afforded himself a polite laugh.

'Rather a splendid plan, don't you agree?'

Bald spat out of the window. Trying to get the bad taste of sewage and sweat out of his mouth. The bad taste of Land too.

'You're a cunt,' he said.

'Perhaps. But I'm a cunt with a brain and a six-figure income.'

Hands gestured to the BB and pointed to himself. He hadn't been able to hear Land down the line. But he could sure as hell glean enough from listening to Bald to know that the call was nearly over. And he still needed his end of the bargain.

'One other thing,' said Bald grudgingly. 'Hands has a demand. In return for his cooperation.'

'What is it?'

'He wants back in with the Firm.'

Land exhaled wearily. Then he said, 'Fine. Tell him to report to me once the mission is complete.' He coughed. 'I trust you don't need reminding that failure tomorrow will cost you dearly. The clock is ticking, John. Good luck.'

Click.

Bald watch the phone's screen fade to slate. Then he turned to Hands and said, 'Your wish is granted, Davey boy. But only after you've done a little job for me.'

He laid out the plan to the other two. Skinner listened and licked his lips. The guy was practically creaming in his pants at the thought of finally getting in on some action after a lifetime of paperwork and Ben & Jerry's. When they were a kilometre from the Seven Wonders Hotel, Skinner fished out his old Nokia and wedged it in the fold of flesh between shoulder and chin. He made a call to the hotel's restaurant and booked a table for two. Scribbled the reservation number on a Post-It note.

They swooped past souks and lines of fish stalls and sped through a tunnel that burrowed under Dubai Creek. Bald wiped himself down with one of Skinner's fine cashmere sweaters from the back seat. He poured water from a half-empty plastic bottle onto its sleeve and dabbled it across his face to give himself a modicum of respectability. If he looked like a tramp he'd never make it past hotel security.

Bald tossed the bottle at Hands and told him to clean himself up.

The tunnel ejected them onto the western side of the city. The Seven Wonders coasted into view above the myriad beach hotels. The first time Bald had seen it had been during the ride over from the airport in the late afternoon. Back then the façade had been a sleeve of brilliant white from top to bottom. Now strobes of outrageous colour were playing across the façade, and countless room lights sparkled. Bald felt his jaw muscles stiffen.

Somewhere inside is Viktor Klich, he thought. My passport to a new life.

As the Panamera rolled up to the front gates, a security guard in Ray-Bans and a dark suit rapped his knuckles on the driver's window and took the reservation number from Skinner. Ran his eyes down his clipboard. Stepped back and waved them through. The gates opened onto a forecourt that circled an extravagant marble fountain jetting streams of water some fifteen metres into the air. The forecourt was lined with Camry cabs. The hotel's entrance was lined with four-metre-high palm trees and a red silk carpet stretched like a tongue between the forecourt and the revolving lobby doors.

As Skinner slowed again, Bald cast his eyes around. Valets were climbing in and out of Maseratis, Ferraris, Bentleys. The Seven Wonders was possibly the only hotel in the world where a guy could drive a Porsche and feel poor.

Hands tapped Bald on the shoulder. 'It's all sorted. We'll report to the penthouse suite and get you suited up.'

'That's it? They don't want to grill me first?'

Hands patted Bald on the back.

'I told you, me old mucker. My word is golden. I tell 'em you're good, they believe me. Besides, Klich ain't got time to read your fucking CV.'

'What about you?' said Bald to Skinner.

'I'll get everything set up for the shot tomorrow.'

'Ever fired a .22 before?'

'Yeah, on the ranges.'

'This is for real. We get only one crack at grabbing Klich. So make sure you don't shaft us both.'

Bald left the UMP stashed in the footwell. It wasn't the kind of weapon he could conceal and anyway, he figured the BG team would probably pat him down before allowing him into the same room as Klich. Then he stepped out of the car and swaggered down the red carpet. The central shaft of the revolving doors was made of gold and the panels on each of the four doors were trimmed with gold. Mounted on the central shaft was a small glass enclosure filled with water and populated with exotic fish.

The hotel was the opposite of the minimalist style Bald had seen in most classy Western hotels. The Seven Wonders screamed opulence. The floor was polished marble and imprinted with gold patterns that looked like a Persian rug design. The walls were walnut trimmed with gold. A chandelier hung from the ceiling like a diamond-encrusted claw. Strewn across the lobby there were bronze replicas of the Leaning Tower of Pisa, the Taj Mahal and the Empire State Building, flanked by boutiques selling designer jewellery, cosmetics and other luxury goods.

Hands was crossing the lobby fast. Bald strode after him. They muscled their way through a throng of Asians with their faces pressed to the shop windows. Bald and Hands still smelled like dead rats. The Asians parted to let them through. Amid the throng, Bald noticed a few moody white couples. Men with sloped noses and podgy bellies and women half their age draped tastelessly over them, looking like expensively dressed versions of the Eastern European hookers Bald had seen in the Scorpion Bar.

'Russians,' said Hands. 'They can't get enough of the place, mate. They clean the place out of raw oysters and caviar.'

They rode the lift to the eighteenth floor. Hands led the way down a corridor lined with abstract paintings, the kind that Bald guessed cost a fuck-off-sized pile of wonga. The penthouse suite had a walnut door with a card reader to the right.

Bald could hear something coming from the other side of the door. He pressed his ear close and listened. The moans and grunts of a couple screwing each other's brains out reached his ear. He swapped a puzzled look with Hands. Then Hands switched his gaze to the door.

It was very slightly ajar.

Hands pushed the door open and waited, listening. Then he inched inside, Bald right behind. They entered a high-ceilinged foyer with a dining room to the left and what looked like a private cinema to the right. Straight ahead was the lounge. The shagging sounds were coming from that direction. Bald and Hands edged into the lounge and spread out. Three black-leather sofas were arranged around a leopard-skin rug. There was a set of sliding doors fanning out to a trellised balcony overlooking the Gulf. There a porno movie was playing on a forty-two-inch plasma TV fixed to the wall. Bald reached for the remote and turned it off, killing the exaggerated sounds of fucking. That's when he noticed two blonde women, both passed out, each on one of the sofas.

Straight away Bald recognized them as hookers. He knew a good hooker when he saw one, and these two were top-drawer. They wore platform shoes and latex mini-skirts and every inch of their bodies had been Botoxed and surgically enhanced. A glass coffee table in front of them was laden with half-filled champagne flutes and a bottle of Moët in an ice bucket. Lines of toot were laid out on a mirror.

'Guess how much a night,' said Hands.

'Five grand,' said Bald.

'Not even close,' said Hands, now standing over one of the hookers. Her nose was snotty and her eyes were whiting out. He waved his fingers in front of her, then clicked them. Nothing. She was out for the count.

'Fuck it. Ten?' said Bald.

'Twenty.'

Bald nodded his appreciation. If this was what twenty grand bought you, he thought as he gazed at the hookers, then it was value for money.

'And that's not including the food, the chauffeur, the entertainment,' Hands continued, nodding at the girls. 'Know what, these two are probably the cheapest fucking things in sight.'

They climbed a set of marble stairs leading to up to a separate bedroom area on the first floor, then split up to investigate the rooms. Bald entered what appeared to be the master bedroom. There was a four-poster bed draped with Egyptian silk duvets and a dozen down-filled pillows. There was a complimentary iPad on each of the bedside tables, and an en-suite bathroom with marble and gold fittings and a whirlpool bath, tailor-made, thought Bald, for getting frisky with the high-class hookers. There was all this, but there was no sign of Klich.

'Where are all the fucking bodyguards?' Bald said as he emerged from the bedroom.

Hands was standing in the corridor. He was gripping a dark suit by the hanger in his right hand, had a crisp white shirt and a towel in his left. He offered them to Bald and said, 'I just got a text from the boss man. He's popped out with the rest of the team. Had to take care of some urgent business. Says he's due back in a few hours.'

'Any idea where he went?'

Hands shrugged.

'Grab a shower, mate. Clean yourself up and get changed. I'm gonna do the same. I smell worse than a fucking raghead running a marathon.'

'And then you'll introduce me to Klich?'

Hands nodded and said, 'Soon as he's back.'

'What about shoes?'

'Take a pair of the boss's. He has so many he won't notice one pair gone.'

Bald was grateful for the change of clothes. He took a power shower in the guest bedroom. Hot water blasting off the layer of shit and sweat and dirt that had formed a crust on his skin. It felt good. It felt like the best shower in the world. He tried on the suit. The jacket was a little short in the arms and the trousers a bit tight around the waist. He liberated a pair of black leather brogues from the rack in the wardrobe. Size ten. His size. Fucking nice shoes.

Then Bald decided to get some shuteye. In his experience lack of sleep was the number-one reason for missions going tits up. Tomorrow evening he would need to bring his A-game to the plate. A few hours' sleep now sounded like a fucking good idea. He thought about kipping in the guest bedroom. The bed looked enticing. But as he was about to crash on the pillow he stopped short and thought that the boss might not like it. Bald wouldn't, if he was Klich. Taking the man's shoes was one thing, but sleeping in his bed would take the fucking piss. So he retreated to the lounge and crashed on the free sofa. The two hookers didn't stir. They were off their nuts on toot and champagne. The tiredness swooped over Bald like a blanket. He didn't fall asleep, he fucking nosedived into the abyss.

He was woken by the heavy slam of a door and the click-clock of footsteps. Hands was sweeping past him in a grey suit whose jacket was too broad in the shoulders and a couple of inches too long. Bald sat up, stretched. Sunlight was cashing through the windows and spraying the room gold and bronze. The clock on the wall read 0615 hours. He turned to see Hands standing a couple of metres away. He was talking to somebody. Laughing at something they'd seen. Bald couldn't see the other person, who was hidden behind Hands. Then Hands stepped aside, and Bald set eyes on the figure standing in the doorway.

She was dressed in a black two-piece suit with a white blouse and grey court shoes. She was clutching a pistol and eyeing Bald and Hands warily. Hands smiled at Bald as he turned and said, 'John, mate. Come say hello to Odessa Stone.'

twenty-two

Bald and Odessa stared awkwardly at each other, the temperature rising with every second, until the silence became scalding, and Hands must have felt it too, because he made a smile like someone was shining a torch in his eyes and said, 'This is the new fella I was telling you about.'

'Pleasure to meet you,' said Odessa.

The words had to practically prise themselves from her sealed lips. Bald was aware that his own face had gone dead slack. Last time he'd run into Odessa had been at the villa in Caracas two days ago. She'd helped him escape, saved his fucking life. But then she'd disappeared. Now he was bumping into her again on the other side of the world. And she also knew that Bald had been on the hunt for Klich. One word out of those ruby lips and his cover was blown and the mission dead in the water.

'Where are the others?' Hands said.

'On their way.' Odessa was stashing her pistol in a leather belt holster. Eyes on Bald the whole time. She still looked damn good. Her hair was covered, in keeping with local custom. The overhead lights picked out the electric green in her eyes. She asked Hands, 'Did you find out who was tailing us?'

'Russian agents. Just like the boss figured.'

'And you took care of them?'

Hands scratched an itch on the back of his neck.

'They're not a problem any more,' he said.

Footsteps sounded behind them in the foyer. Another black woman entered from the corridor. She was built like a fridge. Six-two, wide shoulders, hefty legs that touched at the knee, and hair in cornrows. A man was standing at her shoulder. He wore a ridiculously large pair of Ray-Bans. Bald recognized the traditional black shirt, stonewashed jeans and the red and yellow striped boots of the Russian playboy. But the guy wasn't the one he'd seen at the labour camp. He was leaner and taller. His hair was pulled back in a ponytail. And no sign of a mullet. Bald realized the guy he was looking at was the real Viktor Klich. The one at the camp had been bait.

Klich marched across the lounge. Hands bowed in deference like the Russian was a king. Klich beelined for the master bedroom and slammed the door shut behind him. Fridge-woman didn't follow. Instead she stopped in front of Bald. Sizing him up. The face she was pulling, it was like she didn't what she was seeing.

'You must be the new guy,' she said. 'What's your background?'

'Kidnap and ransom,' Bald said. 'I work as a security expert. I'm meeting up here with my business partner.'

Fridge took a step closer to Bald. Said, 'I've got contacts in K&R. They must know about you. What's your company?'

Bald hesitated. Shit, what had Land said? The company's name had slipped his mind. His eyes were darting left and right, like maybe someone had scrawled it on one of the walls. Then he had another idea. He dug out his BlackBerry, pulled up the contact listed as the imaginary company's PA, and chucked the phone at Fridge. 'Love, I've pulled shifts at so many companies over the years, it's like women: it's hard to keep track of their names. Why don't you call my assistant? She'll happily answer any questions you've got.'

Fridge eyed the BlackBerry suspiciously. Then she snatched it and pointed to Hands. 'Wake the girls up. The boss wishes to spend some time alone with them.'

She hit 'call' and tapped her foot while she waited. After five rings she introduced herself to a voice at the other end of the line, and Bald breathed a sigh of relief. Hands withdrew and shook the two hookers awake, Bald staring daggers at his back. Hands was supposed to vouch for him and now he was fucking off. The hookers lazily stirred. Bald looked sideways at Odessa while Fridge fired questions down the phone. The mission was poised on a knife edge. If Odessa spilled her guts Bald would be in big trouble. But so far she had held back from blowing his cover. Bald wondered why she would do that. Unless . . .

Fridge interrupted his thought by tossing the BB at him and saying, 'Your story checks out.' She turned to Odessa, the two of them swapping one of those mystifying female looks that Bald was fated to never really understand. Fridge told her, 'I want to do some more digging on this guy. In the meantime he can guard the corridor. Once you've briefed him report up to me.'

Odessa escorted Bald towards the entrance to the penthouse suite. There, Hands was guiding one of the hookers up the stairs, Fridge holding the door of the master bedroom open for him. From inside the room Bald heard Klich laughing heartily. Being really fucking loaded sounded like a lot of fun. Sounded just as much fun as Bald had imagined.

Looking directly at Bald, Odessa whispered, 'What the fuck are you doing here?'

'Like I said, I'm the new bodyguard.'

Odessa didn't reply. They were standing alone in the hallway outside the suite. Odessa leaned in close to Bald. For one blissful moment it looked like she was going to kiss him and his balls went blue at the thought. Instead she whipped out the pistol.

'You think that little trick with the BlackBerry fooled me?' she said. 'Think again.'

Bald recognized the weapon. A Sig Sauer P230 semi-automatic. It weighed 500 grams unloaded and was less than seven inches from muzzle to hammer. Unlike other close-protection guns, the P230 had reasonable stopping power. The weapon was chambered for the semi-rimmed straight-walled .32 ACP cartridge, a bullet that had been invented by John Browning more than a century back and had stood the test of time. Sometimes the oldies really were the goodies. At short ranges the .32 ACP could do a lot of damage. A good gun for close-protection work.

A bad gun to have pointed at your head.

'I'm not tugging on anyone's dick,' Bald said, holding up his hands. 'I got this job through Hands.'

'You're friends?'

'We go way back. He asked me to fill in on this BG team at short notice. I needed the coin, so I said yes.'

'Drop the act,' said Odessa. 'You're a lousy actor.'

'Makes two of us,' said Bald. His eyes were grinning, his hands dropping to his sides. Odessa stared at him for a few moments. But then she blinked and Bald sensed an unease stirring in her. 'Let's face it,' he said. 'If you wanted to dob me in you would've said something to your mate back there. But you didn't.'

'So?'

'So, that means you have something to hide too.'

Odessa curled her lips into a weak smile and laughed in her nose. She lowered her left hand to lightly brush against his groin. 'Well, look at us,' she said. 'Keeping secrets from each other. Like a real couple.'

Bald felt Odessa cupping her hand around his ball sack. Then she squeezed.

'I know you're here for Klich.' Her voice was still a whisper, but lacerating rather than soft and seductive. 'That's why you were in Venezuela. At the villa. You and your friend. The one who got arrested.' She squeezed harder and Bald writhed in pain. 'Joe Gardner.'

Bald felt nausea tickling his tonsils. 'How do you know his fucking name?'

'Answer my question first. What are you doing here?'

Feet were clumping down the stairs inside the penthouse. Odessa glanced at the door and released her grip on his balls. 'Look, we don't have much time, so you'd best level with me. I know Joe. Used to work with him.' She paused a beat, lost in her thoughts. 'I kind of liked him.'

'Joe was a fucking idiot.'

'Was?'

Bald gasping for breath. 'He's doing chokey in Venezuela. He lasts twenty-four hours I'd be amazed.'

Odessa dug the Sig's muzzle into his cheek. 'Last chance to come clean.'

Bald didn't panic. He'd had plenty of guns poked in his face over the years. He looked at his predicament with a cool, detached logic. Figured that if Odessa knew about Gardner, that could only mean one thing. She had to be on the same side as him. He also knew that if Fridge saw Odessa holding a P230 to his head he'd be kicked off the team and the plan would be fucked.

'I'm here on official business,' he said. 'Now put the fucking gun away.'

'Who sent you?'

'The Firm.'

A wave of uncertainty passed between them. Footsteps so close now that Bald imagined they were only a few paces on the other side of the door to the suite. He needed Odessa to stow the gun. Odessa seemed ignorant of the approaching footsteps. She said, 'I'm with Six too.'

Bald did a double-take. 'Fuck off.'

'It's the truth.'

Bald just stood there, gun in his face, the feeling sinking out of his extremities.

'My handler says there's no other agents assigned to Klich,' said Odessa. 'So tell me, who are you reporting to?'

Bald was about to answer when the door flung open and Odessa spun away and tucked the Sig back into her holster.

Fridge, filling the doorway, glowered at Odessa. 'We're leaving,' she said.

Odessa nodded. Then Fridge gave her back to them both and stomped back through the foyer, towards the lounge and the two comatose hookers. Odessa went to follow but Bald gripped her upper arm.

'What's going on?' he said.

'The RV has been pushed forward.'

'To when?'

'To right the fuck now.'

Bald waited until Odessa had disappeared up the stairs and tapped out a text to Land – 'ON THE MOVE' – and sent it. Three minutes later she returned. 'Dave Hands is a friend of yours?'

'Depends.'

'On what?'

'Whether your definition of a friend is someone who's a flaming cunt.'

'Maybe you should get new friends.'

Bald shrugged. 'Maybe I should get a new job. Hands reckons he's raking it in on the security gig with your boss. Couldn't stop saying much how much bacon he was bringing home each week. He's landed on his feet.'

Odessa laughed. 'And you believed him?'

'Why not?'

'You're an idiot. Hands gets paid a pittance. Klich is broke. He hasn't paid any of his staff for months. Hands lives in a broom cupboard in the labour camp with a Filipino who cleans toilets for a living. And believe me, she looks like she cleans toilets for a living.'

Fridge was first out through the door, P230 secured in a shoulder holster, dour look plastered across her face. She paused a few steps beyond Bald and Odessa and looked back at Klich, who followed her out of the suite. He was adjusting his manhood and looking pleased with himself.

Bald realized this was his first proper look at Klich. He had a belt of uneven stubble on his face and his eyes were greener than they had appeared in the photos. Maybe that was a trick of the lens. He'd ditched the black cotton shirt and the gaudy boots and opted for a washed cotton chambray shirt to go with his distressed jeans. He wore a pair of worn-in suede boots.

Klich had an odd way about him, Bald thought, for a one-time billionaire. Rich people he'd seen tended to march around with a sense of authority and entitlement, secure in the knowledge that they were superior to pretty much everyone else around them. Klich, though, acted nervously. His left hand was trembling and he repeatedly quelled it with his right. He looked warily at the world around him. Then again, thought Bald, he'd be bricking it too if he had the Russians and the Brits on his case. Klich didn't acknowledge Bald. He ran a hand nervously through his grey hair on his way past. Bald smelled whisky on his breath and suddenly craved a drop of the hard stuff himself.

Hands, in his ill-fitting suit, was the last to emerge. He walked behind Klich. Then Odessa closed the door to the suite and hurried after the rest of the team, Bald jostling alongside her, the two of them bringing up the rear as tail-end Charlies.

'No matter what happens, you stick close to me,' Odessa said.

'Because you're concerned for my safety?' Bald was smarting.

'Because I don't trust you.'

As they reached the end of the corridor leading into the hotel, Bald received a new message alert on his BlackBerry. He slyly checked the message while Fridge thumbed the call button beside the lift. 'SKINNER ON HIS WAY,' the text read. 'ETA TWO MINUTES.' Bald hastily deleted it and stashed the phone.

The lift arrived and sounded its nonchalant ping. Klich was first inside. Then Fridge and Hands, and finally Odessa and Bald. Even with five of them inside, it didn't feel crammed. Bald was aware of Klich looking at him, as if noticing him for the first time.

'What the fuck are you doing here?' he said. His voice was surprisingly light and jumpy. Like a kid anxiously trying to please its parents.

'I'm your new bodyguard, sir,' Bald replied.

Klich scratched his stubble. 'You know how many body-guards I have hired in last three years?'

Bald shrugged. He didn't give a fuck, but he'd have to humour the man. Klich removed a miniature hip flask from the back pocket of his jeans and tipped a generous measure of what smelled like Crown Royal down his throat. 'Eighteen,' he said. 'Most of them dead. I hope you do not consider this a permanent post?'

'I don't think about tomorrow,' said Bald.

Klich grunted his agreement as they plummeted down in the lift. A quick flick of his eyes across the lobby and Bald could tell they were the only guests up and about at this early hour. A few tired-looking staff were lugging breakfast trol-leys into other lifts. Bald smelled fresh coffee and scrambled eggs and toasted croissants. He realized he hadn't touched a morsel of food since the in-flight meal twenty-three long hours ago. He made a mental list of the things he would do once he had Klich in the bag.

Tuck into an English breakfast.

Have a pint of Guinness.

Bang the Thai prossie at the Scorpion Bar.

The BG team arranged themselves in a diamond around Klich. Bald was shunted to the back of the diamond with Fridge at the spearhead and Hands and Odessa to the left and right. The rear was the last place Bald wanted to be. He had to manoeuvre himself to the spearhead in order to get into position for the shot. But he was still at the back as Fridge swept through the lobby doors and Klich and the rest of the BG team followed and they emerged into the breaking dawn. The sun was a stab of red amid a coat of purple and grey. The air was sticky and moist. From deep in the city came the morning call to prayer.

Bald made a quick recce of the area ahead of him. The water fountain was switched off. There was a single security guard on duty at the front gates. Pacing up and down, thumbs resting on his utility belt.

Fridge stopped. Klich stopped.

Everyone stopped.

Fridge said, 'Where's Nikolai?'

She meant the chauffeur for the Lincoln Town Car, Bald figured. The Lincoln was nowhere to be seen. Outside the hotel, to the right, stood a tattered old bus with a front like a crushed soda can and tyres worn down to tar-grey strips. The doors of the bus opened and disgorged a throng of sad brown faces dressed in maid and waiter uniforms. Must have been thirty of them, Bald thought. They flocked towards the hotel's revolving doors, moving with the slumped shoulders and heavy footsteps of the fuckers at the very bottom of the food chain. Bald recognized that look, because he had been there himself. The slow human wave shuffled on, obscuring the BG team's line of sight beyond the bus.

Bald sensed his opportunity. He used the confusion to draw behind Hands, gesturing to him to swap positions. Hands took a couple of sly steps back so Bald could take his place. Then Bald cast his eyes out across the main drag. But he wasn't looking for the Lincoln. He was searching for Skinner.

Couldn't see the guy anywhere.

'Fucking Nikolai,' growled Klich, swigging from his flask. 'I'd fire him, if I could find a Russian who didn't drink vodka for breakfast.'

Fridge said nothing. She dug out her iPhone 4S and pressed the handset to her ear. Calling the famous Nikolai, Bald thought. Then he saw something glint in the periphery of his vision. Coming from the main road. Sixty metres to the left. A beast of a car. Diamond black, with a grille like bared teeth, bulleting towards the hotel. Bald squinted.

Not a Porsche Panamera.

But a Bentley Continental.

Was it Skinner? Bald wasn't sure. Land hadn't said which vehicle to look out for. It occurred to him that since the Panamera had been compromised during the shootout at the camp, Skinner would have taken the precaution of changing his wheels.

Yeah, he thought. This must be Skinner. The plan is still on.

Thirty metres from the hotel the Bentley slowed to a fast walk. Bald estimated that it would take another four or five seconds for Skinner to have lined himself up directly opposite Klich.

'There!' Fridge said. Bald snapped his head away from Skinner. Fridge was pointing through a gap in the flock of workers, at a point beyond the bus. The last of the workers, the old-timers, were taking longer to climb off the bus and schlep towards the hotel. Now Bald looked through the gap. A chauffeur was coming towards them. Guy was twirling a set of keys and behind him Bald could make out the elongated hood of the Lincoln. The chauffeur had been forced to park farther away than he would have done, because of the bus, leaving a four-metre gap between the two vehicles. Now he threaded his way through the workers single-filing into the hotel.

Bald looked back ahead. The Bentley was at their two o'clock. The bus was six metres to their right. Fridge raised a hand to indicate to the BG team to wait for the crowd to filter past.

The chauffeur had practically reached the team.

Four seconds to go. The Bentley was almost lined up. Klich was totally oblivious to the threat unfolding around him. Bald counted down the last few seconds. Fridge was examining the faces of those still stepping off the bus, hand resting on the butt of her P230.

Three seconds.

The Bentley's brake lights beamed and the car eased to a graceful standstill. Bald saw the tinted window lowering. Skinner preparing to take his shot. Now Bald sprang into action and threw Klich to the floor. The Russian fell back, his hand outstretched and grabbing hold of Bald's wrist and dragging him down with him. Bald tugged his arm clear. Then he looked up and saw a rifle barrel poking out of the Bentley window. He couldn't see Skinner in the wan light inside.

The barrel lit up as a tongue of flame licked out of the muzzle. Then there was a loud *ca-rack*, like an invisible whip rushing through the air, and everything happened fast. Fridge ducking and rushing towards Klich, Odessa shouting, Hands dropping to the ground. It's all going to plan, thought Bald.

Then he felt a searing pain graze his ribs.

He looked down and saw he had been shot.

twenty-three

Bald lay still for a moment, a lone thought repeating on him. Skinner was told to fire a blank at me. So why the fuck am I bleeding? Then the thought changed tunes and told him he'd been shot for real. There was a lot of blood. A dark, glistening patch on the right side of his T-shirt ran from the mid-point of his ribcage down to his hip. He felt a pain like someone thrusting a screwdriver into his stomach. The pain quickly dissipated as adrenalin and endorphins flooded his bloodstream.

There was a second shimmer of light at the Bentley's window, and a second *ca-rack*, then Bald saw a bullet strike the revolving doors at his six o'clock. Glass shattering. Shards hailstoning the ground. Workers at the doors screaming. Skinner's lost the fucking plot, Bald was thinking.

Fridge and Odessa had reached for their holstered weapons and were raising them as a third round zipped out of the rifle in the Bentley. There was a gasp from Fridge. Her head snapped back as a bullet thumped into her neck, and she dropped a metre to the right of Bald. Fingers clawing at her throat, rasping and gasping, like she was choking on a pretzel. A bright-red carpet pooling beneath her.

Bald spotted movement at his two. The security guard at the front gates was fleeing across the street. Bald turned his attention back to Klich. The oligarch was sprawled beside him on the ground and numb with shock, his expression confused rather than terrified, like he had just seen a billion pounds wiped off his shares. Klich began to pick himself up. Shaping to flee. Classic fight-or-flight syndrome. Bald thrust out an arm and kept him pinned down. Thinking, three shots, one BG dead and he got me too. This is some fucking surgical shooting.

Can't be the work of Skinner.

Keeping hold of Klich, Bald turned to Odessa.

'We need to get behind cover,' he shouted.

'Yeah. I'll take him,' she said, discharging two rounds from her semi-automatic in quick succession. Compared with the roar of the rifle targeting them, the P230 sounded puny, and the rounds sparked and glanced off the Bentley's bodywork. Fucking great, thought Bald grimly. Bulletproof armour.

Panic was spreading among the camp workers dashing towards the revolving doors. They were blocking Bald and the others from reaching cover behind the bus. Now Odessa hauled Klich off the ground and ushered him towards it. Hands sidestepping Fridge and joining them, the three of them darting towards the bus. The rifle barked again and three rounds spattered into the back of a stubby maintenance guy. He stumbled forward like he had only just remembered he had legs, blood gushing from his stomach and splashing the ground in front of him. He blundered on for a couple of steps before he fell onto Bald and sent them both crashing down. The old fuck let out a death groan and puked blood all over Bald's chest.

A second three-round burst sounded. Two more workers were cut down. Bald didn't see them fall. His view was blanked out by the dead guy on top of him. But he heard their cries cut short and the slap of dead weight against concrete. Bald had to get to the others at the bus before he got nailed too. He planted his palms firmly on the dead guy's chest. Then he puffed out his cheeks and pushed up, locking his elbows and straining his pectoral muscles, as if he was doing a bench press. He lifted the body, took a deep breath and rolled him off to his side. The guy tumbled into a heap beside Fridge. Bald pulled the P230 from her cold grasp.

Bald looked up to see that Hands, Odessa and Klich had reached cover behind the bus. Now he scuttled towards them. But he spotted movement in the corner of his eye. Two figures carrying rifles had debussed from the rear of the Bentley. They had slipped out of the passenger door facing away from Bald and knelt down by the boot to gain cover from his fire. Three gunmen, thought Bald. Two on foot, plus the driver.

The two gunmen popped their heads above the Bentley's boot. They were decked out in matching white shemaghs and each was levelling a Colt Commando assault rifle in his direction. Buttstocks tucked firmly into shoulders, jaws resting against the upper left sides of the weapons.

The two gunmen fired as Bald made the bus. Three-round bursts barked out of the Colt Commandos, six rounds hammering the side of the vehicle, the wretched jangle of metal yawing through metal. Who the fuck are these guys? Bald asked himself. There was a brief lull in the gunfire and he peered around the corner of the bus to see what was going on. Then he clocked the gunmen racing out from behind the Bentley, heading towards the fountain at their twelve o'clock, and Bald got his answer. They were here to snatch Klich.

Bald snapped into action. He raised the Sig level with his shoulder and put down four rounds at the two men as they dived for cover behind the base of the fountain. A sequence of flames throated out of the P230's muzzle. Bald maintaining his grip, the weapon kicking up in his hands, the slider bar crashing back and forth. Spent brass showered the ground around him. He missed the targets. Thirty metres with a semi-automatic firing .32 ACP rounds: he was always going to miss. But at least he'd put the brakes on their advance, bought himself a precious few seconds to figure out a counter-attack.

He heard a soft moan and turned to see Odessa clutching her right shoulder. She'd taken a hit. Blood slicked her smooth neck like a velvet wrap. Odessa was trying to staunch the shoulder wound with her hand.

'Any idea who our new friends are?' Bald shouted at her.

'Russians,' she said. 'Someone must have tipped them off.'

'What about Klich?'

'He's OK.'

He didn't look that OK to Bald. The guy was feeling his body in a blind panic, terrified that he had been shot. He was breathing heavily and mouthing prayers in Russian. Odessa got Bald's attention and jerked her head at the gunmen concealed behind the fountain.

'What are we going to do?' she said.

'They've got assault rifles and an armoured car and fuck knows what else. We've got pistols and we're low on ammo. If we wait here they'll overpower us eventually . . . nab your boss and slot the rest of us. Our only chance is to hold them off long enough for us to bug out in the Lincoln.'

'Looks like we're already too late,' Odessa said, nodding at the fountain. Bald joined Odessa at her shoulder. One of the gunmen was bolting towards the Lincoln while his mate put down rounds along with the Bentley's driver. Three, four, five rounds forced Bald and Odessa to pull back, the rounds ricocheting throughout the bus and puncturing its tyres.

Bald said, 'On my mark, you put down cover fire and I'll put the drop on the prick.'

There was the slightest pause in the gunfire, Bald shouted, '*Now!*' and Odessa displaced to a spot two metres clear of the front of the bus to give her a line of sight to both the gunman still behind the fountain and the driver. She had to hold her P230 in a one-handed grip as the wound on her shoulder made it impossible to bear any weight on that side. She trained the P230 at the gunman by the fountain, opened fire, and in the same blur of motion Bald pulled out from behind cover and targeted the gunman who was making a break for the Lincoln. The guy was nearer to Bald now as he pounded across the open ground. Twenty metres. Close enough for Bald to stand a much better chance of an accurate shot. He smiled inside as he lined up the guy's head between the notched front and rear sights on his P230. The gunman's head was a white smudge. Bald was about to make it a red one.

His first effort kicked up and whizzed over the guy's head. Shit. Bald lowered the P230 a couple of inches and fired again. The second round whistled in his wake. The pain flared up again in his guts and Bald struggle to focus on his target. He gritted his teeth and fired. This time his aim was true and the bullet nailed the target's shoulder. The guy howled in agony as hot lead sliced and diced muscle and bone, and he instinctively loosened his grip on the Colt Commando. Bald gave the trigger another squeeze as the guy went horizontal. The fourth round penetrated the gunman's upper chest, did a little jiggle inside his torso and exited out of his right shoulder blade. Blood was jetting out of both entry and exit wounds.

Odessa and Bald retreated behind the bus as shots rained down on their position.

'That should buy us a few seconds. Take Klich and get to the Lincoln,' Bald told Hands. 'You got the keys, right?'

Hands nodded.

'Good,' said Bald. 'We'll put suppressive fire down on the two shooters left standing. Get the engine started and wait for us.'

Hands didn't mess about. He hauled Klich to his feet. The Russian was shaking and dazed but he was otherwise OK. He was in better shape than Bald. Blood continued pumping out of his stomach wound. But at least it was a steady, slow trickle rather than a squirt, which meant that the round hadn't severed any major arteries. All the same, he was still in danger of bleeding out if he didn't get medical attention soon.

Now Hands was escorting Klich to the rear of the bus while Bald and Odessa were nearer the front, closer to the gunman at the fountain, giving them a better chance of an accurate shot. They now wheeled out from the side of the bus, Odessa taking aim at the Bentley's window while Bald loosed off two rounds from the P230 at the other guy. The rounds veered wildly off target but they kept the enemy subdued long enough for them to leg it to the Lincoln.

Hands had the longer gait and the quicker stride and he reached cover behind the Lincoln ahead of Klich. He looked back. The Russian had tripped up over the outstretched hand of a dead guy. The chauffeur. Bald hadn't noticed his corpse before. Figured he must have been caught in the crossfire. Bald put down another round at the gunman behind the fountain. Then he went to put down a fourth and—

Click, click.

'Fuck it! . . . Displace!' Bald shouted to Odessa. They sprinted back towards the rear end of the bus. Towards Klich. Towards the Lincoln. The gunmen sensed what was happening and directed their fire at the car. Round after incessant round punched into the bodywork. The sound was deafening, like sheet metal being forced into a shredder.

'Fuck this,' Hands shouted. He flipped open the driver's door of the Lincoln and slid inside, and Bald understood immediately what he planned to do.

He was going to bug out by himself.

You cunt, Dave, thought Bald. He and Odessa rushed forward. They were eight metres from the Lincoln now. Klich was four shy of the motor.

Almost there.

Then Hands started the engine.

Bald was blinded by a shaft of white light. He saw Klich thrown through the air. Then he felt a powerful wind blow him backwards, and Odessa too, a scalding backdraught lifting them both off their feet. A furious noise crashed his eardrums, like someone had let loose a bandolier of hand grenades in a diamond store. And as Bald hit the deck, his bones crunching with the force of the impact, he was aware of a figure landing a couple of metres in front of him. Bald's world shuddered and dissolved. And when it straightened out again he found himself staring into the dead eyes of Viktor Klich.

twenty-four

A ball of heat swelled and belched at the Lincoln. Bright-orange flames swallowed the car, red lashes of fire pouring out across the road, followed by capes of black smoke. The flames gorged themselves on the bus and shattered the remaining passenger windows and tarred the seats.

Bald heard the screech of rubber on tarmac and the roar of a car engine. Lying on his back, he had a two-inch line of sight between the underside of the bus and the road. Amid the spent brass and the shards of glass he could see the Bentley racing out of the front gates of the hotel, rear door yawning opening as the surviving gunman thrust himself into the back seat. The Russians were bugging out. Bald was still for a moment, his mind trying to put together the pieces. The Lincoln had exploded as soon as Hands had started the engine. It had to have been a booby-trap, he told himself. But who? The Russians?

Why would they bother to ambush Klich if they had already rigged his wheels?

The numbness disappeared. He was left with a million aches and pains in his bones. Everything hurt. Bald somehow scraped himself off the ground and lugged his weary body towards the Lincoln. The explosion had perforated his eardrums. He saw Klich lying face down beside the car and knew that there was no way the Russian could have survived. Chunks of shrapnel were embedded in his back. Bald could smell his burning flesh. Funny thing, he thought. Billionaires burn just like regular people.

Hands is dead too, another voice said.

Yeah, but fuck him.

Bald staggered towards Klich. He kicked aside empty cases streaked across the four metres of ground separating Bald from the Russian. Charred air suffocating him. He put a hand over his mouth and nostrils to block out the smoke. He stopped by Klich and rolled him onto his back with his foot.

Klich was dead all right. His body was in rag order. His guts had been blown open and he had a Z-shaped slash across his belly. The skin around the wound was a mesh of brown and black from where the material of his shirt had been fused to his flesh. His guts were coiled up on the ground in front of him. A weird smell of burnt plastic hung in the air. With the mission fucked, there was only one thing left to do. Bald reluctantly reached for his phone and dialled Land.

No answer.

Bald was still listening to the sixth or seventh bleep carrying down the line when he heard a metallic click at his back. He left his hand dangling and the phone ringing. Did a slow one-eighty and came face to face with Odessa. She was training her P230 on him. A strip of material torn off her jacket arm helped to stem her shoulder wound. Her hair was sprinkled with glass and dirt. He could hear the faint nasal tone of Land's voice on the answering machine 3500 miles away.

'Turn around and get on your knees,' she said.

'You can't kill me,' Bald said. 'You'd be killing one of your own.'

Odessa shifted on the balls of her feet. 'Except I don't believe you are one of us. Now on your fucking knees.'

Bald figured she was bluffing. She had no good reason to waste him, and the unsteady undertone of her voice told him she also had her doubts. He shrugged, turned his back to

Odessa, dropped to his knees and clasped his hands behind his head. Six minutes ago everything had been going to plan. He considered Klich's roasted corpse and thought that six minutes felt like a long time. Felt like it had all happened years ago. His thought was punctured by the cold tip of the barrel digging into the back of his skull.

Odessa said, 'Since I know you're not from Six, tell me who you're really with.'

'I report to Leo Land. Don't believe me, ask your handler. This is getting really fucking boring.'

Bald started to climb to his feet. But Odessa pressed the muzzle harder against his head and he stopped and tensed, feeling his heart pound and the blood raging in his neck. For a split second he thought maybe he was wrong and maybe Odessa really would slot him. Then he heard police sirens coming nearer, and the pressure from the gun lifted, and he heard footsteps scramble away from him, their sound like a sheet of ice cracking. Odessa was sprinting towards the front gates.

What the fuck? Bald thought about giving chase. But then his eyes wandered down to Klich and he noticed something odd. He stooped down to investigate. The guy's jawline was dripping like candle wax. Like it was melting. Bald was no fucking scientist, but he had seen enough charred bodies to know that skin didn't melt like this. He pinched a flap of the skin between his thumb and forefinger. It was hot and plasticky. He pulled on it and to his shock the face started to peel away. Like pulling a plaster off a wound. Bald went on peeling. Another face revealed itself underneath. This one was bleeding and real. Bald gave the face a final yank and it came clean off.

Then he felt the blood drain from his own. Into an invisible hole beneath him.

Bald was holding a prosthetic mask.

The man in front of him was not Viktor Klich.

twenty-five

Torn from the face of the dead guy sprawled on the ground, the prosthetic mask didn't look much like Viktor Klich. Didn't look much like a face at all. The brow had been singed black and the skin paint rubbed off. Then again, the dead guy himself didn't look much more real. His head had been scorched down to the scalp, like the tip of a struck match. Bald stared at him for a second, wondering who he was. Thinking that it didn't really matter: he was just another dead guy.

Then his BlackBerry vibrated. 'Number withheld,' said the caller ID. Bald took the call. Chucked the mask into the fire raging around the Lincoln Town Car. Silence, broken only by the crackle of the flames, then a voice crawled down the line.

'Where the fuck are you, fella?'

Bald's face twisted like he was being forced to watch a torture movie. 'Skinner,' he said. 'You fat cunt. You left me in the shit.'

'It wasn't my call,' Skinner said. His voice was lost for a beat beneath the growl of a car engine revving. 'Listen to me, mate. You're in trouble. Now, where are you?'

The sun beat down on Bald. The lead particles from the shots he had fired mixed with the sweat on his skin and formed a kind of grease. Where the fuck am I? he asked himself.

I'm in a world of shit, he thought.

'John,' Skinner said urgently.

'Who ordered you to pull out?' said Bald. 'That wanker Land?'

Skinner said nothing.

Bald shook his head and went on, 'I'm looking at the face of the guy who was supposed to be Klich. A body double.'

'You're still at the hotel? Jesus!' Skinner seethed down the line. He paused a beat. Sighed. Said, 'Listen carefully, mate. You need to get out of there right now. Make your way east on the main road. I'll come and grab you soon as I can.'

'Yeah?' Bald spat. 'And why should I believe you after you just fucked me off?'

'Because you don't know what's about to happen to you, and I do.'

There was a tension to Skinner's voice that made Bald pause. He frowned at the flames and said, 'What're you talking about?'

'Remember the contract that the Iranians put on your head?' said Skinner.

'I try not to,' said Bald.

'There's two guys on their way to you now. They're coming to collect the reward.'

Bald killed the call and wheeled away from the Lincoln. Hurried over to Fridge. The bodyguard had that newly dead look about her. Eyes sprung open in shock, like a couple of opened shutters, mouth agape like she was waiting for someone to pour water down her throat. Bald liberated the spare clip of .32 ACP rounds from her belt, ejected the empty clip from his Sig Sauer P230 and inserted the fresh one into the feed on the underside of the grip. Gave the chamber a decisive tug. Then he tucked the pistol into the waistband of his trousers, concealing it under the tail of his jacket.

Darted through the gates and into the street.

He hooked a left onto the main road as a wave of sirens blasted the air. Cops. Close. Hard to judge how close. The earlier gun battle was still playing high-pitched notes in his ears. He figured the cops were no more than three or four blocks away. He upped the pace, running in a kind of stagger down the block. Could feel the bullet lodged in the lower right side of his stomach.

Fifteen metres clear of the hotel, Bald spotted them. They were forty metres ahead of his position. Four police motors. White Beemers sledding down the two-lane tarmac, lights pulsing in the morning heat and dust. Bald lowered his head and pressed his left hand to where he'd been shot. Jesus fuck, that hurt. Bald needed painkillers. He needed a doctor. He needed a bottle of Jim Beam.

But more than all that, he needed the truth.

The plan had been stupid-simple. All Skinner had had to do was roll up outside the hotel and discharge a blank round at Klich, and Bald would dive in front of the Russian and make himself a hero, earning Klich's trust and leading him into the welcome embrace of MI6. Collect his payment and head off into the sunset, like all top heroes. But then Bald had ended up taking a real bullet and found himself in a firefight with three Russian gunmen armed to the teeth.

The cops rocketed past Bald and skidded through the open gates of the Seven Wonders. Bald pushed on. Each draw of breath triggered a shard of pain under his ribs. Bald put the pain on ice. Every second step was a limp. Every limp accompanied by a scratch of a thought at the base of his skull.

Where the fuck's Skinner? He's let me down once today.

Twice and Skinner would have made an enemy of Bald for life.

Blotches of colour shot across Bald's vision. His lips were dry and his tongue felt like sandpaper. He needed fluids. With this injury he wouldn't be able to go on much longer.

Then he saw it. An old-school Mercedes Benz E-Class, lipstick red, angular and muscular. Probably twenty-five years old. It slowed. Skinner had driven a Porsche Panamera around Dubai, thought Bald. Not a Mercedes. But then the headlamps flashed twice at him and he thought, thank God. Skinner had made it. The Merc stroked into a parking slot fifteen metres ahead of Bald. Came to a halt outside a Bulgari jewellery store. Between Bald and the Merc stood the entrance to the local Al-Arabiya metro station.

Bald hurried towards the car. Ten metres away he quickened his stride. His body didn't like that, and his muscles screamed. Back at the Seven Wonders a dozen cops were now swarming around the blazing Lincoln and the dead hotel workers. Spent brass glimmered on the ground behind a shimmering curtain of heat.

Eight metres from the Merc and Bald temporarily forgot about the bullet in his guts and the coppery taste in his mouth. He was getting out of here. If he had any say in it, he wouldn't be returning to the Arabian Gulf any time soon.

Then a couple of figures swung out of the Merc, and Bald stopped dead in his tracks.

One look at the guys told him his problems were about to go from big to supersize. They had Rolex faces and suntan suits and an angry gleam to their shades. They were dark-skinned and dark-haired, and they were packing Skorpion Vz. 61s. Czech-built submachine guns. Compact weapons with the buttstocks folded up and extended mags curving like inverted shark fins out of the mag feed system.

The Iranians.

twenty-six

Bald rapidly weighed up the odds. Two of them, one of him. They had submachine guns. He had a semi-automatic pistol. They weren't bearing bullet wounds. He was. Bald made his decision in a snapped second, as the Iranians went to train the Skorpions' sights on him. He bolted a hard left and sprinted the four metres across the street and ducked into the Al-Arabiya metro station. Stumbled into the ticket hall, the two guys yelling after him. A wall of cool air greeted Bald, blasting away the fifty-degree sweat lathered across his face.

The hall was like a five-star hotel lobby. Chandeliers lit up in greens and blues. Marble floor so polished Bald could make out every cut and bruise in his reflection. He elbowed his way through the lazy Arabs and their fat wives slugging towards the ticket barriers. He followed the signs directing him to the Red Line, and headed for the eastbound platform. Bald had a rough idea of the layout of Dubai, knew that the city ran left to right, hugging the coastline. If he took the Al-Rashidya train east, he'd swing right past the RV with Leo Land at Port Rashid.

Bald pulled his jacket tight across his chest, like he was bracing himself against a bitter wind, and hoped that nobody would notice the blood splatters on the cuffs and collar of his shirt. He looked back at his six o'clock. The Iranians were shouldering their way through the throng. They were fifteen metres behind Bald and the crowd blocked them from taking a clean shot at him. As he shuffled on, he discovered that he couldn't go any faster. His calf muscles were burning. His glutes ached. He knew that soon the Iranians would break clear of the crowd. Then they'd corner him and he'd be shafted. He needed to get onto a train before they got the chance to cash in their cheque on his head.

Bald climbed clumsily over the ticket barrier. A guard shouted at him but Bald ignored him. Carted down the platform in a lopsided gait. Behind him the Iranians vaulted cleanly over the ticket barrier, and the gap between them and Bald had now narrowed to ten metres.

Bald scrambled along the eastbound platform. He wasn't quite sure why, but most of the commuters were crammed onto the westbound one. Only a few commuters lined the forty-metre-long eastbound platform. Fibre-glass doors separated the platform's edge from the tracks. 'Train approaching,' said the overhead sign. The Iranians were bursting onto the platform. A pale guy in a crumpled suit flipped through a newspaper ten metres behind Bald, blocking the Iranians' line of sight. Bald glanced ahead as he heard a powerful hum beyond the far end of the platform. A spear of bright light shot out of the tunnel. A futuristic train bulleted along the platform and sleeked to a halt. The platform-edge doors sounded a cheery ping as they sucked open. Bald hobbled the two metres towards the nearest carriage doors.

Almost there.

A voice barked at Bald from his twelve o'clock. '*Stop, I said. Fucking stop. Don't move!*' He looked up, and did exactly as the voice said. Six guys stormed off the train and onto the platform from the last set of doors, twenty metres ahead of him. His first thought was that the Iranians had brought backup. But these guys were in uniform. Assault suits with elbow and knee pads, ballistic vests and helmets. They had to be some kind of police or paramilitary force. Bald watched as the operators simultaneously trained their weapons at him. Heckler & Koch UMP submachine guns. Iranians behind him, Dubai operators ahead. He was trapped. His eyes flicked frantically left and right, looking for an escape route that didn't exist. A clunking thought struck him: there's no fucking way out.

Then the weapons' muzzles lit up, tangerine flames licking out of their snouts, and Bald thought nothing else. His mind was swamped by the crash of supersonic rounds echoing off the walls. Screams from the crowd. He stood there, frozen with fear. Expecting the bullets to thwack into his body, ripping him to fucking shreds.

Yet Bald didn't feel the impact of the rounds. They've missed, he thought, only half believing it. A split second later he heard a shriek and he realized that the operators hadn't missed. It wasn't him they had been aiming at.

They were shooting past him.

twenty-seven

Bald spun around. He watched as the two Iranians dropped like a pair of rag dolls, their torsos stitched with bullets. The operators had been aiming at them, Bald realized. He breathed a sigh of relief as the Iranian on the right took four rounds to the chest. The guy desperately tried to plug the leaks in his body while his mate lay sprawled on the floor just to his right, blood gushing out of his slashed bell as a set of carriage doors repeatedly thunked against his skull. Passengers screamed and rushed along the platform, away from the operators and the bleeding-out Iranians. Bald watched one of the operators storm over to the still-breathing one, roll him onto his back with his foot and double-tap him in the head. Bald couldn't have done it better himself.

From the ticket hall came the mechanical wail of alarms.

The operators circled the dead Iranians, kicking away their weapons and padding down their bodies as they jabbered into their walkie-talkies. Bald used the distraction to beat a hasty retreat down the platform towards the ticket hall. He didn't know why the operators had rescued him. He didn't know why they hadn't chopped him in half too. He didn't intend to stick around long enough to find out. Somehow I've got to get to Land, he thought.

The ticket hall was in chaos. People screaming as they scrambled for the escalators, shoving others out of the way or grabbing at arms and legs to drag them aside, climbing over each other on the escalators. The crowd created a fleshy bottleneck where the escalator met the hall.

'*Hey! Hey!*'

Bald glanced over his shoulder as two of the operators bombed into the ticket hall, twelve metres from him. They had spotted him in the crowd, one pointing him out to his mate with the tip of his UMP. Bald began elbowing his way through the bottleneck. He'd made it three or four steps closer to one of the escalators when he found his path blocked by a swarthy Arab dressed in a full-length *thobe* and a shemagh on top secured with a black rope circlet. Bald tried shoving the guy out of the way. He didn't budge.

'Out of my way, raghead,' said Bald.

The Arab turned around slow and heavy, like an oil tanker. His shadowed face was grinning at Bald from under the shemagh.

'John,' he whispered, clamping a hand on Bald's shoulder. 'It's me, fella.'

Skinner.

The fat bastard's smile made his lips droop in the middle like a slack rope.

'Hey, you! Stop right there!' the operators screamed. Skinner flicked his eyes from them to Bald, then jerked him away from the bottleneck, towards an unmarked, green-painted door with a crash bar. Bald was staring at him, wishing he could lamp the prick.

'Stop looking like I fucked your mother and follow me,' said Skinner. '*Quick!*'

Bald reluctantly followed Skinner towards the green door. Skinner slammed the crash bar, shouldered the door open. It gave onto an ascending flight of concrete steps, the air hot and tangy with dust. Skinner struggled for breath as Bald motored up the stairs. He had his second wind now, and the bullet wound had become so much background noise. With six powerful strides he hit the emergency exit door at the top of the steps.

'Through here,' Skinner gasped as he joined Bald. The colour had drained from his face. He waddled along like he had to take a shit right about now. Bald smacked down the exit door's crash bar and booted it open. A thousand blades of sunlight unsheathed. Bald squinted. He was in a side street. A row of wheelie bins lined up against the far wall, a couple of rats scurrying along the gutter and, parked in the middle of the street, Toyota Camry. Silver and slick, like a bullet.

'Get in,' Skinner said, making for the driver's door.

Bald didn't move.

Skinner stepped into his face.

Bald snapped like a stick of wood. He thrust an arm out and clamped his fingers around the guy's ample neck. Squeezed. Like squeezing a bean bag. Skinner choked. His face went from white to blue. He croaked, 'Easy, fella.'

But Bald didn't go easy. 'What the fuck happened?' he growled.

'We had to abort.' Skinner's voice was squeezed down to a whisper. 'Land gave the order. I'm sorry.'

'Sorry isn't a word I know,' said Bald. He dug his fingers so hard into Skinner's flesh he was surprised he didn't draw blood. 'Here's some words I do know. Go fuck yourself, you fat wank stain.'

'Leave it out, John,' Skinner rasped. He pawed at Bald. Tried to wriggle free. Bald loosened his grip a little, let him talk. 'I'm getting you out of this mess now, aren't I? Christ, why do you think the Iranians got slotted at the station? I put in a call to the head boy in the Dubai Defence Force. Old mucker of mine. They hate the Iranians almost as much as we do. Told them they had a couple of renegade Iranian agents running amok. If it hadn't been for me, you'd be a dead man.'

Bald said nothing. Skinner had a point. His arse had been on the line at that station. He released his fingers. Skinner coughed and keeled over. Hacked up his guts. Then he stood upright. The colour slowly returning to his face, like sand spilling into the bottom of an hourglass.

'Look, mate,' he said, soothing his neck. 'There's a doctor at the RV. He'll patch you up. What do you say, eh? Jump in.'

Bald chewed on his rage. Tasted like tarmac. Then he climbed into the Toyota.

Acting like Bald had never lost his rag, Skinner said, 'Land has got some big news.'

Bald glared at Skinner. 'I never want to hear from Land again.'

'Oh, but you'll want to hear this. Trust me.'

That droopy grin again, like it was about to slide off his chin and drop into his lap. Skinner reversed the Toyota carefully out of the little street, then put his foot to the floor. He sped west along Jumeirah Beach, just another Dubai motorist with a total disregard for speed limits. They swept past the Seven Wonders and the double-dozen other glamorous hotels laid out along the coastline like diamonds in a jeweller's window. Bald closed his eyes and concentrated on riding out the waves of pain, which had returned in spades.

They took the road south for three kilometres before swerving north on a busy road that straddled Dubai Creek. The moored dhows Bald had seen earlier had now disappeared. They arrowed through a dust-choked industrial district. A further kilometre on and the Gulf came into view, its waters like a giant sheet of wrinkled metal. Skinner promptly slowed. Port Rashid loomed to their ten o'clock.

The RV.

A hundred metres shy of the Gulf Skinner banged a hard left and snaked the Toyota around a sequence of roundabouts, and eventually rolled onto a deserted road that led

them directly to the old Port Rashid. The road was flanked
by stacks of discarded car tyres and mounds of gravel. To his
eleven o'clock Bald spotted a concrete harbour stretching out
six hundred metres into the sea. Another, shorter, one lay fifty
metres beyond the main harbour, littered with rusting shipping containers. The berths at the longer harbour were occupied by cruise ships and gin palaces in various states of repair,
all of them dwarfed by an ocean liner. Hull three hundred
metres long and the colour of midnight, funnel perched atop a
stack of brilliant-white upper decks, like a candle on a wedding
cake. Bald recognized the liner immediately from its striking
orange-red funnel. The *QE2*.

Skinner dropped speed to a fast walk. 'The Arabs snapped
her up,' he said, nodding at the ship. 'Planned to turn it into
a hotel, or some bollocks. Then the recession put the skids on
near enough every project in the Emirates. She'll probably
just sit there for the next ten years gathering dust.'

'The *QE2* is the RV?' said Bald disbelievingly.

'Nah,' said Skinner. 'Bit more modest than that.'

'Where the fuck's everyone?' Bald asked, peering out at the
empty berths, the rusty containers. The lack of activity.

'Port Rashid used to be a big deal,' Skinner replied. 'Then
the city chiefs decided to build a brand spanking new port on
the western side of the city. Put this one out of business. Now
it's just a parking lot for old cruise liners and knackered trawl-
ers. You won't see a soul out here until gone midday.'

Skinner killed the engine. They had stopped at a spot
between the two harbours. Skinner climbed out of the car.
Not easy for a guy his size. He had to swivel in his seat,
squirming and farting as he swung first his left leg and then
his right across it, his chubby hands gripping the upper frame
of the door to support his weight. The vast rest of him slowly
squeezed out of the door like pus oozing from a boil. Bald
watched Skinner struggling and laughed. Then he stepped

out himself and nearly doubled up with pain. He grimaced as he caught sight of the sticky, glistening patch of blood on the seat. He had lost a lot of blood. He needed that doctor, and quick.

'Wait here,' said Skinner. 'I've got to make sure we're in the right place for the RV.'

Bald watched him waddle along the harbour towards the shipping containers. Sunlight spilled and bubbled like champagne over the concrete. Bald tasted sea salt. At this early hour the smell of the sea was overwhelming and clogged his nostrils, bringing on surges of nausea. He was barely able to stand up. He felt faint on his feet. His muscles were all locked up, but he managed to schlep round to the back of the Toyota and prop his arse up against the boot.

He looked down and his brow puckered. A hole the size of a ten-pence piece had been cut into the centre of the door, half an inch above the number plate. The hole had been stuffed with some kind of a cloth dyed grey to blend in with the bodywork. From a distance, Bald guessed, the trick might work. But up close the colours were mismatched and the outline of the hole was clear. But what it was for? A makeshift air vent? Bald took a step away from the car. Peered along the harbour. No sign of Skinner. The guy had disappeared behind the containers a hundred metres away.

Then Bald popped the boot. Sunlight flashed a torch on the contents. At first he thought there was a body lying inside. He saw what looked like an arm. Then he made out the shape of a rifle.

He recognized the design immediately from his time in the Regiment. A Ruger 10/22 semi-automatic rifle fully a metre long and modded up to the eyeballs with an eighteen-inch bull barrel and illuminated-reticle scope. Bald cast his eyes over the rest of the boot. The space reeked of gunpowder. Two spare clips of ammo were stashed in the smooth trench to the right where the spare tyre would normally be stashed. He spotted a single spent cartridge case and picked it up. It was warm. He identified it as a .22 Long rifle round.

'John!'

Bald slammed the boot shut and slipped round to the front of the car. Skinner was standing at the far end of the harbour beside a bright-blue container. His right hand shielding his eyes from the sun as he beckoned at Bald with his left to join him. Bald walked towards him, passing rows of gantry cranes and old forklifts, along with the dozens of decaying shipping containers. Each container was twelve metres long, two and a half wide and three high.

When Bald reached him, Skinner looked like he was about to drop dead. Sweating like a fat girl writing her first love letter. Bald turned to the blue container. He noticed an ISO reporting mark stamped on its doors, which were ajar. Skinner took a shifty look around before cranking the doors open and squeezing through the gap.

Bald stepped inside after him.

The container was dark and dense like soil, heavy with the stench of diesel and saltwater. Bald spotted four spotlights mounted on tripods set eight metres deep into the container, casting white pools of light onto a cheap plastic table. Beside the table stood a plastic chair and a trolley with a tray of glittering surgical instruments. A figure was standing beside the trolley. At first Bald thought this might be Leo Land. As Bald neared him, he figured the guy was Indian, with a face like a bruised knuckle. Dried spots of blood freckled the floor around the chairs.

'What the fuck is this?' Bald said to Skinner. 'Where's Land?'

'Right here, old boy.'

The voice came from Bald's six. He spun around. Saw Land seeping out of the shadows, decked out in khaki trousers and a pastel shirt with the sleeves rolled purposefully up to the elbows and a fedora resting atop his sunburnt head. He was clutching a bottle of whisky in his right hand. He took a step closer to Bald. Smiled as he thrust the bottle at him. Bald studied the label. Four Rose Kentucky bourbon. Single barrel. His favourite. He swivelled his eyes to Land. The smile was wavering on the MI6 agent's face.

'A peace offering,' he said, nodding at the Indian-looking guy. 'This is Aziz. He's your doctor.'

'Whatever,' said Bald. 'Let's get this over with.'

Land exchanged a knowing glance with Aziz. Looked back at Bald. 'I'm afraid it's not that simple.'

'What are you talking about?'

'You and I have unfinished business with Viktor Klich.'

'Forget it,' said Bald. 'I'm through with the Firm. Klich is your problem now.'

Land stepped closer to Bald until their faces were practically touching. His eyes were bloodshot and the colour of weathered marble. 'Allow me to spell it out for you in plain terms,' he said. 'Either you complete your mission, or I tell Dr Aziz here to pack his bags without so much as dabbing TCP on that injury of yours.'

Bald said nothing. Land's eyes blackened. Like a pair of screws being tightened in their holes.

'I hear that it takes a long time to perish from gut wounds. Days, in fact. Quite a terrible way to die, John. You'll be squealing like a pig. You'll wish you were already dead.'

'I'll take my chances at the hospital,' said Bald.

'Be my guest.' Land waved at the open doors. 'But remember, you have no passport, no cash, no medical insurance, and you're wanted for questioning on three counts of murder. Plus, your picture is all over the news. You're quite the celebrity now, John.'

Bald shrugged. 'I'm no good to you now. Klich has seen my face. He knows who I am. If you think he's gonna trust me, you've smoked too much wacky baccy. Klich won't let me get anywhere near him.'

A strange smile passed over Land's face. 'I don't need Klich to trust you.'

'What do you mean?'

'The plan has changed. We don't need you to capture Klich. We need you to kill him.'

twenty-eight

Bald broke the seal on the Four Roses as he slumped into the chair. He took a powerful swig. It went down like lighter fuel. Better. He set the bottle on the table, wiped his mouth with the back of his wrist. Looked up at Land pursing his lips and folding his hands behind his back.

'Allow me to explain,' said Land. 'When we first became aware that Klich was privy to our intelligence secrets, we worked on the basis that we could return him to the fold. Entice him back to the Firm. The logic behind this was simple. Klich is an intelligence goldmine. He was our once-in-a-life-time opportunity to unravel the Russian security network.'

'So what changed?'

'Klich decided to sell his secrets on the free market,' he said.

Bald looked around for Skinner. The guy had vanished.

Land went on, 'Late last night Klich flew in one of the world's leading prosthetic surgeons in order to trade places with a body double. Appears you can do rather a lot of surgery these days. Silicone moulds, layered prosthetics, wax lips. Klich walked right under your nose, John.'

Land stroked his chin. 'I don't suppose you let slip to anyone about our plan to lure Klich?' he said.

Bald said nothing.

'Because somehow he learned of our plan and gave us the slip.'

Bald thought about Odessa Stone. He thought about her fine arse. But he thought too about how the bodyguard had told him that she was working for the Firm. At the time he'd believed her. Now he wasn't so sure. He was starting to think she'd grassed him up to Klich and played him for a cunt.

'No way,' he said.

Land scrutinized him for a long couple of seconds, the way a driver scrutinizes a scratch on his pride and joy.

'Well. What's done is done,' he said. 'But any hope we had of establishing a bond of trust with Klich is finished. Unfortunately, he presents us with a problem. Thanks to his rumpy-pumpy with the aide to the defence committee chap, Klich knows our dirty secrets. Every last little one. Selling them to anyone in exchange for protection represents a threat to national security that we cannot afford to let go unchecked.'

Aziz plucked a syringe from the tray of instruments. Bald made the mistake of looking at the array of forceps, clamps, retractors and scalpels, and felt his stomach muscles constrict. But needles he hated in particular.

'What about the Iranians?' he said. 'Why did they want Klich dead? I thought they were supposed to be helping him escape.'

Land inspected his fingernails. Frowned. 'Do you recall the Stuxnet virus?' he said.

Bald made a static face. Computers weren't his rag. He could hardly work an iPhone.

'Stuxnet is the name given to a computer worm distributed across the internet,' Land continued. 'The virus was specifically designed to target embargoed Siemens industrial equipment procured by the Iranians, for use in their uranium enrichment programme. Stuxnet severely disrupted the Iranian centrifuge machinery. Set them back years, as I understand it. The regime believes that Klich had a helping hand in the sabotage. He was, of course, intimately familiar with the security procedures at the enrichment facilities, since he helped build them. The Iranians lured him to Dubai with the promise of asylum, but they planned on killing him all along by rigging the car to blow. That would also send a message to anyone else involved in weapons procurement for the Iranian regime: screw with them and you pay with your life. And the plan might have worked. Only Klich never showed.'

Bald down at his hands. They were sticky with blood. He necked another slug of whisky. Was mildly surprised to see that he'd polished off half the bottle. But the booze had helped take the edge off the pain. He saw Aziz hovering at his side, removing the cap from the syringe, giving the needle a tap. A big old grin plastered across his mug, like he couldn't wait to cut Bald open and root around in his guts.

'Dave Hands is dead,' Bald said.

Land harrumphed. 'Don't tell me you're upset about that worthless chancer kicking the bucket? You always told me you hated the man. Have you forgotten what he did to you in Rio?'

'Rio was a long time ago. Hands was a cunt, but he was a Blade once too.'

'A touching sentiment,' Land said, straightening out his voice like it was a tie. Then he sighed, fished a piece of paper out of his inside jacket pocket and handed it to Bald.

'What is this?' Bald said.

'Read it and find out.'

Bald unfolded the paper. It appeared to be a letter. He ran his eyes along a few lines: about half of the words were blacked out. The letterhead carried the logo of SIS, the Secret Intelligence Service. At the bottom of the page Bald noted the scrawled signature of the Director General of the Firm. Both the logo and the signature had a grainy, pixellated quality to them, like they were photocopies.

'This is a letter from the chief,' explained Land. 'Authorizing that your record be expunged and you be given a brand-new identity. The letter also grants the purchase of a five-bedroom property on Madeira and the transfer of £250,000 to a bank account, both in your new name.'

Land snatched the letter back from Bald before he could properly read it.

'This is it,' he said, waving the letter in front of Bald. 'Your new life. Just like you wanted. Everything has been agreed. All I have to do is click my fingers and it'll happen. Of course, if you refuse to accept the deal, then there is a second letter of authorization signed off by the chief. A letter rubber-stamping your assassination, John.'

Land folded the letter, running his thumb and forefinger smoothly along the fold lines before he tucked it back in his pocket.

'I kept my word,' he said. 'Now you have to keep yours.'

Pain stabbed through Bald's skull. He felt the hard lines and edges of the world slipping into a murky, pond-like blackness. A few more minutes of this shit, he knew, and he'd lose consciousness. He considered the blood stains on the ground for a cold, hard moment. Probably the Firm used this place as a torture facility whenever the need arose. Thick walls, abandoned port. A good place to make a man bleed.

His eyes met Land's.

'Five hundred thousand,' he said.

Land guffawed. 'You're taking the proverbial, John. We've agreed a fee already.'

'We agreed a fee to snatch a man alive. Now you want him dead, the price is double.'

Land jangled loose change in his pockets. Looked away from Bald.

'Killing doesn't come cheap these days, it seems.'

'What does?' said Bald.

'Fine,' said Land. He nodded to Aziz. 'Get on with it.'

The doctor rubbed his hands with glee. Bald sat there on the plastic chair, wondering why Land was grinning at him after he'd just squeezed the guy for another quarter of a million. Then Land sucked his teeth and said, 'There's just one small thing.'

'What?'

'Aziz doesn't have any anaesthetic. All a bit last minute, I'm afraid. Hence the whisky.' Land slapped Bald heartily on the back. 'Bottoms up, old boy.'

Bald hobbled out of the container twenty-eight tortured minutes later. His wound had been sutured and dressed with a strip of fluffed-out gauze but his mind was still groggy and loose like a piece of string. He spied Land at the harbour's edge. He was gazing out across the Gulf. Bald staggered over to him, his stride stiff and ungainly, knuckles kneading his bowels. He stopped a step behind Land. The MI6 man lifted the fedora from his head and dabbed a handkerchief to his brow, then asked, 'How are you feeling?'

Bald ran a hand across the dressing strapped across his stomach. Felt the Braille-like bumps of the treated wound. 'Terrific,' he said.

Land was gazing towards the reclaimed islands a couple of kilometres along the coast and connected to the mainland by the Deira Corniche. Like everything else in Dubai, the development had been put on hold, now nothing but a spread of bleached and lonely sand. Bald tried to imagine the mansions and Ferraris that would one day line the site. He couldn't, so he drained the last of the Four Roses and tossed the bottle into the filthy water of the harbour.

'Now that you're ready to resume the mission,' said Land, 'Let's get down to the nitty-gritty. Klich is currently en route to the French Alps. His Gulfstream departed from Dubai International approximately two hours ago. Right about the time you were getting shot, come to think of it.'

'Just give me the spread.'

Land shrugged. 'According to the flight plans, his plane is headed for Courchevel. That's a ski resort for the super-rich Eurotrash mob. Eighteen hundred metres above sea level. This week it's brimming with wealthy Russians gathered to ring in the Orthodox Christmas and New Year.'

Bald squinted at a spot in the sky. 'Why would Klich go somewhere where all of his enemies are throwing a party?' he said.

'We're not quite sure,' Land said. 'I want you to find out what before you kill him.'

Now he turned around to face Bald. 'Of course, Klich looks somewhat different after his facial surgery. We've created a composite of his new face. We had a little word with the surgeon. Managed to tease the details out of him. Here.'

He chucked Bald a Samsung Galaxy Tab. The phone was chunkier and larger than those Bald had used in the past. Almost the size of a brick. He noticed that the photo gallery app had been loaded and the screen filled with a set of composite pictures of Klich. Bald realized this was the first time he had seen the face of the real Viktor Klich since Land had shown him the original snaps in Kazakhstan. He'd never encountered the oligarch in the flesh. Klich had remained tantalizingly out of reach. The difference between these shots and the ones he'd cast his eye over in Kazakhstan was immediate. Here the jawline was pronounced instead of flabby, the nose suspiciously smooth and straight, the wrinkles smoothed out and the blemishes cleaned up. About the only thing that Bald recognized were the eyes. Glassy and black and wolf-like. Eyes that told Bald they were always looking for a fucking angle.

'Klich should be easy to find,' Land said. 'He owns a chalet high up in the mountains. As far as we're aware, he travelled alone. His bodyguards have been decimated, so this really ought to be a simple in-and-out job. No fuss, no mess.'

Bald nodded. 'I'll need a gun.'

'I don't expect you to kill him with your bare hands, John. I've arranged for a courier to come up with a delivery from Nice. Reliable chap, worked for Six for several years. Name of Karim. I'll text you the details of the RV upon your arrival.'

'Whatever.'

'One more thing,' said Land. He looked fidgety now. 'It's absolutely imperative that Klich's murder cannot be traced back to us. To that end I've arranged for a clean-up crew to come in once you're done. As soon as Klich is dead, call the 'Cleaner' contact number stored on the phone. It transmits on an encrypted frequency and sends your GPS coordinates to the team. They will make Klich look like the Iranians killed him, then smuggle you across the border into Switzerland. After that, we go our separate ways.'

'Sounds good to me,' said Bald, pocketing the phone.

'Skinner will escort you to the airport,' said Land. 'And for God's sake have a shower and a change of clothes before you fly.'

He paused and chewed on his bottom lip.

'The consequences of failure would be catastrophic to Six, John. If you cannot take down Klich, I will hold you personally responsible for the whole fiasco and that letter from my boss will be consigned to the dustbin. Our agents will hunt you down. Make your death look like suicide, of course. Something perverted. I quite fancy the idea of death by auto-asphyxiation. What do you say? You, a gimp suit and a stack of gay porn mags.'

'Fuck off,' said Bald.

'With pleasure, dear boy.'

Land indicated with his eyes that he wanted to talk to Skinner alone. Bald left them to it, walking uncomfortably back towards the Toyota. Skinner made no eye contact as Bald passed him. Bald hadn't gone far when he felt something digging into his thigh. He stopped, shoved a hand into his trouser pocket and felt something metal stuffed in there. He dug out a lead nugget a little over five millimetres in diameter and a millimetre thick at the tip, not much bigger than a drug capsule. Bald pinched it between his thumb and forefinger. The fragment of a bullet that Aziz had pulled from his guts, he thought as he held it up to the sun and examined it more closely.

He'd assumed that the Russians had been the ones who had shot him outside the Seven Wonders. Bald had ID'd the weapons they had been armed with as M16 assault rifles, chambered for the 5.56mm bullet. Removed from its jacket, a typical 5.56mm bullet was about the size of an AAA battery.

But the round Bald was pinching was much smaller.

Exactly the same size as a .22 round, he thought. Exactly the same size as the .22 round used by the .22 Long rifle he'd discovered in the boot of the Toyota.

twenty-nine

The cold slapped Bald as he got out of the Renault Mégane at the parking lot outside the Carrefour. He trudged across the road towards the Opera Hotel, keeping his head lowered and his shoulders hunched to shield his face. The snow crunched like gravel underfoot. The sky was a splatter of blood-reds and oranges, as if the mountain peaks had carved open the belly of the sun. Bald pulled his North Face jacket tighter across his chest. He'd ditched the blood-encrusted suit at Dubai International and got kitted out in thermal jogging bottoms and vest, jeans on top and a thick woollen lumberjack shirt. A pair of Belstaff Tourmaster brown leather boots, a beanie hat and the North Face jacket finished off the look. Even with all these layers, the cold still managed to somehow pick away at him.

On the road to his right a black Chevrolet Suburban 4x4 slithered towards him. The number plate read, 'GIGN'. Bald recognized the acronym. National Gendarmerie Intervention Group. It was his business to know about SF forces around the world and he'd bumped into a few former GIGN operators on the circuit. They specialized in counter-terrorism and close protection, and he figured they wouldn't be wheeled out in a place like Courchevel for any old shits and giggles.

Bald stepped back and allowed the Chevrolet to chug past. Then he carried on to Rue de Martin. Worked some feeling back into his legs, tired after two hours behind the wheel of the Mégane he'd rented at the Hertz desk at Lyon-Saint Exupéry Airport. A drive that had contoured east and risen through Albertville and Moutiers before the road wound its way into Courchevel. And before that, ten hours on a Swissair flight from Dubai. He was cream-crackered. He'd gorged himself on airplane food and airplane sleep, and neither had properly replenished his energy. Right now Bald was running on fumes. He craved a bacon double quarter-pounder with cheese piled high, fries, buffalo wings, and a crate of Stella Artois to wash it down.

But first up, he had to kill a man.

A thunderous noise cut through the air. Bald craned his neck up at the bleeding sky, caught sight of a lightweight twin-engine Eurocopter EC135 transporting a stack of concrete slabs towards a chalet high on the slopes. He watched the chopper hovering above the chalet as he hooked a left at Rue de Martin and passed a row of posh restaurants. Couples were strolling arm in arm down the street. The men wore a uniform of grey hair, podgy bellies, and stress lines engraved into their foreheads like knife cuts. Every woman was a ten-out-of-ten, confirming Bald's long-held suspicion that you could be as ugly and dumb as a stack of elephant shit, but if you had wonga you were never going to be short of good cunny.

The Fleming Hotel stood like a turret at the end of Rue de Martin. Looked kind of out of place, with its rammed-earth walls and medieval windows and a giant flag of Savoy draped above the entrance. The hotel had once been the local Nazi Party headquarters, Bald had read in a brochure. The hotel seemed like a good fit. From its position at the epicentre of the village the Fleming had a view of the streets fanning out in every direction. To the north were the Carrefour and the parking lot and a bunch of municipal buildings. Further north, four hundred metres from the village and perched on a plateau on the lower part of the mountain, Bald noticed a derelict farm-house. To the west were Michelin-starred restaurants and to the east chic designer outlets. South afforded a view of the dozens of cables criss-crossing the slopes, black veins linking gondola cars and aerial tramways with the surrounding pistes, where hundreds of specks slowly tumbled like loose dirt down the slopes. Skiers getting in one last run before nightfall. A chalet stood perilously on a mountain ledge to the north. It belonged to Klich.

Bald barged through the lobby doors of the hotel. Kicked an inch of snow off the toecaps of his boots. This had been advertised as the cheapest one in Courchevel. But inside it wouldn't have looked out of place on Park Lane, he thought. The walls were mahogany panelling, on which were mounted antique sconces. Animal-skin rugs lay on the wooden floor. He slipped the receptionist a wink and his room reservation number and his fake passport, and paid for the room in cash. Six hundred euros from the kitty of two grand Land had given him for the op. The petty-cash advance from Land had struck Bald as odd at the time. The SOP for doing the Firm's dirty work was an AmEx card with an unlimited credit line. When Bald had asked, Land had muddled his way through an excuse about logistics on an op with such a short time-scale.

The unease had been building up in Bald since he'd found the rifle in the Camry. At the time his gut reaction had been to confront Skinner and Land about it and find out who the fuck had shot him, and why, because the ballistics proved it hadn't been the Russians who'd dropped him. But then Bald had considered the half a million waiting for him, and figured that neither Land nor Skinner would give him a straight answer anyway. One more bullet in the back of an oligarch's head and Bald wouldn't have to see Land or that fat fuck ever again. So he'd kept quiet about the rifle, and he kept his mouth shut too when Land handed him a wad of notes rather than an AmEx.

He focused solely on the mission.

Now Bald pounded up the softwood stairs and along to the end of the corridor on his right. Classical music played out of Bose speakers set high up where the walls met the beamed ceiling. At the door to Room 19 Bald paused to check no one was watching him. Then he swiped the door open and stepped inside. It was like stepping into a fairy tale. He could see way across the Alps. There was a mahogany king-sized bed with a champagne-coloured cover, and opposite it a dressing table with a painted finish simulating ivory. Crystal-drop ceiling lights poured iridescent light onto the rich wool carpet. Bald noticed a forty-eight-inch HD TV mounted on the wall. This had been tuned to the hotel channel, where a soothing voice welcomed him to the Fleming and hoped he enjoyed his stay. Bald hoped so too. He flipped channels before taking a deeply satisfying shit.

Next he checked out the mini-bar. Looked longingly at the miniatures of Bell's and Smirnoff, but told himself, a few more hours of sobriety then he could shower in the stuff. Instead he grabbed a can of Coke Zero, some roasted cashews and a Snickers and refuelled while channel hopping. Most of them were in French, talk shows with plasticky women and guys with doughy faces and steel-rimmed glasses. He found a sports channel. The guy beaming out at him was an ugly bastard, podgy-faced with hunched shoulders and no neck, like a stubbed-out cigarette butt. He was standing beside a football pitch, proudly holding a replica shirt of a major French Ligue 1 side with his name printed on the back. 'FAVORSKY 1,' it said.

The name hit Bald like a fist. Favorsky. Valery Favorsky: the oligarch and great rival of Viktor Klich for the favour of the Russian President. Bald recalled his initial briefing with Land, back in Kazakhstan. Five days ago. Felt like five years ago. Land had told him, 'The President needed to silence Klich. He used Favorsky to achieve that goal.'

Seemed like Favorsky was splashing the cash big time. Bald spoke French about as well as he handled talk of gay marriage and multiculturalism, but you didn't need to speak the lingo to understand the numbers ticker-taping at the bottom of the screen. Two hundred million euros spunked on a football team.

A three-time knock on the door interrupted Bald. He pressed the 'mute' button and stumped over to the door. He dropped quietly to the floor and peered at the quarter-inch gap at the bottom of the door. Saw a pair of black biker boots tapping impatiently on the polished floorboards outside in the corridor.

The courier.

'Yeah?' Bald said.

'Delivery for Mr Palmer,' the courier said, using the code-name Bald had agreed with Land. His voice sounded anxious through the big hollow door. Bald unhooked the chain and twisted the latch. The courier had a face like a shadow. He wore black motorcycle leathers and gripped a helmet in his left hand. He stepped inside, set the helmet down on the desk near the door and shook the cold off his shoulders. He was on the edge of the edge.

'Where's the package?' said Bald.

'First,' the courier said, 'I want my fifteen thousand.'

thirty

Bald spat a glare at the courier and stepped into his face, breathing heavily through his nostrils and thinking, I don't have time to stand here haggling with this raghead like I'm in some fucking Moroccan market.

'I don't know what you're talking about,' he said.

The courier wavered but wasn't about to back down. 'I agreed fifteen thousand euros with Land,' he said. 'Cash. Unmarked bills.'

Bald shrugged, flagging up the cold, hard truth that he couldn't give a fuck.

'Look, brother, I don't want any trouble,' the courier said, quickly ditching the tough-guy act now, trying to act like he and Bald were bestest best friends.

'Give me what I want, I give you what you want. Simple, eh?'

Bald hardened his glare. 'What do I look like, his fucking bagman?'

The courier folded his arms. Took a step back. Said, 'Then we have a problem.'

'The only problem is with your attitude. We have a deal.'

'No. We do not. My deal is with Land.'

'I don't have time for this bollocks. Call him yourself.'

'I got no number for him. Land, he calls me. Not other way around, man.'

Bald silently cursed his bad luck. He couldn't immediately see any sign of the gun on the courier. He wasn't carrying any type of package or bag. Maybe the guy had half a brain, and had secreted the gun in a safe location until he received his funds. That's what Bald would have done if he'd been in the same position. If the courier had been thick as shit and carried the gun into the hotel room, Bald could have ended this nonsense with a single punch to the bridge of his nose. But as things stood, he had no choice but to make the call to Land. He needed the gun. The sooner he put a bullet in Klich, the sooner he could put all of this shit behind him.

'Screw it, then,' he said as he fished his Galaxy out of his jacket pocket and tapped in Land's number.

'No, wait,' the courier snapped. He reached into a pouch pocket on his leathers. 'Use mine,' he said, chucking Bald an iPhone 3 with a shatter in the screen. He nodded at the Galaxy. 'You don't get a decent reception with those up there.'

Bald shrugged, took the iPhone and called the number. After four rings, he got an answer. Heard a bunch of voices warbling around Land, and the polite tone of an announcer. Sounded like he was at an airport.

'Yes, what is it?' Land said irritably.

'It's the courier,' said Bald. 'Wants his money.'

A hiss came down the line. 'Christ!'

'Guy says I don't get the package till he gets paid.'

'Ah, yes,' Land said, making fidgeting noises. 'There may have been some kind of glitch with the bank transfer. Computers, eh?' He chuckled. 'More damn hassle than they're worth.' The MI6 agent paused for a second, then said, 'But you need your gun. Well, I have an idea. Listen carefully.'

Bald listened in grim silence as Land laid out a plan. He kept one eye hooked on the courier, who was shifting on the balls of his feet, like he was desperate to piss. When Land was done Bald killed the call and offered a fake smile to the courier.

'Is he going to transfer my money right now?' the guy asked.

'Better than that,' said Bald. 'I'm gonna give you cash. The bagman is waiting for us a couple of klicks outside of town. I'll take you to him now.'

The courier snarled. 'Why didn't you tell me this before?'

'Because there was a fucking change of plan, all right?' Bald said, rolling his eyes. 'Relax. It's all cool.' He slipped on his North Face jacket and beanie, stepped over to the door and swung it open. 'Come on then. You want to get paid, or what?'

The courier stood uncertainly on the spot. Finally he nodded and headed for the door. Bald followed him out of the room. He tucked his head low and slipped on a pair of cheap sunglasses he'd stashed in the pocket of the anorak. With his face pretty well concealed from the hotel's security cameras, Bald hurried after the courier and dived into the lift. Positioned himself to the right and a half-step behind the guy's right shoulder, shielding his front profile from the CCTV camera mounted in the lift's top-left corner.

A delicate ping announced their arrival on the ground floor. Bald tucked his chin tight to his neck and tried not to draw attention to himself as he led the courier down the lobby towards the main doors.

The sun had sunk low behind the mountains and the temperature had slumped way the fuck below zero. The chill gnawed at his bones. Bald spied the Eurocopter swooping across the valley. Engines throbbing. The sky was now a tango of deeper reds and oranges, the snow hard underfoot. Bald tramped towards the Carrefour parking lot and the Mégane.

With the courier sitting beside him, the guy's left leg nervously tapping, his breath crystallizing in the cold air, Bald started the engine. It gargled and cleared its throat. He whacked the heating all the way up to Ibiza and steered out of the lot. Twenty minutes later he found the perfect spot. A lonely, snow-ploughed road linking Courchevel to another village. The left bank was like a cliff face. Beyond the knee-high snow on the right ran a thick clump of conifer and birch trees, with a glimpse of a frozen lake behind.

Bald took one final look in the rear-view mirror.

Coast was clear.

'Where's the bagman?' the courier asked.

Bald grinned. 'On his way. First show me the gun.'

The courier shrugged as he unzipped his jacket and pulled out a brown parcel stuffed inside. He handed it to Bald and said, 'You don't know the shit I had to do to get this here.'

Bald didn't reply. He tore open the package and the stainless-steel chamber of a Beretta M9 semi-automatic pistol winked at him. Bald could tell it was the newer A1 model by the bevelled grip and the Picatinny rail system fitted to the underside of the barrel. A Trinity 9mm suppressor was screwed to the muzzle. Nestled snugly alongside the Beretta were two fifteen-round box mags loaded with 9x19mm Parabellum.

'Cops everywhere, helicopters too,' the courier went on. 'Never seen anything like it.'

Bald calmly retrieved the Beretta. It was chill to the touch, and its weight told Bald the weapon was empty. He took one of the Parabellum clips and slid it into the feed on the underside of the grip. Smoothly, not forcing it in, because that would cause a round to choke in the chamber and ultimately lead to a stoppage. Then Bald shunted the slider back before releasing it, so the slider crashed forward into the loaded position and the resultant pressure boosted the initial round from the clip into the chamber, primed to discharge.

The decisive click startled the courier. He shot a look at Bald.

'What the fuck are you doing?' he said.

'Nothing,' said Bald coolly.

Then he pressed the tip of the suppressor to the side of his skull and capped the cunt.

The suppressor dampened the noise. Reduced the discharge to a squib, like an underwater *phtt*. The courier gave a death-grunt and then his head snapped back against the head rest and his eyes rolled back. Last sound he made was his blood splashing against the window. *Phtt-grunt-splash*. The sounds of a man dying. Blood sliding down the glass, a soup of brain matter and bone and gristle that slowly slicked its way to ground zero.

Except that some residual part of his brain still functioned. His left leg trembled. His right hand twitched spasmodically. Bald grimaced. The problem with Parabellum was the size of the round. Smaller than many of its counterparts, the stopping power of the round was limited. Bald shoved the suppressor between the courier's cracked lips. Gave the trigger a squeeze and tapped a second round into the roof of his mouth. The guy's body jerked once more as if somebody had wired him up to the national grid.

Then he stilled.

Bald set to work quickly. He wiped down the window with a shammy from the glove compartment, then got out of the car. He shoved the Beretta into the waistband at the front of his trousers and hurried around to the passenger side, next to the snow-ploughed bank. He opened the door and dragged the courier out of his seat. Hauled him over the mound of fresh snow. The ground beneath him was strewn with the rotting petals of edelweiss and mountain pine. The thick cluster of trees blocked out the sunlight and Bald felt the already mean temperature drop a couple of degrees. The cold pressing against his cheeks.

He dumped the courier behind the bank and scattered snow over his corpse. He figured that at this time of year, when the snow fell thick and fast each day, the snow ploughs would be clearing the roads every hour or so. They wouldn't see the body covered with snow and concealed in the shadow of the bank. And every time the ploughs cleared the road, they would bury the body under more and more snow. Only when it melted in late April would they discover it. By then Bald would be long gone.

He returned to the Mégane, grabbed the spare clip from the parcel and stuffed it into his jacket pocket. Figured he'd OP the chalet so he'd be well prepared and accustomed to the lie of the land before he stormed in and brassed Klich up that evening. All being well, he could be out of Courchevel by midnight.

Bald had driven back about a kilometre when he noticed a vehicle blocking the road.

A Volvo XC90 SUV. Tinted windows, Swiss plates.

A slim figure standing beside the vehicle, palm outstretched, gesturing for him to stop.

Oh shit, thought Bald as his bowels belly-flopped. I've been fucking rumbled.

He killed the motor and pulled to the side of the road. Shot a panicked look at the passenger-side window and saw a couple of tiny drops of blood that he'd missed. Gears clicked inside his head. How the fuck would he get out of this hole? He felt down for the butt of the Beretta. Bald made up his mind to drop the cunt if he caused trouble.

Then he watched as the figure swaggered over to his window, wearing a pair of oversized Tom Ford sunglasses and a pair of black dewline pants, with a graphite-grey boulevard jacket with a high collar and a fur trim. And he recognized the face even behind those enormous shades. He'd know that pout anywhere.

Odessa Stone.

thirty-one

Bald eyed Odessa warily. She stopped six inches from his face and motioned for him to get out. He did, slowly. She took off her Tom Fords, slowly. Flashed her bottle-cap eyes at Bald and said, 'You really ought to be more careful, you know.'

'I don't know what you're talking about.'

'Oh, come on, John. You didn't exactly make life difficult for me. I've been tracking you since you entered Courchevel. You were easy to follow. Didn't even take a roundabout route to your RV. And you're supposed to be ex-SAS?' She tut-tutted playfully. 'You must be losing your touch.'

Her scent tickled his nostrils. Even in thermal winter wear, Odessa looked smoking hot.

'There's a dozen Six agents nearby,' she said. 'Lay so much as a finger on me and they'll drop you like a bad habit.'

'You're bluffing,' said Bald. 'I'm here on a lone-wolf op.'

Odessa smiled at Bald the way a parent smiles at the first shitty drawing their kid shows them. He half-expected Odessa to pat him on the head and tell him the sketch was going on the fridge. 'What's the matter?' she said. 'Don't trust me?'

'I don't trust my own mother,' said Bald, recalling how Odessa had put a gun to his head after the shootout at the Seven Wonders. She'd threatened to cap him, then legged it at the first squawk of police sirens. 'I definitely don't trust someone who did a runner when the shit hit the fan and blew back in my face.'

Odessa dropped the smile. Glared at Bald. Stepped even closer.

'I know you're here for Klich,' she said in a low and lethal voice. 'So you can either come with me quietly now, or I can get the guys on the extraction team to sweep in and drag you to the nearest cliff. Trust me. That won't end happily for you.'

Odessa smiled professionally at Bald.

'You and I want the same thing,' she said.

'What do you mean?'

'We both want Klich. And you can either work with me and get him, or you can work against me and find yourself in a world of trouble. Your call.'

Bald said nothing. He wondered whether Odessa wanted Klich served up in a body bag, or still breathing. He figured it didn't matter either way. As long as Bald had Klich in his grasp, he could slot him.

'Last time we met,' Odessa said, 'you were about to tell me who your handler was.'

'Last time we met,' Bald replied, 'you had a gun to my fucking head.'

'I don't suffer fools or liars.'

'I should have slotted you when I had the chance.'

Odessa didn't reply. She wheeled away from the Mégane and trudged back towards the Volvo. 'Why do you think I'm talking to you?' she said.

Bald grinned. 'Because you can't resist my Scottish accent?'

'My handler asked me to reach out to you. We're both here to achieve the same goal. We both want what the other one wants. And I need your help seizing Klich and getting him back to London.'

Bald nodded. My luck is in, he was thinking. Odessa doesn't realize I'm here to kill Klich. She thinks I'm still trying to snatch the bastard. That means she wants him alive. A warm feeling spilled open like honey in his guts. I can string her along, he told himself. Give Klich a double-tap as soon as I get the chance. Game over.

'Go on,' said Bald.

'My orders are simple. Protect Klich from outside threats, and wait for a Six extraction team to arrive and detain him. Simple, right?'

'Simple,' Bald repeated.

Odessa said, 'Klich isn't alone.'

Bald tried not to look surprised. 'Land told me he'd run out of bodyguards,' he said.

'Klich has got reinforcements. Three six-foot stacks of hired muscle.'

'When the fuck did he have time to recruit and vet them?' Bald said, narrowing his eyes.

'Beats me.' Odessa blew air up her face with her bottom lip. 'Point is, with the extra muscle around we've had to change the plan. The extraction team is setting up an RV outside of Courchevel. I have to detain Klich and escort him to the next village down. But I need to distract the muscle to get to Klich.'

Odessa stopped by the door of her car. Smiled at Bald with her eyes. 'That's where you come in,' she said.

'Klich is still at the chalet?'

Odessa nodded. 'He's hosting a party.'

'Party? But Land told me he wanted to keep a low profile.'

Odessa shook her head. 'That guy is a party animal. The party is the talk of the town. All the great and the good of Russian society are expected to be there. All the oligarchs. A few politicians. Invitation only, of course.'

'Why would Klich invite his enemies to his party?'

Odessa shrugged. 'Your guess is as good as mine.'

Bald put the lid on his puzzlement and glanced at his Aquaracer: 1920 hours. Night had swooped down on

Courchevel. Lights flickered like candles high up in the mountains, where the grandest chalets jutted out of the slopes and afforded their owners sweeping views over the budget hotels and chalets of the village centre, down in the base of the valley. In the Alps, the higher you lived, the bigger the price tag. Klich lived right at the very top of the mountain. One bullet would change all that.

'Fuck it, then,' he said. 'Let's do it.'

Then a thought struck Bald. 'He'll recognize me,' he said. 'Klich. The moment I set foot through the door.'

Odessa laughed and shook her head at the same time, like she was recalling a dirty joke that Bald hadn't been privy to. 'Klich won't recognize you,' she said, 'because you'll be wearing a mask.'

Bald frowned.

'Why the fuck would I be wearing a mask?'

Odessa locked her eyes on his. They glowed with excitement.

'It's a special kind of party.'

thirty-two

Odessa drove. Bald sat in the front passenger seat and gazed out of the window. They had climbed the steep road leading up from the bottom of the valley and were now high above Courchevel, en route to the chalet. Way down below Bald could see the Fleming Hotel lit up from within, although from this high up it looked about the size of a soup crouton. In the distance Bald made out the runway at Courchevel Airport. It was level with their height, shaped like a giant black horseshoe and perched some two thousand metres above sea level on the side of another mountain.

'Seventh most dangerous runway in the world,' said Odessa.

Bald craned his neck. The approach looked hairy as fuck. 'If that's seven, I feel sorry for the fucker who has to land at the most dangerous.'

'Princess Juliana International, on Saint Martin,' Odessa replied in a flash, and Bald wondered how the fuck she knew all this stuff.

Red and yellow lights blinked on the runway. There was a deafening roar, and then the lights catapulted towards the bend in the horseshoe and vaulted high into the night sky, like a skier jumping off the side of a cliff. Quickly the shape resolved itself into the distinctive form of a Beechcraft Baron. The twin-engined plane droned above Bald before cutting through the cloud cover and disappearing.

The bends tightened at each corner as they climbed the mountain road. Odessa took them fast and a little too close for Bald's liking. A sign warned them of avalanches and rock fall. Another indicated they were now fifty metres from the summit.

'When we arrive at the party, locate Klich and keep an eye on him at all times,' said Odessa. Her manner was business-like, the sweet-eyed look and honey smile now wiped away. 'Don't let him out of your sight.'

Bald nodded.

'What about you?' he said.

'I'll locate the three BGs and distract them long enough for you to bundle Klich into the back seat. Then we head to the RV. It's forty-five minutes' drive from the chalet. Any luck, we'll be finished before midnight.'

Odessa stiffened her grip on the wheel. 'You never told me what happened to Joe,' she said.

'That's because I don't give a crap about him,' said Bald.

'He said you were friends.'

'He was mistaken.'

'How so?'

Bald peered down at Courchevel way below as he answered. 'I made certain choices. He made certain choices. Joe never got it. He didn't have a brain on him. He always did as he was told, followed orders. But this is a shitty world. You want to have the high life, you've got to be prepared to screw people over. Tread on some fucking toes. Joe was too naive.'

Odessa said nothing.

'Friends?' Bald asked himself, spitting the word out like it was cold tea.

As they reached the summit Bald spotted a cable-car terminal to the north. Two passenger cabins were suspended four metres above the ground, fixed by two-metre-high metal shafts to a two-track overhead steel haulage rope that looped out from the terminal, over the precipice and down to Courchevel. Each cabin looked capable of holding around a hundred passengers. An electric motor unit occupied the base of the terminal. The terminal roof was built from corrugated steel and a spiralling metal staircase ascended from the ground to the doors of the cabins.

Bald looked due east, to Klich's chalet. Poised close to the edge of a cliff, it had a wooden-tiled roof and a timber frontage punctuated by baroque decoration. Beacons flickered either side of the carved columns at the main entrance.

Odessa slowed right down as they neared the chalet. They passed a line of limousines parked at the side of the road. Chauffeurs passed the time, some leaning against the driver-side doors and smoking cigarettes, others gathering in small groups and passing round a hip flask. They eyed the Volvo suspiciously. Once they were just beyond the limos, Odessa pulled over, fifteen metres short of the chalet's gates. Lights were on inside the building, glowing apricot in the powdery darkness. Most chalets were built to look outwards across the valley floor and Klich's was no different. The windows were all south-facing, and from his position in the Volvo Bald could get no view of the interior of the chalet. He could see little except a pair of wrought-iron gates guarding the entrance, and foamy snow wedged on the slopes of the roof and compacted by a row of logs, preventing the snow from tipping over the edge.

Bald shaped to debus from the Volvo. He seized up in pain. The stitches on his gut wound were fucked up, the pain told him. Aziz had botched it. He was sure of that. He pushed the pain to one side.

'Don't forget this,' Odessa said as she popped open the glove box and fished out a black masquerade mask decorated with lace braiding and with silk ribbon ties. She passed the mask to Bald. Then she got out of the car and said, 'Follow me.'

Bald slid out into the steel-cold night. He walked as fast as the pain allowed him, just about keeping up Odessa as she beelined towards the wrought-iron gates. Snow crunched underfoot. Bald recognized the outline of a Rolls-Royce Phantom in the driveway. Odessa and Bald snuck through a gap between the gates and approached the front door. Bald heard voices coming from inside. Boisterous singing and maracas and accordions and mandolins. Some kind of traditional music, he reckoned.

Odessa led Bald into an entrance hall about five metres square. A rich smell of mahogany and leather greeted them, along with, from deeper in the chalet, the expensive pop of champagne corks and a chorus of giggles and excitable voices.

Somewhere in there is Klich, Bald thought. All I need is one moment alone with the guy. Double-tap him and leg it. I don't give a shit about Odessa and her agenda.

He followed Odessa through an arched open doorway into a main living area the size of a tennis court and a beamed ceiling three metres above their heads. The living area was furnished to perform all the separate functions of lounge, reception and dining area, with leather sofas grouped around an elaborate stone fireplace and a massive dining table positioned next to a pair of sliding glass doors serving as a partition between the living area and a marble-floored balcony. Bald was impressed. The decor looked like someone had tried to replicate the palace at Versailles in a chalet. He looked up at the huge chandelier hanging from the ceiling. Cyrillic letters were etched in gold lace on the walls.

Bald estimated there were sixty men and women in the room, chatting away in their native Russian. The crowd appeared to be engrossed by a band seated on wooden chairs in front of the fireplace, dressed in traditional Russian shirts, red silk with an embroidered ribbon running around the collar and down the middle. The band members, Bald noticed, were the only ones not wearing masquerade masks. Everyone else in the crowd had their backs turned to Bald, watching the band perform. Earlier Bald had been privately worried about rocking up to some high-class gig dressed in jeans and an anorak. But now he saw that half the blokes in the chalet wore the same kind of clothes. Like they were having a private competition to see who could be the world's scruffiest-looking billionaire.

At his ten o'clock, outside the room, Bald noticed two wooden staircases, one leading up, one down. Every few minutes he saw a couple slipping away from the crowd, making for the stairs. All of the couples headed downstairs.

'I'm going upstairs,' Odessa said.

'What's up there?' Bald asked, noting that no one seemed to be headed that way.

'Klich's private office and gym. His BGs are up there.'

Odessa left before Bald could get a word in. He turned away from her and scanned the sixty or so masks covering the guests' faces. Thought, how the fuck am I going to identify Klich?

'Having a good time?'

The voice was borderline comatose and came from his back. Bald did a one-eighty and saw a redhead in a black, sequinned halter dress, a diamond necklace snaked around her slender neck and gold bracelets on both wrists. Her figure was mostly tits and arse, and totally fake. Bald's favourite kind of girl. She looked like the girl next door, if you called Beverly Hills home. A Venetian mask covered her face from her cheeks up. The mask was brilliant white, the colour of sugar, and criss-crossed with gold ribbons to create a Harlequin effect. Tiny diamonds studded its rim. Her get-up probably cost more than I've earned in my whole life, Bald reckoned.

'You are not Russian,' the redhead said. 'Russian men old and fat.'

Bald pursed his lips. He needed to find Klich. But sod it, a snakish voice piped up in his guts. Why not enjoy yourself until you get a mark-one eyeball on the guy? Bald lived by the mantra that you never turned down good times, especially when it came packaged as a pair of fake tits. He smiled right back at the redhead. She drained her champagne and gestured to a passing blonde in a bunny-girl costume for a top-up. Bald grabbed a flute from the silver tray and gobbled down cana-pés from another tray. He swigged on Bollinger, all the time casting his eyes across the crowd, seeking out the oligarch.

The redhead said, 'Looking for someone?'

'Mate of mine, yeah.'

'What's his name?'

'Viktor Klich.'

The redhead did a spit-take, then smiled, amused. '*You're* a friend of Viktor Klich?'

Bald nodded. 'We go way back.'

'Come,' she said, taking him by the hand. 'He's downstairs.'

Bald polished off his Bollinger and let the woman guide him through the crowd, goosing him more than once. He was glad to be going downstairs as the folk music was pissing him off. The musicians got another round of applause as Bald hit the first step. He launched down the stairs after the redhead, his heart thumping against his breastbone.

At the foot of the stairs she led him down a narrow, dimly lit passageway. The floorboards were wooden and the walls exposed rock. Candles located in pockets along the walls threw flickers of gauche light over the passage. It was like descend-ing into a cave. Bald couldn't see clearly more than four or five metres in front of him, but vague silhouettes danced around. He saw the shimmer of what appeared to be a pool set amid a circle of rocks. He heard the trickle of water and the clink of champagne glasses, and moans and cries of ecstasy coming from the silhouettes.

The redhead smiled at Bald as she led him out of the passage and into a big room about twelve metres square. Neon lights were attached to the exposed rock face at his nine o'clock, bathing the room in a lunar-blue glow. The music from upstairs dribbled through the ceiling, dull and warbled, and Bald was grateful for the quiet in this room. He glanced across at the shallow pool to his left, and shot a look so wide-eyed it had wings. Two old farts were by the water. Bald recognized them by the details on their masks. They were spit-roasting a dark-haired woman wearing knee-high fuck-me boots. To his right stood a sauna. Bald could see two couples through a glass door. The women were going down on the men. The men looked pleased with themselves, high-fiving each other. Within moments he'd spotted a dozen other couples, ploughing away on the floor, against the rock face, or standing up.

thirty-three

The redhead licked her lips at Bald and fondled his crotch. He hardened. Tried to look around, tried to concentrate on the mission. But he couldn't make out the faces behind the masks. One of these guys has to be Klich, he thought. Which fucking one?

'What's the matter?' the redhead said coyly. 'Don't you want to have some fun?'

Bald said nothing. He definitely wanted to have fun. But first he had to get his hands on his target, then bug out to the Volvo. After that he could have all the fucking fun in the world.

'Where's Viktor Klich?' he asked.

The woman shrugged as she loosened her shoulder straps, her fake tits calling out for Bald to caress them. He should have been gearing himself up for the fuck of his life. But his focus was on the other silhouettes. Where is Klich? he wondered again. He spotted figures at the far end of the room. Shadows. But they were partially blocked by a skinny guy who was biting off the clothes of a morbidly obese woman, to bury his face in her cunt.

Standing in front of Bald, the redhead slowly traced a finger down his stomach, lightly touching his wound, making him wince. Then she stepped out of her dress and moved even closer, her tits brushing his chest.

'Stay a while,' she said. 'Your friend can wait.'

'I don't think so,' said Bald. He shrugged the redhead off and gave her his back, then investigated the depths of the room. Stepped around a guy and a girl locked in a reverse cowgirl position. The guy was about ninety, the girl about nineteen. Just my luck, thought Bald. The one time I get to go to an orgy and I have to focus on killing a man. He saw a couple right at the back of the room. A man standing, still in his dinner suit and wearing a full-face gold joker mask. A woman was on her knees, sucking him off. The man carried a metal briefcase with a pair of chunky, silver key-lock latches and a central combination lock. The briefcase was handcuffed to his right wrist. This figure intrigued Bald, who moved towards the man. He was stopped short by a hand grabbing his bicep and the redhead's voice at his six o'clock, whispering, 'Don't you want me?'

Bald spun around. He'd had enough of being messed about for one day. He seized the redhead by the wrist, clamping his hands around her gold bracelet. She tried to retract her hand but Bald had a rock-hard grip and yanked her arm just enough to get her compliance.

'Ow,' she said. 'You're hurting me.'

'Where's Klich?'

'Over there,' she said, jerking her head at the figure in the joker mask.

She tried to wrench herself free and Bald reacted by shaking her, causing her mask to fall off. The skin on her face was like doner kebab meat. He pushed her away and now saw that she was an old trollop. Her legs were mountains of varicose veins and cellulite. Bald was disgusted with himself just for looking at this hideous old bag. Then he spun around and strode towards the man in the joker mask.

'Hey!' the redhead yelled. 'Stop him!'

A dozen heads shot looks at Bald. Klich suddenly jumped back, away from the woman giving him head, zipped himself up and stopped for a cold second to look at Bald. The joker mask smiling at him. Then he rushed off, lugging his metal briefcase, towards one side of the room. Bald shaped to give chase, but a pair of hands clawed at him from the sauna. A naked middle-aged guy with a beard tried to prevent him gaining on Klich. Bald quickly kneed him in the balls. The guy doubled up in pain as Bald hauled him over to the sauna stove and in the same quick move shoved his head onto its hot stove surface, then grabbed the pail of water and tipped it over his head. The guy howled in agony as scalding hot steam blistered his face and tore away his flesh. The other men in the room looked on cagily, pondering the wisdom of trying to stop Bald. But the redhead didn't get the message. She hit Bald on his back with a torrent of pathetic fists. He sent her flying into the rock wall. No one helped the redhead to her feet.

The oligarch was already scaling a ladder running up the wall to a trapdoor. He was halfway up. Getting away. Bald increased his pace. Five metres, and Christ, he was so close he could almost reach out and grab the prick. At two metres he saw Klich's top half disappear through the trapdoor. He lunged for the guy's shoe before it disappeared. But Klich had anticipated the move and punted a foot at Bald. The tip of his shoe poked Bald in the eye. He stumbled back a couple of steps and by the time he had recovered his balance, Klich was already gone. The trapdoor slammed shut.

No, Bald thought. Not this time.

As Bald propelled himself up the rough wooden rungs of the ladder, his palms burned. At the top he punched the trapdoor in rage. It shuddered on its hinges as only a crude lock held it in place. Then Bald punched it a second time, harder, the lock snapped, and the trapdoor swung up on its hinges. Bald heard the panicked crunch of footsteps on snow and saw above him a square of night sky, studded with stars so bright they seemed to be dangling right in front of him like diamonds. Hauling himself through the opening, he crawled onto a blanket of soft snow. The trapdoor lay just a few metres back from the edge of the cliff. To his right stood the chalet, to his left a stand of birches.

He whipped out his Beretta and looked around. No sign of Klich. Where the fuck is he?

Snowflakes were drifting down onto him, thick and fast, obscuring his vision, but he spotted footprints cushioned into the fresh snow, tamping it down. He traced these north, towards the wrought-iron gates at the front of the chalet. Bald looked up at the gates just in time to hear the roar of a car, husky and softened by the snowfall, and then he saw Klich racing towards the Phantom. The oligarch dived into the back seat as the chauffeur reversed out of the driveway and did a ninety-degree turn. The car was now pointing towards the road leading away from the chalet and back down to the village. Its headlamps were chopping the falling snow, fumes pumping wildly out of the exhaust, tyres squealing. From where Bald was standing, he had a side view of the car. Twelve cold metres away. Another couple of seconds and the Phantom would be joining the road and Bald would be waving goodbye to Klich.

Goodbye to his new life.

What Bald did next was automatic. Hardwired into his blood. The result of years of training in the Regiment, in the Killing House and on the training ground, and in the field. Actions that had been practised hundreds of times until they had become instinctive movements ingrained in his muscle-memory. He brought the Beretta to bear, keeping his elbows locked and tucked tight to his sides and his arms raised level with his upper chest. Peering through the iron sights at the driver's window of the Phantom, he focused on the front post centred between the two rear notches on top of the receiver. The rear notches were heavily blurred like an out-of-focus dovetail, the driver's window marginally out of focus. Bald breathed out to relax the muscles of his neck and right shoulder but kept his forearm sturdy and his wrist fixed. Just enough tension to keep the shot centred on the target. Not too much tension, or his aim would be stiff.

He pulled the trigger.

The Beretta kicked up a fraction in his grip as he discharged the first shot. The bolt and barrel recoiled as the first round barked. The bolt was still shunting backwards on the slider even as the barrel fired forward again, ejecting the spent brass from the side of the receiver. Bald could almost feel the individual parts moving inside the Beretta. All those components working in tandem. The energy of the movement compressing the recoil spring inside the gun. The bolt shuddering forward, releasing the spring and forcing a fresh round into the barrel from the clip.

Bald unloaded two more shots in quick succession, the weapon's parts moving decisively. The *phtt* of each discharge was smothered by the snow. Bald doubted anyone inside the chalet would hear the shots. There was only the polite shattering of glass as the first two bullets starred the driver's window, the third embedding itself in the door below it. Bald couldn't see inside the car, but a split second after the first two rounds' impact, the Phantom lurched to a halt, and Bald knew that they had worked their magic, and nailed the chauffeur. Just ahead, Bald saw the chauffeurs from the line of parked limos diving for cover: some into the bushes, others into the backs of the cars, dashing their cigarettes into the snow.

Bald stepped forward. Still lining up the Phantom between the sights. Index finger vigilant on the trigger. The Phantom sputtered. Bald did the maths. Fifteen rounds to a clip. Minus the three bullets he'd fired now and the two he'd expended on the courier, and he was down a total of five rounds. That left him ten bullets in the clip, plus the spare clip. He had twenty-five rounds of 9x19mm Parabellum left to play with.

More than enough to slot Klich.

He dropped his aim a couple of degrees. Like he was aiming at an imaginary waist. Then he popped two rounds at the front tyre. The first missed. But the second round punctured the tyre clean. The Phantom sagged to its left. The tyre hissed its distress. The engine groaned.

I've got him, thought Bald as he hurried clear of the chalet. Ten metres to the Phantom and he quickened his stride. Eight metres now. Bald began manoeuvring towards the rear passenger door. Figured he would prise it open and introduce Klich to the Beretta M9.

Then the door swung open and the business end of a Heckler & Koch UMP slid out of the gap. Trained on Bald. He didn't see the shooter. Just saw the weapon and the hand fastened around the grip. Then the flames licking like a tongue out of the muzzle as the submachine gun opened fire at him. A three-round burst. Three hot balls of lead gashing the snow a footstep ahead of Bald, showering him in a heated slush that had him frantically pepper-potting away from the Phantom. He ducked for cover behind the birches at his five o'clock. Hit the ground as the UMP unleashed a second three-round burst. This time the bullets spattered into the trees above Bald as he lay prone on the ground, spraying him with splinters of hot wood. The noise of the shots was muffled by the snow.

Ca-rump! Ca-rump! CA-RUMP!

The third round torpedoed into a trunk six inches from Bald and level with his head. Shredded wood spat in his face. He hunkered down lower and crawled deeper into the trees, using his knees and elbows to haul himself across the snow. Crawling like a spider. Putting more wood between himself and the shooter in the Phantom. He hunkered down behind a thick trunk as a third burst flashed from the car, crackled in the night air, scythed through the trees, gnashing at the trunks and branches, the bullets whizzing and skidding past Bald and disappearing over the cliff edge. He gripped the Beretta and caught his breath.

Then the shooting stopped.

Bald waited a double-beat, then glanced back at the Phantom.

All four doors were popped. Fresh footsteps were sunk into the snow, leading away from the car. Bald followed them. Through a break in the driving snow he made out four shapes twenty metres away. One of them had a briefcase strapped to his wrist. A rage brewed inside Bald as he watched Viktor Klich escape. He had what appeared to be a three-man BG team comprising two monstrously bulky heavies in suits and a third figure, skinny but tall and wearing a bright-yellow beanie hat. The two heavies looked like brothers. Had broad shoulders and chests shaped like beer kegs. One of the guys was shaven-headed, for that neo-Nazi look. The other had cropped black hair. All three were brandishing UMPs.

Seconds later Neo-Nazi unleashed another three-round burst at Bald from thirty metres. The rounds walloped into the trees and Bald got a faceful of splinters for his troubles. Their aim was off. Back-pedalling through snow, firing a submachine gun from the hip, at that distance and in this kind of light, the chances of anyone hitting Bald were remote.

He wondered where Klich was headed. He had no wheels. And what had happened to Odessa? She was nowhere to be seen.

Then he watched Klich and his bodyguards break right.

Hurrying towards the cable cars.

thirty-four

Twenty metres stood between Klich and the cable-car terminal. Bald darted out of the stand of trees and ran falteringly towards the Phantom to secure himself some decent cover. The UMPs lit up and doused the snow in flashes of waxy light. Shots slapped into the snow behind Bald as he slid behind cover by the Phantom's grille. The chauffeur was lying on the ground a metre to the right, his vacant eyes staring at the snow. There was a curious look on his face, like he was trying to remember where he'd left his wallet. Bald shaped to displace from behind the Phantom and unload shots at Klich but the din of three rounds *ca-racking* and the bullets perforating the rear end of the car forced him back down to a crouch.

A pause in the shooting. Bald did a three-count. On three he sprang upright, hoisting the Beretta up in the same motion. He spotted Klich and the BG team fifty metres ahead of him. Klich lumbered up to the terminal, then shuttled up the metal staircase leading to the passenger cabin docked at the left-hand platform. Briefcase swinging from his wrist and banging against the railings. The three BGs moved in close order behind Klich, clumping up the stairs in giant, cumbersome strides, as if they were stepping over dead bodies.

Bald thought about loosening off a couple of rounds at the passenger cabin. But the distance between him and the cabin was some sixty metres. On a good day the Beretta M9 boasted an effective range of up to fifty metres. Today was a not-so-good day.

Beanie Hat slammed the door of the passenger cabin shut. Bald broke clear of the Phantom and hurried across the summit towards the cabin. His guts were squirming. He couldn't feel his toes. He couldn't feel his balls. He couldn't feel his face. Could hardly make out the terminal behind the thick curtain of snow. He heard the electric motors at the terminal grinding into life. There was a pause as the track cables shunted forward on the steel haulage rope and a moment later the cabin glided out of the terminal. Teetering along on the steel cables down the precipice, slowly at first. But the cabin quickly picked up speed, moving at eight metres per second, and before Bald was able to properly line up his shot the cabin was over the precipice and beyond the Beretta's range.

Bald lowered his weapon, allowing a grim thought to enter his mind. I was within seconds of nabbing Klich. So close I could have spat on the guy. And now he's escaping. He thought about chasing him in the Volvo. But the horizontal distance from the summit to the terminal at the bottom of the valley was six hundred metres, and vertically it was a drop of a hundred and fifty metres. At the current rate Klich would hit the terminal down in Courchevel in under a minute. The journey up to the chalet had taken nineteen minutes by car. Klich would be long gone by the time Bald made it back down to the village.

Then he looked over at the terminal, and the kernel of an idea sprouted in his head.

The second passenger cabin. I can shuttle after Klich. I can still catch him.

Bald raced towards the building. His leg muscles were ragged and torn. Blood seeped from his ruptured gut wound, washing down his shirt and trousers. Warming his genitals. Didn't matter. Adrenalin was pumping freely, quelling the pain. He still had a chance to kill Klich.

Twenty metres to the terminal. The cabin containing Klich and his entourage had travelled two hundred metres horizontally and fifty metres vertically. Still a long way to go to the bottom of the mountain. Bald raced up the stairs of the terminal after stashing the Beretta into his waistband so he could grip the railings with both hands. Halfway up, he had a vertiginous view over the precipice, down to the village three hundred metres below. He asked himself why Klich would be heading back down there.

He wondered, too, what was in the metal briefcase Klich had handcuffed to his wrist.

Now Bald cleared the last tread and hit the grated metal walkway. Lugged himself towards the passenger cabin on the right-hand platform. He yanked open the door and bundled inside, eyes flicking left and right in a frantic search for the override controls. He knew that the cabins were ordinarily operated by a tram manager and his assistants at the terminal itself. Cheaper and more convenient than having a guy shuttle back and forth in the cabin all day. But an attendant accompanied the passengers on each journey in case a problem developed and he needed to take control of the cabin and guide it to safety. He needed to do what the guys in Klich's cabin were doing, and turn on the manual override. Bald spotted the control panel at the front, a boxed unit protected by breakable clear glass. He drove a fist through the cover. Cleared the shards away and studied the controls.

The buttons were colour-coded. The instructions were in French. Bald pressed the green button. The universal colour for 'go'. The cabin wobbled for a beat, pulleys and gears and winches graunching in the metal shaft directly above. Then it lurched forward. Bald almost fell back on his arse. The engine growled and the cabin steadied itself and began trundling out of the terminal on the haulage ropes. Bald could see Klich in the cabin ahead of him as it bobbed along the ropes on a gentle decline. He could see Beanie Hat and the heavy with black hair by his side.

But he couldn't see Neo-Nazi.

Then there was a clang at Bald's six o'clock, and he wheeled around. Someone had sprung off the terminal and dived through the cabin door. The guy dropped heavily, like a cement sack being dumped from a great height and the cabin lurched violently. Bald steadied himself with a hand on the controls as Neo-Nazi scraped himself off the floor and charged at him, roaring.

thirty-five

As Bald reached down for the Beretta he already knew he was out of time. Less than two metres separated the two men. Neo-Nazi made it zero metres in an instant, and he pounced at Bald on the balls of his feet, surprisingly quick and agile for his bulk. His shoulders were broad, his chest wide as a beer keg. He had no definition: just muscle layered over muscle and a cheap black suit on top of that. Had a face that had taken a beating or two in its time and bulbous knuckles that looked like they had returned the beatings with interest.

Bald felt a fist whump into his guts. Right on his wound. The pain was like someone had stabbed him with a cattle prod. He keeled over. Couldn't breathe. His hand fell limply away from the weapon and he dropped to his knees. Felt vomit rising in his throat. Felt the Beretta grip dig into his ribs. He snatched desperately at the cold air. He coughed up blood onto the heavy's black leather brogues. One of them shot up into his face, hitting him with the force of a truck. He heard the crack of his jaws, like a plank of wood being chopped in half. His skull jarred as his head banged against the wall of the cabin.

Then he saw the heavy drawing his UMP.

A second more, the lizard part of his brain told Bald, and he'd be slotted.

His survival instinct kicked in. Breathless and disorientated, he had no chance of swinging an accurate punch. So he did the next best thing. He shot forward. Steaming into the guy at his midriff, leading with the bony part of his head and using it as a battering ram. He slammed his dome into Neo-Nazi's abdomen. The guy wheezed and took an unsteady step backwards. But he stayed on his feet. With that much muscle, bringing him down would be like pushing over a tank. Bald kept driving on, putting every last ounce of energy in his body into pushing Neo-Nazi backwards, his neck muscles pumping, his shoulder muscles stinging. He pushed the guy two steps back. Then a third. Then a fourth. But then a burst of pain electrified his spine and speared down his back as Neo-Nazi slammed the butt of his pistol down on the back of Bald's neck. One last push was all Bald could manage. It was enough. The guy lost his footing and tumbled to the ground. The impact winded him, forced him to relinquish his grip on the weapon. It clattered on the floor, half a metre from Bald. He swiped a hand blindly in that direction, his palm sending the submachine gun skimming across the floor. Out of reach.

But now Bald had Neo-Nazi pinned down. Right where he wanted him. He swung a flurry of left and right hooks at his face. The hard ridge of his knuckles connected with cheekbone. Stunned the guy. Bald rained down blow after vicious blow. Scored no points for artistry, but then again in a real fist fight you didn't worry about how good your moves looked. You fought dirty and you fought with sheer intensity. Bald gave away four inches in height and maybe fifteen kilos of muscle to the man on the floor. In a straight slugfest, he'd lose every time. The only advantages he had were speed and agility. He had to keep swinging at the guy, making up for his lack of power with the sheer number of punches and kicks.

He went to swing again. But his shoulder muscles were weary and the blow took a long beat to wind up. Advertising his intentions to Neo-Nazi. The guy shot a hand up at Bald. Enormous fingers clamped around his face, locking his head.

Bald kept on hitting at the guy's face but his punch was weak now. Neo-Nazi slid his index and middle fingers up towards Bald's eyes, trying to gouge them. Bald shut his eyes and wrenched his head as far away as possible. Managed an inch or two. Neo-Nazi had a vice grip on his skull. Bald bit down on the hand, chomping on the outer palm. It was sinewy and rubbery, like chewing on pork rind. But he bit as hard as he could. His incisors tore through flesh and he drew blood, which gushed into his mouth, warm and brassy. Neo-Nazi howled, whipping his hand away and striking out at Bald with the other, balled-up like a kettlebell. It smashed into Bald's temple and sent him rolling off to the left of his opponent.

'Get back on your feet,' a voice urged Bald. Any fight, the last place you wanted to be was on the floor.

Bald acted on the voice. Pushed himself up on the palms of his hands. Neo-Nazi was now vertical as well. He shot Bald a killer look. Blood oozing out of the palm of his right hand and drenching his shirt cuff dark red. He moved in on Bald, his punches wild and flailing, throwing his arms in a wide arc. Bald took a step back. Tucking his chin tight to his neck to protect the fragile triangle of his face. Raising his forearms up to his nose, ready to block each punch. Bald glanced over his shoulder. Neo-Nazi was backing him into a corner. If he got stuck there, he'd never get out alive. Neo-Nazi would swarm him with blows, beat him to a pulp.

Bald stood his ground. Dropped his defensive fists, inviting a punch. Neo-Nazi enthusiastically took up the offer and launched another reckless haymaker at Bald. Swung his right arm at Bald in an arc so wide it came at the ex-Blade from another time zone. Bald pushed back on his left foot, lifting his right off the ground a couple of inches and twisting his torso to the right, like he was stepping out of the way of an oncoming train. He was sideways and a half-step to the left when the fist came at him. He left Neo-Nazi swiping at thin air.

The momentum of the punch carried Neo-Nazi forward and now Bald found himself to the side of the guy and unleashed his counter-attack, side-stepping until he was positioned to Neo-Nazi's five o'clock.

The heavy had stopped in his tracks now, realizing, too late, that the momentum had left him exposed. He started to turn around. Bald had the pick of body parts to fuck up. He went for the legs. Easier than trying to crack open his skull, and the guy had packed so much muscle on his lats and delts that you'd need a wrecking ball to strike a decisive blow on his back. And like most bodybuilder freaks, this one had spent half his life bench-pressing but neglected his leg exercises. He was top heavy, and his legs were vulnerable. Bald raised his right foot until his knee was level with his waist, then stomped down on Neo-Nazi's right calf. The guy grunted as the blow put him off-balance. He stumbled forward, almost crashing to the floor, stopping himself by planting his palms on the cabin window.

Now Bald moved in for the kill. He wrapped his left hand around his right fist and formed a point with his right elbow. Then he thrust his elbow at Neo-Nazi, catching him on the small of his back. He struck again, then again, the helmet-like bone of his elbow cracking into the ridge of the man's spine, stunning him. After four blows Neo-Nazi let his palms droop off the window and his head sagged. The fight was seeping out of him. Bald now grabbed his shoulders and rammed his head through the window. Shards of glass tumbled through the air into the valley below. They were suspended high above the mountain, Bald saw. Shattered teeth of glass remained fixed to the window frame. Bald gripped Neo-Nazi's head and plunged it down towards them.

But Neo-Nazi jabbed an elbow backwards at Bald. It smashed into his ribs, a stabbing pain exploding in his chest. The pain knocked Bald back on his feet, his hands involuntarily releasing Neo-Nazi before he could spike his neck on the broken glass. Then, before Bald could shake his head clear, Neo-Nazi yanked his head back into the cabin and spun around to face him. His jacket caught on the spikes of glass as he turned, yanking the jacket off his back. This flapped and fluttered in the wind, the pockets spilling their contents over the mountain floor. Neo-Nazi scowled at the window and stormed into Bald with a brutal combination. Jab, jab, uppercut.

Bald had nothing left in the tank. Yet he blocked two out of the three punches. The third crashed into his jaw. And then he was falling to the floor, and Neo-Nazi followed through with a series of kicks and stamps, hitting him in the ankles and chest and forearms. Bald reached for the Beretta in one last attempt to take the guy down. Neo-Nazi brought down a huge foot on top of Bald's hand as he grabbed the grip, grinding his fingers like they were cigarette butts. Then he stooped down, seized the gun and stuffed it into his waistband. Next Neo-Nazi moved around to the side of Bald and scooped up the UMP that Bald had earlier swiped out of his hand. Checked that the UMP was functioning. Nodded with his bottom lip.

I'm fucked, thought Bald.

Neo-Nazi wiped his lips with the back of his hand. Grinned at Bald. Half his teeth were gold and silver. The other half were blood-red.

Bald waited for the bullet.

But Neo-Nazi frowned as he padded down his trouser pockets. The passenger cabin had almost reached the base terminal and they were skating forty, maybe fifty metres above the village when he turned back to Bald and said, 'Give me your phone.'

Bald blinked his confusion.

'You cost me a phone,' Neo-Nazi said, his grin deforming into a scowl as he jerked a thumb at the jacket impaled on the glass teeth around the window and fluttering in the wind. 'Give me yours.'

'You're not going to kill me?' Bald said.

Neo-Nazi shrugged. 'Boss man says he wants you alive. You and the other MI6 people. Says he wants to kill you himself. Make it last long fucking time.' His fat fingers motioned at Bald. 'Phone.'

Bald didn't move. Just evil-eyed Neo-Nazi. The guy stood there for a moment. Then he whipped Bald with the UMP. The blow triggered a million pain neurons in his skull, sent them crashing around like a pool break. Neo-Nazi reached down and grabbed the Galaxy Tab from Bald's trouser pocket. Stood up. Spat at Bald, a knot of bloody phlegm the size of a hailstone hitting him on the fucking chin. Neo-Nazi turned his back to Bald and tapped a series of digits into the phone as they drew into the terminal.

He looked briefly back over his shoulder at Bald. Grinned.

'No hard feelings,' he said as he pushed the green dial button.

The Galaxy exploded.

thirty-six

The passenger cabin shuddered to a halt. They had arrived at the base terminal. Bald sat up. Neo-Nazi didn't sit up. Mostly because he had a hole in his fucking skull big enough to accommodate a grapefruit. Bald was momentarily hypnotized by the sight. The Russian had died instantly. Soon as he hit the dial button. He was dead before he'd even finished slumping to the floor.

Bald picked himself up, seized by a single paralyzing thought. Land booby-trapped the Galaxy. If I'd pressed the dial button, I'd be the one with the hole in the head.

He shook his head clear of that shit, and took the UMP from Neo-Nazi. The weapon had a vertical foregrip attached to the underside of the Picatinny rail system. The logo stamped on the side of the receiver reminded Bald of the motto Heckler & Koch printed in their literature. 'In a world of compromise, some don't.' Bald liked to think he was cut from the same cloth. The curved clip inserted into the mag feed told Bald that the UMP was the 'niner' variant, chambered for good old-fashioned 9x19mm Parabellum. Good news for him, since the effective range on the UMP9 was a hundred metres, twice the killing distance of his Beretta. Bald thumbed the fire selector to the safety position, pushed the magazine catch forward and removed the clip. A quick check told him he was down by ten rounds. A UMP9 took thirty rounds to a clip.

Meaning he had twenty rounds left. Throw in the Beretta and business was looking good. He noticed blood dripping from the UMP's barrel, like black syrup, gritty with bits of brain. Bald wiped it clean on Neo-Nazi's shirt and clambered out of the cabin.

Time to kill Klich, he thought. Then I'll find out why the fuck Land tried to blow my fucking brains out.

He lumbered down the stairs of the terminal stairs, his wound throbbing. Wasn't easy. The snow still fell heavily. If anything, Bald reckoned, the snowfall was thicker lower down the mountain. Squinting, he discovered that the cable car had dumped him at the limits of the village. At his six lay the village. Nobody on the streets. This kind of weather, people were wrapped up nice and warm in their chalets, so Bald doubted they would have heard the explosion. The tiny amount of explosive material in the phone, and the fact the explosion had occurred inside the cable car, would have kept the sound down.

Bald looked to his twelve o'clock, to a gently sloping plateau on the lower part of the mountain. There, a hundred and fifty metres from him and twenty metres above him, illuminated by the moonlight on the crystal snow, was the tumbledown farmhouse he had noted on arriving in Courchevel. Faint footprints in the snow led in that direction. That's the way Klich went, Bald told himself. He figured the oligarch had a couple of minutes' head start. Quickly he scanned the area ahead. The terrain between the terminal and the farmhouse was staked with three rows of perforated bright-orange temporary snow fencing to accumulate the drift. At each end the snow fences were bordered by conifer trees, and behind the farthest fence, at the left-hand end, stood a Snow Trac clearance vehicle, its roof caked in two inches of snow. The snow was purple and the sky was tar, making it difficult for Bald to pick out details beyond the Snow Trac. But he perceived a darker smudge on the slope, breaking clear of the last of the snow fences. Klich. Bald identified him by the metal briefcase glinting in his hand. Where the fuck are the other two BGs? he wondered, but he didn't have time to worry about them.

Klich had already pulled the best part of a hundred metres clear of him, and he needed to put the brakes on him before he disappeared into the swampy night.

The target was at the threshold of the UMP's effective range. Bald sprang into action, unfolding the buttstock and raising the weapon level with his target. Thumbed the fire selector to semi-automatic. He liked the heft of the UMP. Its polymer case weighed the slim end of three kilograms, making it easy for Bald to hold and keep level with Klich even in his exhausted state. He tucked the moulded buttstock tight to his shoulder and rested his cheek on the smooth comb.

Exhaled.

Fired.

A mechanical bark rattled across the valley.

The round missed, landing eight inches short of Klich, thwacking mutely into the farthest snow fence. The oligarch flinched at the shot and stole a glance over his shoulder at Bald before he broke into a run.

Bald adjusted his aim. Zeroed in on Klich, hiking the UMP up a notch, framing his head a fraction below the rear aperture and the vertical ring of the front post. A simple flex of his index finger, Klich would drop and Bald could start getting the beers in. He experienced a mild pang of disappointment as he depressed the trigger. Hunt a man halfway across the world and it came down to a long-range shot in the middle of nowhere.

Then something flashed amid the speckled darkness. It seemed to come from the Snow Trac. A blade of a second later the ground in front of Bald erupted into a slush as a bullet zipped into the snow. Instinctively he ducked low, reducing his size and presenting himself as a smaller target to the shooter. He spied Beanie Hat and the crop-haired heavy kneeling either side of the vehicle. Caught the glint of their barrels in the moonlight. They'd been lying in wait to ambush Bald. The two of them, secured behind good cover, would be able to keep him pinned down long enough for Klich to escape. The ex-Blade had walked into a fucking trap. Now Beanie Hat and his mate trained their UMPs on him and Bald jolted into action, putting a single round down at the Snow Trac. The round hammered into the cabin but it brought Bald a precious couple of seconds to swap his exposed terrain for some better cover. He made for the nearest of the three snow fences, twenty metres in advance of his position, thumbing the fire selector to the two-round burst setting and pumping a couple of shoot-and-scoot rounds at the Snow Trac as he displaced. Giving them something to think about. As Bald moved he kept a running tally of expended rounds in his head. He'd now used up three more rounds from the clip. Seventeen left in the UMP. Then he'd have to switch to the Beretta.

He struggled to achieve a decent pace in the snow. It was two fists deep in places and each step sapped his energy. Bald was five strides from the first snow fence when Beanie Hat popped out from behind the Snow Trac and unleashed a two-round burst at him. The bullets slapped into the snow four inches to his left. Bald continued in a zigzag towards the fence. He put another two-round burst down at the Snow Trac. Fifteen bullets left in the clip.

Another step, and Bald dived towards the fence as a couple of rounds chewed up the top of the dense drift of snow on the other side. There was a pause in the fire. Bald peered above the fence, saw Klich fifty metres from the farmhouse, his silhouette barely visible in the darkness. But before he could eliminate the oligarch, he would have to deal with the two BGs. Outnumbered, outgunned, he needed a fucking plan.

Then he rested his hand on the snow and found the stuff was flakier and looser than he had expected, and a plan began to form in his head.

Bald hunkered down behind the drifted snow as Beanie Hat popped up again, and the other guy too this time, both putting down rounds at him. Hot lead chopped up the fresh snow inches above his head. Bald counted six rounds. Then there was a lull in the fire. This was his chance. Bald rose to his feet and thumbed the fire selector to fully automatic. He opened fire at the Snow Trac, spraying it with half a dozen rounds. Keeping Beanie Hat and his mate pinned down behind the vehicle while he made his move. He vaulted over the fence, rolled onto the other side of the packed snow. Sprang up and staggered towards the middle fence, almost losing his footing in the snow. Dropped behind it as another torrent of rounds blitzed over his head from the two BGs. Bald had closed the gap between him and them to forty metres. Two three-round bursts spat out of the snow fence at his six. That told him the BGs believed they still had Bald trapped at the first snow fence. They didn't know he'd advanced to the middle one.

He waited for another lull in the fire and climbed over the second fence, hurried towards the last one, twenty metres short of the BGs. Now he crawled around to the left edge of the fence and scooped away the snow from the top until he had created a U-shaped hollow that gave him a good view of the Snow Trac. Bald watched the dark-haired heavy pop out and train his sights on the snow fence that Bald had just displaced from. The guy had a tense finger on the trigger. Waiting for a flicker of movement. Itching to kill Bald.

Now Bald bolted upright to fire, and the BG spotted the abrupt movement at his two o'clock. He froze in shock to see the ex-Blade much closer to him than he'd expected. Bald had levelled the UMP and pulled the trigger before the fucker could arc his own weapon across at him. He put nine rounds down on the guy. Properly brassed him up. The *ca-racks* were dampened by the snowfall, like they were suppressed. The heavy jerked and jolted as bullets pinballed around inside his system. Fragments of lead perforating his vitals and nicking away bone and muscle.

One down. One to go.

Bald couldn't see Beanie Hat. Figured the guy must be hiding behind the Snow Trac. He stayed crouched in the hollow and focused on the vehicle. But then he detected a slight movement in the corner of his left eye, coming from the conifers bordering the fences. Beanie Hat was trying to out-flank Bald. The ex-Blade displaced from the hollow, swinging his aim in the direction of the conifers. He clocked Beanie Hat storming out from the tree line. UMP sights already locked on Bald. Closing in for the kill. Bald had the drop on this cunt. He squeezed the trigger.

Click-click.

Shit!

Bald ducked low again behind the snow fence as Beanie Hat unleashed six rounds in his direction. The bullets whipped through the packed snow and lashed the ground around him. Ditching the UMP, Bald pulled out the Beretta and did a three-count. He had to nail Beanie Hat before the guy out-flanked him and had a clear line of sight across the fence.

On the count of two Bald shot upright. Spotted Beanie Hat charging at him from the conifers to the left of the fence. He seemed emboldened by the belief that Bald was shit out of ammo. But he hadn't counted on Bald packing a second-ary weapon. First rule of any operator going into battle, Bald recalled from his Regiment days: always plan for a stoppage. Beanie Hat had his UMP drawn but not zeroed on Bald. In a blur of motion Bald angled his torso at the BG and levelled the sights with the sizeable target of his upper chest. He discharged two shots before the guy could vittle off a round of his own. The first bullet struck Beanie Hat in the throat. Blood graffitied the snow fence. Beanie Hat dropped, making all kinds of fucked-up gargling noises.

Bald lowered the Beretta.

Two good kills.

He turned his attention to Klich. The Russian was now sixty metres from Bald and had reached the farmhouse, his charcoal silhouette merging with the building. Bald saw a worm of light as Klich burst through the front door. A couple of beats later vicious barking came from the farmhouse. Bald watched in horror as a pair of attack dogs tore down the slope towards him.

Boerboels, he guessed from their lean, imposing build. South African mastiffs, over two feet tall, snarling, growling, and very hungry-looking. They tore towards Bald. The first dog was forty metres away, the other a few paces behind, when Bald frantically lined up his shot. By the time he'd managed to squeeze off a few shots, the leading dog had halved the distance from him. He popped four rounds into its ugly fucking face. The animal whined, skidded to a halt, pissing and shitting itself as it pawed at thin air.

The next moment the second mastiff – eighty kilograms of pure muscle – was on Bald. It sprang forward with its powerful hind legs and the impact knocked him onto his back. His fall was cushioned by the snow, but he dropped the Beretta. Instinctively he thrust his hands up to the animal's neck before it could sink its teeth into his face. Snarling with fury, the dog tried to wriggle free of his grip. Bald twisted its neck hard with an anti-clockwise jerk, like turning a rusted wheel. The mastiff yelped. The life drained out of it. Bald rolled the dead weight off his chest and picked himself up. Watching the dog die, he told himself that from now on he was a cat man.

He scooped up the Beretta and headed for the farmhouse. On the way, he stopped at Beanie Hat and knelt down beside him. He ejected the empty clip from the Beretta M9 and inserted the fresh one. Pulled the slider back. He was sure Klich was not armed, but he didn't want to take any chances. He didn't know why Klich had fled to the farmhouse. Maybe he had a gun stashed in there somewhere? Maybe he just had nowhere else to go.

Fifty metres became forty, then thirty. He willed his legs to go quicker.

This is it, Bald told himself as he approached the farmhouse. This is where the mission ends. Right here, right fucking now. A burning sensation seared across his guts. Like someone had stabbed him with a branding iron. He touched a hand to his shirt. Felt a circle of warm, sticky blood. The wound had split open and was bleeding.

Fucking Aziz. Fucking Land too.

He applied pressure to the gauze dressing. He felt giddy and nauseous. He was dehydrated. His jaw was lumpy and swollen like Plasticine. And the cold lashed him, freezing and burning hot at the same time, scalding his cheeks and stinging his neck and hardening the blood from his wound. Ten metres to the farmhouse now. Bald was collapsing through the steep snow. Falling into each step. His body begging him to stop, his mind willing him to go on. His feet crashed through the fluffy top layer of snow, the slush underneath squelching and sucking at the soles of his shoes. Like he was treading grapes.

As he drew near he could see just how dilapidated the farmhouse was. The walls were warped, all the visible windows were smashed and the terracotta-tiled roof had caved in, pulling down part of the stone façade with it and exposing some of the beams. Cracked blocks of stone were heaped to one side of the house, like a collapsed staircase. The only new thing was the hefty padlock on the front door, left undone by Klich.

There's fuck all here, Bald thought. Maybe Klich hadn't planned to come here at all. Maybe he'd hoped his men would dispose of Bald, and now he'd run out of options. Doesn't matter, I've cornered Klich.

Bald heard a scream. Blood rushing through his ears, he yanked the door open and stumbled into a gutted kitchen. Rusted pots and pans were stacked on the stove. Broken china, piles of dust, and the bones of dead rats littered the stone floor. The air was filled with a foul stench, like burnt hair and faeces. Flies buzzed around Bald's face. He couldn't tell where the scream had come from. He heard the scramble of footsteps from somewhere in the farmhouse, then a door slam. A hallway led off from the right-hand side of the kitchen and Bald figured Klich had bugged out in that direction.

He was about to give chase when he caught sight of something in his peripheral vision. Something that caused him to stop dead in his tracks.

A body was hanging from a ceiling beam at the other end of the room, swaying slightly on a short length of rope. Bare feet suspended six inches from the ground and smeared in dirt and blood. Legs mauled. Torso slashed open like a bag of coffee beans. Entrails slopped on the floor at his feet. Bald studied the face by the waxy moonlight that poured through the great hole in the ceiling where the roof had fallen in. He took a step towards the body. Prodded a leg with the muzzle of his Beretta M9. The body swayed a little more, like a pendulum, and the face sagged forward and caught the moonlight.

Bald didn't move. He listened to the sound of death reverberate around him, the flies buzzing and the dust crackling underfoot. He felt his bowels doing somersaults. He looked at the face of the corpse dangling in front of him.

It didn't belong to the man he'd been sent to kill.

But to an old friend.

thirty-seven

2150 hours.

Joe Gardner had been dead longer than a little while, thought Bald. His skin had a puffy and mottled texture that reminded him of the layers of fat on the morbidly obese people who appeared on reality TV shows. His eyes were wide open, but only because someone had cut off his eyelids. His hands were bound behind his back with a length of rope and there were burn marks and knife cuts on both his forearms. His legs had been chewed on by the dogs: Bald could make out the teeth marks on the calves. The dogs had also been feasting on the disembodied intestines, and thick streaks of blood running from the anus told Bald that someone had buggered Joe Gardner, either before or after he left this earth. Joe was naked except for a note pinned to his abdomen. Bald unpinned the note from his old mucker. It was just a crude scribble on a scrap of lined paper, written in thick letters so the message wouldn't be lost amid the pints of blood seeping from the corpse.

Bald raised the note to the moonlight. 'Do not follow me,' he read. 'Or follow – and join your friend. Your choice.'

He felt his body go rigid, rage gripping him like hands around his throat. He screwed the note into a ball and tossed it at the stove. It fell to the floor not far from a second body sprawled there. Bald rushed over to the body. Clocked the black hair and black skin. Lowered the Beretta. Stooped down beside Odessa. She wasn't dead. Her lips were purple and swollen and she had cuts on her cheeks and nose. Her wrists and ankles were bound up with parachute cord. She looked like the face of a domestic abuse awareness campaign. She coughed and spat blood, looked up at Joe and gasped.

'Oh, Jesus, no. Joe—'

Bald looked Odessa hard in the eyes. 'What the fuck happened?'

'Klich was here a minute ago.' Odessa tried to sit up. Grimaced in pain. 'He found out I was working for Six. His people brought me here. They said he was going to kill me. Said he'd have fun with me, the same way he'd had fun with Joe. You got here just in time. He left the moment he heard you arrive.'

Bald fumed as he picked out details in the darkness. He had initially assumed that the kitchen had been a dump. Now he made out a table that held knives, a screwdriver, pliers, a blowtorch, and a battery-powered drill with a range of bits. Several meat hooks hung from the beams overhead. In one corner of the kitchen stood a garrotte chair. Another table was crusted with old blood and had a vice attached to one end. A chainsaw lay in another corner, the teeth coated in blood. Some of the bones on the ground were too large to belong to rats, Bald thought.

'What the fuck is this place?' he whispered.

'Klich's personal torture chamber,' Odessa replied. 'He likes blood—'

'And Joe? Klich did this to him?'

Odessa nodded painfully. 'Klich said you had crossed him and fucked up his plans, and now he was going to take out his rage on the only friend you had. But I didn't know he meant . . . this.' She dragged herself to her feet and evil-eyed Bald. 'This is all your fault.'

'Fuck that,' Bald rasped at her. 'I didn't carve up Joe. Your mate Klich did.'

'Only because he knew you were chasing him. We had the situation under control. We were going to detain Klich quietly. No gun battles in the Alps.' Odessa sniffed up a tear. 'No Joe hanging from a rope.'

Bald steeled his gaze at Joe. Took one last look at him. He didn't feel sad. He didn't feel anything at all, except perhaps a slight regret that he hadn't been here to see him suffer. All the shit Joe had done to him, he figured they were about even now. Enjoy the afterlife, you prick, Bald silently said to the corpse.

Then he strode into the hallway, Odessa at his back, shouting, 'Wait. Where are you going?'

Bald gripped his Beretta M9. 'I'm going to find Klich and kill him.'

'No! You can't!'

Bald made a face at Odessa. 'Bollocks! I'm about to become a hero.'

'By killing Klich?'

'That's about the size of it.'

'That man is an MI6 asset. He is to be protected at all costs.'

'That's where you're wrong, love. I have orders from the very top. Klich needs to die.'

'Your orders are wrong.'

Bald had no time to argue this shit with Odessa. He had a mission to complete. A life to take. The hallway was damp and cold. Up above it was where the roof had collapsed, and tiles had fallen through down and shattered on the floor. The door at the far end of the hallway stood open. As Bald rushed towards it he was assaulted by the incessant *whump-whump* of a helicopter from some distance behind the farmhouse.

Klich was getting away.

As the slow *whumps* accelerated into a staccato rhythm, Bald decided not to head back through the kitchen. Beyond the door he found himself in a large room strewn with trash and human skulls and a few scurrying rats. On the far wall, five metres away, was a substantial door that had to lead to the back of the building. The *whump-whump* grew louder and faster, telling Bald that the helicopter was almost powered up for lift-off and he must get a line of sight on Klich in the next few seconds.

Bursting through the door, he emerged in the back yard of the farmhouse, to see an old well with a few snow-covered birch trees behind it. A set of footprints in the snow led past the well and away from the house. They continued through the purplish snow until, two hundred metres away, the snow itself seemed to be swallowed up by a pitch-black hole.

Dread in his guts, he made for this black mouth. Klich had to be there. Out of sight. Bald lowered the Beretta and staggered on. I won't let him get away. Can't. This has to end here and now.

Ninety metres from the black hole, Bald could see it was a crevasse. Then a sudden wind whipped up, blasting him to a standstill. He lowered his head and shielded it with his hands. Just beyond the crevasse, powerful rotor blades were lifting a Eurocopter into the sky, the same model Bald had seen earlier. The blades whipped the trees all around him into a frenzy, reducing his world to a snowstorm.

Then the wind dropped and Bald looked up at the chopper. Through the window of the front cabin he could see a figure in each of the two pilot seats, lit up by the light from the control panel.

On the left sat Viktor Klich.

The oligarch looked pleased with himself. He seemed to be staring at something in the distance. Then he noticed Bald and looked down at him. Bald seethed, powerless to stop Klich. The pilot pitched the Eurocopter forward. The nose dipped and the tail fin lifted as the chopper entered translational lift, preparing to commence forward flight. Last thing Bald saw was Klich turning the wave into a middle finger.

Flipping him the bird.

thirty-eight

Courchevel, France. 2211 hours.

His eyes lingered on the Eurocopter as it thundered away from the farmhouse, its lights blinking high above the mountain slope. John Bald felt the arctic cold sucking the blood out of his face and his hands. The lights quickly shrank to pinpricks. Then they disappeared into the mouth of darkness cloaking the jagged mountain range.

Viktor Klich was gone.

Bald stared into the darkness, his fingernails almost drawing blood from the palms of his left hand. He saw failure written in the sky. Bald had been sent to Courchevel to kill an oligarch, and he had cocked it up. By rights Klich should be in a coffin by now. Instead he'd bugged out in a helicopter, leaving Bald turfed out on his arse on a plateau high above the village with nothing but spent brass and dead muscle for company.

And snow, he reminded himself. Lots of fucking snow.

His survivor instincts kicked in. Told him, you need to get the fuck out of here.

He unclenched his fists and trudged through the snow towards the rear of the farmhouse. The sky had cleared a little and the snow glinted on the ground like tiny grains of glass. Somehow it felt colder inside the ramshackle building than outside. His facial muscles hardened like concrete as he strode down the hallway and back into the debris-strewn kitchen.

He passed the tables with their torture instruments, the meat hooks hanging from the wooden beams, and Joe Gardner, hanging limp and dead, from one of the beams. Bald looked down again at the pile of guts on the floor beneath his old mate's feet, then glanced up at him and smiled to himself.

'Fuck you,' he said.

Then he turned to Odessa Stone. The MI6 agent scraped herself off the floor, eyes trained on the Beretta M9 semi-automatic Bald gripped in his right hand. She said nothing. Just stood there looking about as good as it was possible for a woman to look after she'd had the crap kicked out of her. Which was still pretty good, thought Bald. She had a body ripped straight off a Hed Kandi cover and in normal circumstances her arse would have had him foaming at the mouth. But these were not normal circumstances. Since rocking up in the French Alps things had gone from bad to FUBAR for Bald. He'd been ambushed by Russian heavies and screwed over by Odessa, and his handler at the Firm, Leo Land, had tried to kill him from a thousand miles away courtesy of a mobile phone wired with explosives. A heavy had confiscated the phone from Bald and ended up with a hole in the side of his head. Now Bald needed an exit strategy, and Odessa Stone was his only option. He drew the Beretta level with her head. Her eyes bulged in their sockets to twice their normal size.

'What the fuck do you think you're doing?' she said.

'You're going to get me out of here,' said Bald. 'Set me up with your handler.'

Odessa shot him a look that could skin a rat.

'Or what? You'll kill an unarmed MI6 agent? I don't think so.'

'Try me,' said Bald in a voice that told her he meant it. 'Where's the RV?'

'With my handler?'

'No, with Justin fucking Bieber. Of course your handler.'

Odessa pursed her lips. 'Geneva,' she said after a beat. 'My orders are to report to Room 219 at the Metropolitan Hotel. But only once Klich had been successfully handed over to the extraction team.'

Bald said, 'You and me are going on a little trip.'

Odessa made a puzzled face. 'Why do you want to meet with my handler?'

'Land is out of reach. I don't have any way of contacting him.'

'So?'

'I want to get paid.'

Odessa laughed disbelievingly. 'You're crazy. The Firm won't pay you a penny.'

'Land showed me a letter from your big chief,' Bald said. 'Signed off and everything. What I'm owed. Half a million and a home on a nice island called Madeira. They'll pay up in full, or I'll make them sorry.'

Odessa's eyebrows shot up so high they almost hit the roof. 'You turned a top-secret Six mission into a train wreck. I think that probably terminates any agreement you might have had, tough guy.'

Bald said nothing. Odessa rolled her eyes as her confidence grew. 'What exactly *was* your mission, John? Arrest Viktor Klich? ' She took a step closer. '*Kill* him?'

'That's about the size of it.'

'And how's that going?' She nodded towards the back of the farmhouse. 'You let him slip right through your fingers, but only after you'd shot up half of Courchevel. You seriously think that the guys at Six are going to reward you for a botch job?'

Bald stewed inside. He clenched his left hand into a rock.

'*You* fucked up,' he snapped. 'Not my fault. If you hadn't interfered, I would've delivered the oligarch to the pearly gates by now. I came here, followed orders, did my part. Whatever happens next is not my fucking problem.'

Odessa folded her arms across her damn fine chest.

'What a convenient motto to live by.'

Bald pointed at the front door with the M9. 'We can take my wheels.' He recalled the Mégane ditched at the side of the road on the outskirts of Courchevel. Ten hours ago. Felt like ten years ago.

His heart thumped furiously. Echoes played out in his throat. Every second he spent in that farmhouse put him at risk of capture. Earlier in the day the village below had been crawling with operators from GIGN, the National Gendarmerie Intervention Group. Bald had to assume the French SF operators would have heard the gunshots from the shootout at the farmhouse. Sounds always carried loud and clear on a crisp night. Any minute now, Bald figured, the GIGN fuckers would be all over the farmhouse like Romanian lap dancers over a stag party.

Odessa said, 'I'm sorry about Joe.'

'Don't be. He was a spineless cunt. None of the lads in the Regiment ever respected him. He always played it safe. Never questioned the ruperts. He made his choices. Fuck him.'

Odessa shrugged. 'You'll be joining him soon enough, I guess.'

Bald frowned. 'What the fuck are you talking about?'

'Klich has seen your face,' Odessa replied, lowering her eyes to the floor. 'You know why they call him the Elephant Man?'

'Because of his good looks?'

Odessa shook her head. 'Because he never forgets. Sooner or later Klich will find you, John. And he'll do the same things to you.'

They took a winding route to the Mégane. Getting out of Courchevel was easier than Bald had anticipated. The GIGN team had simply melted away from the village. Bald wondered aloud why they had suddenly fucked off.

'You mean you didn't know?' Odessa said.

'Know what?'

'The GIGN guys were here to guard the President.'

'As in American?'

Odessa shook her head. 'As in Russian. He always takes his New Year holiday in Courchevel. Everyone knows that.'

'Not me,' said Bald. He didn't follow politics, any more than he read the papers or drank chai lattes. He imagined there were pleasant people who lived in pleasant towns with pleasant cars and pleasant gardens who did that kind of thing. But that life wasn't for Bald. It had never even been an option.

'The President checked out of Courchevel early,' Odessa continued. 'Some kind of threat made against him. At least that's what I heard.'

She kept the Mégane to a steady 110 k per hour. Bald slouched beside her with the Beretta M9 on his lap. Twenty kilometres before the Swiss border, he ordered her to pull into a service station and drive on past the petrol pumps and the restaurant to the parking lot. The lot was empty except for a couple of long-haul lorries, and Bald told Odessa to park some way from these. He unbuckled his belt and before she had a chance to escape he bound her to the steering wheel by her hands.

'You're just gonna leave me here while you go and stuff your face?' Odessa said.

'I'll bring you back a doggy bag.'

'But I need to pee.'

'Too bad,' Bald said, stroking her cheek with his thumb. Then he pocketed the keys and debussed from the Mégane, stuffing the M9 down the front of his jeans with the butt concealed under his shirt. He moved across the parking lot at a brisk pace. The asphalt was slick and greasy and the air was heavy with the smell of hard recent rain. He passed the lorries and swept through the door of the restaurant. It was as

drab and weary as the humourless exterior suggested. Kind of
like France itself, he thought. A miserable Eastern European
waitress with a nose like a knuckle directed him to the toilets
at the rear of the joint. A cheap clock on the wall was broken,
the hands permanently set to 2.18. Bald made his way past a
table loaded with grim-faced lorry drivers, a thought twisting
like a screwdriver at the back of his skull.

Why hadn't Land told him about the Russian President?

Bald shrugged off the thought and locked himself in a cubicle. Lowering the seat, he sat down and attended to the gauze
dressing on the lower right-side of his chest. He peeled up
a corner and got a whiff of mouldy cheese coming off the
wound. Removing the dressing, Bald counted four sutures
threaded across his ruptured flesh. They were black and sore.
Pus seeped out of the gaps between the stitches. The wound
was in a dire state and he was at risk of septicaemia if he
didn't get proper medical attention soon. He would make it a
priority after meeting the handler. Money first. Health later.
Another motto Bald lived his life by. He splashed soapy water
over the wound and wiped away the seepage with a clutch of
paper towels. Then he replaced the dressing and returned to
the Mégane. He released Odessa, ignoring the scowl she was
shooting at him.

They hit the road. Bald kept the Beretta concealed for the
border crossing. Odessa stuck to the back roads, steering
clear of the motorways where the Swiss border patrol units
were known to prowl. They made it over the border at two
in the morning. No one gave them trouble. Dawn was still
just a rumour by the time they rolled into Geneva. A swirl of
colours brewed on the horizon, below the charcoal night and
bleached stars.

The streets were cold and empty. Odessa steered past
luxury watch retailers and fashion brands Bald had never
heard of. They snaked by a dilapidated train station splashed

with graffiti, a double-dozen Eastern European men huddled outside. They had the look of illegals, their hands stuffed in their pockets and their collars popped against the cold, their eyes hungry and grey as they waited for the builders' vans to roll up, desperate men on the lookout for dirty, untaxed work. Europe's dark economy, working away in the hours before well-dressed bankers rose from their duck-feathered slumbers and commuted to their open-plan offices.

It was twenty past three when they crossed the Mont-Blanc Bridge over Lake Geneva. The mountain itself brooded in the distance. Bald spotted the Jet d'Eau near to where the River Rhône enters the lake. In the gloom it was doused in alarm-red artificial light, spurting water a hundred and forty metres into the air, like blood fountaining out of a slit throat.

Then he spotted the Metropolitan Hotel on the other side of the river. It looked like the kind of place exiled African despots and cokehead Saudi princes liked to call home, with its name in gilt letters and a fleet of Bugattis and Ferraris on parade in the front car park. The façade was the colour of vanilla ice cream and intricately detailed, and the windows of each room gave onto a private balcony. Odessa arrowed the Renault into a car park just south of the Metropolitan. She and Bald left the car and approached the gilt-plated revolving doors.

Inside the lobby, oil paintings of Lake Geneva and the Mont Blanc *massif* lined the pastel-coloured walls. Chandeliers bathed the marble floor in diamanté light. A pale receptionist was working the graveyard shift. Odessa checked in using her fake passport and driving licence. She paid with an AmEx, black. Then she and Bald rode the Otis lift to the Royal Suite on the second floor. Bald checked out her arse in the mirror. Odessa caught him and smiled a cheeky smile.

Every piece of furniture in the suite looked like it cost more than Bald had earned in ten years in the Regiment.

The bedroom had a four-poster bed, the frame studded with Swarovski diamonds, and a bottle of Bollinger was chilling in an ice bucket on a side table. French windows overlooked the lake. The room smelled of perfume and the air tasted like the pages of antique leather-bound books. Whatever cutbacks the MoD had been making, they hadn't affected the Firm's expenses account, Bald told himself. If he hadn't been a man on the run, he might have sat down and enjoyed a glass of bubbly. But he had a mission to complete, a cheque to cash. A new life to begin. He cast his bloodshot eyes over the lake. It was dark and smooth, like black ice. He tucked away his Beretta in the drawer of the bedside table while Odessa was in the lounge, distracted by a message on her iPhone.

'Where's the handler?' Bald said, turning back to speak to her.

Odessa frowned at the screen for a second or two before looking up at him. 'We're early,' she said. 'The RV's not until 1500 hours.'

Bald was about to ask who she was texting when she smoothly tucked her phone into her hip pocket and flashed that sweet smile at him again as she catwalked over to him. He was hypnotized by the elegant swagger of her hips. He forgot all about the doubts digging like metal hooks at the back of his mind. He forgot about the pain of his wound. Odessa carried on swaying towards him. She stopped right in front of his face with her tits four inches from his chest. Her warm, easy breath caressed his lips. This close, Bald could smell her. Strawberry and cheap perfume. A dirty smell. A good smell. Her eyes were black but somehow they glowed. Looked at him, into him.

Odessa whispered, 'I wonder what we can do . . . to pass the time?'

She brushstroked a hand down his side and rested it lightly on his waist. Bald tensed up a little. She pulled him closer.

They touched at the hips. Bald had the kind of hard-on that could crack a safe.

'Any ideas, mister?'

Bald grinned. 'One or two.'

'I can think of a hundred,' Odessa replied sweetly as she reached down to his groin.

Fuck me, he thought, it hasn't taken long for Odessa to change her tune. He'd been hoping to work some of the John Bald magic on her before he sodded off to Madeira. From the moment he'd first set eyes on Odessa in Venezuela he'd been sorely tempted to pump his muck into her. But he could feel his jaws swollen like he'd been chewing on a bag of stones, and he knew from examining his face in the mirror at the service station that his forehead was purpled and bruised and his left eyelid was all kinds of puffy. He could smell his own potent stench of sweat and gunpowder. Maybe she likes it rough? he wondered.

She took his hands and planted them on her breasts. Bald stopped wondering.

'I need to get you out of those clothes, mister,' Odessa said.

Her fingers teased his balls as she leaned into him, standing on the tips of her dainty toes and pressing her lips tight to his. For a second Bald thought she was going to kiss him. But instead she started licking the cuts on his lips.

Odessa did a little pirouette. Gave him a sneak preview of her rack. She slipped out of her clothes and revealed a white-lace bandeau bra and matching hipster briefs. Nothing but a thin strip of satin between Bald and a legendary shag.

He pulled her close to him.

Bald woke up with the sun wafting like cigar smoke over his eyes and the pain from his wound buttoned down to a dull ache. He cast his eyes down at his dressing. Odessa had patched him up in his sleep. A bunch of sterile plaster wrappers lay on the bedside table. He patted the dressing and checked his Aquaracer: 1414. Forty-six minutes until the RV. Time for round two. He stretched his recharged muscles and rolled over towards Odessa. But she wasn't there. Her head had left an imprint on a well-fluffed pillow. Then he heard the hiss of a shower, and saw the trail of clothes leading from the bed to the closed bathroom door. He smiled. Sex in the shower it is, then, he thought.

He was all set to jump out of the bed when Odessa's iPhone 4S trilled.

Bald hesitated. Odessa had left the mobile on the floor beside her discarded knickers. Puzzled, Bald rolled out of bed and knelt down by it, craning his neck at the display. There was no name on the screen, just the number. Bald noticed the +44 at the start and felt a coldness rising in his guts as he recognized the following sequence of digits at once. He mouthed the name of the caller.

Leo Land. His direct line.

The warmth drained out of Bald, from his head to his toes. He grabbed the phone and stepped across the bedroom so that Odessa wouldn't hear him. He kept one eye rooted to the bathroom door as he tapped the 'Answer' icon. A fuzzy sound scattered down the line. Then silence, followed by a hesitant voice.

'Yeah?' said Bald.

Land sighed like a pressure valve being released. 'Thank God,' he said in his silvery voice. 'I tried this number as a last resort. I've been trying to get hold of you for the last six hours. Where the hell have you been, man? What happened to your phone?'

Rage boiled inside Bald. 'It blew up.'

Land paused. Then he said, 'What the hell are you talking about?'

'You tried to fucking kill me.'

Land laughed. 'Nonsense.'

'The phone you gave me was booby-trapped. You were waiting for me to finish the op. Soon as I'd put the call in to the Firm, the phone would blow up next to my ear. Turn my skull to mush.'

Land made a sound like he was snorting up a pile of toot. 'That's ridiculous. Why would I do such a thing? No, John, you've got it wrong.'

'You gave me the phone. You must've known it was fucking rigged.'

'Think it through, John,' Land said impatiently. 'Who else could have had access to the phone? Hmm? Odessa, perhaps? She could've tampered with it while your back was turned. Replaced the battery. Did you consider that at all?'

'Odessa? The fuck are you talking about?'

Bald shifted on the balls of his feet. Odessa was taking her time in the shower. Steam puffed out from the crack between the bottom of the door and the fine carpet.

'Listen,' Land said. 'I'm afraid there's no time to rake over old coals. You have to trust me. I'm calling to help save your life. Presumably Miss Stone is nearby, given that you've answered her mobile?'

Bald pursed his lips.

'She's around,' he said vaguely, narrowing his eyes at the bathroom door.

'Good. Then there's no time to lose. You have to do it now.'

'Do fucking what?'

There was a pause and a crackle came down the line like metal being crushed. For a moment Bald thought the signal had cut out. Then Land came back and said, 'You have to kill her, old bean. You have to kill Odessa.'

thirty-nine

The shower hissed. The line hissed. The hisses mingled in the air and built up a relentless pressure in Bald's temples. He'd been free of migraines since the clusterfuck at Caracas. Now they returned again. Dim footsteps in his skull, clicking and clocking. Getting closer and closer.

'John? Are you still there?' Land said.

Bald clenched his jaw. 'Here.'

'Listen to me. Odessa is working for the Russian security services. They sent her to lure Klich into a trap. They badly want him back in Russia.'

The hissing ceased. Bald popped his eyelids.

'Odessa told me she's with the Firm,' he said. 'I'm here to meet her handler.'

'She's lying to you, you bloody fool. Odessa never had a job with Six. Not in procurement, not in the field. Not even as a bloody temp. She's pulled the wool over your eyes.'

Bald didn't reply. Blotches nudged at the corners of his vision. The lights seemed impossibly loud and sharp, like knife points. Any moment now Odessa would step out of the shower. He had to get off the phone.

'Odessa led me to Klich at the chalet,' Bald said. 'Why would she have helped me if she was working for the Russians?'

'She knew you were going to kill Klich. Remember the old adage, John? The one about keeping your enemies closer than your friends? She plans to eliminate you once your guard is down.'

'What about the handler? She said the guy's arriving in about half an hour.'

'Did she give a name?'

Bald said nothing.

'The chap coming to visit you is a cleaner,' Land fumed. 'The kind who works for the Russians. Kills anyone who is a threat. Odessa must be taken out now or you'll end up the same way as Joe.'

The handle of the bathroom door twisted.

'Kill her,' Land snapped. 'Now.'

Bald tapped 'End Call' and quickly hid the phone behind his back as the bathroom door flew open. A mouth of steam coughed out into the bedroom. Bald watched Odessa slink out of the steam, naked and brown and curved in all the right places. She leaned slenderly against the door frame, her right arm draped across her breasts, a delicate hand paused between her legs.

Land's order was scratching at the base of Bald's skull. 'Kill her.'

'You really should try that shower,' said Odessa. 'It's so refreshing.'

Veins of water trickled down her breast and dripped to the stone floor.

'You look good naked, John. Come here. Join me.'

Bald wanted to move. Didn't. He said, 'Your handler. What's his name?'

Odessa angled her head at him, smooth, relaxed, not flinching at all. 'Why do you ask?'

Bald shrugged. 'Just wondered.'

'You'll find out soon enough,' she said playfully. Then she tossed her hair back and winked at him. 'Are you just gonna stand there or are you actually gonna come into the shower?'

Bald didn't like the way Odessa had ducked the question about the handler. Only one reason why she wouldn't tell me, he thought. She didn't have a handler. Land had to be on the money. Suddenly Bald understood why she had come on to him so aggressively. It wasn't because of his rugged face and Scottish accent. It was because she needed to buy some time with him before the cleaner crashed through the door and brassed him up.

'Give me a minute,' he said, thinking, I really need to change my taste in women.

Odessa blew a kiss at him and slid back through the curtain of steam. The shower spurted into life once more. Bald carefully set the iPhone down next to her knickers. He checked the time: 1430. Thirty minutes until the cleaner rocked up. This could get messy. He didn't have a moment to lose. He retrieved the Beretta from the drawer, the Trinity 9mm suppressor still fixed to the muzzle. Then he fished two thick bath towels from a pile, wrapped one around his waist and gently slipped the weapon between the ample folds of the second. He wasn't sure why he was concealing it. A security against the cleaner? Or because he'd been told to pop Odessa? He kind of liked her. She had a certain way about her. Not elegant. Not classically English. But tough. Feisty. Didn't take shit from anybody. Bald liked that. He still hadn't made his mind up whether to slot her as he tucked the towel containing the pistol under his arm and made for the bathroom.

'Hurry up,' Odessa cooed. 'It's nice and hot.'

Bald stepped through the steam. He found Odessa leaning across the cubicle, adjusting the temperature dial with her left hand and testing the water with her right. The way she was propped, Bald had a grand view of her arse. Odessa glanced back at him and smiled suggestively. He returned the smile with interest as he set the towel with the gun down on the vanitory unit outside the shower. He checked to make sure that the grip of the weapon wasn't visible.

'What took you so long?' Odessa said. 'You're mean, making a woman wait like that.'

'You know what they say, about good things and those who wait.'

'Meanie,' she teased. 'Patience never was my strong point.'

Odessa gently wrapped her arms around his neck and pulled Bald close to her. She pushed her tongue into his mouth and kissed him, hard. She tasted of vanilla. She didn't let go. She kept on kissing him, her thighs stroking against his. She coaxed him into the shower, pushing him back against the wall. She sank to her knees. Hot water gushed furiously down over her head as she tickled his balls. Bald closed his eyes. Let the tension percolate from his body and gurgle down the drain. For a brief moment he was able to forget about Land and Klich and the mission, and enjoy a blowjob so good it made him want to punch a hole in a wall.

Then Odessa slid away from him and hopped out of the cubicle. Curled her lips as her hair streamed down, caressing her shoulders. Bald came charging out of the cubicle and violently spun her around. She was grinning, thinking this was some kinky new sex game he'd read about in a manual. She went along with it, purring sweetly as her spread her arms across the vanitory unit and placed a hand on her back. Then he spread her legs and cast a hungry look at her snatch. He felt a brief pang of regret. Then the pang faded and he reached across for the towel he'd placed next to her left elbow. He saw her eyes in the reflection of the misted wall mirror, following his hand as he slipped it into the folds of the towel. He saw the smooth lines of her face wrinkle in confusion as he whipped out the Beretta and pressed the tip of the suppressor to the back of her head.

Saw her puzzlement turn to fear.

'No, wait—'

The semi-automatic jolted as Bald depressed the trigger and a round flamed out of the snout. There was a sharp crack as the bullet thwacked into her skull and punched its way through her brain before spitting out between her eyes, spraying a confetti of brain matter and cranium across the mirror. Her legs twisted and buckled. Her head slumped into the sink and made a clunk as it smacked into the porcelain base. Blood spewed out of the exit wound and into the sink. The weight of her legs dragged her upper body down. She slumped into a heap on the stone-tiled floor.

Bald took a step back from Odessa. Kicked her in the ribs to check she was dead. The noise of the discharge had been suffocated by the suppressor and the furious blast of the shower. He switched off the shower and wiped down the bloodied end of the suppressor with a hand towel. Then he put the weapon to one side and laid both the bath towels on the floor to stem the blood gooing out of her skull. He didn't want it to seep under the bathroom door and stain the bedroom carpet. He imagined a maid coming in to clean the room. There would be a minute, maybe even less, between her walking in and seeing a blood stain on the carpet, then opening the bathroom door to find Odessa's body. That minute could prove vital to Bald when it came to making his escape. His hands were lacquered with blood. He scrubbed them at the sink with liquid soap and his fingernails. Then he grabbed the Beretta, returned to the bedroom and shovelled Odessa's clothes under the bed. It was as if she had never set foot in the room. He slipped into his shirt and jeans, then tucked the Beretta down the back of his waistband. Shaped to leave.

He was halfway towards the door when the iPhone vibrated for a second time.

Land again? Bald thought as he picked up the mobile. He'd left it on the floor while he'd been busy clearing away the rest of Odessa's junk. Now he paced over to it and knelt down.

'DANIEL CAVE,' the display showed.

The name was familiar to Bald from a previous assignment with the Firm. Danny Cave was a subordinate to Land, one of his lackeys, with an attitude and haircut lifted from *The Apprentice.* What the fuck does he want? a voice poked Bald in the chest. He didn't know, and he didn't want to know. He let the phone ring out. Knew he had to get out of the hotel before the cleaner arrived. Bolting to his feet, he took one final look around the room. He slipped the iPhone into his pocket and hurried towards the door leading out into the corridor. Figured he'd bug out of the place first before telling Land he'd done the job. And collecting his money.

Bald was almost at the door of the suite when they swung open and a figure burst into the room. The cleaner, he thought as he reached around for the pistol. Then he froze for a numb second as he recognized the figure standing in the doorway.

'John Boy!' Danny Cave said in his throaty Essex accent. He didn't look surprised to see Bald. 'Small world, ain't it?'

'Too small,' Bald replied, burning up inside, wondering what the fuck Cave was doing here. The MI6 man smirked as he stepped further into the lounge. And he had company: two blokes in badly cut suits trying on the tough-guy look. It didn't fit either of them. Bald had woken up next to scarier-looking women in his native Dundee. The stiffs filed into the room after Cave and took up a position either side of him. They were armed with Glock 17 pistols, Bald noted.

It had been a year since he had last laid eyes on Cave. The agent wore a slim-fit blue herringbone suit, a pastel-blue shirt and a pair of black Oxfords. His collar dug into the folds of his neck. It struck Bald that the booze culture of Vauxhall had slowly taken its toll on his physique. Cave had skin like pewter. The fire that used to flicker in his blue eyes had long since petered out. Now they were smoky and weak. His hair had thinned at the front to a wiry few strands. About the only thing that had stayed the same was the toxic aftershave coming off him in waves. He looked and smelled like the kind of guy who sold car insurance. Cave cast his eyes about the lounge as the stiffs closed the door behind them. The one on his right carried a manila envelope.

'Where is she?' Cave said, craning his neck past Bald, peering around the room.

'Where's who?'

Cave swung his eyes to the ex-Blade. 'You know who. Odessa Stone. My agent. She texted me an hour ago. Told me she was holed up here with you. I've been trying to reach her ever since.'

Oh shit, Bald thought. Odessa really was with the Firm. Cave's her fucking handler. I've just slotted an MI6 agent.

'She had to leave,' he said, with a quick glance at the bathroom door. 'Why don't we go grab a coffee somewhere?'

'Coffee? You? Don't fuck me about, sunshine.' A frown tied Cave's eyebrows in a knot above the bridge of his nose. 'She was under orders to keep an eye on you until the cavalry arrived.'

Bald shrugged. 'She left, that's all I know.'

'She didn't say where, or why?'

'I didn't ask. I'm not her fucking handler.'

'For fuck's—' Cave cut himself off mid-rant and sighed. He looked harassed. Bald got a kick out of wiping the smarmy look off his face. But he knew that if Cave or his two mates opened the bathroom door, he was supremely fucked.

'You,' Cave snapped at the stiff on his left. 'Find Stone. I want to know why she's gone AWOL.'

The guy slammed the door as he left. The shudder straightened into a cold silence. Cave swivelled his gaze back to Bald. His famous dental-floss smile had returned.

'You're in big trouble, John Boy. You've spent the past week pissing over a highly sensitive and covert operation. My bosses are going to have your head on a stake and your balls in a vice.'

Bald said nothing. His mouth suddenly felt dry and he could taste the dread surging back up his throat. Tightening his breath. Beads of sweat traced down his back like cold fingertips as Cave marched right up to him.

'Listen to me you inbred Scottish prick,' the agent snarled. 'I'm gonna give you one chance to level with me. You're gonna tell me everything I want to know. Mainly, what business you have with Viktor Klich, and who you're working for.'

'I was following orders,' Bald protested. 'You got a fucking problem, speak to that wanker boss of yours. He's the one who hired me as an asset.'

Cave stared at Bald.

'What boss?' he said quietly.

'Land,' Bald replied. 'Who do you fucking think?'

Cave was white-eyed as he said, 'Leo Land hasn't worked for Six for nearly a year.'

forty

The migraine exploded inside Bald's skull, a tidal wave of sound and fury. He shook his head uncertainly, over and over, and backed away from Cave, as if he could shake the words out of his head. Forget about the nightmare unfolding in front of him.

'Land cleared his desk last Christmas,' said Cave, his face locked in neutral. 'I took his old job. I'm a director now. Know what that means, John Boy? I'm practically your boss.'

Bald blazed up. Someone had doused him in petrol and struck a match. 'Why did Land quit the Firm?'

'He didn't walk. The chief sacked him.'

Bald backed up against the wall. Pins and needles machine-gunned from his elbows to his wrists and riddled through his jaw.

Cave said, 'Ever since the Intelligent Dust scandal, Land has been a dead man walking. It was the worst-kept secret in Whitehall. The top brass spent ages trying to get rid of that stuck-up old bastard. But a stain like Land ain't easy to shift. He's got friends in high places. Old Eton chums.'

Bald closed his eyes, sought refuge in the darkness. *Intelligent Dust.* Memories of his last mission for Land rushed back at him. Then, Bald had been tasked to hunt down and eliminate a sleeper cell attempting to sell a top-secret US technology, Intelligent Dust, to the Chinese. The mission had ended with

Bald and Gardner decimating half the Chinese military at an underground bunker close to the border with Kazakhstan. Gardner had left Bald for dead. But Bald had survived, nursed back to health in a hippie commune in the Kazakh badlands.

'Land carried the can for the mission going sideways,' said Cave. 'In revenge he decided to cash in on the Intelligent Dust and sell it on the black market. To your old mates the Iranians.'

Bald popped open his eyes. Said, 'Impossible. Impossible with fucking bells on. Me and Joe destroyed the stuff in the underground bunker. I rigged the place myself. Nothing would have survived that explosion. Not even a cockroach.'

Cave looked so smug and sure of himself he could probably get a job at Hollister. 'You could've turned the bunker into the next Hiroshima, of all the good it would've done. The Intelligent Dust wasn't in the bunker when you pressed the red button. It had already been removed to a safe location. Land gave the order.'

Bald his eyes widened as he said, 'You think *I* took it?'

Cave said nothing. His eyes saying everything.

'Joe,' Bald whispered darkly.

Cave nodded with his eyes.

'Joe was just following orders,' he said, clearing his throat. 'Land was the one pulling the strings. Soon as the top brass discovered that Joe had handed over the Intelligent Dust to Land, the chief organized a dummy swap. Had a guy posing as an agent with cash to burn. We caught Land with his pants round his ankles.' Cave chuckled to himself. 'You should've seen the look on his face. Looked like he was about to piss himself.'

'Why the fuck would Land sell the stuff to the dark side?' asked Bald.

'Money,' he replied. 'You forget, the modern world makes no sense to an old-timer like Land. He's a dinosaur. He belongs in a world of telegrams and colonies and stiff upper lips. He can't work email. He's not on Facebook. He saw the writing on the wall. Guys like me, we're the future. Old bastards like Land can look forward to a shitty pension plan and a bungalow in Eastbourne. Land figured the Firm owed him more than that, so he decided to cash in on the Intelligent Dust. Planned to use the money to buy a big old slab of real estate in South Africa.'

Cave inspected his fingernails. Then he went on, 'After the chief handed Land his P45, the stuck-up twat vanished off the radar. We thought he might have taken a job in the private sector. Some cushy position in the Emirates. Somewhere he still had friends. Then last week I get a call from the main man at the Venezuelan Justice Ministry and he tells me they got a former SAS legend by the name of Joe Gardner in silver bracelets accused of killing one of their cops. Said he'd been sent there by a Six agent called Leo Land. I tell you, John Boy, when I heard the news I nearly fucking choked on my prawn sandwich.'

Glancing at the bathroom door, Cave said, 'We cut a deal with Gardner in Venezuela. In exchange for making the murder charge disappear, Joe agreed to come on board with Six and help us track down Land. Find out what his game was and bring him down.'

Bald snorted. 'Joe turned fucking snitch.'

'Not a snitch. An informant. Joe's a good man.'

'Was,' said Bald. 'Klich chopped him up in Courchevel.'

'Really?' Cave feigned sadness. A well-rehearsed look, Bald thought. The guy was probably an expert in faking a lot of things. 'There's casualties in every war. But bottom line, mate, Land played you for a fool.' Cave chuckled. 'Thank God you're crap at your job, otherwise Klich would already be six feet under, and we'd be having this conversation through a cell window.'

'Why would Land want the oligarch dead?'

Cave scratched an itch at the nape of his neck. 'He still needs that payday after he missed out on the Intelligent Dust deal.'

To Bald's ears, the faint drone of the fan whirring in the bathroom swelled to the proportions of a jet engine. He needed a drink. He had never needed a drink so badly in all his years. He remembered the Bollinger beside the bed. He brushed past Cave and stumbled into the bedroom and over to the side table. He popped the cork and necked it straight from the bottle. He instantly regretted it. Dry and vinegary. A poofter's drink.

'Land told me Klich didn't kill the girl,' he turned and said slowly, as if trying to clumsily assemble his thoughts in front of him, like pieces of a puzzle.

'Land is full of shit,' Cave said, folding his arms, standing a couple of paces behind Bald. 'Thing is, Klich likes his torture. Gets a kick out of it the way other people get kicks out of porn. Normally he doesn't take it too far. But the parliamentary aide, fuck me. He really went to town on her.'

Bald thought back to the farmhouse, and the torture implements and meat hooks, the human bones scattered like ash over the floor. 'You have proof that Klich butchers women for shits and giggles, but you still want to protect him?'

'Everybody has their vice. The richer you get, the more shit you can indulge in. You get a million, maybe you want to eat caviar for breakfast. You get ten million, maybe you feel like wiping your arse with rabbits. Then, when you get to a hundred million – who knows? Special Brew keeps you happy, John. Torture ticks the same box for Klich.'

Cave clicked his fingers. In the corner of his eye Bald watched the stiff by the door hand him the manila envelope. Cave opened it and fished out some photographs clipped together. He placed these sunny side up in front of Bald. Tapped his index finger on the top one. On the face of Leo Land.

'In case you don't believe me,' said Cave. 'Have a look.'

The snaps showed Land in his best linen suit pressing the flesh with a portly businessman in a black suit, black tie, white shirt, and a chin that drooped down like the tongue of a thirsty dog. The meeting appeared to be on the deck of a boat.

'Know who this is?' Cave said.

'Valery Favorsky,' Bald replied. 'The oligarch who elbowed Klich out of the way so he could snuggle up to the President.'

Cave looked surprised. 'You've done your homework, son.'

Bald necked a hard measure of Bollinger. 'What the fuck is Land doing meeting with Favorsky?'

'He's the middle man. We believe Favorsky set Land up to negotiate with the Russian security services. Doing the President a favour by taking Klich out of the equation. At first they wanted Land to kidnap Klich. Return him to Moscow. Interrogate him in that special way only the Russians can do. But after the shitstorms down in Venezuela, then Dubai, they decided he was better off dead. The order was passed on to Land, and then to you.'

A pain stabbed at Bald's wound. The pain was elastic. Then the elastic snapped, and he swiped a hand across the photos and sent them flying across the room as he rushed for the door.

'Walk away from me and you'll regret it, John.'

Bald stopped. He glared at the stiff. Got a fuck-you grin in return. He spun around and caught Cave stooping to pick up the pictures scattered across the carpet. Anxiety seized Bald. Cave would spot Odessa's clothes under the bed. Bald was about to bolt across to him when the suite door flung open. The second stiff returned wearing a frown. Cave stood upright. Forgot all about the photos. Bald darted past him and scooped them up.

'Well?' said Cave.

'Nothing,' the stiff replied. 'Nobody saw her come or go.'

'Shit! And she's not answering her phone?'

'I can get them to check the security footage?'

'There's no time.'

Cave turned back to Bald. 'You're sure Odessa didn't tell you where she was going?'

'Not even a hint,' Bald said, coolly handing the photos back to Cave.

The agent continued to stare at Bald for a long moment, his lips and eyes twitching at the corners. He snatched the pictures. Harrumphed, then said, 'Grab your things. We're leaving. Now.'

'Fuck off. I'm not going anywhere.'

'Klich is still at large,' said Cave. 'He represents a clear and present danger to our national security interests. His mind is a treasure chest of secrets we need to keep secret. We've got to bring him back to Six before the Russians trap him. And you're going to help.'

'You have your own people,' Bald said. 'Take care of him yourself.'

Cave pinched his shoulders. His lips tightened and his eyes narrowed viciously. 'I don't think you appreciate the situation, John Boy. So let me lay it out for you. You owe the Firm. Walk out of that door, I'll make one call to my boss and an hour from now Interpol will issue a red notice and you'll be the most wanted man in Europe.'

'But why me?'

'My best agent is missing. It'll take time to get another asset reassigned and dispatched. Time that we don't have. But you, mate, you're right fucking here. Really, you don't have a choice and you know it.'

Bald made a face, his gaze fixed on Lake Geneva. Its waters glistened like tin foil. He grimaced as he polished off the Bollinger, burying the migraine under layer upon layer of booze. Footsteps retreated at his back.

'Fuck this,' Cave said. 'I'm busting for a piss.'

Bald spun around. Clocked Cave beating a path towards the bathroom door. He was four or five steps from stepping on Odessa's corpse.

'Fine!' Bald shouted. 'You've got yourself a deal. I'll do it.'

'Good man,' Cave said, walking back to Bald and patting him on the shoulder. His phone buzzed in his pocket. He swiped the display, studied the message. Dislodged a morsel of food trapped between his teeth with a fingernail. 'That was the top brass. Things are moving quickly. Let's go already.'

'Why?' said Bald. 'What's going on?'

'Klich is in Antibes. Hoping to parlay with a friend.'

'I thought he'd run out of friends?'

'He has one left,' Cave said, eyes glinting like polished metal. 'Favorsky.'

forty-one

1520 hours.

As they took the lift down to the ground floor, it seemed a lot more crowded with four bodies than it had with two. Bald dared not look at Cave. He was bricking it about Odessa. His mind insisted on replaying the image of her lying face down in a pool of blood and piss.

The two stiffs led the way through the lobby towards the revolving doors. Cave glanced at his watch. It was a good watch, Bald noticed. A Gucci Timeless number, stainless steel and black. 'Did Land give you the lowdown on Klich and Favorsky?' the agent asked.

'What's to know?' Bald said. 'They hate each other. That's all there is to it.'

Cave shook his head. 'We're talking about Klich, the man who used to be the most powerful oligarch in Russia, and the guy who took his place at the top table. Oligarchs don't hate, John Boy. They scheme. That's why they're rich and you don't have two fucking pennies to rub together.'

'Now you're trying to hurt my feelings.'

'Trying to make you see the light,' said Cave as the four men swept through the reception. Winter sunlight flooded through the lobby windows and spilled across the marble floor. The stiffs marched ahead of Cave and Bald.

'Why did you think Klich went to Courchevel?' asked the agent.

Bald thought back to what Land had told him in Dubai. 'To get away from the Russians.'

'Wrong again. Klich was going to do business with the Russian security chiefs. Not run away from them.'

'Why the fuck would he do that? They want him dead.'

'Ah, but the truth is a little muddier than that. The intelligence he has on Six is a powerful bargaining chip – if he plays his cards right. Klich isn't a wimp. He doesn't run away from things. He reckoned if he could sell the intelligence to Favorsky he might be able to get the security services off his back. You know, do a favour for the President's poodle and work his way back into his good books. Unfortunately for Klich, he was late to the party in Courchevel. By the time he rocked up, Favorsky had already checked out.'

Bald recalled the twin-engined Beechcraft Baron he'd spied taking off from Courchevel airport as he and Odessa had made their approach to the chalet on the mountain. Soon after it had departed, the heavy security presence in the village had melted away.

'When Klich found out that Favorsky had given him the cold shoulder, he was properly hacked off. Took it out on your mate Joe.'

The revolving doors spat Bald and Cave out onto the front steps. The air smelt suspiciously clean in Geneva. Already the stiffs had bombed down to the bottom of the steps, eight paces in advance of Bald.

Cave paused, lifted his head, squinted into the sunshine. 'Three hours ago we received intelligence that Klich had landed his chopper at a helipad in Antibes. Know what's in Antibes, John?'

'Fake tits and suntans?'

'Millionaires' Quay,' Cave said. The stiffs made for an Audi A5 parked behind a row of supercars. 'That's where the super-rich park their yachts and host all-night parties.'

'So?'

'Favorsky has a berth there for his yacht. I say yacht but it's more like a fucking cruise liner. It's called the *Seraya Sowa*. Means "Grey Owl". We believe that Klich has pursued Favorsky to Antibes with a view to having a little talk on his boat.'

Bald watched the MI6 man turn on his heels and thread his way towards the Audi. The stiff who'd carried the manila envelope was now behind the wheel, he and his mate having flat-packed themselves into the car. Bald shuffled slowly behind Cave. The champagne had formed a fog behind his eyes. Thinking on booze. Never a good idea, he remembered. He struggled to marshal his thoughts. They were murky and disparate. Despite the snaps of Land and Favorsky getting chummy, Bald still didn't trust Cave. At least Land was upfront about being a cunt, he decided. Whereas Cave would try to act like your best mate. Now the agent held open the rear passenger door of the Audi and waved for Bald to hop in. In the grating light his features appeared blotchy and waxen. His eyes were tattooed with blood.

'We'll escort you to the airport,' Cave said. 'There's a private jet waiting to fly you across the border. You'll land in Nice around half four. There's a vehicle waiting for you at the airport. It'll have your phone, your gun, expenses, travel documents, the usual. Take you about forty-five minutes to drive to Antibes. Once you're there, your mission is to locate Klich and bring him home in one piece.'

'What about my money?'

Cave blinked. Feigning his fucking innocence.

'I had a deal with Land,' Bald went on, anger surging through him. 'Five hundred grand. A new identity. A house on Madeira.'

Cave looked incredulous.

'Tell me you're joking! What's a soldier like you going to do in a place like Madeira? Drink sangria and play fucking eight holes on the course? Give us a break, mate.'

Bald skimmed his eyes across the lake. Sharp rays of light bounced off the water. 'From where I'm standing, civvie street sounds like paradise.'

Cave went quiet for a moment. Jangled loose change in his trouser pockets, like he had thoughts there instead of coins. Then he nodded repeatedly at Bald. 'Fuck it, ' he said. 'A deal's a deal. You shook hands in good faith with Land that he was acting on behalf of Six. Tell you what. I'll honour our side of the bargain – but only as long as you honour yours. Bring me Klich and you can have the house, the money and that brand-new ID. But a word of warning. You're not built for civvie street. Like all your tribe.'

'I'll take my chances.'

The MI6 agent spun away from Bald and ducked into the back seat of the Audi. Bald did likewise. The driver nosed the car out of the hotel parking lot and joined what seemed to be a procession of limos.

'What do I do once I get my hands on Klich?' Bald asked.

'Notify us on your encrypted iPhone. We'll give you an RV to take Klich to on the outskirts of Antibes. Escort your quarry to the location and we'll take care of the rest. No problems, no complications.' Cave's eyes narrowed like a pair of blinds shutting. 'No fuck-ups this time, John. We need Klich alive to find out what he knows about the Russian intelligence agencies. He has the answers to some questions we've been asking for a long time. He knows who poisoned Litvinenko. He knows who assassinated Bystrov, the journalist shot dead on her doorstep in Islington. He knows about the connections between the oligarchs who are buying up Mayfair and the Russian state intelligence agency. Klich dies, our deal is off the table.'

Geneva's refined streets were replaced by a landscape of primary-colour fields full of grazing cows, with barren roads running alongside them. Switzerland, thought Bald.

No wonder people came here to die. The place was already half-dead.

'How will I know where to find Klich?' he said.

'This is the really beautiful part, mate. We thank Odessa for this. She did right by us before she decided to vanish into thin air. You've seen that metal briefcase Klich has been lugging around?'

'The one filled with secret files?'

Cave nodded. 'Odessa sprayed it with microscopic GPS transmitters when Klich's back was turned. These transmitters are *tiny*. A courtesy from our friends in the US, as a thank you for retrieving the Intelligent Dust. According to the signal we're receiving, Klich is holed up in a hotel in the south of Antibes.'

'Why wouldn't he just head to the yacht for his parlay with Favorsky?'

Cave smiled again, and Bald was sure that the guy had had work done on his teeth. They were whiter than a picket fence. 'The *Seraya Sowa* isn't due to dock until eight this evening, when Favorsky rolls into town from St Tropez. Once a month the guy hosts this legendary party on his boat.' There was an almost wistful look in the agent's eyes as he reeled off the party list. 'Designer drugs, Europop stars, TV presenters—'

'And until then Klich plans to lie low?' Bald thought aloud.

'Normally he'd be less inconspicuous. Hole up in a five-star hotel someplace near to the Quay. But Klich is flat broke. We froze all his assets. He has no bodyguards left. He's running scared. He's barricaded himself in a cheap hotel room. He won't budge until he knows Favorsky is in town.'

Cave glanced back to his phone. Bald had an almost overwhelming desire to grab it and shove it down his smarmy fucking mouth.

The agent went on, 'Your mission is to make your way to the hotel and grab him before Favorsky berths his yacht in

Antibes. Klich has got no bodyguards, so even you can't fuck this one up. And make it quiet. I don't want you going in guns blazing and leaving a bollock-load of corpses in the streets.'

'What about Land?'

The question irked Cave. 'What about him?'

'Is he in custody? I'd love a couple of minutes alone with that cunt.'

'No sign of him,' Cave said quietly as he tucked away his phone and fidgeted in his seat.

'What happens if I clock him in France? He might be going after Klich too.'

Cave didn't reply for a few beats. He stared out of the window, the pale landscape whooshing past. Then he said, 'Do what you like to him. To the Firm, Land is already dead.'

forty-two

Bald rolled into Antibes at dusk, a stark and naked sun at his ten o'clock. He'd bolted down from Côte d'Azur Airport in Nice in good time. An Opel Vectra had been waiting for him at the airport's short-stay car park courtesy of the Firm, along with a Ruger SR semi-automatic handgun and two clips of ammo stowed in the glove compartment, a GPS handheld navigator tucked under the driver seat, a fake British passport in the name of Adam Broady, and a clip of euro banknotes totalling a grand. Traffic had been thin as Bald headed out of Nice along the Promenade des Anglais. The weekend party-goers were still clearing their heads from Friday night and had not yet roused themselves for another night on the tiles. He had cruised down the Route du Bord de Mer, hugging the eastern seaboard of the Riviera as it sloped south towards Antibes.

Thirty-five minutes later he was nudging the car through the warren of narrow streets in Antibes and closing in on Viktor Klich. When he'd pulled over somewhere along Avenue du 11 Novembre to consult the GPS navigator, it had showed Klich still tucked up in the hotel on Rue Joseph Jourdain. The guy hadn't moved in the three hours since Bald had departed Geneva.

Klich wouldn't get away this time, he told himself. No bodyguards, Cave had said. Running scared. He had Klich right where he fucking wanted him.

He felt his pulse thumping in his neck as he turned right onto Avenue Robert Soleau and veered south through the Old Town. He fought an urge to race through the streets with his foot to the floor. Instead he took his time. Speeding through a sleepy coastal town would attract the attention of the cops and the locals, and the last thing he wanted was to have some crusty old prick noticing an Opel going too fast and making a note of the number plate. Sticking to a respectable speed also allowed him to recce the layout of the town, in preparation for extracting Klich to the RV.

Bald steered onto Boulevard du Président Wilson and headed south and west through a maze of concrete apartment blocks with marzipan façades, dirty laundry draped from crumbling balconies. The cars lining the streets were knackered. The streets were comatose. Antibes looked like the kind of place where nobody had a job but somehow everybody had money. At the end of Wilson Bald slung a left onto Boulevard Edouard Baudoin, handrailing the coast all the way south past the Cap d'Antibes and the hundreds of speedboats, all colours, moored at the port. Towards Rue Joseph Jourdain.

Towards Klich.

The sun melted into the Mediterranean. Bald hit the southern tip of Antibes, joining Boulevard John Fitzgerald Kennedy. Next road off that was Jourdain. He instinctively tightened his grip on the wheel as he rehearsed his plan of action for the fiftieth time. Barge into the hotel room. Grab Klich before he can leg it. Push the gun to his chest in case he tries to scream for help. Then escort him to the Vectra.

Bug the fuck out of Antibes. Out of this life.

Three hundred metres along JFK Bald hooked a right onto Jourdain.

He found himself driving a lonely stretch of road that peeled away towards a clump of boulders on the coastline, four hundred metres away. He dropped to sixty-five k per.

The boulders tapered the road, and formed a barrier between it and the sea. About three hundred metres out to sea stood a line of circular stone ruins shaped like half-demolished gun turrets lapped by gentle waves. Umbrella pines straddled the limestone coastline. On the inland side of the road, a thick grove of olive trees was hemmed in by a decrepit stone terrace. A shrill sound pricked his ears. Like a broken police siren stuck on the same note.

Then, a hundred metres ahead, Bald spotted a stone church with slit windows. Pulled up at the side of the road, ten metres before the building, was a Mercedes CLK Coupé, grey. Bald drew over to the side of the road twenty metres behind the Merc, the wail of its horn drilling its way through his cranium.

He checked the navigator. The GPS transmitters in Klich's briefcase were displayed as a pulsing red dot. But that red dot wasn't indicating the hotel any more. Nowhere near it, in fact.

The signal was coming from the Merc up ahead. Bald climbed out of the Vectra and walked cautiously towards it. Navigator in his right hand, Ruger tucked down the waistband of his jeans, beads of sweating dripping down his spine.

When he was ten metres from the Merc, he could make out the silhouette of a head slumped over the steering wheel, and the spider-web crack of a gunshot starring the rear window. The driver's side door was flung open. A shoe was touching the blistering tarmac, as if the guy had been stepping out of the car at the precise moment someone had pulled up alongside and capped him.

The horn was blaring ever more maddeningly inside Bald's head. Now he was a few metres from the Merc, he could see blood and brain matter splattered over the inside of the windscreen. A stench of piss and shit rammed his nostrils. The driver had obviously voided his bowels on his way over to the dark side. Bald felt a searing stab of anger in his guts. All this way, he thought. All the shit I've been through, and it comes down to this.

He stopped beside the Merc and peered inside. Checked out the features of the head resting its cheek on the steering wheel. A hot wave of relief flushed through him.

The man with the hole in his head was not Viktor Klich.

He was dressed in the uniform of a chauffeur. His suit was cheap and black and his shirt formally white and now stained red. He had a thin moustache and thinner hair, gnarled hands and a head with a gaping exit wound on his left cheek an inch or so below the eye. His eyes were dim and his mouth was open in mild horror.

Bald's relief quickly turned to anger at losing track of the oligarch. And the constant racket of the horn was driving him nuts. He shoved the dead man off the wheel. His body slumped to the right and made a squelch as it thudded against the gear-shift. Silence at last. Bald pinched his nostrils and scoped out the inside of the car. On the back seat he spotted Klich's metal briefcase, the handcuffs lying on top of it. He walked round to the rear door, opened it and flipped the lid of the case.

Empty.

Then where the fuck is Klich? Right at the moment that thought drummed its fingers on his temples, a gust of wind rushed in from the sea and Bald heard a heavy door banging at his one o'clock. He looked up and clocked one of the church's double doors flapping back and forth.

Klich has to be in there. Nowhere else for him to run.

Bald crept towards the church. It was built of massively thick rubble walls with a semi-circular arched doorway and an eroded wooden-tiled roof. Decorative carvings of angels armed with swords and spears had been partially eroded by the salty air. A plaque on the wall to one side of the doors declared the church a World Heritage Site. Named it as the Church of St Jérome. Bald had never heard of it.

He crept up to the entrance. Pricked his ears for any sound of movement within. Hearing nothing, Bald cranked it open and inched inside.

forty-three

Killing his breath in his throat, Bald cast a steady eye down
the aisle. The church was laid out in the shape of a crucifix, with a pulpit at the far end and richly decorated masonry
columns to either side of the main aisle, eight each side, each
column standing thirteen metres tall. Exposed timber beams
extended right across the high ceiling. Bas-reliefs adorned
the walls. The main aisle was twenty metres long from the
entrance to the rear wall, behind the pulpit. Stained-glass
windows depicted saints and angels and reminded Bald of the
Protestant churches down the back streets of Glasgow. The
air was cold and damp, the light gloomy.

The sound of breathing, light and hurried, reached Bald.
He felt under his black T-shirt for the Ruger. The semi-automatic pistol was the SR9 compact model chambered for
the 9x19mm Parabellum cartridge. For once, thought Bald,
the Firm had come up with the goods. The Ruger was ideal
for his purposes, a weapon tailor-made for the concealed-
carry market. It weighed just six hundred grams and came
equipped with enhanced-contrast three-dot iron sights, and
unlike the limited-round magazines of other concealed-carry
guns, this Ruger compact held seventeen rounds to a clip. A
grip adaptor welded to the underside of the clip accommo-
dated the extra length of the clip when slid into the mag feed.
Bald had two clips. One inserted into the mag feed, another

stashed in his hip pocket. A total of thirty-four rounds of ammunition – more than enough for the job of extracting Klich, he thought as he listened to the breathing echo off the ceiling.

He stifled his own breath and stood his ground, wary about moving forward and exposing himself to a potential shooter. Slowly retrieving the Ruger from his waistband, he wrapped the fingers of his right hand around the stippled grip. The breathing, he now realized, was coming from the aisle leading off to the left of the central aisle. Gripping the Ruger hard, he crouched low and shuffled towards the sound. Eyes running over the shadows, finger tensing the trigger. Blood rushed in his ears. Less than ten metres ahead, to his left, he saw a confessional cloaked in shadows.

The breathing came from inside that booth.

Bald froze. Silently bringing the Ruger to bear in a two-handed grip, he edged along the main aisle and into the left one, moving as fast as he could without making a sound. He trained the open sights on the confessional, eyes peeled for the slightest motion. Now he stopped in front of it. The breathing sounded slight as it seeped through the wooden latticework. Then it skipped a beat.

Tensing his finger on the trigger, Bald yanked open the door of the booth.

'Don't shoot!'

A pair of glassy, spectral blue eyes glowed in the near-darkness as they stared at Bald. They belonged to a face with the slightly stretched look that indicates recent plastic surgery. Viktor Klich was wearing a traditional black Russian shirt, stonewashed jeans and a pair of battered sneakers. His face and neck were polka-dotted with blood. A Makarov semi-automatic pistol dangled limply from his right hand.

'Lose the gun,' said Bald, bringing the oligarch's attention to the Ruger with a flick of his wrist.

Klich looked at the Makarov as if suddenly remembering he was holding it. Then he tossed the pistol aside and it clattered to the ground, the noise filling the void. He looked up at Bald and a light flickered in his eyes as they shifted from dim to hundred-watt.

'I know your face!' he said, emboldened now, and stepping out of the confessional. 'You're the Englishman!' His voice had bite. It had teeth. 'You ignored the warning I left for you in Courchevel, I see.'

Bald recalled the scrawled note pinned to Gardner back at the farmhouse. 'Do not follow me,' it had said. 'Or follow – and join your friend. Your choice.'

'I'm Scottish, not English,' said Bald as a migraine clawed across his temples. His vision blurred. Strange lights crawled and spiralled at the edges of his vision. The stained-glass windows looked incredibly loud and violently bright. He closed his eyes.

'Drink?' said Klich.

Bald opened his eyes and saw the Russian offering him a hip flask. He gratefully accepted the flask and took a long swig. His lips shrivelled at the taste. Vodka. Sour and sharp. Not clean. You could taste the dirt in it. Moonshine, Bald figured. Russians had a taste for that shit. To him it tasted like nail varnish. The drinking ads warned against letting good times go bad. But things had gone bad for Bald a long time ago. It was too late in the day to change now. He took another gulp. Aaahed. Felt the alcohol burn a hole through his guts.

'What gives with the dead guy in the Merc?' he said, handing back the flask.

'My chauffeur.' Klich tipped a stream of vodka down his throat and scowled at the entrance to the church. 'That lying piece of shit screwed me over. Told them where I was.'

'Told who?'

'The Russian security services. They don't like the idea of me paying a visit to Favorsky on his yacht.'

'Smile,' Bald replied. 'I've got good news. Turns out the Firm want you alive. You're coming with me.'

Now Klich had emerged from the confessional, Bald saw that he was about six foot two, a good four inches taller than himself. The oligarch had that shine to him that all mega-rich people had. Like he'd been sprinkled with gold dust. He had the soft-toned physique of a man who hopped on the cross-trainer first thing each morning. And he wore a Blancpain 50 Fathoms, stainless steel with a black dial. Bald knew his luxury watches: the Blancpain cost nearly seven grand, enough to keep him in Special Brew for the next century.

'They'll be here any minute,' Klich said, looking straight at Bald. His voice was more stainless-steel than his watch.

'Where are the files?' Bald said.

Klich did a thing somewhere between a shrug and a nervous tic. 'What do you mean?'

'The briefcase. You cleared it out. Left it in the Merc with your dead fucking chauffeur. So where'd you put the files?'

Klich smiled playfully. 'In a safe place.'

Bald stiffened his grip on the Ruger, centring the oligarch's forehead between the softly glowing sights, fantasizing about pulling the trigger. But Klich stared with an unnatural lack of fear at the gun pointed at his head.

'Are you a man of business, John?'

'How do you know my name?'

'I know a lot about you. I know, for example, that you are a man who can be bought. For the right price.'

Bald was about to reply when the urgent thump of a car door interrupted him. He raced to the church entrance and peered around the left-hand door. There was the Merc, the Vectra twenty metres behind it. And now, a few metres behind that, a BMW X5.

Four guys had just out of the SUV. They wore black jeans, blue T-shirts, and combat boots, and they were kitted out with 9A-91 carbine assault rifles and bulletproof vests. One of the gunmen had gold rings on every finger. He had arseholes for eyes, a shaved head, and looked like he meant fucking business. He motioned silently to the other three and they all advanced towards the Vectra to check it out. Then they walked on cautiously and scanned the Merc.

Bald drew back from the door and turned to Klich. 'What the fuck's going on?'

'The security services. They're here to kill me. And they'll kill you too – unless you listen to my proposal.'

'Go fuck yourself.'

'But you haven't even heard my offer yet.'

'What offer?'

'Five million US dollars.'

Bald nearly jumped out of his bones.

'Five million dollars,' Klich repeated, like it was a chant. 'Today.'

'For doing what?' Bald found himself saying.

'For escorting me to the yacht.'

forty-four

'You're fucking nuts,' said Bald.

'I'm many things,' said Klich. 'But crazy is not one of them.'

Bald puckered his brow and laughed uneasily. 'You just told me that the tough guys outside are here to stop you getting to the yacht. My handler says Favorsky hates your guts. Why the fuck would you want to go knocking on the door of the man who's trying to put you six feet under?'

Klich went to answer but was interrupted by the noise of several sets of feet on the road, along with the decisive click and clatter of clips being slid into mag feed systems and hammers being cocked. Rounds being chambered. The mechanical prelude to organized violence. Bald stole a glance outside again. The Russian agents had seen the dead chauffeur in the Merc. Now they were striding the ten short metres to the church. In ten seconds, four heavily armed men would come bursting through the doors.

'I'm still waiting for your answer,' said Klich.

Five million. Bald rolled the words around his tongue. They tasted good. Money always did. Bald had walked on both sides of the divide. He knew the universal truth about money better than pretty much anyone. Money didn't buy you happiness. But it bought almost everything else.

'Well?' said Klich.

They were flat out of time. Bald hauled the oligarch down the aisle towards the pulpit. The ex-Blade glanced over his shoulder as the church doors were flung back and four shadows flooded through the gap. Two figures breaking left, one breaking right, while the fourth Russian gunman bombed down the aisle and bringing his 9A-91 to bear. A laser aim on the underside of the barrel slashed a bright-red beam through the half-light. Bald shoved Klich into cover behind a thick decorated column as the gunman opened fire and a sound boomed through the church like a bag of spanners being dumped into a forty-gallon drum. Bald ducked down behind the next column. Three rounds walloped into the wall at his five o'clock and tore chunks out of an ancient and probably priceless statue. He made sure Klich stayed shielded behind the column in front of him. The shooter unloaded a second three-round burst in their direction. The rounds punched a hole in Bald's column the size of a gaping mouth, spraying plaster across the aisle. The sound of the discharge – deafening but not sharp – told Bald that the guy was using subsonic ammo. Probably the 9x39mm round. Supersonic rounds made an explosive *ca-rack* when fired, but subsonic gunshots sounded duller and travelled slower over long ranges, making them about as lethal as air rifle pellets at two hundred metres or more. But in the confined killing environment of a church, the 9x39 could be devastating.

Outnumbered. Outgunned. Bald saw at once that unless they got out of the church, both he and Klich would get fucking slotted.

'Stay down!' he barked at the oligarch as he used the lull in gunfire to pivot out from behind the column, his index finger steady on the Ruger's trigger. His thumb flicked the safety catch to the 'off' position, then rested next to Ruger's flaming bird logo stamped on the grip. Bald lined the pistol up with the nearest gunman as he scurried towards cover behind a column on the opposite side of the aisle. The guy was eleven metres away. Bald didn't have time to zero his sights. Aligning the Ruger roughly with the target, he squeezed the trigger.

The semi-automatic jerked powerfully in his grip. A hot round of 9x19 Parabellum fizzled out of the snout in a flurry of flames and gunpowder smoke. The round glanced off some kind of metal control panel fixed to the wall. Speakers high up on several of the columns crackled into life.

'Bonjour,' said a monotone voice, surreal amid the gunfire. 'Guten Tag. Ciao. Hola. Hello.' It continued in English, 'Welcome to the World Heritage Site of the Church of St Jérome.'

Bald unleashed two more shots in quick succession, the Ruger jerking as the first round smacked into a confessional booth on the Russian's side of the aisle, punching a hole in the wood and flinging a whirlwind of shattered wood at him. The gunman squinted as the splinters grazed his face and nicked his arms. Bald's second round was the money shot. It struck the agent in the leg, lodging deep in the meaty flesh of his thigh. The gunman clamped a hand to the wound as blood spurted from his leg. Then he stumbled back a couple of steps. Lost his footing. Dropped. The 9A-91 clattered to the floor.

'The Church of St Jérome was inscribed in the World Heritage List in 1999 and—'

Left hand pawing at his gushing leg, the gunman made a fatal grab for his weapon with his right hand. Bald punished him, shifting his aim down a notch and aiming at him through a gap between the pews. He lined up the Russian's head in the rear sight.

Fired.

The shot felt good. Really good. It looked even fucking better as the round drilled a hole in the agent's neck and exited his temple before embedding itself in a pew. Blood spurted from the ragged hole in his neck.

'First built in 1153, the Church is a precious relic of the Romanesque period—'

A spurt of gunfire thundered over the recorded commentary and smacked into the wall behind Bald, six shots in three evenly spaced two-round bursts. The three other gunmen had hesitated by the entrance and looked on as their mate got slotted. Now they were out for revenge. The rounds ripped into a plaster figure on the wall. Some kind of a serpent swallowing its own tail that Bald had noticed earlier. The half-dozen rounds decapitated the serpent, spraying pebble-sized chunks of plaster across the floor. A mist of incinerated dust hung over the interior of the church. Klich hacked up a ball of phlegm. Bald shunted back behind cover and glared at him.

'The Firm reckons you're broke,' he said in a low voice. 'Said they froze your assets. How do I know you've even got five million to front me?'

'My friend,' Klich scoffed. 'Your MI6 colleagues can only freeze what I already have. Which is not so much now.' A trace of bitterness tinged his voice. 'But they cannot seize what I will earn tonight. Once I get to the yacht and hand over my files, I will be the richest man in Russia.'

Bald shot a frown at the oligarch. Something about the guy reminded him of Del Boy. 'Because of a bunch of files about British state secrets?'

'Don't be so fucking stupid!' Klich spat. 'I have something else to bargain with. Something of much more interest. Something you couldn't possibly get your barbaric head around.'

From the shadows near the church doors Bald could hear the gunmen shouting to each other in Russian. Running through their plan, he guessed. Klich went on, 'As I said, the security services are here to stop me from reaching the yacht. Get me there and I'll richly reward you.'

Bald clocked movement in the periphery of his vision, at his two o'clock. A second gunman was inching down the aisle. Bald unloaded a rash round at him. The round slapped pathetically into the stained-glass window above the doors, punching a hole in Jesus's halo and sending multi-coloured shards of glass scattering across the main aisle. But the discharge at least sent the gunman backtracking into the shadows near the entrance.

'The yacht is half an hour away by car,' said Klich. 'Think about it. Thirty minutes' work, five million in your back pocket. It's a good deal, my friend.'

The audio guide droned on, 'Lovingly restored in 1858—'

Bald chewed on a thought. He hated the idea of protecting Klich. Bald had been shot at, beaten senseless and wounded in his hunt for the oligarch. But worse, Klich had got surgical on Joe back in Courchevel. And, underneath the bad blood that existed between Bald and his old mucker, they were still both ex-Blades. That counted for something.

'I already have a deal,' he said. 'With my handler.'

Klich snorted. 'You think I don't know about your little adventure with Leo Land? He's in deep with the Russian agencies. That means you are too. Your bosses will use you as long as it's convenient. Trust me. As soon as you hand me over, they'll throw you to the dogs.'

Bald weighed up his options. Follow orders and drag Klich to the RV? Or take a punt on guarding Klich and getting a big pile of dosh at the end? And the more he thought about it, the more the second option sounded like the better deal.

'*Ten* million,' he said. 'Sterling.'

'Deal!' Klich replied in a snap. Bald kicked himself for not squeezing a lot more out of the guy. 'Now get me the hell out of here.'

Bald spotted a door towards the rear right-hand corner of the church. Solid-looking wood, painted dark red. Bald realized that the door led out to the side of the building nearest the Vectra. Figured his best bet was to keep the gunmen pinned down and allow Klich to leg it outside and race around to the car. Then Bald could pepper-pot back from the church and join him. The plan was sketchy. But it was better than no fucking plan at all.

Grabbing Klich by the upper arm, Bald thrust him towards the door. At that moment he heard hurried footsteps. The three remaining gunmen, including the wounded one, stormed out of the gloom. Two of them broke for the columns to the right of the aisle. The third scurried in a kind of crouch towards the facing columns.

'*Fucking go!*' Bald screamed at Klich as he thrust the oligarch through the side door. 'Keep running and don't look back until you reach the car.'

Klich ducked outside. Bald wheeled around and let off a shot down the aisle. Missed. He hit the deck as six rounds fizzled over him and thumped into the wall behind him, shattering an ancient figurine and showering him with plaster. The three gunmen concentrated a ferocious stream of rounds on him. Seven . . . eight . . . nine . . . ten rounds. Bald hoped they hadn't seen Klich's exit, otherwise they would surely split up, two of them taking care of Bald while the third went after their unarmed compatriot. Gunshots were now thundering through the church like a high-speed train. Demolishing statues and bas-reliefs. Chewing up the ornate columns. Turning the World Heritage Site into a fucking war zone.

Four rounds slapped into the baptismal font at the foot of the pulpit. The font was the size of a large wash-basin and of some kind of hard polished rock. The bullets glanced off it and ricocheted through the church, splintering statues of angels. The air was quickly fogged with burnt plaster, dust and smoke. Lying on his front, his eyes streaming and the powerful tang of gunpowder on his tongue, Bald listened to the Russians discharging a continuous stream of rounds. They weren't bothering to aim, but simply peppering the area all around him with bullets. Another two-round burst shattered the baptismal font. Bald glanced over his shoulder as holy water ran out through the crack and splashed onto the stone floor.

Then came a lull. Bald swung to his right. At head height the fog was impermeable, but from his position on the floor it was thinner, giving him a view of the gold-ringed gunman stampeding at him from twelve metres away, along the central aisle. The ex-Blade hefted the Ruger up and depressed the trigger. The slider came back before crashing forward, then a round roared from the snout and struck the guy's ankle. He screamed as the wound exploded in a burst of bone and tendon, but stumbled on for a couple of steps. Bald unleashed two more rounds of Parabellum at him. Pumped his groin full of lead. The guy groped his shredded ball-sack and fell backwards.

In the right periphery of his vision Bald caught sight of the other two agents surging up the aisle. They were bringing their carbines to bear on him. He twisted his torso in their direction and gave them the good news in the shape of three rounds of Parabellum. But the bullets slapped uselessly into the wall eight inches ahead of the nearest guy. Plaster gushed over the aisle. The gunman hit the deck, looking for cover. His mate quickly followed suit.

Using the pause in the firefight, Bald broke into a run for the side door, kicking aside reams of spent brass. The church had been totalled. Plaster carvings had been punched full of holes. Bullets had taken chunks out of most of the columns. One of the roof beams was so badly split it was creaking. The baptismal font was blown apart, the last dregs of water spewing out of the cracks. Bald stumbled blindly on, his sweating face smeared with plaster. Flakes of it tumbled off his shoulders and down his back. He spat out dusty phlegm and calculated that he'd expended twelve rounds of ammo. Five in the clip, plus the spare seventeen-round clip in his hip pocket. Twenty-two rounds in total. Two gunmen.

Fighting odds.

Bald quickened his step as he crashed through the door. He knew he had to reach Klich before the gunmen did. He found himself in some kind of remembrance garden. There was a derelict water feature of some kind, amid tall wild grass and weeds. A broken-down, knee-high fence surrounded the garden, which became an olive grove at its extremity.

It was dusk now, and the blue canvas of the sky was lacerated with bleeding orange and purple streaks. Bald cast his eyes at his three o'clock. Twenty metres away, down on the road, he could see the Vectra.

So where the fuck is Klich?

Then he heard a sharp breath behind him, and swung round.

Klich was leaning against the wall next to the side door of the church. Struggling to control his erratic breathing. Sweat glistened his face. Why the fuck the guy had stopped running? Then he saw the Russian's face. He had turned the kind of white that you only ever saw on a paint chart. He was truly frozen with fear. That puzzled Bald. Klich struck him as a hard man. Not the type to shrivel up at the sight of blood. He was an oligarch, after all. And from what little Bald knew of those guys, murder and violence were part and parcel of everyday business.

'Let's go,' Bald said, wrenching Klich away from the wall.

The oligarch ran after him in a staggering sprint. They were twelve metres from the road when Bald heard the heavy side door of the church swing open. He stopped. Wheeled around. Saw one of the gunmen charging out towards them. Fuck it! These pricks were beginning to really piss him off.

The gunman already had his 9A-91 level with his shoulder and trained on him.

Bald pushed Klich to the ground behind the water feature. He dropped to one knee as the gunman opened fire. Flames licked out of the carbine's snout, briefly illuminating the darkness that was settling like black snow over the church and garden. Three rounds thudded into the ground a quarter of a metre to the right of Bald. Hot dirt spat at his face. The rounds were fucking close. There was a pause as the gunman zeroed his aim. The next shot, Bald knew, would be the killshot.

He had one chance to take the gunman down.

Bald struggled to target the gunman in the failing light. He had no time to fuck about getting his shots dead-centred. Tugging back the trigger with his index finger, he unloaded three shots in quick succession. The rounds clanged between his ears: *ca-rack, ca-rack, ca-rack.*

The guy didn't drop. The rounds sputtered into the long grass.

Two rounds left in the clip.

The gunman opened fire again. Bald dived to the ground behind the water feature as the three rounds zipped narrowly overhead. Bald nudged Klich, who was cowering face down on the ground, his face spattered with dirt.

'You see my wheels?' he said, pointing with his eyeballs to the Vectra, parked some thirty metres from their position. 'On my count you leg it. Get yourself down behind the rear wheel and don't fucking move until I get there. Clear?'

Klich nodded frantically.

Three more rounds spat at the water feature.

'*Go!*' Bald thundered at Klich. The oligarch darted towards the road and in the same blurred movement Bald sprang up from behind the water feature. Froze. The gunman had displaced. But to where? Then Bald detected a smudge of movement in the messy periphery of his vision. Coming across his right shoulder. Bald spun around. The gunman was circling around to the south of the garden in an attempt to outflank Bald. He was ten metres away and targeting Klich. The laser aim on his carbine loomed over the oligarch as he scrambled towards the Vectra.

One shot, Bald thought. That's all I've got.

Miss, and Klich is dead.

He relaxed his shoulder muscles and tensed his wrists.

Exhaled.

Pulled the trigger.

For a shaved second Bald thought he'd missed. The gunman simply stood there. Then he let his rifle fall limp by his side, and he put a hand to his throat, patting at it, as if trying to swat a fly. Bald saw the blood drooling out of a neat hole in his Adam's apple. The gunman blinked his shock as he dumbly tried to staunch the wound. His legs abruptly gave way and he sank to his knees. Bald rose to his feet as the life seeped out of the fucker. Another kill notched up on his mental chalkboard. Bald had a lot of fucking notches.

He wheeled around to pursue Klich. He spotted the fourth gunman. Shit! For a moment he'd forgotten about the fourth guy. The Russian agent had exited the church by the front doors and was stood there with his assault rifle to his shoulder.

Aiming at Klich.

forty-five

The next three seconds played out real slow. Bald scraped himself off the ground as Klich faltered the last seven metres to the Vectra, exhausted by the short run and totally unaware of the gunman targeting him ten metres away. The gunman stalked Klich. His left hand throttled the mag feed on the underside of his 9A-91, his right hand clenching the rear grip. Bald slung his Ruger up from his side towards the agent. He figured he had either one or two rounds left in the clip, but he couldn't fucking remember which, not with all the shit going down in the heat of the firefight. Two, he hoped. His run of luck suggested one.

He had no time to aim. He needed to put rounds down on the gunman before he opened fire. As he pulled back on the trigger, the motion was hypnotic and smooth, the Ruger as familiar as an old lover. The weapon's moving parts juddered in his grip as the slider shot back and forth and snorted fumes and lead out of the snout, spitting spent brass out of the ejector like a guy spitting a peanut shell out of the corner of his mouth.

The round glinted as it yawed through the moonlit sky and whistled past the gunman. Distracted by the shot, the gunman spun away from the oligarch and trained his sights on Bald. The ex-Blade processed the scene in front of him. Klich was diving behind the rear of the Vectra. Bald was aiming at the gunman. The gunman was aiming at Bald. It all came down to who had the quicker trigger finger.

Then Bald took a sharp breath, the leaden air tangy on his tongue and furry on his teeth. The smell of gunpowder swirled beneath his nostrils. The dots on the Ruger's rear sight notches glowed luminous green. They trapped the gunman. Bald had the shadow marginally out of focus. The rear sight in sharp focus.

He depressed the trigger.

Click-click.

Shit! It *was* only one round.

The gunman fired.

Bald dived to his left. He felt the round before he heard it, a hot razor-blade graze of pain slashing across his right cheek, followed by a dense crump as it slapped into the grass behind him. The gunman had to retain his aim on Bald. He was a smudge of charcoal black twisting towards the ex-Blade. Now Bald pressed the mag ejector on the side of the Ruger as he dug the spare seventeen-round clip out of his hip pocket. He inserted it smoothly into the mag feed. The gunman was still dragging his carbine across as Bald pulled the hammer decisively back and then released it in a flash, letting it slam forward as the first round from the clip crashed into the chamber.

He had fired before the gunman got a chance to unload a second shot at him. The round flamed out of the Ruger. The Russian jerked, as if someone had pumped him full of twenty-thousand volts. He flopped backwards noiselessly and busied himself with the grisly business of dying as Bald congratulated himself on a good job. Klich paused before scrabbling out from behind the car. He dusted himself down, noticed the fatally wounded gunman and marched triumphantly over to him. He was pumping his fists in the air.

'Fuck you!' he screamed as he kicked the guy in the ribs. 'Who's the fucking man now? Who?' He knelt beside the agent. Whispered, 'What's that, my friend? I can't hear you.'

Then he stood up and once again kicked the gunman in the ribs. 'Me, motherfucker. *I'm the man. And fuck you!*'

A soft flopping sound came from the dying man's chest as blood filled his lungs and bubbled in the fresh hole in his throat.

'See how it feels now, bitch!' Klich rasped, planting his feet either side of the man. Then he unzipped his flies and released a hot stream of urine onto the agent's face. The guy whimpered somewhere deep down.

'We need to get out of here,' Bald said.

'In a minute,' said Klich, swaying his hips to piss a 'K' over the gunman's face. When he was done he shook the last few drops out of his dick and zipped up.

'I'm done here,' he said to Bald. 'Now take me to see my old friend Favorsky.'

Klich climbed into the rear passenger seat as Bald hurried behind the steering wheel and twisted the key in the ignition. He U-turned in the road. Put his foot to the floor as he sped north along Rue Alain Grillet, hitting JFK Boulevard at 145 per. He arrowed down the street on an eastward trajectory. He had Google Maps open on his iPhone 4S and the phone suctioned to the dashboard. Millionaires' Quay was due north-east of their location. Half a kilometre along JFK, Bald hooked a sharp left onto Boulevard Christian Lacombe. He checked the rear-view mirror every ten or fifteen seconds to make sure they weren't being followed. After four hundred metres Christian Lacombe transitioned into a parade of sprawling whitewashed mansions hermetically sealed off from the outside world by two-metre-high stone walls, electronic gates and artful hedges interspersed with palm trees.

Bald kept his foot right down as he raced north. He drove hard because he figured that if the Russians wanted Klich dead that badly, they would have sent for more than four guys to get the job done. And the sooner he delivered Klich to Favorsky, the sooner he could get his money and wash his hands of this whole shitty business.

The roads were nearly empty. Bald swerved right on the first turn-off from Christian Lacombe and swung onto Chemin de Revault. This he followed for a corkscrewed kilometre before rolling onto a two-lane road that straddled the eastern shore-line. Google Maps politely informed Bald that he was now just a kilometre south of Millionaires' Quay. The hang-out for the super-rich, the billionaires who could drop three hundred grand on champagne and not feel it in their wallets. The ones who owned Formula One teams and islands on the other side of the world.

Bald at last eased his foot off the accelerator.

'We lost them,' he said.

'No thanks to you,' said Klich. 'You nearly got me killed back there, you fool. You're supposed to be protecting me!' He pointed to his plastic-surgeried jaw. 'If this baby gets so much as a scratch, our little agreement is void.'

'Bollocks,' said Bald. 'You're the one who wants to pay a visit to the fucker who's trying to kill you. What's your business with Favorsky, anyway?'

Klich smiled faintly. 'I have my reasons.'

'You really think your so-called mate is going to be rolling out the red carpet when you show up at his yacht?'

'Don't you worry about the welcome party. Just concentrate on getting me there.'

They swept north past a row of utilitarian apartment blocks facing the sea like a set of bared Rottweiler teeth. A breeze rushed in from the coast. The palm trees shivered. To his nine o'clock Bald could see some kind of medieval fortification, a vast stone structure running almost the length of the bay, with three-metre high arches punched into the base and a gangway spanning it above.

Just a little further, Bald told himself. He couldn't go on much longer. The migraine had been continually murmuring at the spot between his left ear and temple ever since he checked out of the Metropolitan in Geneva. Adrenalin had kept the lid on it during the shoot-out at the church. But now they were clear of the shit it had come back into piercing focus. Just keep it together for another hour, Bald reassured himself. Tomorrow he could put the whole lot of it behind him. Antibes. Europe. The Firm. With ten million to blow and a new identity, the world was full of bright possibilities. He thought he might try Costa Rica. Or maybe Thailand. He'd heard plenty of things about Thai women. All I have to do is put the migraine on ice until I get to the yacht, he told himself. He hoped to fuck that Favorsky had a plentiful stock of booze. With a bit of luck he could mainline some Jim Beam into his bloodstream and delay the migraine.

Now Bald banged a right onto Avenue Maréchal Robert. The road narrowed like a pair of hunched shoulders. He stuck to ninety as they nudged down a single-lane road flanked by sleeping Renaults and battered Peugeots. The pavement was cracked. A row of modest hotels with fanciful names lined the left side of the street. A five-storey, flat-roofed housing block stood on the right, its plain exterior the texture of papier mâché. About a hundred metres further on the road wound to the left. Directly ahead was a warren of intersecting alleyways. Earlier that day Bald had passed by those same passageways. Back then they had been heaving with food stalls and dining tables and trinket shops and tourists on a nice pension. Now they were lifeless and strewn with rubbish picked at by scrawny wild dogs. But just beyond the market, Bald knew, was the Quay. Five hundred metres away.

The migraine split his skull apart roughly four hundred metres from his new life.

It hit him with speed and precision, like an uppercut. His sight blurred at the edges. Then a searing white light flashed across the centre of his vision and speared his frontal lobe, carrying a lightning bolt of pain all the way through his brain to the back of his skull. The pain was instantaneous and vicious. The streetlamps screamed at Bald. He clamped his eyes shut to block out the blinding lights and the noise. He heard a metallic crunch. Felt a shockwave judder through his bones.

He opened his eyes as he lurched forward in his seat. His head slammed into the steering wheel. Then there was a bang. Pain crashed through his head like a bag of marbles bursting open. The lights dimmed.

Then they went out.

forty-six

Bald opened his eyes to the sound of a thick and nasal voice yelling behind him. He shook his head clear. Had no idea how long he'd been out cold for. His back was agonizing and a dull ache was working its way through his jawbone. The windscreen had cracked in several places. The Vectra had slammed into a parked Peugeot 206. Took Bald a couple of hazy seconds to realize that he must have veered off the road during his migraine attack before crashing into the other car. Countless pains shuddered up from his wrists to his shoulder blades, where they flared up for a while before fading out to trembles in his neck. He was dimly conscious of a pair of hands shaking his shoulders. Then he glanced up at the rear-view mirror, and saw that the hands belonged to Klich.

'Wake up, you fucking idiot,' the oligarch scowled. His nose was purple and swollen at the bridge. Bashed it against the headrest in the crash, Bald figured. 'Wake up!'

'Gaaahh—'

Bald tried to speak proper words. No use. His jaw felt like someone had wired it shut. The engine tap-tapped. Smoke fanned out of the grille. He focused on the digital clock on the dash: 1918. He had been out cold for exactly a minute. He soothed his stiff neck and was halfway to piecing his skull back together when he heard a growl thundering to the south. He craned his head over his shoulder. Looking beyond Klich, he spotted a BMW X5 slaloming into view. Sliding and screeching to a halt side-on and ten metres to the rear of the Vectra. Black exterior, black windows, all-black everything.

Oh shit, thought Bald. It was the X5 used by the gunmen who'd ambushed the church. He froze as its front passenger window whirred down and a rifle muzzle poked out in his direction.

'*Get down!*' Bald shouted at Klich.

The muzzle lit up. There was a distinct *phtt*, followed by a noise like a bag of coins being dumped on a table. A single bullet hole starred the Vectra's rear window. Bald dived across the front passenger seat as two more *phtts* sounded from the X5. Like splitting ice. The bullets thwacked into the glass near the first hole. Three rounds grouped in a kind of constellation. Klich was sprawled across the back seat, his legs pulled up, shaking with fear. Another storm of suppressed rounds erupted from the X5 and bullets pierced the rear window again, hammered into the bodywork and the chassis. The rate of fire was overwhelming. Bald couldn't get his shit together. A third burst of gunfire brought the back window crashing down. Shards showered over Klich's face, rained down on his clothes. He shouted some kind of a curse in his native tongue. One round spurted up from underneath the gearbox and zipped between Bald's legs. Missed his groin by four inches, then embedded itself in the roof. Four more bullets pinballed around the underside of the car.

Fuck it, thought Bald. He'd come too far to let these arseholes get in the way of his payday. Rolling onto his back, he lifted his head a few inches and peered over the dash. Ninety metres of exposed road separated Bald from the market. He was sure he and Klich could shake off the gunmen if they could make it into the alleys without getting riddled with hot lead. He reached across to the front passenger seat and grasped the Ruger. Sixteen rounds left in the clip, he reminded himself groggily. Adjusting himself so that he was lean-ing slightly forward, he pointed the pistol between the front seats, and through the shattered rear window he could see the side-on X5 clearly. Klich, now flat on his stomach, looked badly shaken, as if someone had rattled him close to their ear, listening for loose change. Bald unloaded three steady rounds from the freshly chambered clip. His aim was marginally off. The rounds fractured the lowered window of the X5's front passenger door. Spent brass sprang out of the ejector, landing like hot coals in Bald's lap.

Thirteen rounds left, he said to himself.

Another brutal burst of rounds exploded from the X5 and flacked the back end of the Vectra. Bald didn't panic. He let off four assured rounds, spattering the passenger window. The rifle muzzle withdrew into the darkness inside the SUV. There was a brief pause in the gunfire.

Nine rounds. Don't fucking waste them.

Bald sprang into action. He booted open the Vectra's front passenger door and popped three more rounds back at the X5's damaged window. The glass finally disintegrated, show-ering across the road. The gunman had ducked out of sight, Bald guessed. Six rounds remaining.

'*Get the fuck out now!*' he boomed.

Klich vaulted out of the rear of the car as Bald pumped out two more rounds, now aiming lower, at the bodywork below the blown-out window. There was a piercing din as the bullets ripped through the metal. A howl came from inside the SUV. This time Bald was sure he had nailed the shooter. With only four rounds left he couldn't afford to piss away any covering-fire rounds. Every bullet had to have a fucking name on it now. Klich was scrabbling past Bald and racing towards the maze of alleyways as the same door of the X5 flew open and a head popped out. Must be the driver this time, Bald reck-oned, then unleashed two rounds before the guy could fire.

The driver's head exploded like a pineapple. His body rolled into a lifeless heap in the middle of the road.

Satisfied that he had done enough damage to stop the gunmen in their tracks, and with just two rounds left in the clip, Bald swung around and ran towards the market. He almost did a double-take when he saw how far ahead Klich had raced. He was forty metres ahead of Bald and fifty metres short of the alleys. Bald hurried after him.

Twenty metres clear of the Vectra, Bald stole a glance over his right shoulder. He saw another shooter debussing from the bullet-ridden X5. Guy with a goatee, dressed in black slacks, holding an assault rifle in his right hand. Blood spurted from a wound in his left shoulder. He stumbled a few metres towards Bald with a lopsided gait. Then, tottering, he stopped to raise his weapon in a feeble one-handed grip. He fired twice at Bald. The rounds slapped into an old-school Citroën Xantia four metres left of Bald on the other side of the road. An alarm wailed.

Now Bald increased his pace, putting more distance between himself and the shooter and gradually catching up with Klich. Twenty metres from the first alleyway and seventy metres clear of the X5, he drew level with him. He heard a clatter behind him and grabbed one last look over his shoulder. The shooter had given up the chase. He was slumped against the side of the Vectra, his eyes glancing at the skies and his mouth agape as he gasped for breath. His assault rifle lay on the road beside him.

Bald ushered Klich into the alley. His plan had fucking worked. They were clear of the X5 and the shooters. The market was empty. The stray dogs had scarpered at the first sound of gunfire. Now the air was filled with the sound of Bald and the oligarch breathing heavily as they pounded down one cobbled alleyway after another, Bald leading the way past peeling shop fronts and lines of parked scooters, recalling the layout of the market from Google Maps.

'How much further?' Klich asked. He breathing was distorted by his busted nose. Made him sound like he was sucking air through a straw. He was flagging badly. They both were. They had come a long way.

'Nearly there,' Bald replied confidently.

Bald blocked out the pain in his knee and the weariness in his muscles. All he focused on was getting to the port. He knew that he couldn't afford to run into any more gunmen. Down to his last two rounds of ammo and with no spare clip, it was the yacht or bust.

A minute later they dashed into a short, pitch-black alley. Bald knew from the map that it opened out at the far end into a seafront promenade, and the sight of this gave him a second wind. Almost there. He hurried on. He could see rows of pleasure boats arranged at Port Vauban beyond the glitzy promenade. He could taste the sea salt in the air now, and hear the waves slapping the breakwater. He sighed with relief.

Klich gave him a hearty slap on the back. 'We're going to make it,' he wheezed.

As they neared the end of the alley Bald felt his iPhone buzz in his pocket. He looked at the display.

Cave.

He let the call die. Five seconds later his phone told him he had a new voicemail. Bald listened to the message as they cleared the alley and headed into the port. He pressed the iPhone tight to his ear and found himself listening to the voice of a desperate man.

'Pick up for Chrissakes,' Cave said, his voice on the edge of the fucking edge. 'Jesus, John. I told you to do it quietly. GCHQ is going fucking mental about the noise at your end. Get Klich to the RV asa-fucking-p. Before I change my mind and put in that call to Interpol—'

Bald tapped 'Delete'.

'You have no new messages,' the screen reassured him.

He tossed the phone into the sea. Bid goodbye to the Firm.

Then he turned to Klich. The oligarch had stopped. Bald shot him a puzzled look. They couldn't piss about now. Not when they were so close to the prize. But Klich simply stood in a trance at the edge of the port. Bald chased his line of sight. He counted at least a hundred boats moored at the jetties, laid out like white coffins at their berths. Neon-blue spotlights illuminated the jetties and one of them, maybe eight hundred metres away, extended further out into the sea. The further out along this quay he ran his eyes, the bigger the boats. The pecking order was speedboats, then sailing yachts, then gin palaces. Some of the gin palaces featured two upper decks and had hulls more than forty metres long. Their lights glittered like distant fires in the flat black night.

'Christ, look at this place,' said Bald. 'I bet these boats cost a bloody whack.'

Klich snorted. 'These shitty things?' he said, waving his hand like he was wafting away a bad smell. 'They are nothing.' He nodded at a yacht moored at the far end of the huge quay, which jutted out six hundred metres into the sea.

He said, 'Now *that* is a fucking boat, my friend.'

forty-seven

The yacht that Klich pointed to occupied a large berth at the very end of the quay. Bald had a side-on view of it. Ropes helped to anchor the vessel, hooked to bright-yellow mooring buoys floating like the hats of drowned wizards on the water. Fuck me, thought Bald. Cave was right: it does look like a cruise liner. The yacht was like the kind of vast boats you find at the port in Miami, disgorging medicated retirees on world cruises. It was about a hundred and seventy metres long and its hull glowed a brilliant white, brighter than the moon. A helicopter pad was perched on top of the uppermost deck and a submersible vessel was fixed to the port side of the hull. A flag hung lazily from a mast at the stern. It had a Union Jack in the top-left corner, a coat of arms in the bottom right, and the British red ensign in the centre.

'The *Seraya Sowa*,' Klich announced. 'Not bad, eh?'

'One way of putting it,' Bald replied.

'Pah! I had a bigger one once. Not so long ago, in fact.' Klich grinned at Bald. 'This time next year, I'll build one twice as fucking big!'

Rows of lights sparkled like champagne on the upper decks. Bald counted four upper decks, stacked like the layers on a wedding cake. A whitewashed gangplank led from the lowest deck to the quayside. Music thumped out from the upper decks.

'Sounds like someone's having a party,' he said.

'Ha!' Klich hacked up a laugh. 'My parties were better than this shit. I'm talking mountains of cocaine. Prostitutes. Real classy, you know? Rolexes for every guest. Caviar. Pop bitches singing me "Happy Birthday". I had the world eating out of my hand.' He shook his head ruefully. 'Then I made a mistake. Just the one. But a big one.'

Bald grinned. 'You got too greedy?'

'I got too soft. I stopped killing my enemies.'

An image blinked at Bald. Like a subliminal shot in a movie. He saw Joe Gardner hanging like a slab of meat from the hook in the farmhouse, his belly slashed open and his uncoiled bowels glistening beneath his blackened toes. Joe had met his end at the hands of Viktor Klich. Bald asked himself how many other men and women Klich had butchered down the years. He looked at the man and saw no remorse. No fear. No nothing. Just a cold, hard certainty about the world and his rightful place in it.

They had walked briskly along the promenade and were nearly halfway down the quay leading to the *Seraya Sowa*, the dull thud of their footsteps as fast as the beating of Bald's heart.

'I'll let you in on a little secret,' Klich said. 'Getting rich? That's the easy part.' He coughed. 'But staying rich? You have to have balls of steel.'

Bald said nothing.

'Take that MI6 agent I killed,' Klich said, clicking his fingers in an attempt to jog his memory. 'What was his name again? Jim? Jake?'

'Joe,' Bald said. 'Joe Gardner.'

'Ah, Joe! Now I remember.' Klich clapped his hands. 'Know what else I remember? The way he screamed when I cut his dick off. I mean, he really *cried*. Like a little girl.'

Bald balled his left hand into a fist. Ten million was a lot of cash, but Klich bragging about slicing up an ex-Blade stung him. He felt a powerful urge to punch the guy in the face. Instead he tried to get Klich to speed up, as he had slowed to a stroll in his excitement. All he wanted to do was get the guy onto the boat before he lost his cool.

'See, this Joe, he tried to fuck with me,' the oligarch went on. 'I had no choice but to deal with him. Send out a message. Fuck with Viktor Klich you end up dangling from a rope. Yeah . . . Favorsky should have known not to fuck with Klich.'

'Joe was . . . a friend,' Bald said in a low voice. Well, it was true in a way and he felt a pressure building between his temples. Twisting his arteries and pulling at his neck muscles.

Klich laughed. 'Your "friend" was a piece of human shit. He got everything he deserved.'

Bald flipped. He launched his right hand at Klich, the pent-up tension in his muscles released in a sudden burst of aggression. A cross-punch to the middle of the chin. The Russian moaned as his jaw crashed upwards and slammed into the roof of his mouth, grinding up the mass of nerves located just behind the jaw pivot. He let out a light moan. Then his jaw went slack and his eyes rolled into the back of his head. He slumped to the ground. Bald soothed his stinging knuckles. He'd knocked Klich out cold.

For a moment Bald was seized by anxiety. Klich was his ticket to ten million. Putting the guy unconscious suddenly didn't seem like such a bright idea. Then Bald shrugged. You promised to take Klich to his parlay with Favorsky on his yacht, a voice reminded him. You didn't promise he would be conscious when he got there.

A dull chugging came from the *Seraya Sowa*, three hundred metres away. Like someone revving up a chainsaw underwater. The water trembled. Then the sound modulated to a turbine drone. Four figures scurried across the main deck and untied the mooring ropes.

A thought swept away the rage fogging Bald's mind. The yacht was preparing to leave.

He had to act quick. With Klich KO'd he had no choice but to carry the guy on his back and lug him up the gangplank before the yacht sailed. Hooking his elbows underneath Klich's shoulders, Bald hoisted him up to his knees. Then he grasped Klich by his right wrist and slung the Russian's arm over his right shoulder before dropping to a hack-squat posture, bending his knees at a right angle and keeping his back parallel to the ground. Now Bald slung Klich over his back. He left the oligarch's left leg and arm hanging by his side. A fist of air surged out of his throat as Bald pushed up on the balls of his toes, and his hamstrings burned with the weight of the man. He rose slowly. He rose stiffly. Like he was squatting a heavy barbell. By his reckoning he was a hundred and fifty metres from the rear deck of the *Seraya Sowa*.

Better get a fucking move on.

Bald kept a close eye on the four men working the ropes. They didn't appear to have noticed him approaching. He wanted to keep it that way, in case they sounded the alarm and cut the yacht adrift from the port before he could reach the gangplank.

The going was tough. Despite Klich's relatively lithe physique Bald reckoned that he weighed north of eighty kilograms, much more than a Regiment Bergen with standard-issue kit. Those first few steps Bald almost lost his footing, his ankles threatening to buckle under the load. A circle of pain scorched his lower back. A voice of doubt whispered in his ear. Told him he couldn't do it. He was in a rag-order state. The urge to stop and unload Klich was constant. But Bald reminded himself of his Selection training on the Brecon Beacons. Of the harsh days and cold nights slogging his guts out. He'd done it then. He could do it again now.

He staggered on.

A hundred metres now.

Sweat gushed down Bald's back and glued his T-shirt to his skin. Seventy metres from the yacht. The propellers were churning the water violently. Bald pushed harder. His legs ached. His lungs inflamed with each snatch of breath, as if the air was laced with glass. Klich roused at his shoulder with a groggy groan. Fifty metres now. They were going to make it, Bald thought.

Then a quadruple *ca-rack* erupted at his six o'clock, and shocks of white light seared along the quay like flashes of lightning in quick succession, pitching the world into shards of black and white as four rounds whooshed past Bald, thwacking into the ground ahead of him. Up on the main deck, the crewmen scattered for cover.

Bald glanced back across his shoulder. Three hundred metres behind him he made out several shadows racing down the quay in his direction, illuminated by the lights from the line of smaller yachts moored there. They had to be mates of the gunmen he had dropped at the church, and he figured they were probably armed with the same assault rifles.

Less than fifty metres to go, but now Klich was sliding off his back. Bald jerked his shoulders and leaned forward, re-shouldering the oligarch before pushing grimly on. He saw no point in taking cover. At three hundred metres he and Klich were beyond the two-hundred-metre threshold of the 9A-91's maximum effective range. All he had to do was maintain his current pace. The carbines' 9x39mm subsonic cartridge had an air pocket built into the tip which allowed the round to yaw heavily through the air after being expelled from the chamber and pierce flesh at a ninety-degree angle, fragmenting on impact and stabbing the target's vitals with hundreds of tiny fragments of lead. Its stopping power meant that even at the maximum range of two hundred metres, a couple of shots that were on target could quickly promote Bald and Klich to glory.

Before long a second volley cut through the air like four quick lashes of a whip. The quay sparked up again, the world reversing into white for an epileptic beat. Bald didn't look over his shoulder to see where the rounds had struck. Didn't need to. He could hear the *ker-rang* of each bullet striking the ground, distinct and close, landing five metres to his six o'clock, maybe six.

The gunmen had closed the gap to two hundred and ten metres. Another few steps and Bald and Klich would be in target range. Bald knew he couldn't outrun the gunmen. His legs were struggling to keep up the pace. When they were twenty-five metres from the yacht he laid eyes on a waist-high coil of sailing rope. He lumbered up to it and deposited Klich behind its cover. His muscles breathed a sigh of relief. But Bald hadn't dumped Klich off his back for a quick breather. The Regiment voice in his head told him he'd need to delay the fuckers shooting at them before he could load Klich onto the *Seraya Sowa*. Spinning around and dropping to a kneeling firing stance, Bald brought his Ruger to bear. Two rounds left. One in the clip, one chambered in the snout. Four gunmen. Any which way you sliced it, the numbers didn't look good.

The gunmen had divided into two pairs. Two of the guys had raced twenty metres ahead of the others, and were now a hundred and fifty metres from Bald and Klich. The Ruger had a maximum range of a hundred metres. A hundred and twenty with a bit of luck. A few seconds and the first two guys would be within Bald's range.

He slid Klich to the ground, knelt down beside a coil of thick rope and took aim at the shooter to the left. The guy was a hundred and fifteen metres away. Then a hundred and five. On a hundred Bald brassed him up with a quick tap of the trigger. A single shot. The guy pawed at his throat. If he'd been on Twitter, his final tweet would've been '#dead'. Now the second shooter surged recklessly past his fallen mucker, firing as he moved and directing a three-round burst at Bald's kneeling form. Bald saw a tongue of flame at the carbine's muzzle. Heard the *ca-racks* melding into a hammering din. Didn't flinch as the first two rounds landed a half-metre shy of his feet. But the shooter's aim had skipped up a fraction as he discharged the third shot and the jerk corrected his aim. The round thumped into Bald, penetrating his left shoulder and taking a bite out of his rotator cuff before ripping out at a spot just above his elbow.

The pain was intense. But Bald had already depressed the trigger on the Ruger and he reflexively discharged his last bullet at the shooter before the pain overwhelmed him. The round punched into the guy's right leg, shattering his knee-cap. He lost his balance, tumbled sideways and fell into the water.

The shooters twenty metres further back now split up, one breaking left and the other breaking right as they sought cover along the sides of the quay, removing themselves from the fatal funnel of fire. Bald was out of ammo. He'd have to chance making it to the yacht with Klich before the gunmen had a chance to nail him. The yacht engine droned urgently in Bald's ears. He realized he couldn't haul Klich across his shoulders. Not with his arm leaking blood. Instead he grabbed the oligarch by the collar of his shirt and dragged him like a heavy sack towards the yacht.

Twenty metres.

Bullets slapped into the ground somewhere behind him. Two three-round bursts. Bald risked a look back down the quay. The last two shooters were putting rounds down behind cover at a couple of wooden loading crates. Weary joints creaking under the strain, Bald hauled Klich towards the yacht. He felt nauseous and dizzy. His shoulder felt like someone had taken a blowtorch to it.

Ten metres to the gangplank now.

Ten million quid. Fucking do it!

Six more rounds swished through the air and slapped into the coiled rope. Bald charged on. At last he reached the gangplank. He dropped Klich and swung a step ahead of the oligarch onto the gangplank. Then he wrapped his arms under Klich's shoulders and around his chest and dragged him up the gangplank, his expensive shoes scraping against the metal. A foghorn blared. Bald looked back down the quay in horror at the approaching gunmen.

The yacht still hadn't departed. Thank fuck. Now hurry. Bald could see the gunmen had closed the gap to two hundred metres. Target range. Two thoughts punched their tickets in Bald's frontal lobe. One, he was clean out of ammo. Two, both he and Klich were badly exposed in their elevated position halfway up the gangplank.

They were fucked.

But then the gunmen did a curious thing. They stopped dead in their tracks and lowered their weapons. Their shoulders relaxed. They even appeared to be sharing a joke, laughing to themselves. The guy on the right waved at Bald. The ex-Blade wondered why the fuck they hadn't gunned both him and Klich down when they had the chance. Then the yacht's engine growled, and the gangplank wobbled and Bald forgot all about the gunmen as he desperately dragged Klich the remaining distance in a race to get on board before the yacht pulled clear of its berth. His muscles howled. Klich groaned. Bald hauled him onto the lowest deck just as the yacht broke away from the quay, like a crust of ice breaking off an iceberg, slow and powerful. The gangplank fell away and was soon swallowed by the glistening water. Bald laid Klich out flat on the deck. He was exhausted and drenched in sweat. But they were sweeping into the night. He watched the gunmen melt into the soft light of the quay.

I fucking did it, he thought.

He stood up and tended to Klich. Slapped him on the cheeks. The guy was fucking out of it. Mumbling under his breath, his eyes clamped shut, like he was having a bad dream.

Footsteps sounded at Bald's six. He turned around. Looked up. Saw three men striding purposefully towards him from across the deck. Not the crewmen from earlier. The guys to the left and right were straight out of the Rent-a-Tough brochure. Square jaws, peephole eyes and shovel-like hands. Their black suits were tight at the chest and their shoulders bulged like basketballs in sacks. Their white shirts were stiff at the collar and two inches short at the sleeve. It was tough getting smart threads when you were the proportions of a gorilla, Bald guessed.

The guy in the middle gave away a foot in height and about a hundred pounds to the other two. Next to them he looked like one of the smaller figures in a set of Russian dolls. He wore a black suit that fitted him perfectly. Tailor-made, Bald reckoned. The thick, pristine collar of his white shirt suggested silk. He had no tie, and his collar button and top buttons were popped to reveal a triangle of chest hair. His was the physique of a man who did triathlons at the weekends. His skin was somehow whiter than his bleached hair. The rest of his features were thin and insubstantial. Except for his eyes. They were long and narrow and grey like a couple of nails. But they didn't look directly at Bald. Maybe he was afraid to look anyone directly in the eye, in case they saw something he didn't want them to see.

The two bodyguards trained their Makarov semi-automatic pistols at Bald.

The man in the middle folded his arms across his chest. Considered Bald for a moment, the way a guy considers a turd on the sole of a brand-new shoe. He gave a signal to the rent-a-toughs. They grinned from ear to cauliflower ear as they lumbered over to Bald. The guy on the right unloaded a fist into his guts. Bald keeled forward, choking on the air, fighting vicious waves of nausea. The other one grabbed him by his bleeding shoulder. Pain drilled down deep into the core of his skull. Bald tried with all his evaporating strength to shake the guy off.

'What the fuck are you doing?' he croaked. 'I'm here to get this guy to Favorsky. They've got a meeting. Where is he?'

'He's busy,' said the man in the middle.

'And who the fuck are you?'

'Nikolay Nakrasov,' the guy replied. 'The President of Russia.'

forty-eight

A chill froze Bald. The toughs tried dragging him towards a closed door. He struggled against their weight. They all stopped what they were doing when a groan came from Klich. Four sets of eyes swivelled towards the oligarch as he came back to the land of the living. The Russian President waved abruptly at the toughs. They unclamped their hands from Bald, pounded over to Klich and hoisted him upright. Klich rubbed his jaw and grunted. He scowled at Bald. Then he set eyes on the President. Frowned. Like he was trying to work out if he'd really regained consciousness, or this was just some bad dream.

'You've got guts. I'll give you that,' the President said as he stepped towards him. Music and voices filtered down from the upper decks. 'I speak English, for the sake of your comrade here,' he added with a curt nod at Bald. 'You should have stayed away from this place, Viktor. You're not welcome.' He did a sweep of the deck with his hands, like he was showing around a prospective buyer. 'You should have fled while you still had the chance.'

Klich said nothing. Nakrasov shrugged at Klich then cocked his head at Bald. Somehow his eyes managed to linger on the oligarch as he spoke. He said, 'So you're the fucking asshole who's been killing all my men. What's your name, friend?'

'He's just a guy,' Klich answered for Bald.

The President grinned.

'Congratulations,' he said. 'You just followed Viktor into an early grave.' He nodded at the bodyguards. Gestured at the guy on the left. 'This is Zorin.' Then at the guy on the right. 'This is Karpin. They torture people. They're very good at their job. Be nice to them and they might make it quick.'

'Wait, Nikolay! Please!' Klich said.

Zorin and Karpin paused. Simultaneously looked to the President. The most powerful man in Russia clicked his tongue disapprovingly. 'Trying to buy my favour again, Viktor?' He chuckled, his chin melting into his neck, like he was stifling a hiccup. 'You forget that you have no money. You're as poor as a fucking Greek.'

'I have something that you will want to see.'

The President's face flickered with uncertainty.

Klich pressed on. 'Why do you think I came here, Nikolay? To give you the satisfaction of seeing me die? I risked my life getting to this boat because I had something very important to share with you.'

'Then you have wasted your time,' said the President.

'There's a plot to assassinate you, Nikolay!'

Nakrasov briefly lost his sheen. His eyes widened. Then he laughed. 'Bullshit.'

'It's true,' Klich continued, his voice faltering. 'The plot is from someone in your inner circle. Someone very close to you plans to kill you. I swear, everything I am telling you is the truth. I have the proof. Let me show it to you.'

'You've lost your grip on reality, Viktor.'

'I have come a very long way to speak to you. Would I do that if I wasn't completely sure about what I have to say? I have risked life and limb. Please, Nikolay. At least consider the evidence.'

The President stared at Klich for a long beat, his eyes

strangely absent. At last he nodded to the bodyguards. They released Bald and Klich and stepped back.

'Give it to me,' the President barked in a sergeant-major voice, his hands out in front of him, palms uppermost.

Klich unstrapped his Blancpain and chucked it to Nakrasov. 'There's a micro-SD card built into the casing,' he said. 'You need to plug it into a laptop to listen to the recording.'

'What recording?' The President cocked an eyebrow at Klich.

'A conversation between Valery Favorsky and Leo Land, plotting to kill you.'

'Land?' the President asked, he and Bald both shooting the same what-the-fuck? expression at Klich. 'Who is this man? I've never heard of him.'

'He used to be with MI6. But he got too dirty even for those snakes,' said Klich. 'Land conspired with Favorsky to kill you. They intended to pin the blame on Islamic separatists. Land told Favorsky he had a man who would do the job for him.'

The President showed no reaction as he held the Blancpain up to the moon and squinted at it. He sighed heavily, deep in thought. Then he tossed the watch to Karpin and clicked his fingers at Zorin. 'Where is our friend Favorsky at this moment in time?'

'In the pool, sir. With two of the prostitutes.'

'Bring him to me,' the President snapped. He turned to Klich as Zorin trudged off. 'You'd better not be playing games with me, Viktor.'

'No games,' Klich said.

'Good.' The President offered a gaunt smile. His lips were as thin as matchsticks, and the same whitish-pink as his cheeks. 'Because if you are I'll make your death a hundred times as painful. Both of you.'

With that the President turned on the heels of his expensive black lace-ups and gestured to Karpin to go ahead with Bald and Klich, up to the main deck. There they passed down a long corridor with cream floors and ceilings and lined with Aztec carvings mounted on marble plinths. Bald's arm throbbed from the bullet wound. The flesh around his shoulder and upper arm was painfully distended. At the end of the corridor they turned left and entered a suite through an ornate door guarded by another pair of rent-a-toughs.

The suite looked like the Oval Office recreated in a discount furniture showroom. Everything was cream- or walnut-coloured. Sofas and tub chairs congregated around a low coffee table to Bald's right. A standalone bar and drinks shelf occupied the middle of the room. A series of minimalist clocks were fixed to the wall behind the bar, giving the current time in Moscow, New York, London, Istanbul, Tokyo and Rio. To his left Bald spotted a big dining table in front of a curved-glass window that ran the length of the room. Spotlights glowed on the ceiling. Bald counted half a dozen guys sitting at the dining table, gorging themselves on caviar and lobster.

Nakrasov guided Klich over to the coffee table and plugged the watch, via a USB connector, into an open laptop with a diamond-encrusted shell. Klich rubbed his hands in expectation.

Bald hovered in the background. Figured he was in the clear. Klich would play the recording to the President, forgiving handshakes all round, and Bald would collect his pension fund and fuck off. He feasted his eyes on the bottles arranged on the shelf, and name-checked a rare Macallan single-malt whisky. Eighty-seven years old. The best. Twenty grand a bottle, Bald knew, which worked out to fifteen hundred quid for a two-ounce measure. More than a Blade earned in a month, for a shot of fucking whisky. Bald reached out for the Macallan, figuring he could blot out his migraine. It had been trembling in the background since the car crash. A drop of expensive whisky, he reasoned, might put the migraine to bed once and for all.

'Hey!' Bald froze. He turned to the President. The guy stared at him with a sharpened face. 'Touch that bottle and I'll cut off your balls and feed them to my dogs.'

Disappointed, Bald pulled his hand away and watched the President turn back to Klich. A scratchy audio recording played through the tinny laptop speaker. The President listened in silence, arms crossed, foot tapping impatiently. Land spoke in Russian with Favorsky. Bald had no idea Land could speak Russian. The President said nothing for the two minutes of the recording. When it finished he kept on staring at the screen, at his murky reflection in the dim display.

'Why would Favorsky want to kill me?' he said in a low voice to Klich, shaking his head in disbelief and kneading his knuckles. 'I gave him everything. Without me, he's nothing.'

'That may be so,' Klich replied. 'But you forget that Favorsky pays you certain fees each year. He does not wish to pay them. But he knows that if he stops paying you he will be outcast and lose control of his companies. So he decided to kill you instead.'

'And why would this MI6 agent assist him?'

'Money.' Klich pointed to Bald. 'And influence. Favorsky knew that if he killed you, he would be seen as your natural successor. He already has significant support in the media and security services. In return for Land's help, he would have transferred stakes in state assets to a shell corporation owned by Land.'

'Bullshit!' the President said. 'What you say makes no sense. If Favorsky really wanted me dead, he didn't have to go cutting deals with our enemies in Britain. He could've colluded with any number of those spineless bastards in the Duma who'd like to see the fucking back of me!'

'But Favorsky couldn't take the risk that a Russian national might report back to you on his plot. Besides, your death had to look like an attack on Russia itself. And who better than a British special forces operator to do the killing?'

The President stroked his chin.

'What about that bitch they say you murdered in London?'

Klich gave the floor a solemn shake of his head. 'I was framed,' he said. 'As soon as I learned of the plot against you, I became a problem. It was a priority for Land to kill me before I had the chance to warn you. He reached out to his contacts and secured the services of a man who used to be in the SAS.'

The President laughed. 'Thank God he found someone so incompetent to kill you! Otherwise we might not be having this conversation.'

'Indeed.' Klich joined in the laughter. Bald stood there, thirsty and tired and wounded, watching a couple of minted Russians point at him and chuckle at his misfortune. He suddenly felt like a prize cunt.

But his rage didn't last long. The President buried his laugh in his throat and nodded at him. His lips were thin and straight and looked like he only ever smiled out of the corners of them. 'You are expecting some, uh, payment, for bringing Klich here? Don't tell me you did it out of the kindness of your heart!'

'Ten million,' Bald said eagerly. He glanced at Klich, then looked back at the President. 'I want it paid as a lump sum, in sterling, into an account registered in the British Virgin Islands. Those are my terms.'

'But how do we know we can trust you?' said the President. He was standing in front of the bank of clocks, flicking his eyes between each time zone and stroking his dimpled chin. 'For all I know, you might be working undercover for MI6.' He paused, before turning to Bald and jabbing a pale finger at him. 'You want your money, you must prove your loyalty to us. We need to know you're on our side. Show your word is as strong as oak, and you will get your reward.'

Bald shrugged. The pain in his shoulder sparked up again. The President's proposal sounded a fair deal, he thought. He'd come this far. He wasn't about to turn his nose up at a job and miss out on his ten million. Besides, he figured he was in no position to negotiate. He'd cut his ties with the Firm. There was no going back now.

He said, 'What do you have in mind?'

The President said, 'I want you to kill Valery Favorsky.'

'No problem.'

forty-nine

The Mariner outboard engine gurgled in the crisp night like blood in a throat. Bald operated the tiller. Steered the life-boat into the midnight abyss. They were some sixty kilometres clear of the French coast, on the edge of the Ligurian Sea. A hundred kilometres from Corsica.

'Please,' Valery Favorsky said. He was sitting opposite Bald, snot dribbling onto his bruised lips. The gorillas had given him a battering before throwing him on the boat. 'I can make you rich.'

'Nah,' said Bald with a grin. 'I've already got my money.'

Favorsky looked away in despair. His eyes focused on the yacht looming on the horizon like a giant iridescent rock. Bald took a perverse pleasure in listening to Favorsky bawl his eyes out. The oligarch had heavy bags under his reddened eyes. He'd been crying since Karpin and Zorin threw him into the lifeboat. His arms were tied behind his back and bound at the wrists with plasticuffs. The shirt of the football team he'd recently purchased in the French Ligue 1 was smeared with tears and snot. He mumbled prayers in Russian and Bald thought it kind of funny, a guy that rich and powerful, having to resort to the power of prayer.

The three-metre lifeboat had a top speed of twenty-five knots, and they had been cutting across the water for three minutes. Bald had put two and a half kilometres between the two of them and the *Seraya Sowa*. Far enough. He killed the engine. There was a crust of silence, broken off at the end by the tears coming from the man sitting opposite him, and the soft churning of the propeller in the water.

Bald picked up the closed-circuit rebreather lying next to him. Movement was easier since the on-board doctor had patched up both his new shoulder wound and the earlier one to his body. The fact the bullet had exited had made the clean-up job on his shoulder easier, since the doc hadn't needed to remove a lead nugget from his joint. Both wounds had been properly cleaned and dressed and Bald had been injected with a cocktail of antibiotics to combat any potentially septic infection, although he figured the warm glow in his stomach was from the fact he was about to get rich. Now he strapped the D-ring belt around his chest and secured the oxygen cylinder to his front and connected the cylinder via the breathing tube to the mask covering his face. Favorsky's death had to look like an accident, so Bald had been tasked with taking the oligarch out to sea in the lifeboat, dragging him overboard and then holding him underwater until he stopped breathing.

'I give you money,' Favorsky begged. 'Women. Men. Anything.'

Fuck this prick, thought Bald. He had big money waiting for him back on the boat. But this wasn't just about the money. Bald told himself he was playing with the big boys now. I'm a player on the world stage. Pass this test and that ten million on the table could be just the beginning. Impressing the President had other advantages, besides his payday. He'd be inserting himself into the highest echelons of power. He smiled as Favorsky sobbed. Bald was going places. But the only place the oligarch was going was a couple of feet under the surface.

Bald twisted the oxygen valve. Tasted chalky air in his mouth as the oxygen circulated through the rebreathing system.

Favorsky screamed as Bald threw him overboard.

Maybe I'll have myself a sip of the Macallan when I get back on board the yacht, Bald told himself as the Russian hit the water. Fuck it. One swig, when the President's back was turned. He wouldn't notice. He smiled as he turned back to the task in hand. Favorsky was flailing his arms, coughing and spluttering as salt water flooded his nostrils, filled his mouth, stung his eyes. Bald leaned over and wrapped his arms around the guy, like he was performing the Heimlich manoeuvre on him.

Then he dragged Favorsky under the choppy water.

The Russian kicked and screamed wildly. Made a sound like a guy in a gimp suit calling for help. Bald shoved him down deeper. Favorsky gargled a scream, bubbles pouring out of his mouth. After thirty seconds his kicks weakened. After a minute he wriggled his feet. After a minute and a half he stopped moving altogether. Bald held him under the surface for another thirty seconds, just to make sure the cunt was dead. Then he released him. Watched his dead weight drift away.

Four minutes later Bald kickstarted the outboard and steered back towards the yacht. He disembarked and discarded the rebreather. Klich, Zorin alongside, was waiting for him on the main deck. A small bronze key was dangling from a keychain in Klich's right hand.

'The fuck is this?' said Bald.

'Your reward.'

Bald frowned. 'Is this some kind of a joke?'

'My friend, what's in the safe is better than a lottery ticket. It's better than ten million. Think of it as an unlimited credit card. You will be able to draw money using it any time you like. And not just money. With the contents of the safe you can ask for anything. Cars, private jets, mansions. Whatever you want. Here. Let's go and toast your reward.'

Bald's rage cooled when he spotted the bottle Klich gripped in his left hand. Bald took a swig of the vintage Macallan. Jesus, but that tasted good. It tasted like whisky worth twenty large ought to taste. In just a few minutes Bald could look forward to a lifetime of double measures of the stuff. He wiped his sated lips with the back of his hand, passed the bottle back to Klich and snatched the key. Then he followed Zorin through a maze of corridors and up a flight of stairs to the master bedroom, leaving a soggy trail in his wake. Excitement bubbled in his veins. He felt like all his Christmases were coming at once. Finally. After all this time, Bald thought. Now I get my reward.

The President was waiting outside the master bedroom. He swapped grins with Klich. The two of them tittering like fucking school kids. Bald half-wondered what was so funny. In truth he didn't care. He was all about the money. He breezed past the President and the oligarch as Zorin pointed out a key-lock safe built into the wall next to a fifty-inch 3D TV. Bald swaggered up to the safe. Veins pumping. Heart racing. He twisted the key in the lock. The President and Klich were whispering in Russian, and still sniggering together. Fuck them, thought Bald. The safe made a satisfying clunk as the bolt catch released and the door sprang open.

Inside he saw an A4 brown envelope. Slim. His breath cloyed in his throat as he removed the envelope and prised open the flap. There was a single slip of paper concealed inside. Bald pinched it. The paper was glossy to the touch. Like a photo. He unsheathed the slip of paper from the envelope. Studied it. At first he didn't know what he was looking at. Then he realized, the blood drained from his head to his toes, and the envelope fell from his hand. Behind him Klich and the President bellowed with laughter, slapping their thighs and going red in the face. Bald glowered at them. Karpin had joined Zorin at the door and the bodyguards were chuckling too, their arms folded across their barrel-like chests, their enormous shoulders bouncing up and down. All four men were growing hysterical with laughter, their eyes streaming with tears. They looked like they were about to piss themselves.

Bald clenched his jaw and turned back to the photo. Almost as if he couldn't believe what he was looking at. It depicted a middle-aged man engaged in a despicable sexual act with a boy no older than eight or nine years old. The shot was grainy and low-res, as if lifted from CCTV footage. But in a beat Bald recognized the man's face. His knuckles burned with cold. He felt an urge to rip the picture in half. The Russians kept on laughing behind him, and Bald kept on boiling at the photo.

At the image of Leo Land violating a young boy.